SUCCESSION

SUCCESSION

The Faithwalker Series Book 4

Darryl Markowitz

FAITHWALKER PUBLISHING

The Faithwalker Series
Book IV: Succession

Copyright © 2021 by Darryl Markowitz

Published by:

Faithwalker Publishing
An imprint of Darryl Markowitz

Cover Artwork: © 2010 Tori J. Holes
Interior Design: Creative Publishing Book Design

ISBN Paperback: 978-1-7374936-2-4
ISBN eBook: 978-1-7374936-3-1

Printed in the United States of America

Acknowledgment

I have found this life to be more than difficult, more than a small amount of pain and suffering. Yet, the Reality of Goodness and how that is revealed to those who search in spite of evil, is a reality worth living, worth loving, and worth having faith by. There is nothing else real. Real and merely existing are not synonymous.

The *Faithwalkers,* who are too often unknown, will . . .

CHAPTER 1

Freedom

His freshly cut willow switch whistled through the air, catching Matthew by surprise as it slashed through the flesh at the back of his neck. The boy half-screamed and half began to turn in anger, but his mind was quick enough to make him blurt out, "Forgive me, Judge Ezekiel."

With black robe billowing as he silently eased in front of the terrified youth, he bent down to within inches of Matthew's face. "How old are you and why are you here?"

"Ten, Sir! One year for each of the Ten Commandments means I'm ready to be a man, Sir, if you'll teach me."

Judge Ezekiel swatted Matthew's hands away from hiding a piece of paper on his desk, then snatched it up. A caricature of the good Judge, and not just a fair representation of his officious-looking face. While turning a deeper red, the Judge spoke calmly to hide the rage that any moment could take control of him. "Do you have any idea how important this lesson, every lesson I teach is? It requires your undivided attention, your undivided loyalty. We don't hide the past like our heathen neighbors to the North do, we learn from it. The reason why the United States failed and allowed terrorists to destroy us was because of *exactly* the kind of thing you are doing *now!* You are *not* paying attention, and you are weak. We allowed the Godless to distract us. We let all their blasphemies and whoredoms go unchallenged. So God got angry and punished us along with *them.* Now, it is my responsibility to punish wrongdoers quickly so that God won't be angry with *me.* You wouldn't want Jesus to be angry with me now would you, Matthew?"

Unfortunately for Matthew, he allowed himself actually to think about an answer. Soon as the other students saw his hesitation, they knew he was doomed. The good Judge grabbed the boy by his ear and yanked him out of his chair. He threw open the top of the boy's desk, retrieved the Holy Bible, then slammed the top down and slammed the Bible on top of that, all in one seamless motion. Grabbing the boy by the back of his bleeding neck, he shoved his face into the Bible and softly spoke. "We will not suffer our future Judges to be *weak,* Matthew. Even though we can't be perfect, it's my job to get you as close as possible. God has greatness in store for you. Write the First Book of Moses out by hand, and do *not* get up out of this chair until you are done. And I better not find a single mistake." The judge went to the back of the room, retrieved a roll of plain, unlined paper, and gave it to the boy. "Write it as they did in ancient times on a scroll, and every line had better be straight."

Matthew's eyes widened, but he hurried to fish his pencil from his desk. *How am I to write all that? It'll take me all year… I'll… I'll starve to death before I finish!"*

Vaughn shook his head again while slouching upon a stump in the middle of the woods in what used to be the southern United States. When they'd fled, almost a year ago last spring, the complications of the word 'freedom' as they now manifested were unimaginable. Burying his head in his hands and rubbing his eyes could not remove the oppressive weight from his mind. Neither was there respite from the aching in his heart, or the eternal flame that burned to be with Stephanie.

Freedom, he thought, *is a lot more than just crossing a border.* Yet running for both their lives, for all the poor people who followed him, did not allow any deeper consideration of freedom, than merely finding a place where they wouldn't immediately be murdered. Unfortunately, now their fate had become apparent to Vaughn as he assessed what one year of freedom had gained them. *There's also a slow death, just as sure as the quick one.* One year of their so-called *freedom* had not produced anything of hope, but only brought them closer to disaster.

Vaughn had grown a full two inches this last year, and was sure there wasn't a muscle on his body that hadn't been conditioned, reconditioned, then somehow given automatic-battle thought. However, his physical preparedness could not ease his foreboding. Jargono's impeding invasion, the earth-demons' maturation and undoubted reproduction, and the eventual unnamed punishment from the theocratic Christian government to which they now owed their meager, continued freedom, all these were knots in his gut.

Vaughn reflected upon being sealed in the sacred cave with Glen, remembering how trapped he'd felt. *But at least I sealed us in to protect Stephanie from him. But what am I doing now?* Looking up, he frowned at an irritating, screeching blackbird flying through the treetops. He wondered about his cleverness in escaping Glen who later turned half demon as a product of Jargono's experiment with the cursed Black Oil.

Vaughn hung his head yet, again, wondering. *Has my cleverness in coming here gotten everyone into even more trouble than before? And only maybe two more years and I'll have to deal with hundreds of Glen's offspring! How am I going to do that? I'm not gaining anything here. I can't believe it. Every time I think I'm free, I'm more trapped than ever. And whatever happened to Trevor? He was supposed to keep me informed. Was I wrong to send him into that devil's den?*

'Learn as much as we can about this new country, but tell them nothing more than necessary about us, especially about the mysterious happenings during our escape lest they fear us.' That had been Vaughn's kingly orders. He laughed at the thought of being named King a year ago by his impoverished escapees, not long after just turning sixteen. Yet, his loyal subjects still kept growing in numbers as his spies continued to guide more of the condemned across the border to freedom because the people kept fleeing the brutal, strictly atheistic country now ruled by its supposed savior, Jargono.

So much knowledge to share, but Vaughn certainly didn't have to worry about the theocracy or the religious people of this Christian country wanting to learn *anything* from him. No, not at all. Not about the atrocities done back home, not about how dangerous Jargono is, and certainly not about demons. Here, the unidirectional flow of knowledge proved in some odd way to be both their sole reliable safeguard and a curse for Vaughn's people. Their true nature wouldn't be discovered, hence they would be neither threat nor help to the United for Christ, which was the name given to what used to be the southern half of the United States right after the Second Civil War. A good hundred years ago that Civil War had been spurred by the Great Religious World War. After Muslim terrorists had destroyed all the major cites of what they called the *heathen*, all the Muslim countries were completely obliterated, turned into a smoking wasteland of righteous retaliation was what Vaughn's new Christian teachers told him.

Such worldwide destruction obliterated trade, access to energy supplies, and most of the world's industries. The small town populations who were spared were left to rebuild in a world that had quickly regressed in social, industrial, and technological development. It became painfully clear to the initial survivors just how dependent their lifestyles had been upon world trade which supplied rare materials needed to construct advanced technologies. It also became apparent that the destroyed cities had grown so large due to their geographic locations being ideally suited for trade and industry. All gone in one month's time along with much of the knowledge that sustained society, and any legitimate currency exchange. The most pressing question arose as to what would be the basis of value? And when Vaughn's religious teacher asked that question, it was with extra emphasis implying so much more.

Equally destructive was the massive loss of populations that affected cultures worldwide. One main imperative became repopulation so marrying age became synonymous to reproductive potential. With the early onset of family responsibilities, guidance from the theocracy became essential. Due to the past failures of religion, it became crucial that the ruling clergy, otherwise called Judges, correct the errors of the past and maintain purity and order as never before. And when Vaughn's instructor said the word '*purity*', he glared at Vaughn with silent accusation.

Who are the heathen? Vaughn mumbled to himself, knowing that his people were now considered to be *heathen*, in dire need of salvation. That need was even more than dire. Left unspoken between the lines of Christian instruction was the requirement, the unstated *threat* that if you don't convert… well, that threat was only implicit, but Vaughn knew that their growing population of *heathen* settling outside Jericho wasn't going to be problem-free. *But as long as we continue to consent to learn their ways, we might be safe for now.* He shook his head again. *I've been through all these thoughts already.* However, Vaughn had begun gathering an increasing sense of discord between what their Bible said, or at least what he thought it said, and what the clergy said the Bible said, and what they said to do and actually did. *Does that make sense?*

Ancient King Mafferan, who had visited Vaughn in spirit a whole year ago had told him that the holy words lived in Vaughn's heart, passed down through the blessing of generations. Vaughn wondered why he hadn't realized his ancient heritage any sooner. But once he immersed himself among his people, it was obvious he belonged to them. Not just his wavy dark hair and dark eyes, but even his posture and unconscious manners were common to them all. *Heritage. Just another circumstance called a blessing that brings additional suffering. How long can we keep* this *a secret?* According to the United for Christ's tenets of Christianity, Vaughn and his people were the worst of the heathen.

Who are the heathen? Vaughn remembered calling upon the Lord God to help him push away the great stone that blocked the sacred cave. That stone had moved, crashed and crumbled to dust and pieces, then he and Stephanie fought Jargono in that cave. Vaughn recalled how she died, and the Seed to the Tree of Life entrusted to Stephanie's care had gone to ash, giving its sacred life to return hers. Later that precious Seed, the hope for all humanity, mysteriously restored itself to them as a wedding gift!

Ha! Wedding gift! Since Vaughn couldn't do anything about Stephanie and his current situation, he simply laughed and reflected upon the weak reason for the Seed's return. He knew the Seed's importance far outweighed any supposed wedding. He was sure the rules of the truce between Heaven and the demons had been broken somewhere in that timeline, but he wasn't sure how or who breached first. *Somehow, this may be our most pressing problem, Earth becoming their open battleground.* He tried to imagine human beings caught between their epic war, but quickly shook the thought away. *What's the point?*

All the battles he and his secret wife, Stephanie, had fought flashed their short-lived greatness in his mind. Yet the most magnificent development of all occurred when his people asked them to teach them the truth about God. They knew absolutely nothing, any such knowledge having been forbidden in the country from which they came. It was only through Vaughn and Stephanie's tenacious introspection, reaching out, searching for real meaning that they found themselves now blessed as they were.

Ha! Blessed! Vaughn grumbled in sarcasm. All their trials to win their *freedom*, and their people's sincere faith in him and in his wife, whom he couldn't be with because of this country's law, pained him beyond relief. Still, despite such duress and danger, the secret predawn spiritual lessons continued to be taught by the young couple. They mysteriously brought more peace to his people than he could feel now or had felt since learning the contorted dynamics of the United for Christ's government.

There were two branches of government here. All executive leadership gushed from the ruling theocracy and their guided interpretation of a book called the Holy Bible, which Judges at all levels of government flawlessly administered. But actual physical enforcement of all laws and security came via the military.

Ahhh, the Military. It was the logical choice of occupation for Vaughn when their host government learned he was a Ranger in his former country. Besides, the rigorous military training melded well with his self-taught lessons from the *Art of Fighting* series, those seven books from back home that remained in Vaughn's possession because a young military officer claimed the books were of tactical value. The captain, only twenty-three years old with short black hair and a proper gray uniform, happened to be in charge of the military force in the town of Jericho. Vaughn smiled, remembering the tense standoff over the fighting series between Captain Joshua and Judge Matthew, a fat, balding man with official-looking jowls and black robe, the head of the whole district.

After forcibly confiscating almost everything from Vaughn's people, the Judge piled up the heathen's possessions in the center of town and burned them as directed by the Holy Bible. If it had not been an affront to decency, the Judge would have stripped the people naked as well. Of course, he had needed the military close at hand to enforce his orders. When Captain Joshua heard Vaughn trying to explain the value of the *Art of Fighting*, he stepped in and deemed the books militarily significant and *that* was the end of the story, so to speak! Apparently, proclaiming military value was one unquestionable right that military officers could declare. Vaughn intended to gain at least that much for himself in joining the Captain's forces.

Fortunately, Stephanie fared better upon their entry to this new country since Vaughn's claim that she was the official head and ambassador of an oppressed group of people in the Northern country bestowed her with diplomatic immunity and honorary citizenship. She could then marry any *real* citizen of the country if she wished. The fact that people kept pouring across the border with deference to her did well to maintain her position. Captain Joshua had smiled warmly at her as he commanded that none of her belongings be touched. The Book of Wisdom, an extraordinary spiritual gift from Stephanie's ancient ancestors, had been safely hidden among her stuff.

Captain Joshua also informed a disgruntled Judge Matthew, who also couldn't keep his eyes from Stephanie, that she should have special quarters within the Judge's complex. As he swept another gaze at Stephanie, the Judge agreed but his musings were quickly cut short by Captain Joshua's order for two round-the-clock guards for her. The Captain's serious attentiveness to the young lady and the Judge's keen interest in her gave Vaughn more than pause. Nonetheless, he couldn't help his strong positive feeling, an instant deep respect for this Captain, as he also realized that his fondness for Stephanie could be a blessing.

Now visions of Stephanie's long, fiery red, wavy tresses filled Vaughn's senses, as he recalled how he loved to run his hands through them. Her firm but soft body, the glorious glow to her flesh, the longing these precious memories evoked was driving him insane. Yet, to be true to the Tree of Life, as the letter from her ancestor King Mafferan explained, Vaughn knew they couldn't really come together to begin a family until the proper, right time. *Whenever that will be!* As it goes, the times they really got to see each other had only been when she snuck off to their secret lessons, her guards oblivious to her abilities to travel in the spiritual corridor and pop up anywhere in the *real* world.

ↀ

Captain Joshua looked deeply into her rich brown eyes. As he went down on one knee, her heart thudded and sank. "Stephanie, I love you with all my heart. Marry me!"

While sitting on the floor playing dolls, Lynnara's head full of bouncy brown curls snapped up. The now five-year-old, adopted by Stephanie and Vaughn prior to coming here, leaned over and whispered into her best friend Rebekah's ear. "Vaughn's already my Daddy. I don't think I'm allowed two Daddies."

Rebekah, a year older and with longer, wavy dark brown hair, had been the girl in Vaughn's heart vision that said 'save the child and save the world!' Rebekah responded to her best friend by whispering back. "You're not… I don't think."

Stephanie removed her hand from Joshua's, took his hand in hers and pulled him to his feet. "You're so dear. I do love you for what you are, but you know I can't marry you. Your government forbids it. I'm not Christianized yet."

The children nodded to each other, glad they were right.

Joshua shook his head. "The military, especially officers, have all kinds of extra privileges." Then he sneered as he seemed to look off into the distance. "Besides, all is not what it appears to be with our *religious* leaders."

Stephanie knew full well of what he spoke. Her favorite hobby now was investigating the seedier haunts of Jericho. After locking the door to her apartment, she regularly popped into various underground business establishments. There was no worry about being recognized for everyone who patronized such places weren't supposed to be there. In fact, such places were not supposed to exist at all in this now *holy* country. With different dress, hairstyle, and a return to makeup for disguise, Stephanie reveled in her alter-persona. In fact, she now relished dropping into various people's lives as she had done in her old country.

Even while Captain Joshua kept gazing at her, waiting for her to respond to yet another marriage proposal, Stephanie's mind was elsewhere. *I wonder if the Black River is still solid. I hope so… maybe I ought to go back there and make sure.* The Dead Forest was where she and Lynnara had been mysteriously deposited when they escaped Jargono's fire during their public face-off. The trap set there by the demon that had caught them backfired, resulting in the Black River of Death turning to stone. Stephanie suddenly chuckled, and Joshua immediately looked hurt.

Red-faced, Stephanie put her hand to his cheek. "Oh, no! Joshua, dear Joshua, I wasn't laughing at you… my mind was elsewhere."

"Yes, I notice you do that a lot. I'll repeat…"

"No need. I still heard you. Please, Joshua, you know I've many responsibilities as representative of…"

"You also deserve a life for yourself, and you're well into marrying age now, you're *sixteen!* How're we ever to repopulate from the Religious War catastrophe if we don't marry and have children? Actually, our law requires that we be fruitful and multiply." Then Joshua turned dark and Stephanie considered it, *Very similar to what often surrounds Vaughn.* It was the spiritual manifestation of righteous anger, not the dark radiance of evil.

"Stephanie, there's more. Judge Matthew has had his eye on you for some time. His wife is old, past childbearing, and he seeks a second wife. He wants you! If he declares it…"

Now the children's eyes popped open. They whispered into each other's ears again then nodded.

"But he can't ask for me! First, I'm not Christianized, and second, I'm a representative, and third, I…" She cut herself off, just before getting carried away with her answer.

"You love Vaughn, I know. It was obvious from the first time I saw you two together. And even though you don't see each other that much anymore…" Stephanie narrowed her eyes at him. "That's not really my fault. I'm training him to be an officer like myself. That's what's best for him, but it requires a *lot* of extra time. Besides, I really like him, Stephanie. In fact, I would have to say he's my best friend, because I *know* I can trust him. That just makes my proposal even more crucial since you know you can't marry Vaughn. Judge Matthew would never allow it, he wants you for himself, and if he knew you two loved each other, Vaughn will *never* be granted citizenship. But he can't disallow me if I get you first, and I think even Vaughn would rather see you with me than with that…" He cut his words off, turning even darker.

Lynnara whispered again. "We can't tell anybody King Vaughn is already married to my Mommy. They made it a secret 'cause they got here too young to be married. But they weren't too young… I don't know. It's confusing!"

Rebekah sighed. "Right, I don't know either!"

"Well, like I said. I'm not *Christianized*." Stephanie emphasized her lack of religion.

But Joshua shook his head. "Look here. That game won't wash much longer. First of all, there are rumors you've been healing sick people." Stephanie tried to look innocent but Joshua could read her too well. "Oh God! It's true?"

"I told them to keep it secret."

"We did, Mommy!" Lynnara insisted, while Rebekah nodded, too.

Joshua stared at the children, his eyes widening by the moment. He lifted Stephanie's chin back up to look into her eyes. "My dearest, my love, I don't know, but somehow I knew you were special from the first time I saw you. Somehow, I even believe you're far closer to Jesus Christ than… any of us! But this just makes matters worse, Stephanie! If Judge Matthew hears of your miracles…" He paused with realization of her extra-nature then whispered, "Is there more… ahhh, anything else out of the ordinary I should know about?'

Stephanie looked away, her eyes darting around from instant recollection, and Joshua now knew the situation was far worse than he thought. He stared questioningly at the children who looked away and picked up their dolls again, so he took Stephanie's hands firmly in his. "Look, if Judge Matthew really believes all this, and he probably knows by now, then he's thinking two different things. One, he can't let this go much longer because you're doing miracles without the church's approval, and you're not even Christianized yet. Do you want to be burned at the stake?"

Stephanie chuckled. "Already been there, done that!"

"I'm not joking." Joshua warned her. "Thou shalt not suffer a witch to live."

"She's not joking, Captain. I was there!" Lynnara spoke with all truth and innocence.

Joshua stared at her, his mouth dropping open, but Stephanie shot her a look then Rebekah whispered again in her little ear.

Stephanie smiled coyly at him. "Dear Joshua, are you calling me a witch?"

Every time she gave him that kind of look, he indeed felt under some kind of spell. Joshua studied her for a brief moment then shook the ridiculous thought away. But he could feel some annoying pressure, subtle but definite, that wanted him to betray her, and knowing that presence, it angered him. *Why would the devil want me to betray her, if she isn't a true soul for Christ? Besides, I know she's true by my own mind. So I don't even need such reasoning.*

Stephanie could see the transparent gray arm reaching inside his head, and how a light shined within him and drove it back. If she didn't love Vaughn, she knew she could marry Joshua.

Joshua saw her looking over his head and fancied she could actually see the devil trying to influence him, making him all the more determined to help her. "Look, Stephanie. I've only heard or read about miracles and I *doubt* Judge Matthew could do them." Then he thought a bit. "I guess what I'm really saying is that I don't think that Jesus would hear Matthew even if he asked, and I doubt very much that he'd even have the faith to ask for such things."

Stephanie took hold of his muscular forearms, and implored him. "But dear Joshua, believe me, anything *I* do, I do through true faith… I'm gifted! And no one outside my current people knows this, but I trust you with my secret. I'm what the Lord has made to be… a *faithwalker*. At least, that's the name that my ancestors, the Appendaho, called us. I haven't yet found the term for it within your Bible, or your religion, but I'm sure it's there somewhere, because I know the Book is true!" *Some of it, anyway.*

Joshua shook inside but couldn't let her know. His spies had reported on what had happened to her people that were accused of sedition in the Northern country, and massacred a year ago. But he knew even more, because his own father's life had once been saved by them. His father, a spy, had been chased into the woods and hidden by those very same, rare people. He spent six months with them before he left and found a way back a changed man. *Destiny?*

Joshua struggled against the code of secrecy he always kept and decided to break it since Stephanie just confided in him. "Judge Matthew is soon going to *require* you to Christianize. Shortly after that, you *will* have to marry him. No choice!"

Stephanie acted as if nothing of consequence had been said. "You said he was thinking two things. What's the second?"

"That being married to you, as gifted as I'm coming to realize you are, would make him appear very important. He'll use you, the fact that *he* saved you and that God delivered you into *his* care. He'll use that to demonstrate God is favoring him very highly, and that means the arch clergy should elevate him to a higher church office, giving him more authority in the government as well. From then on, all your gifts… whatever they all are, from then on you'll use none of them except when and how he orders you. *He* is the head of the house, besides being a Judge."

"Joshua, he can't force me against my will! That much is in the Bible, in your laws."

Tears crept into Joshua's eyes and for the first time, the hairs at Stephanie's neck prickled, knowing she was about to hear a truth that she didn't want to hear. "My dear

Stephanie… you are naïve. *You* are considered a heathen, and different laws apply to you. If he wanted, he could just marry you even now! But he wouldn't have to because… well, he could simply make you do whatever he wanted!"

Tears were creeping into the corners of the *faithwalker's* eyes before her mind even knew the answer, but her heart obviously did.

"How?"

"What would you do if he brought you to his private chambers, accused you of being a witch and that your people are your followers and must all be burned alive?"

Stephanie's hand went to her stomach and must have looked faint, because the next thing she knew, Joshua was carrying her to the sofa. Vaughn had warned her that things here were not as safe as it seemed, and that her playful attitude with this ignorant country did not do the situation justice. But being housed in the Judges' complex in luxury, perhaps that had softened her too much. Or, since she really did have that new will from the Lord Jesus Christ, she now knew she had received the Holy Ghost, though she had received it strictly through the meaning of Goodness from the Tree of Life without knowing Christ's name or history at that time, well, perhaps that knowledge had also somehow made her complacent.

She weakly said, "But he's a Christian. He won't do…"

But Captain Joshua cut her off. "Never underestimate the power of lust, either for flesh or for power. And since when did a claim to a name ever dissuade people from sinning? You've studied about the crusades? We're taught that our new

Christianity is now foolproof from corruption but I don't know…"

The children went over to Stephanie who hadn't looked so troubled since they came to freedom. Lynnara squeezed between Joshua and her third mommy then laid her head down on Stephanie's breast. Rebekah crawled up on her other side, cupped her hands and whispered in Stephanie's ear. "Don't worry! Ranger Vaughn will know what to do."

Stephanie fought hard to keep tears away. *I can't let the children see.*

Joshua stared at the three girls, watching the intense love between them all. *Lord Jesus, help her understand what she has to do.*

∽

Jargono smiled, being careful not to concentrate too hard on Stephanie, nor get too close to the spot in the spiritual corridor corresponding to the physical world where Stephanie resided. He knew she would detect him if he did. "Well, well, my Sweet. You didn't want me. Ha! Let's see how much you'll love the fair Judge Matthew. A little time in his bed, in his *religion* and you might not think my presence is that bad. I wonder what Karen would say if I had you as my *second* wife." Jargono couldn't contain his laughter and so quickly popped out of the corridor back to his new palace in his new modern city.

∽

Karen peered through the dirty blue orb as the Highest Councilor ScrabaGag adjusted its focus for her while his hideous serpentine body rippled and floated in mid ether. Her long blond hair seemed to radiate in contrast to his black shimmering body. She became increasingly amused at how she could finagle, she could even say force the highest demon to do what she wanted. She knew his great glistening black Eye in the center of his huge bulbous head drooled to consume her, and that no human had ever been allowed into any demon's personal ethereal chamber. She also knew that what she offered to the demon was too good to pass up and that the power she'd accumulated was only the start. *Hmmm, their Eye consumes others thereby acquiring all the power and abilities of their prey, gobbled up forever a prisoner inside their devourer. I wonder if there's some way I can do the same.* Her thoughts of the future were a bit whimsical as she wondered what a demon would taste like, and imagined consuming the Highest Councilor, but the present demanded her attention.

In the vision of the large blue orb that floated in the middle of ScrabaGag's room, Karen could see her husband, King Jargono, watching the one human being in all the Earth whom she wanted to suffer beyond all imagination. *Well, well, when the cat's away, huh? We'll see about that, though it might even be better to let his hand play out some.* She still remembered the stupid doggie look Stephanie wore as she began to suspect Karen had murdered her mother. *I don't think she'd appreciate my husband's fondness for her the way I do, especially when it's against her will. Maybe I can do the same to Vaughn. Yes! That would make us even, wouldn't it? Hmmmm.*

Karen turned to the demon. "I've seen enough. Everything's going according to plan. Send me back now."

The Highest Councilor narrowed his Great Eye at her. "What plan is that?"

She smiled at him sweetly and tickled him under what she thought might be a chin, ignoring her immediate pain and revulsion from the contact. "You show me yours, I'll show you mine!"

ScrabaGag looked on in amazement. Certainly, new things were happening under the sun. *Is she actually saying what I think she is? She actually knows now.* He never dreamt of any human female consenting to mate with full knowledge. His eye drooled profusely now, but then he shook his bulbous head. She laughed, knowing she had actually played him for a fool again, and knowing he knew she knew. The Highest Councilor waved his single arm attached just below his aching bulbous head, and she disappeared.

His underling swished his tail. "Master, is there any human female in history even remotely like her?"

"No, I don't believe so… but in order for our plans to work, we need her to be exactly that clever. Besides, the more power I grant her, the tastier she'll be so I'm really not losing anything. In fact, the power I give her, she'll nurture, it'll grow, and like the interest on their bank accounts, my investment will eventually bring a greater return.

"I think I still prefer the redhead to the blond, Master."

"Yes, yes, I see that Grinchback. They're certainly different flavors, with far different abilities to add to ours, so maybe you actually liked it when the redhead left her handprint burned into your neck?"

Grinchback changed the subject. "When is the official meeting with your glowing friend? I can't believe he's been able to stall it for so long."

ScrabaGag folded his long tail in his arm and began tapping. He tapped because his underling used the term 'friend' for his heavenly adversary, Mafferan.

"Perhaps Grinchback, you would like him to turn you upside down and stuff a *glowing* ball in your mouth again?" After he saw his underling flinch, ScrabaGag relented. "Well, unfortunately, it appears that Alpha stupidity allowed him to stall. Apparently, when the truce was created, we insisted that a one year proviso be added to all summons so that any serious issues could be researched effectively."

Grinchback ignored his Master's embarrassing reminder and concentrated on the business at arm. "All our documents are in order. I've crafted them particularly to our personal needs." He leaned in close to his Master's ear and whispered about the head of all demons. "The Father won't be able to discern what we hide for ourselves. I've been careful in the summons and have adjusted the orb technology accordingly. That old demon is no technological marvel so when he reviews the records…"

Highest Councilor ScrabaGag hushed him. "We'll see what we can gain from Mafferan, how badly he wants to try to preserve their imposed *balance*. I don't know why our ancestors ever agreed to such a truce. I wish I could find someone who had consumed someone who had been there. Anyway, I'm told that the Father himself has consumed everyone with such knowledge so it's all sealed away."

"Master, are you sure we have Mafferan boxed in?"

"You did exactly as I told you? *Exactly*?"

Grinchback frowned at his Master. "I can't believe you don't trust me."

Highest Councilor ScrabaGag narrowed his Eye at him even more. "Show me."

Grinchback floated over to the orb, and proudly retrieved the stored copy:

> '*Mafferan has been duly summoned by seal of the Father of All to appear before His Highest Councilor ScrabaGag to answer charges of the* glow's *violations of the BALANCE that has been* imposed *upon all reality.*
>
> *Bring documentation of all events listed below for further inspection and investigation.*
> 1. *The Cursed Object's reappearance;*
> 2. *Various threats made upon the Highest Councilor;*
> 3. *Wanton destruction of the Black River (Compensation shall be required);*
> 4. *Abuse of an underling.*'

After examining the summons, ScrabaGag pointed to number four. "What's *that?*"

Grinchback smiled. "That was necessary, Master." And he floated close to whisper more in his Master's ear.

CHAPTER 2
Who's Who

No one understood. "Why should we be summoned to *his* room? He's *not* the Father." Yet, all their rippling suddenly cramped.

"Don't be cowards!" First High Councilor sneered.

"But the Father summoned us *here*," Second retorted.

Although HrorrarrAggrang wasn't even a High Councilor, every Alpha had an unexplained visceral reaction to his very presence. When the last of the Alpha chiefs who belonged under the three High Councilors finally arrived, the doors instantly sealed and the Father's deepest blackness suffocated them all. The unique orb, floating at the room's center, lit up with a terrible *glow,* and all Alphas, except the Father and HrorrarrAggrang, shrieked, fled, and smacked into the ethereal dark gray walls. Some of them hit their bulbous heads so hard, they bounced off and floated dazedly back to the center. With his massive tail, the Father scooped up all three High Councilors, and icily commanded, "Watch the orb!"

The orb review of very recent history began in slow motion with a few thousand *glowing* trees that became people, but not glowing so much as to impair visibility nor cause excessive discomfort. But suddenly, the orb exploded with *glow* and everyone pressed into the ethereal walls again, except for the three High Councilors still held by the Father close enough to the orb to be singed just a bit. Amidst the Councilors' howling, the orb returned to the beginning of its historical loop. The anticipation of that countdown to catastrophe made every Alpha cringe, yet stare ever more intently into the orb though that was the last place each wanted to focus their large, singular oculi.

The Father's own massive Greatest Eye lowered to mere inches away from all three High Councilors. Another *glowing* explosion hit them simultaneously with the last word of the Father's question. "What's *that*?"

After the shrieking subsided, while attempting to regain his ethereal presence, First forced an answer. "It's something … Pentecost … they call it *grace*."

All the chief Alphas began nodding their bulbous heads, mumbling various phrases like "We're doomed!", "No inroads.", "Gone completely!"

The Father's growls shook every ethereal fiber. "I want solutions!" And right there, before everyone's ethereal Great Eyes, he consumed all three High Councilors simultaneously. No one knew that was even possible, *And now three new High Councilors need to be appointed,* was the common thought.

HrorrarrAggrang slowly floated to the center. "Grace shall save us!"

Upon hearing *that,* they all convulsed, daring each other to berate the speaker and even the Father narrowed his massive Eye at HrorrarrAggrang who still held his float as he explained.

"Idiots! *Our* grace. This is a once-in-a-history aberration. The *glow* has perfected for itself just a *few.* After this time, I will see to it that no one ever again believes that to be possible."

The Father placed his tail into his massive arm, tapping. "And what *is* our grace?"

HrorrarrAggrang smiled slyly. "From this time forward, I invent a new religion I'm calling Christianity. At the center of it is *my* grace. Humans will know they can *never* be perfect. They'll be sure of that, and never again will they be totally free of us. My grace is this, that even though they embrace the *glow* in part, as long as they still serve us in part, I will forgive them!"

They scoffed again at his words. Someone in the corner behind all the other Alphas shouted. "First we have *grace,* and now *forgiveness?* Consume him, Father!"

"Fool! My forgiveness is this: We still consider them edible! Besides, deep down, as long as any part of us remains in them, they're *still* ours. *Our* grace is that we allow some of that *glow* to come around them… occasionally."

Another voice yelled out. "But the humans aren't *that* stupid! We can't just tell them *that.* Besides, all those *glowing* people there," his tail pointed at the orb, "know better and they'll tell them so."

HrorrarrAggrang laughed. "What they tell them is of no account. What they write is of no account even if the truth stares humans in the face! Of course we don't tell them like I've just told you. We put it in their hearts and minds that what I say is *their* God's grace, not ours! For the humans, Christian grace is *this,* that even though they're *still* sinners, they're saved *anyway!*"

Every Alpha looked dumbfounded, but one spoke up. "That's absurd! They'll *never* believe *that!*"

"Sure they will, because we'll be telling, *showing* them deep inside our reality that for them, no one can be perfect! So the only alternative, the only reasonable meaning of grace for them, will be that since no one can be perfect anyway, then despite God's grace, sin must remain in man! And all I need to start this new religion is to get someone to start calling those *holy* people that name: Christians. Humans love labels more than anything. Thus, all they need to be forgiven is to be a Christian. Heaven, I'll even throw in a little of *my* glow!"

All the Alphas stared into the orb again, waiting for another *glow* explosion, and once again they pressed hard against the ethereal walls from the excruciating sight of it. And then they broke out into raucous laughter, knowing that their "grace" would succeed over that terrible glowing grace that kept exploding from the orb.

HrorrarrAggrang encouraged them further. "They cannot receive what they don't believe, so just keep telling them 'No one can be perfect. Only God is perfect. Be a Christian. You can only be perfect *after* you die.'"

"After they die … *after* they die …" They all kept repeating, their laughter turning into uncontrolled spasms due to the hysterical irony of it. After they die is when the Alphas consume them.

F inding him sitting on a stump in the woods, Larson hailed. "King Vaughn!" Seeing his leader grimace, he corrected the title. "Err, sorry, Ranger Vaughn. We have a problem!"

Vaughn laughed sarcastically. "Oh, thanks! You've improved my day immensely, we have but *a* problem."

Larson, a stocky blond man in his early thirties, was one of the twelve Rangers who escaped the North with Vaughn. Though these twelve were not of Vaughn's people, they had fallen deeply in love with particular women of his people and were devoted to their welfare. In fact, Vaughn had officially divided his people between the Rangers whom he appointed as peacekeepers. The Rangers and the twenty-five volunteers who headed the secret service fed Vaughn a continuous flow of information from both their former country and this new one.

Larson sighed. "I believe, actually we're quite sure, we've been infiltrated, and not just us, but this country at large."

Vaughn just shook his head. "I'd been wondering!"

"Some of the new escapees just don't... well, feel right."

"Now it makes sense. I was wondering why Jargono allowed so many, even us to escape. He needed a way to get his people in, but maybe we can use this to our advantage. Have you..."

"We've already placed people to watch them. And I hope there's none we're missing."

"I don't want them to..."

"In the beginning, we'd thought it wise to swear our original group to secrecy concerning your orders to form the secret service. I don't believe they even suspect the extent of our intelligence."

Vaughn smiled. "Will I even need to think in full sentences?"

Realizing he'd cut him off several times, Larson chuckled at himself. "Beg your pardon King, err, Ranger Vaughn." Of all the devoted rangers, Larson carried the deepest feelings for

Vaughn who not only had spared his life when they'd fought, but also had saved Rebekah, his daughter, from the minefield.

Folding his hands upon his lap, Vaughn peered up at his comrade. "Larson, we're in a bit of a bind here. My feeling is that Jargono has everything to lose by disrupting us now, because then he'll have no place to hide his existing spies, and can't send new ones anymore. But this country's military isn't stupid, and may already suspect treachery. If something happens, I'm sure the Judges will extend blame to all of *us*." Vaughn paused. "I don't think they like us very much."

"What do you suggest, Sir?" Larson shook his head, thinking of his three children. Up north, his two sons who have their father's features had lived with him, while Rebekah, the spitting image of her mother, had lived with her and her people. That way, his sons were able to blend in and avoid the stigma of the 'strangers squatting at the border'. Here in the new country, Vaughn often saw Larson somehow manage to carry all three upon his person, one son in each arm, and Rebekah straddled around his neck, holding her father's head. Still, there was a continued sadness in Larson's eyes from the loss of his beloved wife, blown up in the minefield while trying to cross to the border by herself with their daughter.

Vaughn wanted Larson to realize the significance of his wife's sacrifice. "You know, my friend, I'm always amazed when I consider what events led us here. If it wasn't for your wife's bravery, I'd never have met your daughter, she wouldn't have led me to her people, and I would've never known her people to be my people. I owe your wife so much! One day, I'll show you where we buried her body."

Larson couldn't help the hint of tears in his eyes. *How does he do that? Turn things around so much, making us feel so worthy when it was all about him and his wife's sacrifice the whole time? I love this young man!*

Vaughn sighed, turning away from the past to more urgent matters. "I think it's time to finally trust someone. Like it or not, our safety depends on this country's security. I'm going to Captain Joshua and tell him a good bit of our situation."

"King Vaughn," Larson saluted by putting his hand to his heart and used the title on purpose, ignoring the order not to address him that way. "Whatever you decide, it will be the best you can do, and that is all we can do."

Vaughn nodded, feeling brought back to a point during their escape at a time when everything seemed lost and he had read Stephanie's glowing letter to all the escapees. Her words had contained that same message. *It certainly could quickly become that way now. I'm tired of always sitting on the edge of a sword. Whatever happened to just being a kid?* But on further thought about all his peers back north, he concluded. *Ehhh, it wasn't all it's been cracked up to be. I guess it's really all about being true to life, whether being a kid or grown up. Hmmm, am I grown up yet?* And for some reason, Vaughn burst into almost hysterical laughter while Larson stood silently studying him.

❧

"Captain Joshua, a word in private, Sir?"

Joshua nodded and walked off the training field into the woods, knowing Vaughn would follow. "I've been meaning to talk to you as well, Corporal Vaughn."

"Corporal?"

"Yes. You've more than earned it. In fact, your test scores, the extra classes in strategy that you took, your battle simulations on the computer are all beyond most with even five years training. You should be a Sergeant, a full officer already, but the Judges would never hear of it because you're not even a citizen, and also because you're so young, ahhh, looking, and also if I ignored all that, I'd cause you undue problems from jealous individuals in the company."

"I understand, Sir!" Vaughn hesitated, wondering if what he was about to say would ruin his promotion. "You may not want to promote me that fast after you hear what I'm about to tell you."

The Captain's eyebrows rose, his silence indicating Vaughn should continue.

"I…" Vaughn sighed because he could barely proclaim it. "I'm…"

"You're King Vaughn!"

Now Vaughn's stunned silence begged Joshua to explain. Stopping to put his hand upon Vaughn's shoulder, the Captain said, "I want you to know something. I consider you my best friend! I know most of our encounters have been official, but I know you. There's no one I'd trust my life with more than you! I don't know much of what's going on. You're actually very good at secrecy. I know you're dearly loved by all your people, that they'd die for you in the blink of an eye, and that you and Stephanie love each other with a love I could only dream to have. If you weren't an impeccable soul, there's no way you'd command such love and respect from such excellent people!"

Vaughn swallowed the unexpected lump in his throat. Seeing his Captain stop speaking, he replied. "Secrecy, yes. Ahhh, I have my own secret service!"

Joshua's eyes widened. "You *are* good. Continue."

"They've found infiltrators from the North among our people and they believe others to be in this country at large. We're keeping track of them and I'll share all that I know." Vaughn pulled out a roll of papers and handed them to Joshua. Some had pictures of the suspects.

The Captain forced a serious tone. "No pictures of *your* agents?"

"If you require, I'll do even that. Actually, I don't see that I have a choice. I have to trust someone, and I've found that I respect you even more than on the first day I met you. I would die defending you, if I had to. And I pledge this: This country's security is my security. All my people understand this and agree."

Vaughn grabbed Joshua's arm, holding it tighter than he intended. "Captain, take care what you do with this intelligence concerning Jargono and his powers. I've sworn all my people to secrecy on this, not feeling it safe to reveal such things, and certainly not believing your government would receive such information in the right way. Frankly, they're too pig-headed. But Jargono has far more power than any of you could even imagine. He's even more…" Vaughn cut himself short, surprised he felt as comfortable as he did to almost tell him about Stephanie.

But Joshua figured his thought. "My God! More powerful than Stephanie?"

Shocked again, Vaughn let Joshua's arm go. Noting the concern in Vaughn's eyes, not quite jealousy, Joshua realized Vaughn now knew there had to be an intimacy between Stephanie and him in order to know such personal things.

Joshua cleared his throat, interrupting Vaughn's thoughts. "But I don't understand. Stephanie said she does her… miracles through faith. But from all I've learned about Jargono, the little I've learned as my agents now keep disappearing, he has no faith or even a liking for any greater power."

"It's in the report, Sir." *Stephanie told him?*

"Please call me Joshua when we're like this."

"Stephanie and Jargono are of the same people, Appendaho. They're the last of them, and both seem to have inherited spiritual gifts that…"

"Ahh, I see now. The gifts of God are without calling or repentance. That's an advanced Scripture."

"Sir… Joshua." For the first time in a deeply personal fashion, Vaughn's intense stare met his new friend's eyes, conveying a seriousness Joshua was unprepared for but accepted. "There's more, much more. The Lord God has called both Stephanie and me to somehow deal with the danger. We could actually use some serious help, though. For one thing, besides Jargono's threat, there are human-demon hybrids hidden out somewhere in the North because of one of Jargono's little experiments, but unknown even to him. And if they're not destroyed within two years, they'll multiply worse than any plague you could imagine! The whole Earth will be lost."

After seeing Joshua's reaction, Vaughn realized he'd better qualify what he'd just said. "Just let the Holy Spirit guide you on this. I wouldn't have been led to confide in you if you weren't meant to listen!" After an awkward pause, Vaughn felt the need to explain even further. "This is happening *now*, Sir, not just reading some ancient book! Just let true meaning join with true words! That's the real Word of God!" But no matter how much Vaughn expanded his explanation, it didn't seem to be quite right. *Oh, God! Why don't I just shut up! How can saying true words with true meaning sound so wrong?*

Joshua was certainly confused. Vaughn wasn't *his* King, and part of the Captain rebelled at the sudden role reversal, at the sudden attack on the Holy Bible. *He's not even a Christian yet.* Another set of Joshua's feelings seemed almost to swear allegiance to Vaughn, to his cause… to *their* cause. *He isn't really attacking the Bible, though… I mean, it does say somewhere that the Holy Spirit would be our teacher… somewhere, I think. But… but the Bible IS the Word of God. Hmmm, true meaning to go with true words! If it wasn't for Stephanie, I don't think I'd even come close to considering all this. But she loves him so dearly. There's much more to Vaughn than I can see, now.*

It was Joshua's turn to be educational. "Have you got to the part in the Bible about King Josiah yet? He was a very *young* King. I think you'd love his story. Actually, your spirit kind of reminds me of him. He was eight years old when he became King, you know." *But it was the Holy Scripture that Josiah found that turned him to the Lord… or was it the meaning of what he read? Can words be without meaning? Is meaning bound to particular words, or…*

Vaughn just shook his head. "To be quite honest, Sir, I'm woefully behind in those studies. My heart burns to learn them, but our security seems to be consuming almost all my energies."

Joshua decided it was time to reveal his plan concerning Stephanie. *Well, I have to tell Vaughn but he isn't going to like this at all. How shall I put it?* "Vaughn, kill me now if you feel I've wronged you! Kill me, bury my body, and say I walked off into the woods and disappeared!"

Vaughn's mouth dropped open. He could only wait for his Captain's confession.

"I love Stephanie, with all my heart I do. And I know you love her more, but you and she can't be together. Judge Matthew would never allow it. The bastard wants her for himself."

The unpalatable predicament froze Vaughn but he managed a gentlemanly response though a part of him stayed dazed. "She's certainly a woman worthy of anyone's love, Sir."

He's not receiving this well at all, and I don't think he gets it yet. "None of her or your plans will work in this matter. You don't know Scripture nor Matthew as I do. If I don't marry Stephanie soon, *very soon*, Matthew will take her for himself. If he has to, he'll blackmail her by using you and your people's safety. My intelligence has verified as much!"

Feeling kicked in the gut as well as shocked at even more government intricacies, Vaughn chose to respond to the latter. "My God, you spy on the Judges?"

"We do, and they spy on us, but Matthew doesn't know my plan for Stephanie because I've been very careful, and neither does he suspect I'd challenge him like this, but I will. I love her, but he doesn't."

Feeling betrayed, Vaughn turned away and walked off as sobs forced themselves out. Rubbing his forehead didn't ease the swirling quagmire in his head. *He doesn't understand. Stephanie and I are married, bonded by the Tree of Life for the Tree of Life to bring forth children unto it. Has this somehow changed? What good would it do to tell him? She hasn't told him, I'm sure. He must've already spoken to Stephanie, probably even proposed. She hasn't told me!*

Vaughn turned back to Joshua, not meaning to be angry, but he sounded it. "What do you want me to say?" Next thing Vaughn knew, he had grabbed Joshua by the shirt and jerked him close, then tossed him far harder than he meant against a tree. Hearing the wind knocked from his lungs gave Vaughn a sickening feeling. *Oh, God! What am I doing?* And he ran to his Captain, easing him down to the ground. "Forgive me. God, forgive me. I didn't mean… I don't deserve to be your corporal."

But Joshua shook his head. "It's OK. I don't blame you. But I suppose if you'd acted any less than that, then I might have considered busting you back down to private! Hell, if I were you, I'd have at least busted my jaw!"

Vaughn helped Joshua stand up. *Oh, that thought had crossed my mind.* "This is why Stephanie told me I *must* receive the new will for just these kinds of things. I lose control of my anger… sometimes. But *damn it*, I just haven't had the time! And she warned me of that, too, saying, 'What if you always have something more important to do, then when will you have time?' When will I have time?"

Joshua looked at him, becoming excited but trying not to show it. "New will. The Holy Ghost? Stephanie has it?" *I knew it!*

"As far as I understand your Scriptures, I did skip ahead, yes, I would say she most certainly does. And far more powerfully then anyone in your country can believe, because she received it through understanding, dire seeking, and suffering for pure meaning of goodness. Isn't that what the testimony of Jesus Christ is really supposed to be about? Loving Goodness fully with all true meaning and understanding? And receiving a new will that defies evil at all levels by its very nature, and creating pure feelings and thoughts? Uniting our mind and heart into one by virtue of that goodness?"

Vaughn felt the Holy Spirit begin to descend upon himself quickly, and knew if he didn't stop now, he would preach to Joshua deeply about the Tree of Life and other things that he didn't believe to be accessible to Joshua at this time. Besides, Vaughn didn't know the Scriptures well enough to transpose into language that would help Joshua understand. *Damn! Now I see I really need to study them to be able to effectively place true meaning with true words!*

Joshua only sighed in response. *I have to give this a lot of thought, but none of what he's said changes anything.* "Vaughn, for all your legitimate anger, it still solves nothing. What do you want me to do?" *Damn it! I hate to put it that way but he really has no choice, neither of us do. And now that I know how very precious she is, even more than I thought, we have to save her from Matthew.*

While feeling such a depth of love, Joshua suddenly felt a connection to Vaughn's feelings with such rich empathy that it startled him, as if he was standing in the very middle of Vaughn's heart. The Captain also could feel the Holy Spirit had descended upon Vaughn, and that scared him even more. *He's the last person besides Stephanie whom I'd want to treat unfairly.* All this undid Captain Joshua who surprised himself with far more of an emotional outburst than he intended. "What do you want me to do? I'm sorry! What can we do? *You* choose!"

Vaughn couldn't speak so Joshua leveled his tearful eyes into his. "My dear friend, silence is a choice as well."

"But I… can't bring myself to…" Vaughn turned his back, fighting back tears.

"Very well… I'll do what I know is best for us all."

Vaughn waved his assent then walked away, now weeping.

Through the woods, the irritating blackbird almost seemed to be following, mocking him with harsh screeches.

☙

Something felt terribly wrong! Vaughn had only walked off not more than twenty minutes when he suddenly found his feet turning him back with increasing urgency to where he left Joshua. Pushing through brush to find a quicker route, Vaughn had thorns tear at him, but he paid them no mind. *Was it some unregistered sound I heard? I don't think so.* His eyes went pitch black, and he felt a familiar power descend upon him. When sensing a deep injustice, his heart sent an automatic plea, and the Spirit of Justice manifested within him. He still wasn't sure if this was in answer to that instantaneous prayer, or if this actually qualified as a spiritual gift, but it really didn't matter because the Spirit was with him now. In fact, his heart pounded, his eyes teared up, and his breathing quickened with it.

As soon as he caught glimpse of something odd, he broke out into a sprint. *That mound wasn't there before!* Diving onto the fresh pile, his arms swished away matted old leaves and loose soil. With a knife stuck in his gut, Joshua lay in bloodied shirt, amidst leaf litter soaked in his blood.

"This doesn't make sense! Why? *My* people wouldn't do this. Jargono has nothing to gain at this point." Vaughn remembered the intelligence papers he'd given to Joshua. "Oh, God!" He pulled open Joshua's vest to find the papers were still there! "This doesn't make sense at all. And who could even get close enough…"

Something caught Vaughn's eye. Seeing a leaf over Joshua's mouth flutter so slightly, he cleared off the debris then pressed his ear against Joshua's chest. "Oh, God! I think he's still alive."

Vaughn's mind raced as did the tears down his face. He'd worked in a hospital, even learned CPR, but what good would it do for a stab wound. The love he had for his Captain, for his new dear friend pounded in his ears. Vaughn knew Stephanie could heal him, but there was no time to fetch her. Another thought hit him, too. *Joshua can't marry her like this.* "Oh, God! No!"

Images of his wife being forced by Judge Matthew flooded Vaughn's mind, racking his heart. "No, no, no!" He threw his hands to his head but that couldn't stop the hideous pictures, they only intensified. "Joshua, please don't die. You're right! You have to marry her!"

Joshua only had minutes left when Vaughn remembered his wedding ring kept on a chain around his neck. Along with its companion ring, it had been left for him and Stephanie in the Sacred Cave, placed there thousands of years ago by Mafferan and Queen Yinauqua themselves. After mentioning in passing to Stephanie that the ring glowed sometimes, they both realized they did so when they were in trouble. *Oh, God! Stephanie, please come to me!* He knew she would be able to sense through the rings where he was then materialize alongside him… but seconds multiplied and nothing happened.

"Stephanie, I need you!" He kept rubbing the ring, but nothing happened. "*We* need you!"

Vaughn's eyes turned even darker. Feeling his Captain and new friend whom he'd just entrusted with the fate of all his people, and Stephanie's only hope dying, anger and pain overcame him. He rocked back and forth, unable to contain himself, then stretched broad his arms, and roared to heaven, "Lord God, Behold the injustice! Right the Wrong!"

Silence. Stillness. Vaughn looked at the dagger. He knew if he pulled it out it would only increase the bleeding, but he couldn't help himself. Unaware of how much force he was actually using, he yanked it out then threw it aside. It struck a nearby tree, some three feet wide, and the tree exploded into wooden shards that showered over Vaughn who threw himself over Joshua to protect him. Then Vaughn repeated his plea with all the life, all the meaning, all the love and anger he had. "Lord God, Behold the *injustice*! Right the Wrong!"

His words seemed to echo, and echo again. A wind out of the East stirred, gathering strength. The trees began to bend. Not understanding, Vaughn threw himself again upon Joshua. "Oh! God, please don't let him die!"

The tempest blew stronger so Vaughn hugged Joshua as tightly as he could, feeling that any more forceful gust would blow them both away. "So be it then, we die together!" In that instant, Vaughn realized he truly would give his life for his friend.

The wind immediately stopped. Vaughn felt a hand touching his back and sat up. Joshua gazed at him, being fully aware of all that just happened. Weakly, he whispered, "Who are you? Who *are* your people?"

Ecstatic, Vaughn answered, "Who is not important. The *what* makes the *who*. I am your *friend*. But if you must know our family background, I am told we are called Jews."

A fire lit in Joshua's eyes as he implored Vaughn. "Tell no one this! *No one!* You hear me?"

CHAPTER 3
Sisters

They all sat around the huge round-table that the King had commissioned. After years of debate he'd decreed it was time for a decision about which books were to become parts of the Holy Bible, and which should not. Everyone had favorites and there were bound to be disappointed souls. However, they also knew that they had better not make too much of an issue over it. And yet, one person raised his hand, who wasn't even assigned an official seat at the table. In fact, come to think of it, no one really knew who this person was, and when he finally did speak, it wasn't a him at all, but a her!

She took off the rather gaudy cap that some were accustomed to wearing and her long red and gray hair tumbled way down past her shoulders. With a tone of direct confrontation but one in which no one could find strength against, she spoke to both their hearts and minds as one. "What *are* we? Have we become the judges of true meaning, or does true meaning judge us, and indeed give us judgment? Do we *argue* over what is to be the Word of God, as if we ourselves were GOD over the Word which is called God?" She waited for some wise man to answer.

Oh, there were many responses rampaging, many spectral and other feelings rushing among them, until the head of the council felt himself obliged to put this *woman* in her place, while at the same time motioning to the guards to seize the intruder. "We live in perilous times and till now there have been outlandish assortments of writings all vying claim to the Word of God. It is incumbent upon us to put an end to this atrocious situation with God's grace to lead us. The people need the Word of God to be clear-cut, unmistakable, and properly approved by those knowledgeable. Now remove her to the dungeon until the King decides what shall befall her blasphemy."

But she whirled around to the guards and her stare seemed to freeze them in place, after which she returned her focus upon the tribunal and their leader. "You think you avoid such a problem by doing *this? As if the Spirit of Truth is *never now* for all time in the people's consciences and as it has been since Christ gave his precious gift of the Holy Spirit, *waiting* for those who care to seek Him out."

The leader's anger grew steadily, as well as his embarrassment, though he could find no reason as to why he should be embarrassed at whom he now perceived as nothing more than a common lay woman. "Who are you to speak against God's chosen, blessed, and sanctified people? But if you must know, the *common* people *must* have a *tangible* Word of God. Even the more common clergy of such laity are not gifted in Spirit as we are. They must have something solid like a granite foundation upon which to focus. From henceforth, the laity and the clergy shall know that *this* version of the Holy Bible *is* the Word of God."

She narrowed her eyes at them all, as they fearfully nodded their agreement with their leader. "Mark my words, gentlemen. The Spirit of Truth, that very Spirit of Jesus Christ which while in the flesh suffered humiliation from such as you, His Holy Ghost will not be mocked, for Jesus testified to us all on his last night here, that only the Holy Spirit would be our leader, our teacher of all things from the inside of each soul. Yes, gentlemen, that such teaching would be given directly between His Spirit and each individual soul. And God Himself witnesses against *all* idols that are stood up in place of the Spirit of God being *now*. You think to replace the Spirit of Truth with paper and ink and men's decisions? You think to teach generations such idol worship, as if they could not learn to recognize directly for themselves the Holy Spirit? And in fact, by such idol worship you teach them that they *cannot* recognize for themselves the Spirit of God which *is* the *True* Word of God. But even those tablets written by the very finger of God himself and delivered to Moses, where are they now, gentlemen? Were they not written in stone as you now desire to do with your Word of God? And where is the staff by which Moses judged the nations of the Earth? I tell you, that staff is hidden away against the very day which your decisions have set in motion!"

"*Guards!* Seize this devil, this *witch*. Bind her mouth so she beguiles no more!"

The trick was to wait until the Lady's Room was empty and then just pop in, no one the wiser. No worry about the guard that wasn't a guard at the inner door, or the one at the outer door, and the one secreted outside the building hanging on the corner. It wouldn't make sense for the Judges to raid any such place, seeing as they used them for *recreation,* but occasionally they had ulterior motives and one just couldn't be sure. Nevertheless, now more than ever, Stephanie needed a break from all her troubles. She desperately needed a diversion and her hobby of investigating the *underworld* had now become an uncontrollable desire.

But tonight the bathroom perpetually filled with an endless stream of young women in various stages of unconsciousness. The bootleg 'more than hard cider, more than wine,' was openly acclaimed to be the Devil's Drink… well, whatever it's called, it must have been extremely potent tonight.

Frustrated, Stephanie peered from the spiritual corridor up and down a side hall then finally took the chance to pop into the physical world. Unfortunately, it was the hall leading to the *men's* bathroom and although far less traveled than the other, a few brave women dared to drop there, too. Just as Stephanie was materializing, a young lady with shoulder-length, straight brown hair urgently staggered around the corner. One second, the hallway was empty, the next second, Stephanie was run over and both girls fell to the floor.

The girl rolled off Stephanie as fast as she could, thinking she was being attacked by something. In her dark-purple knit dress stretched from head to toe as was the unbreakable rule, she tried straightening it and standing twice but fell over each time. All her curves were obvious, and her breasts rippled at every movement.

Observing the style, and looking at her own, black, loose fitting cotton dress, Stephanie recalled wearing a lot more revealing clothing than anything worn in this Christian country. She considered the girl's attire again. *Hmm, that's an idea.* But looking again at the girl and seeing how her nakedness still came through, it began to embarrass her.

Stephanie slowly stood up, rubbing her backside and introduced herself. "Hi! I'm called Red." No one ever used real names. "Looks like the Devil's Drink is really good tonight."

The young woman eyed her, tried to reflect as best she could then made the only semi-logical conclusion. "Wow! You're right! I could swear I just saw you fricken pop in out of nowhere."

Red reached down, and heaved her up by the arm. Barely standing, the girl leaned her back against the wall, just as two young men were coming around the corner. Stephanie heard them before they rounded it.

"I'm telling you, she's as hot as they come, but unlike all the others, she really does! She enjoys it! No guilt! And we can catch her in the men's…" They ran straight into the two girls.

Half startled, not nearly as drunk as most, they squeezed each girl wherever they could accidentally manage, before backing up a bit. They tried to figure out whether they'd been overheard or not, but quickly decided, *Why would it matter? And there are* two *of them. No waiting in line.* "Hey, girls! You're the answer to our prayer. Mandy, who's your *hot* friend?"

Stephanie stared at them blankly, her feelings becoming distant as the men's vibes brought memories rushing back from only two years ago. They seemed a lifetime ago , another life before Vaughn, before knowledge. As she looked at these two men, she saw Gary, her old boyfriend, and her old gang who had intended on brutalizing her if Vaughn hadn't shown up at that window that dreadful night. She looked over at Mandy and saw herself and the past and present collided.

Still leaning against the wall, deciding which one she'd choose, Mandy answered, "This is Red, guys. I don't know if she's *hot* or not, but…"

"Mandy!" There was more in Stephanie's calling her name than just saying it. She called Mandy's name with meaning, and more than when a parent or a teacher calls for order, or even when long-lost friends call out for each other. Stephanie spoke her name with the meaning of both their lives packed into every intonation.

It seemed to ring in Mandy's ears and she couldn't help but look into Stephanie's eyes that were glowing like red-hot coals. The eager young men watched, not understanding, but sensing something amiss, they moved up close to both girls, imposing their presence.

Stephanie laid her hand on Mandy's cheek. Immediately, Mandy turned to vomit all over the two young men who then leapt backwards.

"Shit!"

"Damned *bitch*!"

They stood with arms outward, covered in vomit, while Stephanie ignored them as she propped Mandy up against the wall. Angered, the man who originally asked about the hot friend stepped through the vomit on the floor to strike Mandy. Stephanie, sensing his plan, turned her head sharply towards him. The young man promptly slipped in the swill and went down hard, hitting the back of his head with a loud crack.

Mandy just stared, feeling odd. Stephanie shot the other young man a piercing glance. Something very incongruent assaulted his mind. The physical appearance of Red signaled fair game, but that look! Seeing his semi-conscious buddy wallowing in puke, he looked back at the red fire in Stephanie's eyes then turned to run, not realizing the vomit had crept under his feet. He went down so quickly, the floor mashed his nose into his face.

Stephanie took Mandy into the Men's Room and glared at one man slumped over a urinal. "Out!" The man stared briefly into her eyes then left. Stephanie stared at the door and it locked. She pulled some bobby pins from her small purse, pinned Mandy's hair back, turned on hot and cold water, and bent her over the sink, and washed her face. She cupped cold water in her hand then held it to Mandy's mouth. "Rinse!" After she spit, Stephanie wiped her face clean with paper towels, and announced. "You know, Mandy, you're a beautiful young woman, especially without vomit or makeup."

Mandy thought, *Who the hell is this girl?* "Thanks!"

"C'mon, I'll take you home."

"I'm fine."

"No, you're not."

"If I wanted a big sister, I'd have…" But Mandy stopped in mid-sentence as if wounded in surprise, then broke down crying because she had a big sister once, a whole different life ago. She'd forgotten all about her until she heard the words come out of her own mouth. Something in the way Stephanie looked at her brought back all those feelings, all the pain.

Her sister would have been around Stephanie's age, Mandy thought as she sunk to the floor weeping uncontrollably for a couple of minutes before passing out.

Stephanie sighed, with a tear in the corner of each eye. She gazed around the bathroom, and seeing no one around, put her hands on Mandy then they disappeared.

To travel through the spiritual corridor, at first Stephanie needed to be in contact with the hair ribbon her ancestors had left for her in the Sacred Cave. It had been worn by a girl who had mysteriously disappeared, and Stephanie had descended from that lost child. Not until almost two years ago did Stephanie know about her lineage, and since then had wanted to trace her people's history.

Stephanie's prayer and faithwalking gift had turned a bottle of cursed Black Oil into sacred Light Oil that had saturated the ribbon. The Oil that glowed with a golden light gave her the power to travel in spiritual realms. But having used the ribbon for so long, Stephanie discovered she no longer needed it to transport herself. Either the Oil absorbed into her, or her ability to spiritually travel became quite honed, she couldn't tell which, but the results were a beautiful freedom of movement that had to be carefully hidden.

When Mandy awoke in the morning in such a large, comfortable bed, she knew she wasn't home. She felt around to see if a man still lay beside her, but instantly jerked her hand back. She knew she'd touched a woman's body. Her cursing woke her bed partner.

Stephanie, who had sent Lynnara to Rebekah's, rolled over with a smile. "Good morning!"

Mandy, her head pounding, held out her hands to keep Stephanie away. "I know!" She lowered the volume of her speech. "I know I didn't visit that section of town."

Stephanie stared blankly then realized Mandy's mistake and burst out laughing. "You thought…?"

Mandy pressed her head because of the noise, and groaned. But when Stephanie reached out to touch her, Mandy backed away further, began to slip off the edge of the bed and frantically grabbed at the bedcovers to keep from falling. Stephanie laughed quite loudly again, but managed to pull Mandy solidly back on bed.

"What's so funny?"

"You thought I was…" Stephanie couldn't seem to get the word out. "In *this* country? I didn't know."

Finally, Mandy's full memory returned. "Red?" Stephanie nodded, still amused.

"Where's my dress?"

"Well, when I realized I'd be taking you home, I knew you couldn't go out in the day wearing it. So I took it off, gave you a nightgown…"

"But what am I going to…"

Stephanie had used her *faithwalking* abilities to create a dress for Mandy. "I used to be the same size as you. I've something for you to wear."

She bounced out of bed quite refreshed, having skipped this early morning's spiritual lesson. She brought back a soft cotton dress embroidered in Appendaho design. Equally balanced, black geometric patterns ran around the hem, cuffs, across the waist and then up around the neck, all against a soft, creamy-white background.

Mandy's astonished eyes couldn't pull away from it. She whispered, "It'll never fit."

"Oh, it'll fit perfectly. I'm sure. And I have some undergarments for you as well." Stephanie gave her a somewhat hard look.

Mandy averted her eyes as once again she was reminded of her big sister, Carla, who would have given her that exact same look if she realized Mandy hadn't worn any bra or panties.

Stephanie saw the sadness cross her face, but said, "You can shower, no time for a bath, and then I'll tell you where you are, how to get out, and what to say if anyone stops you."

"Where am I? Who are you really?"

"I'm who they call Ambassador Stephanie."

It didn't register with Mandy. She belonged now to the lowest class of people who rarely mingled with, or cared to know anything about, those upper classes. *She thinks she's so great, all her luxuries, her prissy attitude.*

Mandy pulled off her nightgown and Stephanie made an observation. "Sit-ups?"

"Yea, how'd you know? Makes me…"

"Hot!"

Mandy was surprised. "Drives the…"

"Boys crazy! I know. I used to do the same thing. The flat tummy makes the breasts look even better, too."

Stephanie pulled off her gown as well, preparing to shower, too. "C'mon Mandy, I have to get going." Then Stephanie spoke coyly, giving her a mischievous smile. "Unless you'd like to shower with me!"

Mandy leapt from the bed. "Oh, no… no!"

Stephanie chuckled but Mandy noticed her excellent shape. "But you still look, I'm *not* flirting, but you still look hot."

"I still do sit-ups and a lot of other exercises as well."

"But you just said…"

Stephanie's tone, her demeanor had suddenly taken on a serious depth. "I used to do the same things you do, probably even a whole lot more, but now I exercise for different reasons." When she saw questions all over Mandy's face, she continued. "I still want to look *hot!* But for the one man I will always love, forever, and who would die for me anytime, to protect me."

Oh God, give me a break!

"He will, if you let Him!"

Oh God, did she just read my mind? That's impossible! "Did you… how'd you…?" But Stephanie had left her in the bedroom, having gone to the shower.

Mandy walked over to the large mirror where Stephanie had hung her new dress. She ran her fingers lightly across the patterns on the neck. Even the embroidery felt soft. *It's so beautiful. Just to touch it makes me feel… how? Oh! God, I stink! I'm filthy. I don't want to put this on until I wash.*

Walking around the apartment, studying its furniture, the little knick knacks upon shelves and dressers, Mandy began to peek inside drawers, investigating, and then she found a locked drawer.

Stephanie called out from the shower. "Feel free to look around. Let me know if you find anything of interest!"

This is too freaky! Mandy peered through the study's doorway, and heard Stephanie still in the shower. She used a letter opener to easily slip the lock of the drawer. In it was a beautiful ribbon which she wanted to touch but for some reason, she couldn't bring herself to go through with it. Underneath the ribbon was an envelope that seemed to have waterdrop stains on it.

Pulling out a folded piece of paper from its envelope, Mandy's hand started to shake. Still she couldn't help but continue, and for some unknown reason, tears formed in her eyes even before she read the poem:

The Helpless Finds Help

> *What twisted forsaking*
> *has caused such a disease?*
> *That I should be reared*
> *in ignorance and misery?*
>
> *Where those I looked*
> *even way up to,*
> *have given me emptiness,*
> *raised me to be so too?*
>
> *What terrible canker*
> *has eaten away the root?*
> *Those who were given to sustain,*
> *Have disdained to bring forth fruit.*
>
> *Yet, in spite of it all*
> *I found within myself*

That which had no place
On the tree that brought me forth.

And when they found
this fruit might be good to eat,
they chopped off the branch,
and tried to trample it under their feet.

I thank God for being merciful,
for blessing me with love.
To be disowned for this sake
is my deliverance from this hell.

From Vaughn to Stephanie with all my love
(We can't have all things to please us,
no matter how hard we try.)

As Mandy cried while reading, forgetting where she was, a towel-wrapped Stephanie came up to retrieve the letter gently. It was fortunate Lynnara stayed at Rebekah's.

Now startled, guilty, and rigidly standing half in fright, half seeking something, Mandy couldn't help looking into Stephanie's eyes.

"Thank you!" Stephanie replied in all seriousness to Mandy's silence.

Mandy's confusion mixed with her pain so Stephanie explained, "You've added your true tears to mine and to those of the man I've mentioned earlier."

"You're… not angry?"

"If I didn't see the bigger picture, I most certainly would be."

"Then it's true? You really do have a man like that?"

But Stephanie turned away with pain on her face, a level of pain that Mandy caught making her heart skip a beat. Stephanie stood very still with the letter, then when she turned again, the pain seemed gone. As she placed the letter back in the drawer and slid it closed without locking it again, she urged, "Take your shower, Mandy!"

Oh! God, she so reminds me of Carla! What happened to her? Why did she look so pained? What do I care? She's rich. She has a life. I don't anymore.

When Mandy finished bathing, Stephanie gave her a brand new hairbrush to keep. After putting on new undergarments, she pulled the new dress on and Mandy couldn't take her eyes off her reflection. The dress seemed to have a feeling all its own, somehow more than just what she saw. "I… I don't know if I can accept this."

Stephanie, who had stood back to appraise the dress replied, "It's yours. It fits you. You just don't know it, yet!"

There she goes again. I hate that! "Thank you."

"I'm leaving, but you may stay awhile, Mandy. But please don't look inside that drawer anymore. If you like, just ask me, and I'll show you what's there. My whole life is in that little drawer!"

Stephanie began to walk out and Mandy couldn't understand it. *She's just going to leave me in here?* "But you said you needed to tell me…"

"Oh, yes. That dress is proof that I've given you pass to be here. Anytime you'd like to visit, put it on and come. My door is always open to you. There's a key in your pocket!"

Feelings for her missing sister mixed with confusion and made Mandy begin to cry. "I don't even know you. Why are you doing this?"

"I once was as you are now and a beautiful young woman adopted me as her sister." Stephanie swallowed then continued. "Arlupo gave her life for me in the end. And now I have no sister.' She paused again, and Mandy thought her eyes glistened more. "Maybe I'm being selfish in trying to adopt you because I would like a sister again. After you leave, go down the main street a few blocks, turn left at the main intersection where there are plenty of nice restaurants. Inside the waistband of your dress is a secret pocket with a little gift along with the house key. If anyone stops you, just say Ambassador Stephanie has given you leave."

Mandy searched for her pocket, instantly felt the key and found a carefully concealed overlapping slit at her waist. Inside was a secret pocket with money equal to a month's wages from the shoe factory. Her mouth dropped open as she stared at the empty space where Stephanie had been.

☙

Standing in his righteous black robe, the sign of his official God-given office, of his authority to always be on the lookout for any evil, Judge Matthew issued the order as he pointed in Mandy's direction. "Follow her! Find out what you can and make her useful."

An unremarkable man in street clothing took off down the hall after her as the good Judge scratched the scar at the back of his neck that never seemed to stop itching.

Judge Matthew, full of Godly aspirations, holy desires, and passions, reveled in his official God-given position as being the natural extension of everything that was him, though it was the result of a blessed lineage. His father and grandfather, Judges before him, not only trained him, but made him privy to a special legacy that the fate of humanity centered upon him. *Too many shortsighted people have no idea what is important.* Those thoughts were not only his, though self-esteemed by him to be his own original thoughts, but also held by all the other Judges of the United for Christ. They were 'United for Christ' in principle.

The office was a natural extension, indeed, for the keen abilities of his active mind and heart to search out the utter recesses of humanity, to be acquainted with them so that blessed contact with him helped establish the understanding of order. Who else had the ardor to look upon society with as grand a vision that the classes of human beings evolved because of their spiritual levels.

Of course, those at the top had a great responsibility not to burden those below with more than they could handle. It's just that having to put up with so many lackluster souls, at times drained him, but the blessings that appropriately resulted because of his advanced spiritual achievement did serve to offset the drudgery of dealing with so many hopeless people. After all, they were all given into his hand to do with as he thought best. Quite simple reasoning was behind his oft-repeated words. "Whatever I think of is best, otherwise I wouldn't be a Judge."

"I don't like Mandy's connection to my future wife. What are the chances that of all the people, *those* two should befriend each other? How the hell did they even meet anyway? We've given our *Ambassador* upper-class status."

His underling, a younger man in a gray robe, dutifully nodded. "Yes, Judge Matthew. Actually, Stephanie's quite wealthy even without our favor. But why worry about the friendship? She's going to have to do whatever you order anyway."

"Because I've known women like our *Ambassador*. They have limits. I don't see the need to approach those limits, even if she has no choice."

"I still don't understand. Why does Mandy's connection to Lady Stephanie bother you? You weren't involved."

"But we still protect our own, remember that. Once I put the harness on my little Philly, she's going to want to buck, I'm sure. If Stephanie befriends that little slut, she'll want to help find out what happened to her friend's sister and she'll come to me. If she senses something foul, she'll look to use it to gain an advantage. She may even go to the military knowing we're rivals, then I must let her know about Judge Hiram whom I can't antagonize. He outranks me, and I certainly don't want him learning about Stephanie because he'll take her for himself." Matthew studied the face of his trainee. "How's our other matter proceeding?"

"Perfectly. I have the witnesses in place."

"You're sure they know exactly what to say? I don't want this too clear-cut. If we just convict and execute him, we have nothing to control his people by, plus my soon-to-be wife will never forgive me. I want him locked away for a very long time then I can control him, her, and their people. A dead *King* provides a rallying point. An imprisoned *King* ever hanging at death's door, one so loved, cows the people."

His understudy nodded again. "Wise words, my lord! I've instructed the account to be about a fight. The Captain struck first, unclear why, then got killed."

"Very good! Not enough to execute him on the spot, but enough to deliver him to my discretion. Excellent! The Captain is finally out of my hair. He actually thought he could take her away from me. How *pitiful!* He's as close to a heathen as it gets."

"One more thing, Judge Matthew, there were documents Vaughn gave the Captain that we left to be discovered with the body. We felt it made their connection even more suspect, and provided us with an easy way to explain how we came into their possession."

"Documents? Why wasn't I told sooner? What documents?"

"All we saw was a roll of papers handed over. We discussed whether we should examine them, but felt it better not to have our fingerprints on them at all, not to disturb the evidence that Vaughn's prints were on them."

"I don't like it. I was going to wait until the military reported him missing then discover the corpse, but those documents are an unknown. Have someone stumble upon the body within the next hour, and have those papers brought to me as evidence and I'll decide whether or not they should be made public knowledge."

"What will you do if the military demands further investigation, or if Vaughn's people rebel?"

"If they rebel, we'll slaughter them with good reason, but leave the women and children in accordance with the Holy Bible. They'll be enough to hold her to my will. As for the military, with their Captain out of the way, there's no one else here who can dare challenge me unless they learn something useful. But we *must* neutralize Mandy, she might upset *everything*."

"Why not just reveal her sister is alive? And if she doesn't do as you…"

"Because I don't have her sister, Hiram does. And the way he has her, well, let's just say the masses can't know."

"I didn't realize…"

"Keep your mouth shut! Does it matter what happens to heathen, the foreigners, or our own scum in our town? They're all by our grace only here to serve Christ's chosen."

"How shall we get rid of the girl?"

"I don't see that we actually need to waste her. Judge Aaron at Bethel has been looking for someone special. But before we pick her up, let's see what my spy turns up about how he can use her first. Then next time she shows up underground, make her disappear, she's by herself, anyway. I've never seen a whole family cursed as badly as hers. They must have provoked the Lord's wrath something terrible."

"For sure, my lord."

"Walk me to my chambers!"

They strolled silently together, their robes creating the illusion that they floated down the hall. No sooner than they entered his chambers where he sat for official business, then a rapid knock broke their contemplation. Another man in street clothing entered without permission. "My lord, they've found the body already. The military's quite upset. They've taken the corpse into their private shrine."

"Damn it! The papers! We won't get our hands on them now." But he reconsidered, and added, "But really, the heathen really have nothing of interest to me. It's just that I just don't like unknowns." Turning to the spy, he commanded. "See what you can find out." To his underling, he ordered, "Go pick up our boy *King.*"

❧

God, this steak is so delicious! It's been so long since I tasted anything *like this. And that waiter's so handsome, and he looks at me like… I don't know, but it's not the way all the other guys look at me. I mean, besides being a swanky waiter, he looks at me kind of… special? Hmmm, must be this dress, looking upper class.*

"You look deep in thought, Mandy."

A person would notice when someone sits across from them in a private booth, but Mandy really was deep in thought, so when the man spoke, it startled her. "Excuse me?" Then she realized he called her by name. *Oh God, how does he know my name?* She tried to discern any clue as to who or what he was, but he looked just like an average person, about thirty years old she guessed. She immediately resorted to her sole strength, and leaned forward so he could peek down at her breasts. *Damn! That won't work in this dress.* It dawned on Mandy what the mysterious feeling in the dress was. *I can't flirt at all in this! It's just so beautifully decent, its whole feeling, the designs, the cut, everything about this dress is so right. That must be why the waiter kept treating me like that. He thought I was…*

60

"Look, Mandy, I'm not here to scare you. Frankly, the government needs your help!"

Government! My help! "My help?"

"Yes. You were seen leaving Lady Stephanie's apartment. Well, you see, none of us have ever been in there, what with the guards and all. She hardly lets anyone in, but we're not sure as to her loyalties and some suspect her of possibly being a danger to our country, possibly even a blasphemer. But you seem to have somehow gained access to her. How did that happen?"

"Lady Stephanie? Why do you call her that? Ahhh, I really can't tell you much of how I *gained access* to her 'cause… Hey, wait a minute. I think I know you!" And sure enough, she remembered seeing him in the underground, getting drunk, too.

The man subtly motioned his hand for her to speak very softly. He knew from where she remembered him. "I go there on official business. Is that where you met Lady Stephanie?"

Official business my ass! Come to think of it, I bet you watched my ass more than once. Hmm… "What's in this for me? We don't talk about things from *there*. You of all people know that! And I asked you a question, why do you call her Lady?"

The man smiled and began staring at her as he would have in the underground. *Poor kid, she thinks she can play me.* "She says she's some kind of royalty from up north, from a people now dead. The people with her now call her Lady, more like she was some kind of queen or something to them, too, instead of just a representative. If you ask me, I don't believe any of that crap, do you?"

He's right. She does act like she's some darned queen. That's one of the things that bugs me about her. She thinks she's so perfect. "To tell you the truth, I really didn't talk much with her 'cause I was drunk and she took me home to try and rescue poor me, see?"

"So you met her…" His facial expression indicated the underground and Mandy returned the same kind of answer. This spy wondered. *But no one saw her leave her apartment last night. What the hell?*

"Hey! You still haven't told me what's in it for me?"

The man nodded, reached into his pocket then slid to Mandy some money under his hand. "As long as you're useful, we can continue this arrangement."

Mandy placed her hand atop his with mock affection, slid the money under the table then counted it. *One week's salary at the factory. Damn, this bastards cheap!* "I don't know, this doesn't seem like much for putting my life in danger."

The spy placed his hand over Mandy's with a smile, but suddenly began to squeeze very hard, still smiling as if nothing was happening. Mandy tried to pull away but he held on tightly and shook his head in warning. Suddenly she became terrified, aware that she felt more like a kid in the hand of an adult.

"Listen, Mandy. I know all about you. And in fact, I think we should hook up, too, so I can feel you for myself and see if what the others are saying is really true. You really do look *hot*… except get rid of that awful dress when this is over, OK?" He was still squeezing her hand, and could see tears begin to form in her eyes.

"What do you want me to do?"

"For now, I want you to get real close to her, search her apartment thoroughly then tell me everything you find. After that, we'll see. I may want you to place something in her apartment."

"Like what?"

He eased off hurting her and smiled differently. "You've now become my spy in training. You might place stuff for watching or listening to her, or we might want you to put something there for other reasons. The point is, in the spy world, you never know until that time comes, understand?

Mandy smiled. "This is kinda cool. Only thing I know so far is she's got this locked drawer but I already broke into it, see? I didn't look at everything in there, but a stupid ribbon and a stupid poem. But she said her whole life was in that drawer… and she said she'd show me if I asked.

"See, you're a natural at this. Maybe…" he paused a moment as if in serious thought, "Maybe if you do a good job for me here, you can be placed permanently with an official job in the government, instead of that lame factory you have now. God is blessing you, Mandy."

☙

"That's right, Grinchback! Now, *now* give her the next thought, the next feeling."

Grinchback reached his arm more deeply into the dirty blue orb, connecting to Mandy's tree. Next he turned the tree's image into her real image and reached deeply into Mandy's heart so that her tree's roots would move further away from Stephanie's glowing roots to make her feelings go against

Stephanie. Then he turned her back into her tree to check, to be sure it worked.

Every human is born connected to a corresponding tree in the Dead Forest. And what affects one, affects the other. Grinchback flipped rapidly back and forth between her tree and her true real time-image so that he could observe the tree's continued progress and compare that to how she looked in person. Grinchback spoke into the orb. "Finally, Mandy, you can rise to the top. You can be better than that rich bitch Stephanie. You can be better than her! How's she gonna say how great she is when you bust her for blasphemy or treason or somethin'?"

Mandy thought to herself, *Yeah, what is she gonna say?*

Highest Councilor ScrabaGag watched with extreme satisfaction at his offspring's growing talents in ethereal tree pruning. *Soon, maybe he won't have to look at the ethereal trees in order to tell what's going on with the humans and he'll know how to affect their trees just from looking at their human form. I've never seen any Alpha flip back and forth as quickly as he does and understand exactly what's going on. Our ethereal forest has need of such an excellent arborist as he.*

"Very good, indeed! Remember, they taste best if you raise them up high before you tear them down low. But if you raise 'em up and bring 'em down a bunch of times, you increase their torment beyond just delicious and into exquisite. But besides this, by manipulating her and a few others, we hold all the cards and have much versatility. Being versatile means greater freedom to react and counter whatever the *glow* might bring."

"Yes, Master. And this will help us with the rest of our plans for sure. But let's not forget about HrorrarrAggrang. We're technically invading his area."

"Oh, I haven't forgotten about our crafty nemesis. Let's just assume he's aware of what we're doing, and make plans accordingly."

CHAPTER 4

Word is Bond

He shouldn't have been laughing given the situation he was in, but what the hell! *If there is a hell, surely I'm in it right now and so when this is finally over, well, there's no place else to go but up!* And he broke out into another hysterical laughing fit, making his shoulders hurt even more because of how tightly the rack had been pulled.

The inquisitor eyed him dolefully. "You're salvation is no laughing matter, for without true confession of *Christ...*" It seemed he loved emphasizing certain words by tightening the wrack at the exact times he spoke them. "—you'll surely end up in *hell.*" And he tightened it another notch with even more strain than before.

The poor man didn't want to give the inquisitor the satisfaction of hearing his cry but he just couldn't help it. However, another wretch was suffering an even worse fate. The inquisitor pulled out yet another loop of bowel using a surgical instrument through a cut in the belly, then twisted the intestine so it convulsed amidst the man's howls of agony. The tormentor bent over into his suffering face. "Do you with all sincerity confess that Jesus is the Son of God? Do you confess that you have been only falsely worshiping him, still clinging to your Jewish fallacies?"

The man screamed at him. "Yes… how many… times… do you… want me . . to say… yes?"

That was a good question, but the racked man knew the answer. "Until you're dead!"

Hearing him speak the truth, the inquisitor strolled back to him. "You aren't laughing this time. Why?"

"Because I see the truth."

"And what would that truth be?"

"You can't ever trust that our confession is true, so you'll only suppose it's true if we hold to it on our dying breath. Then you can pat yourself on the back with knowing you saved another wretched soul from the devil."

The inquisitor nodded again. "True enough."

It suddenly dawned on the wracked man that Jesus Christ was in similar fashion hung up as he was now, with the exception that nails pinned him up and his own body weight stretched him. *And all accounts say that he never denied what he was! Even through all that pain! Hmmm… He was either crazy, or … But I've read the New Testament, his words weren't that of a crazy man… but… surely this* Christianity *isn't what he died to bring us.* "Tell me something, *Christian,* if you had heard rumor that some carpenter was suspected of worshiping something other than your religion, would you put him through this inquisition as well?"

"I see your point, but I suppose it's no harm to answer you truthfully. Yes, of course I would."

"I thought as much. So… you are in fact raising to Godly status those who contributed to and finally did crucify Christ, yes?"

After further thought, he confessed. "I suppose I am. They were doing God's will without knowing it, making his confession true."

"I think you're a little confused Inquisitor, because had they been doing God's will, then Jesus wouldn't have forgiven them. Forgiveness is for those who are doing evil, not those doing good." And the Jewish man hanging there, feeling his joints out of place, knowing he was about to die right after his next words, managed to level his eyes deeply into the inquisitor with clarity of heart and mind he never felt before. "I forgive you, Christian."

The inquisitor's eyes grew larger, his face turned red. "You forgive *me*? How dare you? You Jewish *scum*." And he ran at the racked man with one of his surgical tools in hand, but just then the door burst open, and a higher inquisitor yelled out, "Stop!"

If he didn't know that to disobey his lord was indeed punishable by the same torture, he would have gutted the man right there. But he also knew that torture for salvation was strictly prescribed and to deviate from the official methods was also a punishable breach. If his lord had entered a moment later, he wouldn't have had time to cover his transgression. He stopped and bowed to his lord. "Forgive me. I was weak and this *devil*… I allowed him to temporarily overcome me."

"Let him go! His freedom has been bought!"

"But that's… not possible."

"He has friends in high places who offered enough *money* for him, but we won't receive *anything* until his safe delivery. Clean him up and bring him to my quarters." And the lord left.

All through the ordeal of slowly returning the rack to a normal position, for it had to be done slowly, else the joints wouldn't return properly, the Jewish man kept repeating. "I forgive you. I *forgive* you."

And what really bothered the inquisitor was the simple fact that he sounded truly sincere, but he still wasn't sure if it was for the purpose of mocking him, or truly forgiving him. And yet, either way made him angrier by the moment. *I'm not evil.* In fact, once the man was taken down, cleaned up, dressed and about to part from him, the Jewish man reached over with a passionate hug and spoke yet again. "I forgive you! God has saved me from you but I forgive you anyway."

For the inquisitor, it was simply too much to take. He wanted so badly to kill this man, but he knew that would not be Godly, at least if his forgiveness was real. *But a heathen cannot forgive anyone. Besides, I haven't done anything wrong that needs forgiven. But what if he isn't a heathen, anymore? Forgiveness is only for the evil...* It was all too much pressure with no resolution and he began to hear and see those he tortured all saying the same thing to him. "I forgive you. I forgive you..."

And the more he heard it, the more his mind began to slip away until he sat on the floor quite catatonic. The Jewish man bent over and whispered in his ear yet once more. "I *forgive* you." And the man fell over dead.

When Stephanie walked into her apartment, Mandy awkwardly stood in the middle of her living room as if she had just arrived in that spot. *Damn it! I didn't expect her back so soon. What am I going to say?*

Stephanie took a long glance at her, smiled, then turned back through the doorway to kneel down. When she turned back around, her arms were full of a stack of boxes, bags and pouches, then she back-kicked the door shut. "Well, it's good to see you again Mandy, though I didn't expect to see you so soon. Well, actually, your timing is great! 'Cause after seeing you last night, the fashion you were wearing… well, it got me to thinking I needed some better clothes. Maybe you can help me choose. Make-up, too?"

Mandy's eyebrows rose, and then a smile slowly broke over her face. "Oh! I haven't done this in…" Then that same sadness, again, that Stephanie expected to see. "Although… ahhh, I don't think my sister would have approved of the clothes I wore there."

Stephanie nodded, and said, "You know, when I first saw your purple dress… Oh, I had it cleaned for you. Ahhh, it needed it. Anyway, I thought it was really cool. Ahhh, till I saw how naked it made you look, kinda risqué."

Mandy laughed with mischief. "Yeah, well, isn't that the point? I mean, we want to look hot, right? And the closer the hot bod gets to naked, the more it drives 'em crazy."

Stephanie smiled, remembering that very same reasoning. But then Mandy asked, "I don't know, do you still do that if you have a steady man? You said you still wanted to look hot, but, hmmm."

"Like I said, I wouldn't be anything other than pure *hot!*" And Stephanie returned every bit or perhaps even more mischief in her laugh and demeanor.

Mandy studied her. *She's one confusing girl. I give her that. Maybe she's not so bad after all.* "But that still doesn't answer my question, really."

"Well, we look hot to get attention, right? But also we just wanna look *hot* 'cause it's like lively, right?"

The first part Mandy knew was right. "Huh, I never thought about it being *lively*, but ya know, I guess you're right."

Stephanie put on a seductive voice. "Well, I always want to be lively to the man I love." And then she giggled normally. "But the trouble is I got a little confused when I kept attracting crummy guys, then after we did it, I didn't feel like being lively at all. Because… ahhh… well, you know, they sorta ignore you after they get theirs, ya know? Well, some don't exactly ignore you, but they aren't exactly filled with love or even any serious care, either."

I can't believe how she's talking! She couldn't possibly have been…

"Would you like to know how Vaughn and I met?"

Mandy's eyes grew wide. *I love hearing stories like this.* "Sure!"

Stephanie began her story with some background of how she grew up as they both sat on the bed.

Mandy couldn't believe it. "You… were *that* poor? And had parents like *that?*" She reflected on her own life. *At least while they were alive, I had really great parents.* Mandy teared up but didn't want to interrupt Stephanie's story. "Just go ahead, I'm all ears."

When Stephanie described her past behavior, about the drugs, the sex, she had no problem describing the details because, for one thing, they were both the same kind of girls once, and for another, Stephanie knew none of it existed inside herself even in the least bit now so there was nothing to be ashamed of.

Mandy stared at her. *I still can't believe this, and some of that stuff is way past even me, but… she looks like she's absolutely telling the truth! But I don't see or even feel any of that in her anymore!*

And then Stephanie got to the part where Vaughn appeared in the bathroom window to rescue her, then she stopped and stretched. Mandy could almost feel herself being there in Stephanie's story and impatiently pushed Stephanie's knee. "Stop being bad, keep telling. What happened?"

Stephanie finished that part of her life by telling how she spent that night in bed with Vaughn just talking through the night."

Mandy shook her head, amazed, thrilled, but also wondering. "You guys didn't bang that night? Oh, God! I would have been all over him."

Stephanie laughed. "Well, believe me, I wanted him practically from the first time I set eyes upon him, but you see, he was hurt really badly and…" *Oh, I can't tell her how I healed him. I don't want her to know anything about that, yet.* "And frankly, I was pretty ashamed of gettin' him almost killed… I was really shook-up."

Mandy nodded. "But… how'd you come to be…" She searched for the right word.

Stephanie laughed again. "Kinda a prude?"

"Yea!"

Stephanie remembered that Arlupo had never even heard of such a word, but in this country, with its double lifestyles, it made sense that Mandy knew. "Well, I'm not really prudish at all. As I said, I'd love to make love with Vaughn, and that will always be true. It's just that now, I get this funny odd feeling just even considering doing some other guy. Partly because I love Vaughn so deeply, but also if I sense someone doesn't love me, then wanting to have sex with him just feels…" And Stephanie let her sentence hang open.

Mandy considered how to finish it for Stephanie. But in order to do that, she had to empathize with her situation, but had to first imagine what it would feel like to actually be loved by a man. But before she could figure out what Stephanie left unsaid, a conclusion dawned on her. "You mean you haven't had sex with Vaughn?"

Stephanie sighed, remembering their dream love. "There's a lot of my life story left to share if you're interested, but I'm tired of talking about the past. Let's try these clothes and make-up."

Mandy smiled slyly. "You know, you and Vaughn should just hook-up underground."

But Stephanie had already bounded off the bed and began opening boxes. That was all it took to draw Mandy's undivided attention.

After hours of experimentation, laughter, and jokes, there were three piles of clothing. One pile fit Stephanie, one pile was too small for her but just right for Mandy, and one pile of seamless underwear that made them look hot but not quite naked. Since their hair colors, facial features and tones were different, two makeup piles formed as well.

Stephanie took hold of Mandy's arm affectionately, but quickly qualified the gesture. "I'm not flirting!" They both laughed. "You take these piles!"

Mandy pulled away, partly hurt, partly touched by her kindness, and partly angry, "I don't need your charity!" *Oh! God, what am I saying?*

Stephanie could see the transparent very dark gray arm vibrating strongly over her head, reaching deeply inside of Mandy. *What are you up to with her?* "I'm sorry, Mandy. Forgive me. I never meant to imply you did. I'm sure you work hard, or you wouldn't have such nice clothes as you already have. It's just that…"

Oh God! I was so rude. Nice clothes? Ha! Mandy didn't know it but she began turning red from her memories of how she got just about anything nice. When she saw Stephanie begin to pack up the pile that would have been hers, she had to ask. "Why are you so nice to me? I don't deserve *anything* from you." *I really don't. I just fricken searched her whole room. I probably would have even searched her special drawer if she hadn't have come in.* And in fact, it was the last thing left for her to spy on.

Stephanie leveled her eyes into Mandy's. "You may not believe this because you see me here in luxury that I really don't give a damn about, but really my life has been mostly miserable. Yes, Vaughn and I love each other, but as I've said, I still haven't told you very much. The one redeeming factor in my life is that I've learned how to truly love, but not just

Vaughn, but to have love for life, for people, and also for special people like you."

Mandy sneered. "I'm not special." *There she goes* again! *What is it with her?*

"Aren't you special to yourself, Mandy?"

And *that* question just about seemed to smack her across the face, because its whole meaning, tone, and feeling were so darned loving. In fact, there was no escaping the answer.

Mandy leaned back in her stool that was in front of the mirror along with Stephanie and replied honestly. "I don't know." And tears began to roll down her cheeks.

"Don't know, or too hurt to know?"

Turning her head away, she tried her best to hold in her sobs. *She's really good at this. Stephanie must be one hell of a spy for the north or something like that. No wonder the government watches her so very closely.*

Stephanie added, "That's why I offered you the clothes and stuff, Mandy, because I love giving meaningfully to people. I love my friends, and just want to be good to them when it's in my power. Isn't that what friendship is?" Mandy nodded as the pile of new things was placed on her lap.

∾

As Stephanie proceeded down the promenade thinking deeply about how strongly the gray arm influenced Mandy's actions, Barrack rushed up to her. His gray robe rustled in the increasing wind, and his straight dark hair did not fare much better. "Lady Stephanie, Judge Matthew urgently requests your presence."

Stephanie didn't slow her brisk walk since she missed morning time with her people and Vaughn, and intended to visit them now. "My people need my presence first. Tell…"

"You may *not* visit them at this time!"

Stephanie stopped cold, but Barrack answered her icy expression. "Please. I'm not at liberty to discuss it out here. It's why you're summoned. One of your people has committed murder."

Folding her arms, Stephanie waited.

"The man murdered is someone you know, but I'll be in dire trouble if you force me any further."

She felt her heart skip, whirled, and left the understudy behind. When she arrived, she opened the judge's chamber door without knocking.

Judge Matthew rose, came around his desk, and took her arm with solemnity. "I believe you were close to our beloved Captain Joshua. I'm sorry. He's dead. Murdered by someone you know who's been taken into custody. Your people have heard about it and they need you to calm them, lest something terrible happen to them that we hope to avoid."

But Stephanie only stood still then heard herself whisper. "Joshua's dead?"

The Judge, his ever official-looking jowls appearing with even more gravitas, reached his hand out towards Stephanie's cheek. She immediately backed away, trying very hard to control her emotions, lest her powers break through and she begin to glow or manifest them in some other overt way. *God, I finally know who Matthew reminds me of. That damned priest in the government church back home. They're all fricken the same!*

The Judge consoled her. "I'm sorry. I only meant to comfort you. We shall hold the trial later today. We have witnesses to the murder." Matthew was the picture of compassion and delicate concern for her disturbed state. He knew it was about to become a lot worse.

It was obvious Stephanie didn't trust Matthew, nor readily accept his words. "I want to see whom you're accusing. I want to hear it for myself, and I want… what is your protocol? Is there any defense that…"

"I shall sit as Judge as the Lord Jesus Christ has so blessed me to be. I assure you I will judiciously weigh all words and allow His gracious Spirit to guide me in passing judgment."

Stephanie nodded and Judge Matthew, speaking sadly, motioned to Barrack, "Fetch him."

Stephanie's heart began to pound. *Oh God, someone I know. Well, of course, I know* all *my people.*

A man, with his head covered and both hands shackled within a wide crude board that opened and closed down its longer length, was forced through the door and fell at the Judge's feet. Matthew tried to explain. "He was hostile, took down six of my personal guard. I apologize for the treatment."

Stephanie, boiling with rage, and using all her willpower for restraint, spoke softly. "Remove the *bag* from his head, please."

"As you wish."

"Barrack?"

"I'm sorry, Lady Stephanie." Barrack's tone worried her because she knew of his genuine feelings of friendship for her. He ran his hand through his brown hair seeming to steel himself, then he pulled off the hood.

Lady Stephanie's eyes met Vaughn's. She had such a deluge of feelings collide against all her efforts to restrain them that she collapsed to the floor. In some distant place she also knew Joshua was dead and Vaughn was about to die and feeling so alone she felt evil suffocating her. In truth, as the hood was removed, Matthew's heart rejoiced and his spirit kept pouring over Stephanie imagining them being together.

Stephanie wasn't sure how long she was out, but when she came back to her senses and realized the hands upon her trying to lift her belonged to Matthew, she wrenched herself free. "I would like to talk to *Vaughn*... alone, please."

The good Judge nodded and everyone quietly left.

Stephanie crawled over to him. "Oh, Vaughn!" She touched his cheek. "What do we do now? I know it can't be true, it just can't."

He looked away, and that scared her until his silence provoked her to panic. "Vaughn! It isn't true."

"I'm sorry, Stephanie. He told me he loved you, that he wanted to marry you and that he was better for you than I am. I couldn't help myself!"

Stephanie's shock took over and Vaughn thought he could see ripples of something undefined moving through the air. He wasn't sure if that was her power or something else. "No! I don't believe you!"

"You know I have a temper! I reacted badly and before I knew it, he was good as dead. I'm sorry."

"NO! I *don't* believe you. They're forcing you..."

Vaughn looked her straight in the eye. "No one's forcing me to do this. They're cremating the body shortly. I've requested that you be allowed to attend the service because I knew you wouldn't believe me, and I know you love him."

"Oh, Vaughn! But not like I love you. I'll never love *anyone* like I love *you*."

"But you do love him, dear Stephanie."

"I suppose. If it had to be anyone else, it would have been Joshua… I suppose."

"Remember, through our prayers, Lady Stephanie. Remember the last time… through our prayers." Vaughn called out, "Barrack!" And when he opened the door, Vaughn said, "Take her to the funeral, please."

☙

The sound of the funeral pyre seemed so distant though Lady Stephanie could feel its heat on her face, and actually stood arm to arm among a large crowd of military and town officials. She was alone in her thoughts, *Through our prayers … Through our prayers.* She and Vaughn had established that phrase as a secret code a long time ago, before they'd been split up in the North by her mother's murder. That phrase ensured their communication was true. *Remember the last time. Not: Remember* for *the last time, but, remember the last time.*

Her mind went back to when Jargono held her captive. She feared for Vaughn's life and to save him, she decided to give herself to Jargono. She had used a saying that could tell Vaughn she still loved him without Jargono realizing the message. She followed it up with *through our prayers.* That was the last time she'd used that phrase. *Somehow, now, Vaughn is doing the same thing, I'm sure. But what's his meaning? Damn it! I should have just read his mind! I'm such an idiot! Am I not supposed to be able to hear direct meaning though?*

☙

With his tail still tapping in his arm, the Highest Councilor slowly floated in circles around a pedestal that had the official truce upon it. The Demons, or Alpha, as they preferred to be called, were never known to be patient negotiators. And having assigned the meeting time according to Middle Eastern Standard Time, such parameters having been set forth in the finalized truce more than two thousand years ago, Mafferan was now one hour and twenty three minutes late. The Alphas' shimmering lost luster, their rippling seemed erratic. Adding insult to injury, Mafferan finally showed up quite stealthily in the tension packed neither-light-nor-dark room. He materialized behind the Highest Councilor, then tapping his foot impatiently, waited to be recognized.

Highest Councilor ScrabaGag turned slowly, having finally accustomed himself to Mafferan's tricks. He squinted his Great Eye at his 'friend'. "You're late."

"Yes, well… at our next meeting I give you privilege! Balance restored."

The Highest Councilor carefully considered his words. "Our next meeting." *What next meeting?* He hid his anger. ScrabaGag noticed Mafferan carried no documents. "You seem quite unprepared."

"I've been studying protocol. I formally request right to a neutral arbiter. We're at an impasse of differing perspectives."

If it was possible for the Highest Councilor's Great Eye to enlarge, it certainly seemed so. ScrabaGag spoke flatly. "We haven't even begun…"

"Yes, yes," Mafferan waved his hand about, "Your underling… How's the arm, Grinchback? I trust I replaced it well?" Mafferan had reattached it after cutting it off last time they met.

Grinchback, having floated beside and then behind his Master who was also his sire, leaned around him. "Oh, yes! Quite fine, thank you!"

"Quite a piece of work you did, that summons. I had no trouble following it at all. That's how I know we're at an impasse. No need to drag this out. Let's get to the heart of it."

ScrabaGag hadn't anticipated this. He Eyed his faithful underling who looked unaware that he was being scrutinized. *Now I know he didn't do* exactly *as I told him… somehow.* But then it dawned on the Highest Councilor. "Neutral party?"

"Yes, yes. It's in the fine print of the official, codified truce. We sent you the dually approved copy. Would you like me to go fetch the actual document? It has your father's seal on it."

The Highest Councilor fumed, not able to restrain himself. "Fine print? That's ridiculous. No one ever reads the fine print!"

"Well, I did." Mafferan looked straight at Grinchback, who returned to silently hide behind his Master. *Hmm, is he hiding from me, or his Master? I think I saw a flicker of Eye smile, though.*

"Neutral party? I don't even know…"

"I have just the man. Cloud Walker!"

ScrabaGag burst into a demon laugh. "*Him?* He's full of *glow.* That's not neutral. Since you're so fond of my underling, Grinchback here…" And he yanked Grinchback out from behind him and thrust him forward almost into Mafferan.

"Yes, yes! I like him! I like him very much! He's kind of cute, in a demonic sort of way."

Cute? Cute. Cute? Grinchback kept kicking it around in his bulbous head, but Mafferan interrupted his thoughts. "But I'm afraid that wouldn't work. He's too close to you and he'd feel the pressure."

Highest Councilor ScrabaGag cut to the chase. "Define neutral, Mafferan." And ScrabaGag folded his very long black tail in his arm and began to tap again.

"I suppose it would have to be someone with a bit of both of us in him!" Mafferan thought for a bit. "I suppose I could choose *him.*" And Mafferan pointed into the orb at a vision he'd brought up.

Tap, tap, tap… "*Who?*" The Highest Councilor asked before he even looked.

"His name's Vaughn. He's obviously not my first choice."

Surprised, Grinchback burst aloud. "The human who made all those funny noises when he was younger? Who used to pick at himself, screech, and…"

His Master hushed him. "He has a lot of *glow.* I don't see how…?

Mafferan shook his head. "But he's human, on Earth, between you and me. And, if you look closely …" Mafferan waved his hand and a very large blue orb appeared and floated in the meeting room. The ball of glowing blue light manifested no outwardly physical manifestations except simply being blue light. Yet, secreted within it were in fact, many subtle controls. "Hope you don't mind. I borrowed yours and cleaned it up a bit!"

Astonished, Grinchback wondered aloud. "I didn't know they could be moved like that." His Master's tail whipped out, swishing him to the back again.

Mafferan waved his hand and a vision of Vaughn's tree appeared within the now crystal clear blueness. *Oh! What has happened to that boy?*

The orbs had been created from the beginning, or whenever the Earth was. Created along with the Ethereal, now home to the Alpha. The Spiritual Corridor, sometimes called the Ethereal Corridor, connects the Earth and the Ethereal. The orbs were designed specifically to watch, care for, and explore all the mysteries of the Ethereal Forest, which the Alpha now call the Dead Forest. There is hidden speculation as to who was originally intended to maintain and use them. When the Alpha needed a place to go to other than Heaven, they claimed the Ethereal and the Dead Forest as their rightful inheritance.

Every human being born into the world immediately sprouts a spiritually connected ethereal tree which manifests the person's emotional, mental and spiritual conditions through changes in its ethereal form and light displays. Souls may be affected through attempted tree manipulations of either the branches representing the mind, or the roots for the heart, or the trunk for the soul which allows communication between heart and mind.

Vaughn's tree had a mixture of deep blackness and bright glow fading, surging, and it all pulsed together amidst many branches full of large, green leaves. A good number of other branches had only buds upon them. Deeper within the tree were remnants of quite a few broken branches and scars on the trunk that had obviously borne even more branches. A few branches seemed just the slightest bit deformed, although it would take an ethereal arborist to note it and explain it properly.

The Highest Councilor peered closely. *How does Mafferan get such a clear picture? I watched how he did it this time and I almost picked it up.* Pointing his tail into the orb, vibrating its tip for emphasis, "You call *that* neutral?"

Mafferan innocently responded. "Look at that blackness!"

ScrabaGag's Eye frowned. "Fool me once, you know that saying. That's not *our* blackness."

Surprised, Mafferan exclaimed, "Really!" as he concentrated intently upon Vaughn's tree and sharpened the focus even more, while Grinchback stared in amazement. The clarity of the orb's extra-high definition made Grinchback's memory of their usually cloudy appearance seem even cloudier.

But the Highest Councilor had enough of Mafferan's games, and waved the official parchment around. "Look, Mafferan, don't play us. If you'd rather toss this truce away…" *I know I've got the upper arm.* The Alpha have no hands.

He thinks he's got the upper hand. Mafferan pointed at a root deep within Vaughn's tree. He had to fade out a tangle of glowing roots to uncover the root in question. "But that grayness *there*… is yours!" He beckoned the Highest Councilor over but didn't give way.

ScrabaGag had to come up to almost touching Mafferan who was glowing now. His ripples all seemed to be running away from his points of closest proximity as he peered through the orb. Huddled together like that, they almost appeared as best friends but the Alpha also imagined. *Soon, I will consume you... relishing each morsel.*

Highest Councilor ScrabaGag nodded his bulbous head slowly. "So it is. So it is. I recognize that. Definitely ours." *Now that I see it, I know what to do. Idiot! Fool! You should've never shown me. Vaughn's done that on his own, with his own understanding. I'll just encourage him further. Ha! We'll have a meeting of the minds!* "Very well!" ScrabaGag agreed. "Vaughn is neutral."

Mafferan immediately waved his hand and the glowing roots he had faded, returned to their brightness.

ScrabaGag patiently tapped his tail in his arm. "As long as our grayness remains in him, he may represent you. The moment it's gone, he's dismissed."

"Balance struck." Mafferan smiled and offered his glowing hand to shake on it.

ScrabaGag glared at him. "We are not amused."

Mafferan smiled and disappeared, leaving the orb floating in the meeting room.

Grinchback stared at his Master, then at the orb, then back at his Master. The underling tried hard not to let his Great Eye show his amusement. *He left Master's orb here. Can Master return it?*

The Highest Councilor came as close as possible to what can only be described as a demon sigh, a sort of gurgle accompanied by a flattening of ripples and dulling of shimmer. He waved his arm and a wall disappeared, showing the corridor. Floating up to the orb, he put his muscular arm upon it and began to push. Grinchback again gaped but his amusement extinguished when his Master's tail whipped out, grabbed, and planted him firmly beside the orb. Without looking at his formerly smug underling, he ordered, "Push!"

Grinchback set both his tail and arm upon the orb. *I wonder what all the rest of the Alpha will say when they see us? Hmm, no, they wouldn't dare say any anything. There's no demon like my Master.*

And it was true. ScrabaGag had risen faster than any Alpha in known history, breaking only several moderate level rules to get there. Consuming the three High Councilors, who had all been appointed after the Father consumed the original three during Pentecost, was perhaps the most serious infraction. The three had now become one, affording a tremendous locus of power.

However, not to be ignored was the secret that ScrabaGag's underling was his very own offspring. There weren't supposed to be demon dynasties, no family ties to impede the rise to the top of only the most excellent individuals, the absolute best of Alpha. If ever there was a species that proved Darwin's theories of adaptation and natural selection, the Alpha was it. When Darwin came to the fore, many an Alpha cheered, feeling that perhaps even an open and outright agreement could be struck between them and the Earth against the *glow.*

❧

HrorrarrAggrang considered how he would deal with the nuisance of the impending visit of the Highest Councilor. *Why announce it to me? He'll never show up at that specific time. Why would he? That was just to put me on edge, to interfere with my day-to-day activities because he knows I'll be expecting him at some other time. Now I can't meet with her as I wanted. But what's really changed? I'm always careful anyway. I should just continue with my plans as normal. She's a sly one, I'll give her that. Got that buffoon wrapped around her little finger. He'll never suspect the intricacies of what we've devised.*

And then there was what sounded like the blowing of an Earth trumpet, so loud in fact that HrorrarrAggrang scrunched his tail over his head, then, with a deafening thunder, the Highest Councilor materialized in front of him. "Highest Councilor…" He wanted to say more but couldn't find agreeable words to express his revulsion at all the fanfare.

"Yes, Chief HrorrarrAggrang, I know. The introduction lacks… something, but I'm working on that. Perhaps if I add some Earth cymbals crashing at the same time as the thunder… that might add the pop I need. As promised, I'm right on time. I trust I haven't disturbed you, since I actually have arrived when I said I would."

HrorrarrAggrang floated up Eye to Eye with the Highest Councilor, restraining his urge to eat him on the spot. *You're lucky today, Scraback! No one has ever entered my room and left to tell about it, except for the Father Himself… and of course my new partner, but she doesn't count. If I didn't need you for now…*

"Let me be brief, HrorrarrAggrang, since as you know, I'm very busy with many duties, and I've quite a few greater chiefs than you to deal with. I'm here to inform you that I'll be and have been conducting some very important covert activities within your domain. I'll leave my special mark upon all those whom I do not want you to interfere with."

ScrabaGag floated over to HrorrarrAggrang's unique orb, split the screen into several compartments and proceeded to perform certain operations of which HrorrarrAggrang had no trouble following. *Fool. Does he think he can dazzle me with a few simultaneous operations? I run thousands, tens of thousands at once.*

"There. I've adjusted your orb accordingly to remind you to stay away from those I've selected. We're all working towards the common goal, HrorrarrAggrang. I don't want you screwing it up now that we're so close."

"Indeed, Highest Councilor! Is there anything else?"

"You know, there is. I've searched the records concerning you. It's quite unclear as to when you were born. Why is that?"

"Why ask me, Highest Councilor? Is it customary for new offspring to be privy to those keeping birth records?"

ScrabaGag nodded, trying unsuccessfully to penetrate some kind of shroud hidden just below HrorrarrAggrang's surface. *There's a lot more tail to this demon than shows around the corner.* "Just one more thing, don't know if you know, but your orb might be able to do some rather remarkable things. Let me show you." And ScrabaGag proceeded to split the orb into thousands, then tens of thousands, and then he went beyond even that, with part of his very dark arm reaching into each compartment that held a single ethereal tree. Surprised, HrorrarrAggrang began to strain his Eye to keep up with all of the Highest Councilor's machinations.

"I use this, Chief HrorrarrAggrang, when I want to establish a truth for the humans, whether it be a common dislike, or a common lust that everyone knows is part of being human because everyone has it. In this way, these commonalities become like empirical evidence to the humans which helps greatly in rejecting the *glow* whenever it finds random opportunity to introduce its poisonous ideas or feelings through someone. They reject such aberrations of reality because quite simply, the reality we have commonly given them is more real to them. I'm teaching all of the chiefs this method and adjusting their orbs properly so that we may all work together as one." *I watched HrorrarrAggrang. He followed every move I made. No one else could even come close to doing that. Who are you? What are you? His orb is already set to do these things. Hmmm, I only recently achieved this level, but if you've already… hmmm.*

"Thank you, Highest Councilor for your grace! Now, if you will excuse me, I have other business to attend. I shall practice your methods later." And HrorrarrAggrang flipped a switch in his orb and it went black, then he disappeared. Curious, ScrabaGag attempted to turn the orb on again but found he couldn't. *Hmm, I'll have to get Grinchback to solve this one for me.* And the Highest Councilor also disappeared.

❧

"You may all leave." Seeing that the guards hesitated, Lady Stephanie added her expected timeline. "Now!" Her tone left little to be misunderstood, but they gazed at a woman who seemed far too young to be ordering them around even if she had been given standing by their government, which had been impossible for any other woman. The Judge's guards looked at each other, holding back their grins, their rifles still pointed at the gate to the fenced-in village where all the North's escapees had been relegated. Stephanie turned sternly to all her people pressed tightly against that fence. "You will *not* upset the peace of this gracious country. Vaughn would not want that, and neither do *I*. Meet me at our meeting place."

Noting her demeanor, her red hair looking even fierier against her black dress, the crowd humbled themselves to her. They had never been spoken to in such fashion by their Queen, nor felt from her what they now perceived. Everyone obeyed, and when the guards saw how quickly and quietly her command was heeded, they found themselves leaving, too, while wondering why they were abandoning their posts so quickly.

In the center of the little make-shift town, a huge circular tent stood, with another circular tent within, that created a sort of hallway approximately seven feet wide. Guards were easily posted to protect the privacy of the sanctuary inside, and the gap created a perfect sound barrier.

Stephanie mounted the platform in the center of the inner tent where she and Vaughn usually taught the people. It was here that she now gave a new lesson with tears running down her cheeks. Some two thousand and more souls were deferentially silent. Her voice choked so she cleared it then explained, "All of you have been taught so much and joyously received it. The presence within our little village reminds me of the holy presence I felt when I lived with the Appendaho."

They all bowed their heads, rubbing tears from their eyes. They remembered that early morning, months ago, when she had confided to them her personal story. How the Appendaho had willingly, and with foreknowledge, sacrificed their lives to give her the chance to become what God had meant for her to be, a *faithwalker*. Although Lady Stephanie never really elaborated as to what a *faithwalker* is, the more they came to know her and observed the miracles she routinely performed, the more they felt they knew what a *faithwalker* is, and they understood how dearly she loved the Appendaho. Her telling them they reminded her of her people touched the depths of their hearts.

"You have also been privy to some of the challenges Vaughn and I have faced and you remember my letter he read to you. I know…" She caught herself, lest she begin to weep. *Oh God, help me. What do I say? I'm worse off than they are. Help me!* "I know we all hurt." Then she lost it, feeling so very helpless, and feeling as if all had been lost. The people all went down on one knee in front of their little chairs and began to chant. "Long live King Vaughn! Long live Queen Stephanie…"

Her head snapped up. "Stop it!" she scolded them.

Harris, the head volunteer of the twenty-five individuals whom Vaughn had appointed to be secret service, spoke, "Begging your pardon, Lady, but we don't care about the consequences. We will die being loyal to you."

Stephanie clearly had fire in her eyes now. They had seen this before, but this time they knew she was angry. "But I *do* care!"

She paused again as the pain of caring so deeply ripped through her. *And I do know how to deal with such pain now. Thank you, Light, for making me love.* She whispered to them all. "I do care."

Then she raised her voice in power. "This is not the time to die. You all have a purpose beyond Vaughn… beyond me. For goodness sake, even if we lose loved ones, the others must continue on for goodness sake. You people have…" she couldn't stop a sob from interrupting, "You people have enriched our lives more than you can imagine. Don't make us lose that joy by destroying yourselves."

"What would you have us do, dear Lady?" Harris asked, holding his emotions in check as best he could.

"Live. Be peaceful. Pray. We've taught you about faith, taught you about sacrifice. Now is the time to consider them, now that you are required to live them all. Vaughn and I gave our word to this country that you would be peaceful and ally with them. Our word is only as good as each one of you. Knowing that our word stands for the best in goodness *is* your faith to keep it."

☙

Judge Matthew smiled, looking down upon a silent Vaughn who sat on a hard bed in his cell. Matthew, while rubbing his neck, stood very erect, saying, "I'll do you this courtesy. I'll not require her to Christianize until a week is up, after which I'll inform her she'll marry me then I'll not plan our marriage for a month. This will give her time to adjust. I know you two loved each other, but consider yourselves blessed. We could have executed you both, *King* Vaughn." His words spat out like venom hissing from a serpent.

"I did as you asked. Do me one more courtesy. I request religious privilege!"

The Judge's eyebrows rose. It was a privilege for the beginning of conversion. "Yes? Many have found Christ in their hour of need. What would you like?"

"I would like you to provide me two Holy Bibles, the current edition and the oldest edition you can find. I'm sure your library is extensive."

"It is, but why the oldest, our…"

"Because I want to learn the mistakes that were made so I may compare them to my own."

Judge Matthew raised a single eyebrow. This was only the second time he'd actually spoken to Vaughn, the first under extremely unpleasant circumstances. *I'm surprised. I thought the young lad to be a mere deluded power-hungry soul. I have to say I'm impressed. Besides, it's a good excuse for me to get rid of that old book. Every time I see it on my shelf, it annoys me.* "Very well, then. You do know that the older edition was installed by a King, King James?

The Judge once again eyed Vaughn with surprise when he saw a nod. *He has a manner about him that…* "Who are you, really, and your people?

Vaughn didn't know what to say, remembering Joshua's warning, but replied. "People just sojourning in a strange land. We're strangers, that's all." He didn't know why his words so startled the Judge whose visage changed noticeably. Vaughn wasn't sure the change was for the better.

၁၁

"Your fan mail, *King* Vaughn." The guard mockingly bowed, then squeezed the bag through the bars and dumped it onto the cell floor.

Fan mail! Hmmm... Vaughn laid his two Bibles aside, and began opening letter after letter of love and encouragement. Sad to say, reading them actually began to get a little bit boring, so his eye naturally wandered through the heap seeking anything that might break the monotony. Swishing through the piles, his hope became a reality when he discovered at the bottom a different color and style of envelope. It was yellowed, crumpled, and dirty. Seizing it with growing curiosity, he ripped it open and pulled out a single piece of ragged dirty paper:

> *'Old game 45.65-069.59---45.97-068.16*
> *NEW GAME*
> *46.00-83.62---45.63-085.55---45.37-86.90*
> *The devil is in these lucky numbers. Play now*
> *for a small pot, or later for a much larger game.*
> *Trevor'*

What's this? Hmmm, I've been wondering about Trevor. Something about this looks very familiar... but what?

"Well, my boy, you seem to have gotten yourself into a little bit of a jam, again. Fan mail?"

Vaughn smiled at Mafferan who had popped into his cell, and beckoned him close to whisper. "They may have surveillance in here."

"No, I checked. These arrogant bastards are quite confident."

"Come to get me out?"

"Oh, you know the rules. You'll have to make do on your own for that." Looking rather strange, Mafferan paused then continued. "But I can allow you to go on some excursions for me. While you're gone, I'll keep watch here and be your double!"

Vaughn narrowed his eyes at this ancient spirit-man, and what he saw didn't make sense. But he figured it was high time he began to lead with his deeper perceptions, albeit implausible as they may seem. "King Mafferan, you look troubled. Are the human-demon hybrids maturing faster than expected?"

Mafferan shook his head. "You're not the only one on trial, I'm afraid! But I'm more fortunate than you are, I have a defense attorney."

What's he up to now? More tricks? But even so, I know he's holy. What could he ... who could possibly be his...?

"You, my boy! It seems the fate of Heaven, Hell, and the Earth is now in your clever hands."

Still holding Trevor's note in his hand, he couldn't help but peek at it. *But I don't think he's talking about this... is he?*

CHAPTER 5
Trials

"Are you *sure* we have to take it all the way up here?"

As their robes flapped in the dry wind, the ten-year-old boy nodded to his father. "The prophet in my vision came and told me we had to come *here.* But when we get to the cave, we have to go deep within it. There'll be a narrow passage I'm supposed to crawl through that will open into a large cavern, an ancient burial site. I'll place this staff in the outstretched hand of a statue there, and then crawl out. You'll make the rocks fall so that the entrance is hidden."

His father tested his son, staring harshly. "This is ridiculous. Prophet? There are no prophets now. And I've heard many say they possessed this staff. *Liars,* all of them."

The boy nodded, again, smiling. "He said you'd say that. You should believe me, Father. I'm your *son.* I wouldn't lie to you."

"Not intentionally, but being a *child,* you're easily *fooled.*"

With an even broader smile, his son pleaded again. "He said you'd say that too, Father, but he told me what to do! If I were you, I'd just believe me."

What's this boy up to? He seems almost ... smug!

The boy cast the rod down at his father's feet. It turned into a serpent and the man leapt away, much to his son's delight.

He reassured his father, "Don't worry, I'll save you." The boy picked up the snake by the tail, and it became a staff again.

Truly shaken, the father asked, "Why did the prophet want you to do this? Did he tell you?"

"All he said was that one day, this staff will again judge the nations."

"But how will anyone be able to find it if it's buried? We should put it back. Where did it come from?"

"No, Father. He didn't tell me any more than to insist that we do as he asked, and if you still refused, I was to…"

His father held up his hands. "Speak no more of rebellion, my son. I shan't disobey the words of your prophet… whoever he may be."

Pushing to the end of the closet all her other garments she'd been given by various acquaintances, Mandy wept as she hung up Stephanie's wardrobe, saving for last the beautifully designed Appendaho dress she was still wearing. As she pulled it off and hung it by itself, she wondered aloud, "Why is she so kind to me? I didn't ask for her to be my sister. Damn it, she's not Carla! She also saw on the news how a stranger named Vaughn had murdered a Captain who looked very handsome. She recognized the accused man's name. Oh God, I just know it's him! Why do these things happen to us? Oh! Jesus, if you really are there, why do You do this to us?"

She stood weeping, remembering the beautiful gut wrenching words of Vaughn's poem, The Helpless Finds

Help. "Where's the help? Damn, I hate You! Do you hear me, God? I hate You!"

Mandy reached back to where she had shoved her older clothes, and grabbed one of the dresses she wore underground. She then looked at her new underwear, angrily pulled them off, and tossed them on the closet floor.

Mandy had no problem getting men to buy her drinks, but tonight was different. *I just don't want to be drunk. I don't need to drink anymore to fuck. That's all I want, just do it sober! I don't know why people feel they need to be drunk to do it. Why did I? We should just admit it. We're dogs and we enjoy it. No excuse!*

"You're looking ravishing tonight." He wasn't old, but neither was he young like Mandy. Dark hair and incredibly handsome, but with a presence about him Mandy couldn't figure out.

She eyed him, wanting to come right out to say, 'You want to fuck me? I want to fuck you. Let's go!' But the man's presence did something to her. "Thank you."

"You're not drinking."

There were three untouched drinks lined up before her. "No. I don't need them anymore. People should just be honest." And her stare challenged him.

"Honest about what?"

Something didn't make sense and Mandy studied him further. "What are you doing here? You're not a Judge, I can tell, although I haven't bedded one of those yet. You just seem out of place."

"Well, this is my first time. I'm one of the Judge's lackeys and I finally decided that if they can do it, well… I don't have a wife yet, and I figured it's about time."

Oh Jesus, he's a virgin*! OK, he does want to fuck. And I really want to fuck him!* Mandy got up from her barstool, placing her encouraging hands upon his shoulders. "Wait here! I'll be right back. If you need those," she pointed to the drinks, "you can have them."

Better go to the bathroom first. I don't want to have to pee in the middle of this one. But walking down that same hall where she'd met Stephanie, she stopped. *I really don't remember. I don't remember leaving at all.* She shook her head as she heard, again, Stephanie calling her name, *Mandy.* It had so much meaning, whatever that meaning was. Throwing her hands to her ears, she whispered, "Stop it. Stop it."

But she kept hearing Stephanie, and became unsure whether it was the memory of her calling her name. *What is going* on *with me? Ever since I met her… Damn it!* She stormed off to the bathroom, peed, and adjusted her breasts. After checking her purse for condoms, she made her way back to her stool.

"I'm ready. You're in for a real treat." Mandy smiled with anticipation as she held onto the man's arm. For some reason, sex tonight was going to have meaning. *But why?* She pondered it as they strolled down the street, waiting for him to choose one of the many motels. *Because I'm being honest with myself, for one thing… and because I'm not going to be drunk. This is going to be all me tonight, not the devil's brew. But I think, also, because he's a virgin. Yes. That's why. But… does that make me special, too, because I'll be his first? What makes the first time so special?*

Mandy reflected upon her first, shortly after her sister had disappeared. She had to leave school and convince the shoe factory manager to let her take her sister's place. She had to have some kind of job and her sister had explained a lot of what was involved in hers. Mandy had even helped her repair shoes she took home. After their parents' mysterious deaths, Carla had supported Mandy for a whole year, allowing her to go to school. The manager wasn't going to give her the job until Mandy placed a hand upon his chest while staring coyly into his eyes. She didn't know from where those moves came, but she went with it and so did he.

He gave her the job, but became scared his wife or the Judges would find out so left her alone after a few months. She had lost count of her flings after that. *No special feelings for me, but maybe I can be really good for* him. *Maybe he'll even remember back one day, that I was* his *first.* A tear crept into her eye.

"Hey, Mandy! I know a special place, let's go up here."

She just nodded, too deep in thought to pay any attention, or to wonder how he knew her name when she hadn't told him. He took her arm and guided her up a small dark side street. After a bit, Mandy really didn't know how long, two men came out of the shadows while her escort's grip tightened on her arm.

"We'll take her from here."

Mandy realized they all knew each other when her escort nodded knowingly. Hesitantly, she asked, "What's going on?" *There's something in the way that man said, 'We'll take her from here.' Oh God!*

Her escort motioned the men to wait then took Mandy aside. "I'm sorry. It's really true what I told you but I have a job to do. It won't matter that I tell you because of where you're going. We're not going to kill you. In fact, you'll be taken care of… but you'll be hidden away for the rest of your life… just like your sister!"

Mandy barely whispered, "Carla's alive?" But her question didn't get answered.

The sound of a brief scuffle startled them. The two men were lying on the sidewalk, their throats cut. The next instant, a knife was poised at the escort's throat. The attacker warned, "Make the tiniest sound and it *will* be your last."

Mandy stepped up closer, and peered through the darkness into the face of a possible savior. *But it can't be!* She barely whispered. "Captain Joshua? You're dead."

"Not hardly."

Mandy saw her escort's eyes widen at her words and Captain Joshua smiled. "Well, Barrack, seems you have a problem. Now that you know I'm alive, that I can identify who killed me, errr, tried to kill me, and tie them into Judge Matthew, well, he'll probably disclaim knowledge and blame… hmmm, who will he blame *Barrack*? You can accept that fate, if you choose. I won't kill you because I actually respect you! Or, you can help bring all these corrupt Judges down!"

Mandy's heart thudded. She felt strange, exhilarated. Then shame slammed her as she recalled her recriminations against God. She heard Stephanie's voice, too, in her mind, again, *Mandy!* And for the first time, it almost seemed she might understand a bit of the meaning behind the way Lady Stephanie had called her name.

After a while, Joshua said, "Barrack, your silence has chosen for you. I'll lock you away until I get her to safety, then I'll release you to your *fate*."

"No!" he whispered. "How may I help?"

Hearing it, Mandy went a little berserk. "You *bastard!*" With Joshua's knife still at his throat she slapped Barrack as hard as she could across his face. Fortunately, Joshua saw it coming and steadied his knife. "Why don't you *start* by telling me where my *sister* is?"

Then knowledge rushed upon her. Throwing her hands to her face, she couldn't keep that understanding away. All that she'd suffered, all that she'd *done*, could have been avoided if… She balled up her fists and hit Barrack as hard she could in the face, chest, stomach… everywhere she could. Joshua had to remove his knife. She pulled Barrack's hair and clawed at his face but he offered no resistance at all. Out of breath, she screamed. "And I was going to make it… *Meaningful!* Do you know what you've *done* to me? To *us?*"

Joshua saw her plummeting out of control into deeper darkness. "Mandy!" he scolded.

When she heard it, she heard the same meaning as when her sister used to call her, as when Stephanie did, and now Joshua. It made her pain worse, bringing her back to a former self that she'd forgotten after her sister disappeared. It also froze her in place, staring at the man who had rescued her. She knew right then, she had found the man she would love forever, the perfect man Stephanie had described, one who would risk his life for her and she had thought would be impossible to find.

"Actually, Barrack, she makes good sense. Because if we find her sister, then between her testimony, Mandy's, yours, and mine, well, that should be enough to bring the whole Judge system to its knees."

Barrack's eyes widened. *Sweet Jesus, he's right!* Somewhere in the recesses of his heart, Barrack had longed for such justice, for an impossible hope. "She's been secreted away to Judge Hiram."

"Where was Mandy to be sent?" "Judge Aaron at Bethel."

"Does he know what she looks like or who'll deliver her?"

"No. She was to be dropped at a secret location and left alone, tied up in a bag."

Mandy heard herself. "In a bag! Bastards!"

"Well, we'll pull a little switch, and we'll nail him, too. With three Judges' necks in the noose, they should sing pretty loudly about the rest."

But then it occurred to Mandy, as she looked deeply into Captain Joshua's gray eyes. "Captain Joshua…"

"Josh will do."

God, he's letting me call him Josh! Oh, God! But then she wavered. *No. He'll never really go for me. I'm just a slut, a whore. A man like him would never …* Then, even more realization filtered through as Stephanie's words came back to her, 'I used to be just like you, Mandy, even worse.' *Look at her now! She's ahhh, she's… I don't know what she is, but she has Vaughn, a man just like Joshua… though she still might not have Vaughn anymore.* Anger surged through Mandy, empathizing with the pain of being denied the perfect mate. She slapped Barrack again across the face so hard it turned him. "Bastard! Do you know how many lives you've ruined? And you call us *cursed?*"

It was too much for Barrack, and he fell to his knees and cried out. "God, what have I done? What have *we* done?"

Captain Joshua put his hand on his back. "What's more important now is what you *will* do." Then he turned to Mandy.

"You were about to ask me something before you got lost in thought and righteous anger."

"Righteous anger." She heard herself repeat. "Oh, yes. How did you know to find me?"

"It seems you have a very important benefactor. Lady Stephanie posted a watch on you to keep you safe, but *not* to interfere in your life. Just to keep you from harm."

Mandy shook her head, tears pouring out. *Why? God, what have I done?* "And to think they had me spying on her! Oh God, please don't tell her!"

Joshua nodded. "It'll be our little secret and Barrack here won't say anything, either."

"But why would she do such a thing for me? And how did you come to be the man here?"

"I can't answer the why, but I showed up at the same time her orders came through concerning you. There were already people who knew you were being followed."

"People? What people? Followed?" Poor Mandy was shrinking by the moment.

"There are always special people who watch over Lady Stephanie, both good people and bad who saw you. I inquired further about you, and when I found out that your sister went missing, red flags went up. I had heard rumor that the Judges were kidnapping young women, but they were mere rumor. It seemed that there had to be a good reason for Judge Matthew to have you followed. Obviously, you somehow posed a threat or you were of special interest. With him planning to marry

Lady Stephanie who was befriending you, there was something in that connection to the Judge. I volunteered to protect you. Being thought dead set me free to investigate things."

"But Vaughn… and how come everyone thinks you're dead?"

"For now, all you need to know is that I'll help you get your sister back."

"But you can get Vaughn out of jail. And Lady Stephanie loves…"

She saw deep hurt in Joshua's face but didn't understand it. He quickly covered it over with a smile. "We're actually meeting up with her later tonight. She doesn't know yet I'm alive! Now if you'll excuse me, I have to contact someone. There's a lot to be set up and very little time to make it all happen."

Joshua pulled out some kind of communication device and walked between two buildings, back into the shadows.

❧

Only Vaughn, Larson and certain men of the original exodus knew Joshua to be alive. No one told Stephanie because Joshua asked to keep it secret. If King Vaughn trusted Joshua, it was good enough for Larson and the others.

While waiting in a secret place in the forest with Barrack, Joshua and Vaughn's men, Mandy tried to figure it all out. *God, what did he mean by the Judge marrying Stephanie? He can't. She loves Vaughn!*

When Joshua heard soft footsteps, he motioned for Mandy and Barrack to stay put while he ducked behind a tree. As Lady Stephanie came into full view of Larson, she blurted out in surprise. "Mandy! What are you doing here?"

Mandy, not knowing what to say, looked at Larson who answered softly. "My Queen, ahhh, there's something you don't know about."

Queen? Mandy was equally surprised.

Stephanie wondered at how placating Larson sounded. *Something? He's speaking rather oddly.*

"Stephie!"

Turning towards a familiar voice that sounded far more physical than a spirit should sound, Lady Stephanie saw Joshua in the flesh. As tears clouded her vision, she could suddenly see clearly the beautiful life that is Joshua. Through her heart's pounding, she could feel love for him that she didn't even know existed. She was amazed at how even within her own self there was so much to be discovered. While all these thoughts and feelings captivated her, Stephanie found herself rushing into his arms. She kept repeating his name and that she thought he was dead, but then she looked up at him. "But Vaughn…"

"Vaughn knows. A good bit of this is his plan."

"His plan!" *I knew there was something! Dear Vaughn, I'm such an* idiot! *Through our prayers. You were doing the* exact *same thing I was when I meant those words! Will we ever stop sacrificing ourselves for each other?*

Joshua led Stephanie to a log. She looked like she needed to sit down. Mandy couldn't take her eyes off of them, and found no place to sit except beside Stephanie. *They know each other… well, of course they do!*

Joshua took Stephanie's hands in his and narrated the whole incredible story of how he and Vaughn had discussed their relationships, how Joshua was attacked and how Vaughn had prayed and saved his life. He added how they had devised a way to bring the Judges down and protect everyone, and why Mandy was there. When Mandy heard about Vaughn's prayer, she shook, but didn't know why. In conclusion, Joshua said that the one thing Lady Stephanie must do upon Vaughn's order was to marry him.

Mandy blurted her protest. "But she *can't* marry you!"

They both looked over at Mandy, with Stephanie looking deeply into her. When Joshua saw Stephanie shake her head and sigh, he asked, "What?"

Men are always the last to know. Stephanie had instantly read Mandy who spoke up, trying to cover her tracks. "Because… because she loves Vaughn, and because… because the Judge is marrying *her!*"

Hearing the way Mandy said the word *her* made Stephanie wince and Joshua finally understood, too. Stephanie turned fully to face her. "Mandy, there's much you don't understand yet. Vaughn and I love each other with a love that will *never* die. Joshua loves me, too, and he understands. Vaughn understands. If I'm to be protected, I must marry Joshua." Try as Lady Stephanie might, she still felt her last words sounded just a bit hollow.

Mandy's eyes filled with tears. "Joshua loves you? But he and Vaughn are best friends…" She broke down weeping and Joshua looked away, not able to hide his growing embarrassment.

Larson, with his temples already graying past his blond hair, finally spoke up. "Lady Stephanie, Captain Joshua, we have *a lot* to do and a short time to do it. King Vaughn's freedom and this young lady's sister depend upon our timely actions."

At the mention of Carla, Mandy refocused. "Yea, and if we can free Vaughn, then Joshua doesn't have to marry you because we'll bring down the Judges and…"

Stephanie looked helplessly at Joshua and he knew she wanted him to tell Mandy. "It's going to take time to investigate. Your sister's whereabouts are unknown. I don't know how long it'll take to find her. Timing is everything. I'll have to divulge myself before the investigation is complete in order to keep Matthew away from Stephanie. I'm afraid we still have to marry."

Mandy glared at him. "Well, you *love* her. Don't act like it's such a punishment."

But the more Joshua thought about it, the more it felt like exactly that.

Stephanie broke their thoughts. "Joshua, what *is* the timing, exactly?"

Barrack, sitting on the ground in front of them, finally spoke up. "In one week Matthew will force you to Christianize. He promised Vaughn to give you a month before marriage, but I don't expect him to keep his word now. When he finds out that his men were murdered, or even if merely disappeared, which I'm assuming is what you've arranged, he'll check with Judge Aaron to see if Mandy arrived. With your impostor in place, he'll tell him 'yes', but Matthew *still* won't be comfortable. When he feels *that* way, he always acts more quickly."

"You all must let me return to my post!" Barrack held Mandy's eyes in his. "I can't ask you to forgive me… because I don't know that I can be forgiven. I suppose it's possible. The Scripture says it is, but I don't feel it's possible for me. I only ask that you let me do what I can to right these terrible wrongs!"

Everyone looked at this fourteen-year-old girl, and she knew it. "I… I…" Even though Mandy felt terribly jealous of Stephanie, she couldn't keep from looking to her for help. When she did, she felt such a depth of compassion and goodness within Stephanie. "What should I say?" *Oh, my God! I can't believe I actually spied on you, and you saved me! I can't believe the terrible things I thought about you. Oh God, I wonder if you can really read my mind!*

Stephanie reached over, and squeezed Mandy's hand to express her deep love. She knew Mandy felt it, as when Stephanie's best friend Arlupo had first touched her in that same way. A tear rolled down Stephanie's cheek as they stared deeply into each other's souls. *Now I get to give back, dear Arlupo. Now I get to give back. Thank you.* "What's in your heart, dear Mandy? Say what's there."

Mandy looked within. *What is in my heart? I'm so angry about what they did to Carla, to me… but what was I about to do to Stephanie? These bastards were the real evil, but… so was I! Oh, my God! I wanted to be a spy for them, to take their damned money. What if I'd looked inside her secret drawer and found something about her like being a Queen or something and told on her? I think that might have really hurt her and then I'd be even worse than I am now. God, I was working for the very bastards that tried to kill Josh! And this Barrack, he really does seem to have some good in him. Oh, my God! He's a freakin' virgin! Why did he wait so long when he could have…?* Mandy met Barrack's eyes. "I know how you feel! We've all done things… we now would rather not have done." Then she realized if indeed her sister was set free… "Oh God! If Carla finds out what I've been doing, she'll *kill* me."

Seeing the real fear in her eyes, the others burst out into laughter.

"What's so funny?" Mandy asked with exasperation. "She *will!* She'll kill me!"

∽

He treated them all to more drinks so the crowd around him grew larger, straining to hear his whispers. "I tell you it's true. I escaped from the north because I didn't have a job and didn't want to be forced into their labor camps. But they've got a King over there now. And he's trying his darned best to set things right. He has powers, too, and wants to bring peace between our countries and unite us again, but better than before because…" He looked around as if checking to make sure the wrong person couldn't hear him, "--'cause I think God is on his side. Why else would he have all those powers… that none of these Judges here have. He's for the common people, and wants to make all our lives better."

One man scoffed, "Well, why don't you go the hell back there then? Besides, we know about devils that have powers. The Bible describes them *perfectly*."

A few nodded in agreement but the generous man countered. "I told you, he's working to change the old laws but he can't undo all of them overnight. He's already rebuilding the old cities that were destroyed by the plague. Goes into them without a mask or anything, then this powerful glow descends

110

upon the city. He then tells everyone whose specially working there that it's safe to breathe the air, no more plague left. He's reclaiming a lot of the old knowledge and technology. But, I hear he's also adding entirely new technology based on his kind of powers, something the world has never seen before!"

At mention of the old ways that even the South had mostly lost along with their larger cities, the whole crowd gasped. They'd all been taught about the old technology that only now they were beginning to reclaim, but their imaginations couldn't conceive of any extraordinary technological hybrid.

The man continued. "This King Jargon already has giant factories running again… and huge hospitals. People's lives are being saved, like you wouldn't believe, and he's offering *free* health care! I hate to say it but in such short order their medicine is already far better than yours here."

"Free?" One man blurted out, knowing that many people here in the underclass never went to the doctor because they couldn't afford it.

"Free."

So what are you trying to imply?" One man asked, half curious and half intimidated.

"I don't know, except if I read this Jargon correctly, he'll be coming here to introduce himself. All I'm sayin' is just listen, keep an open mind."

Many in the crowd nodded, but a few scowled but knew there wasn't anything they could do, since no one was supposed to be down here anyway. Besides, they knew God was on *their* country's side … even if they themselves strayed from time to time … .only human after all.

CHAPTER 6

Investigations

Nobody knew this would be the last meeting of the Representatives of the United States. No one had the power to see the many transparent gray arms vibrating in synchrony within so many heads. Because so many people had already died, both the senate and house were put together as one to discuss how to proceed. Because of contentions abounding between all concerned parties, meeting in a small town due west of uninhabitable Washington DC was by mutual consent. West didn't geographically favor either north or south.

"The chair recognizes the senator from New York."

"First of all, let's vote on something we *all* can agree upon. I motion to nuke all those damned countries where those damned bastards came from. They sheltered them so they can die along with them. I say to *hell* with the whole damned Muslim world!"

Everyone stood up cheering, cursing, and calling for blood.

"The motion is passed. General, as provisional head of the United States, I hereby order you to coordinate with other assaulted countries across this globe, and one week from now to make an eternal *cinder* out of all Muslim lands."

The General left and immediately set to his task while the senator resumed further business.

"The chair recognizes the senator from Tennessee."

As he began to orate, he brandished the Bible around as if it were a weapon. "All of this happened because we have neglected our responsibility to God. We must return to Jesus Christ in order to rebuild our country. We were destroyed because we had forsaken God. Now we must have Jesus in our government again. We must begin by teaching the Holy Bible in every school…"

As soon as his speech began, the mumbling grew but then increased steadily until it broke out into a full shouting match. The Chair incessantly banged his gavel for order until he and security guards finally imposed silence. "The Chair recognizes Massachusetts."

Red-faced, the speaker pointed at the Senator from Tennessee. "It's *because* of your *damned* religions that all this happened in the *first place*. Look back at history. Your damned crusades, their damned Muslim holy wars, your damned *Christian* holy wars. If you ask me, you're all *damned*. I make a motion: From here now on, *all* religions are *illegal!*"

The cheering became intense, but also did the booing. The senator from Tennessee climbed over several roped-off aisles, chairs, and a minor congressman to reach the senator from Massachusetts. Yelling at the top of his lungs, he shook his Holy Bible at him. "You're *damned!* Haven't you been punished enough for your ungodly rebellion? Haven't the righteous suffered *enough* because of you?"

And as he poked his Bible at the man's face for emphasis, the Massachusetts senator batted the Holy Book away from his nose, whereupon the senator from Tennessee took this to be a direct assault against the very Holy Word of God, itself! And he took his Holy Bible and resoundingly smacked Massachusetts on the head with it! Whereupon Massachusetts doubled up his fist and clocked Tennessee in the jaw! After that, a mini civil war broke out right then and there, resulting in further threats, recriminations, and the forming of two drastically separate provisional governments for which both sides brought troops to the little town to protect and enforce their side's laws.

No one is sure who fired the first shot. Massachusetts batting the Bible away or Tennessee smacking him on top of his head with it, or a firecracker and not an actual gunshot that started the gunfight. The end result was a fifteen-year civil war and the final destruction of the United States. There was a tremendous Ethereal party during those fifteen years and lots of Alpha reproduction due to the steady free flow of nutritious food. At that time, even the chief Alphas were allowed to have offspring so that no food would miss its optimum harvest time.

According to the truce between Heaven and Alpha, direct view into heaven was limited to the original tribe except for the Father of the Alpha. No orb would now work for him in this regard. Hence HrorrarrAggrang felt quite comfortable in his Father's darkest deepest room. Being the last of the original tribe besides the Father, HrorrarrAggrang knew his position to be secure, the others having been consumed by others, who were consumed by others until the Father was sure he possessed all the rest of the original faithful within him.

Much consternation, accusation, and general theory spinning followed the Father's loss of Heavenly vision. Originally, the restriction had been written into the truce's fine, fine print, as a footnote, but unnoticed by all until after the final ratification. Yet, no means of enforcement were provided and for some time the Father had extensive orb abilities unlike anyone's. But one day, his orb disappeared along with all his abilities to access any other.

No one took credit. At first, Heaven was blamed for truce violations and these assumptions geared the Alpha for war. But Heaven opened up all their files and no evidence materialized. Accusations were then made that it was an internal plot. Suspicious, the Father patiently applied his drastic solution though searching all those he now possessed inside himself produced no evidence either.

HrorrarrAggrang was the only one left with heavenly sight. Since at the time of the original Alpha relocation, he had been their youngest member, the Father never considered him to be a suspect. The Father finally assumed that his loss of orb abilities might be due to either eating too much, or even part of his own maturing process. After all, so many changes had befallen them all when they were so rudely asked to move. As to where his orb vanished, well, that was another matter altogether, but hardly an infraction that could be made worthy of war. Besides, his innate abilities to sense and see most of the Ethereal were better than any orb, and if he so desired, he could even directly extend himself into the Earth.

"I watched him closely, Father. Mafferan has even avoided

his wife. He can't look her in the eye anymore. He's defensive. I smell *guilt* in Heaven."

"You're making assumptions."

"I've watched those two from the beginning. They've *always* confided in each other until now. Yinauqua asked him several times what he'd done until he simply vanished away from her without answering. It's been a long time coming, but I told you, eventually our power would encroach enough upon Earth until Heaven would have no good choices so they'd have to choose our way. They'll all fall beginning with Mafferan. In fact, as I've said, I believe he's already on his way down."

"And you have the necessary appeasement to box them in? They'll have to give us Mafferan?"

"Yes. At your order, for flagrant Alpha and truce violations, I will eat the Highest Councilor. Likewise, they will have to give us Mafferan to appease us in order to protect their precious balance. But in doing so, their oneness disintegrates and they all slide down the slippery slope to us."

"What if he simply repents? You know how they do that thing."

"Repentance was *distinctly* left out of any options for rectification. Only *consumption* is decreed for major violations. They were so arrogant that they never thought they'd ever do anything that needed repentance. I'm quite sure we have them, because they'll have to give us Mafferan whether he repents or not. In fact, I hope he does repent because it will make their turning against him all that more criminal! But if they don't turn against him, it'll be clear they're embracing *our* ways by supporting their truce violation. Either way, their oneness is destroyed and their *glow* tainted, then we'll finally be able to reenter *Heaven*."

"How are our Earth fledglings doing?" asked the Father.

"They mature on schedule."

"But when Jargono finds out, he'll destroy them. The Highest Councilor has erred in using and not consuming him."

"Jargono is distracted by women and aspirations to rule the Earth. By the time he realizes, our demon-human hybrids will overrun him." HrorrarrAggrang laughed. "ScrabaGag has visions of keeping him for a pet!"

The Father nodded. "That's one of the reasons I like him. There has never been a demon to match his creativity. Pity he has to be our pawn."

HrorrarrAggrang's Great Eye enlarged. "Pity, Father?"

"Just an odd Earth saying… don't get your Eye all gummed up. And by the way, after you consume him, bring his annoying offspring to me. I want to eat him myself!"

❧

In utter amazement, Vaughn sat on his cell bed with Mafferan. He picked at the lint clinging to an obviously ancient brown bed cover, still trying to digest the secrets that up until now only Mafferan knew.

"You're sure they can't watch us now?"

"No one can. Not from above or below! I threw up a protective barrier, the ancient kind, and created a substitute image of you studying the Bible. We're alone as long as we stay in this part of your cell."

Vaughn couldn't help asking again. "There really was no truce?"

"There really was no truce! How can you make a truce with pure evil? It never works. Look at Earth history! Did truces prevent the first and second world wars? Did they prevent the destruction of Israel right before the Muslims were all blown to hell in the Great Religious War? How can good be balanced by, or strike balance with evil? Only good balances other good, like male balances female. Earth and Heaven are in balance, heart and mind, so on and so forth. Balance *within* Goodness has always been the very secret of creation from the beginning! Indeed, even our Father and the Light, the manifestation of the Tree of Life and the Holy Spirit are all in balance together. A perfect complementary Oneness."

"Then… then…" Vaughn didn't know how to frame the next question so Mafferan tried helping him along.

"Whatever we decide to do, as long as we're true to our nature, it is *always* justified! That being the very nature of pure goodness."

"There is no truce." Vaughn stated again.

"Correct."

"There *never* was?"

"Correct."

"But you're being summoned because you *broke* the truce."

"Correct. And the poor sots believe they'll get to eat me for breaking it."

"But… but… *they* believe there *is* a truce."

"Yes, and everyone upstairs, as well, except, of course, the Lord God. *He* knows better."

"But… but why doesn't upstairs…"

"Simple. They just don't think about it! Perhaps the Lord even withheld that knowledge."

"But not from you?"

"Someone needed to know truly what in the *hell* was going on."

"Accurately put. But why keep everyone in heaven ignorant?"

"Believability? What better way to convince the demons than to have everyone upstairs believe their truce is real? Vaughn, before you go to defend me, you have to be clear on the objectives and realize we're dealing with levels."

"Levels."

"Yes. The truce is one. The Highest Councilor is another. And I believe them to be but at the surface!"

"But he's the Highest…"

"Their father, he's the highest for them."

"But he seems almost nonexistent in this."

"All the more reason to suspect there's a deeper level."

Vaughn studied Mafferan. He shook his head, feeling a strange kind of goose bumps very slowly creep from his belly through his arms and neck to his head, making his scalp tingle and itch. An odd glow began to shine subtly around Vaughn as he announced. "There's still more to this! You're thinking of levels only in a vertical fashion."

Finally, the boy is catching on. "Go on."

"I don't know. It's just a feeling. I need to investigate!"

Now Mafferan's eyes widened. He remembered his first encounter with Vaughn, how he actually went from trying to help Vaughn to chasing him across the Appendaho's burned out village just to hear what he would say next. *Maybe there is a chance!*

Vaughn studied Mafferan as a hint of a smile crossed Vaughn's lips. "Get me a pass!"

"A pass?"

"Yes, a pass!"

"You don't need one upstairs, but it might be a little uncomfortable for you at the moment."

"Not upstairs! I won't learn anything up there if they're as ignorant as you claim, and I think they are!"

"You want a pass *down...*"

"Down below."

"Interesting... I suppose you do have diplomatic immunity, but just what..."

"If I knew that, I wouldn't need to investigate. Besides, it also stalls for time and I'll get to learn my enemy much better from the inside out. As I now understand my *job* as your defense attorney, what I'm really protecting is an *illusion* so all-out war between up and down stairs doesn't decimate humanity. On the surface, it's legal, but deep down it's strictly about power, greed, and need. I have to discover those deeper levels and find out how to neutralize them by some clever maneuver or outright threat. I need to study how far ahead they may be thinking, how much of what I do they'd anticipate, though I'm sure they'll highly underestimate me."

Vaughn explained his thinking further. "The demons know you won't break your word. They know that much about the nature of God and Goodness, and yet they feel that they *have* inadvertently gotten you to step across that line. But knowing how difficult that is for you, I'm sure they won't be expecting any further infraction, so all they'll be defending against is some kind of cleverness. But the truth is, to you there never was a word to break! Your promises to act fairly, to keep balance, could easily be fulfilled if you destroyed them all!"

Mafferan slapped his thighs. "You've got it, my boy. *You've got it!* The truce's language was always put in *exactly* those terms. We promised to act fairly, righteously, and keep the balance, none of which involves giving them a damned thing! Only thing is, we can't destroy them. God never breaks His word. He gave them a free will that depends upon their existence. God would never uncreate any being or spirit. *That would not be fair.*"

The bigger picture came into Vaughn's focus. "But you also don't have a place to send them. That much is obvious, if I understand the *geography* of reality. All of this, this ruse of a truce, is simply to keep them penned in by their own volition and not allow them to think themselves *justified* to enter Earth directly."

"Exactly!" Mafferan got up to go. "Well, I guess I'll leave you to ponder further. I have to go get your *pass*. That's going to be a lot of fun."

"Not yet! I'm not done making my points!"

Mafferan stared at him, remembering how often he watched him use that saying on Stephanie and others, but for the first time feeling the impact on his own person. He nodded to Vaughn to continue.

"But what if they really, or at least one of them, really understands the truth of this like you do?"

Vaughn knew he had surprised Mafferan, whose expression darkened, but he continued to push his point. "Well, like Judge Matthew wants to threaten my wife with blackmail, what if you were threatened? Because they aren't *really* believing in the truce, either!"

It was clear Mafferan didn't like the sound of this. He shifted his weight back and forth as if wanting to walk away but not being able to fully choose a direction. "What do you mean?"

"What if, on a deeper level, all they really seek for starters is you? What would you do if they said that to end this feud, restore the balance, all you have to do is let them eat you? Otherwise, the Earth is lost. Me, your long lost daughter Stephanie, *everyone*, or worse, doomed to eternally feed a growing hoard of demons, our children raised as their food crop while still mortals."

Mafferan's weight shifted back and forth again, his silence seemingly not by choice.

Vaughn studied Stephanie's ancient ancestor, then tried to ease Mafferan's discomfort a bit. "I know how you feel." Vaughn motioned to his surroundings, laughing at the absurdity of his personal situation. "I can truly say it wouldn't help, though, even if you sacrificed yourself!"

I wonder what the young man is thinking. "Why not?"

"After studying the prelude to the Great Religious World War, I found there were appeasements after appeasements after..." Vaughn held out his arms and kept rolling them over and over to indicate the lengthy repetition of concessions. "All the while, the terrorists were infiltrating, putting their plan of mass destruction into play little degree by little degree. They used the more decent of their people to shame everyone else into giving them more and more trust and freedom, but all their negotiation was a ruse, a distraction. They'd always intended to destroy the *heathen* from day one of their religious inception. It's really the same point you made earlier about your truce and the world wars, except in this case *appeasement* has never worked.

"Appeasement is only one side of the coin, but what forced it is the other. While it'd be foolish to ask for everything, the structure or circumstance is created where giving up a little seems to stave off greater consequences. But this is continually repeated to create a slow death. In your case, asking just for your soul might be considered a little."

"Thanks! So what should have been done young man? Maybe you'll teach me something!"

Vaughn peered at him, wondering if he was serious then wondering whether he should be saying anything to wise Ancient King Mafferan. But after examining the truth of what he intended, he continued. "Our spineless fore-parents, those miserable, poor excuses for humanity who sacrificed our lives for their immediate comfort..." The anger hit Vaughn so fast and hard it swept him away. "Those *damned, selfish, hypocrites...* afraid to fight the battle in *their* generation, doomed mine to a wretched life of poverty and corruption." Blackness clearly vibrated around the boy.

"They shouldn't have been so stupid, so fearful, so willing to keep ignoring the consequences or responsibility of their *inaction.* Those idiots who kept shouting for peace, to treat evil people with patience, those so-called peace-lovers doomed us to a life of no peace, no freedom. While hiding behind the façade of fake virtue by screaming for peace, they were really hiding their own morbid fear of true justice or judgment. Whenever human beings abrogate the defense of Justice with as much force as it takes to defend it, then evil will certainly win by overpowering those weak cowards."

"But how should they specifically have acted?" *I wonder what's doing this talking within this boy. Is it really from goodness or from that last gray root of his? He's walking a very fine line here. Hmm, maybe I shouldn't have shown ScrabaGag that root.*

"They should have poured a lot more money into intelligence instead of fearing it. Why fear your *own* country's intelligence *more than your enemies*? I'll tell you why, because their sick consciences were scared of the hand of Justice finding *them* out. And we should have unapologetically attacked our enemies on *our* terms, hit them much harder than they ever would have suspected and not apologize to the world, to the cowardly countries who were so afraid because they'd already let themselves be lethally undermined.

"Their negotiations didn't save them. All their slovenly appeasement while the terrorists cheered at their destruction and laughed at their *stupidity* is, in a way, their just reward! After we conquered them we should have kept our *foot* on them. *Hard.* Nature is nature. A lion eats meat. I don't care how much you shout peace to a lion and feed him vegetables, or how much it purrs, if you stick your hand too close he'll bite it off. And let me tell you, after studying military and political history closely, it doesn't matter how good you treat some countries, they'll accuse you of something and secretly egg on terrorists to do the deeds they are too cowardly to do themselves.

"The only solution is to hold the whole population as a whole guilty. When, by some miracle, they really do internalize a decent sense of justice and sincerely police themselves, only then give them freedom with the warning that if they fail, we'll be back worse than before. An effective, believable *threat* is far more decent, far more peace-producing than all that peace-loving crap that got the world to the shape it's in now. They never faced the reality of the kind of people they were dealing with. But I won't forget that I'm dealing with nothing but demons, so while I really do love peace, I won't preach peace nor expect anything good from them."

Mafferan eyed Vaughn closely. *I'll say one thing for him. He's a fighter. But that's exactly what we really need, now, a real fighter.* "Vaughn, I'll be back. Don't go anywhere." He smiled wryly and vanished before the boy could say to him, *Very funny.*

Vaughn knelt down to pray, "Lord God who is Peace, Life and Love, and who has Justice to protect those, look upon us, Your people. Does it please You that we're always under the feet of evil people? Nonetheless, Lord God, I love You, and if my body were torn limb from limb this very hour, I would still say that I'm glad to have lived this life because of the meaningful goodness You share with me. Enlighten me that whatever it is that keeps me from receiving Your new will, I come to understand and resolve it."

Vaughn looked at the two books setting on the loan shelf in the wall. He took the older version of the Holy Bible and opening it, felt overwhelmed by the Holy Spirit. Directly on the inside cover stretched across to the adjoining page was a map of the Middle East and surrounding territories. There were also the familiar markings of latitude and longitude that all military are taught to remember.

He recalled his first lesson from his military teacher, *Know where you're at, at all times.* And his second lesson was, *Know where your enemy is at, at all times, and if you don't know, you'd better damn well find out!* And then something clicked in Vaughn's mind. Slowly, he pulled out Trevor's letter from his vest pocket. *Oh my God, I recognize these numbers now. Latitude and longitude! Thank you, Trevor. Now I just have to figure out how I'm going to destroy them.* Vaughn thought sarcastically to himself. *Oh, that's no big deal, these locations are just way up north and east. Hmm, makes sense though, that they moved away from Jargono's home, but that means Trevor… How'd he get me this letter anyway?*

Turning the Bible's page over, just before the Scripture, he read, Authorized by King James. *Let's see if you did your job well, King James! I'll know!*

"In the beginning God created… And God said, Let there be Light …"

After reading the first five chapters, Vaughn flipped forward. *The New Testament. Why new?*

"In the beginning was the Word, and the Word was with God, and the Word was God. The *same* was in the beginning with God. All things were made by him, and without him was not anything made that was made. In Him was life, and the life was the light of all men born into the world…"

Word… Word. What is *that Word, truly? What* meaning *does it bring forth?* Vaughn flipped back to the Old. *Let there be Light. It feels like that sentence should just be one word. That* action *of letting there be light* definitely *feels like a single word. Yes, the embodiment of some living, conscious meaning, like the word 'love', only Light would be…* all *goodness! But unlike a word of mere letters, a spiritual word like* love *would actually* be, *hmm… love itself with that quality distinctly embodied to transmit its meaning directly. Which means the Word Light… Oh my God!* And then it hit Vaughn. *The* same *was in the beginning with God. With God… with God… So there's what God is, and then there's the active meaning of His qualities expressed in a spiritual Word. But how does that work? How could I possibly know?*

"In the image of God created he man." *I think this means that I'm somehow structured in the same way God is! There's what I am, along with that part of me that looks at and even appreci-ates myself… that part still possesses the same qualities I have.*

"The *same* was in the beginning *with* God… and the Word was God." *The part of God that looks at Himself knows Him just like the part of me that looks at myself knows me. And this in me is somehow parallel to what the New Testament is describing here about in the beginning was the Word. What if the meaning that was put into 'Let there be Light' was in fact that whole part of God that looks at Himself, that fully appreciates Himself and understands perfectly why!*

Since all truth is really just one tree, the Tree of Life, the branches of goodness like love, peace, justice are all a part of that

One tree. Follow any branch and you truly find all the others so I suppose that *Word is the truest expression of God's nature with the Tree of Life being that singular Word, being that part of God that always looks at Himself and fully appreciating Him for his Meaning!*

Let there be Light! What else could be the true Light, our true life, if not the part of Almighty God that always looks at Himself? How else could God give us freedom if He first didn't bring forth that part of Himself to be free? In fact, that Light is the birth *of Freedom and we live inside of it! We live upon the Tree of Life, free because the Tree is free!* "The Light that lighteth all men." *Just like fruit freely grows out from the different branches of the tree, we're the fruit of the Tree of Life!*

The New Testament. Why new? The Tree of Life has always been, but that Tree is the manifestation of all God's qualities through that particular form.

"He was in the world, and the world was made by him, and the world knew him not. He came unto his own, but they received him not. But as many as received him, gave he power to become the children of God" *Children of God! Yes, I know this is true. I recognize the sound. He was in the world... made by him ... this Word was* made flesh! *My God! MY God! It's the Tree of Life only expressed in human form! If God can do it through a Tree, why not a man? Oh, I need to read further.*

❧

There was a soft knock at her door, a knock she dreaded, but had planned for with hope and determination. *Maybe, Oh Jesus. Yes, I can truly call by that name as well... maybe I can turn this into tremendous good, if Your Holy Spirit just leads me. I've read that all I need to do is just open my mouth and Your goodness will supply me with all I need, but surely, I've lived this for myself already. I don't need to read more to know it. So be it.*

I know you, Jesus Christ. You are the Tree of Life but sent in human form to do what couldn't be done in Tree form! Ha! But your Tree records all You did here, all you have been and are now. So be it. "Come in, Barrack!"

"How'd you know…"

"Before this day is done, you'll have many other questions. Be prepared for surprises! Don't take me to the Judge's chambers. I shall be *Christianized* before the whole country, in your open pavilion at the town center! Ahh, there'll be a lot of company! Why don't you fetch the good Judge so he can meet me there?"

Barrack put his hands to the bridge of his nose, trying not to show his doubt, frustration, or fear. "But Lady Stephanie, if you do that, you will draw the attention of many other Judges to yourself. Is that wise?"

"Wise? We shall see. Are you afraid I'll cause them to fight over me?"

"There wouldn't be a fight as you imagine. The most powerful Judge, highest in the government, simply will decide for everyone else what is *best.*"

"Have a little faith, Barrack, if you want to be redeemed."

"As I said before, I don't think that's possible."

Stephanie placed her hand to his cheek and her soft eyes disarmed him. "It *is* possible, Barrack. And the people are going to need more men like you!" She left him standing in awe as she headed to the center of town. He touched the same cheek, trying to discern more deeply all the meaning he just felt. When he realized he was alone, he ran to catch her.

☙

"What does she mean by all…" The Judge's official looking jowls seemed to lose a lot of their austerity when he saw the tremendous crowd, but before the Judge could think further, Barrack led him through a narrow walkway that had been roped off. Before Matthew knew it, he was standing onstage next to Lady Stephanie, his black robe looking lackluster compared to her traditional Appendaho holy dress of golden and red embroidery upon a royal-blue velvety cloth. Her long fiery hair hung down in two small braids on her front left side and the main larger one festooned with her special blue ribbon with gold trim hung on her right.

"Dear people!" Stephanie's words rang loudly and all wondered about the clarity and easy audibility of her voice without a microphone. "I welcome the whole country to this sacred event. It was my deepest wish to share with you my people's gratitude for rescuing us, and giving us shelter from our atheistic northern enemy. Also to let you know, being the first of our people to Christianize, I will help the rest of my beloved people to find the truth as well. My name is Lady Stephanie, an ambassador for an impoverished and oppressed people from up north."

"The whole country? What's she talking about, Barrack?" His anger was hard to disguise.

As Barrack applauded Stephanie's opening lines, he nodded in several directions, indicating where to look. Much to Matthew's chagrin, television cameras were capturing the

130

live event. Barrack leaned into the Judge's ear. "Apparently, this is a national special presentation, broadcast live to all our stations! Lady Stephanie set it all up without anyone knowing. I really couldn't tell you how."

"I'll be damned!"

"Perhaps not only you, Judge!"

"Dear Judge Matthew." She took his arm and brought him to center stage. "You've been like a father to me. A *father!* You gave me my first Holy Bible. Told me to study, left me on my own, surely knowing that true conversion cannot be forced, but must come about freely from the inside out."

I did no such thing… did I?

"I stand here before the whole country ready to be unashamedly put to the test! Test me like the stern *father* you so rightfully are so that this whole country may know my integrity, and that I'm not ashamed of the blessed name of our Lord and Savior Jesus Christ!"

Father? Test her? I wasn't going to test her. I was jus… "Yes. Ahhh, dear people, it is my greatest honor to bring to you my, ahh, the Lord's greatest accomplishment in a long time, the conversion of such dire heathen to our Lord."

There was raucous applause from the audience, and Stephanie smiled through it all. This was a lot better than her last appearance before a crowd of people. The last time she got burned up as the people cheered. *Alright, you bastard! Let's see how well you enjoy this.* "Ask me your first prepared question, Judge Matthew."

This bitch needs tamed. I didn't know she had balls like this. *I was going to be gentle with her, at first. Forget that.* The judge cleared his throat, then began recalling the litany of questions from back in time that for so long have been glossed over. "For starters, my dear, what form does our God take?"

Stephanie straightened, never having felt the Spirit of Truth come so mightily over her, and knew she couldn't hold back her power any longer. The people hushed, then pointed, questioning each other as they swore they saw her glow with a golden light, and her eyes burn with a red fire.

"What form does our God take? Thou shalt *not* make to thee any graven images, the likeness of which are in Heaven, or Earth, beneath the Earth or in the seas." She waited for Matthew to frown then just as he did, she asked, "Why?" She paused to make sure the cameras froze on his scowling face, then answered. "It wasn't merely to keep people from worshipping idols, false gods. It was to tell them that our true God cannot be conceived of from the outside in! Our God is made out of those inner qualities of goodness, which no form or fashion could describe or do justice. Even the form of the Tree of Life is meaningless to the ignorant. What form would you create to depict Love, or Truth, or Justice? I mean the Capitalized meanings, or even the lower-cased of them. One may depict a human expression, an act of kindness, but certainly not the all-encompassing quality of Spirit.

"So when you ask me what form our God takes, it is as He named Himself to Moses, I AM THAT I AM, abundant in Goodness and Truth. This means that the Almighty God is pure Being. Goodness is the essence of reality and the only quality able to be everlasting Being, because every part of God is complementary to every part, thus being a single unity with no self-destruction within Him. By this, God is not divided against Himself but is One God. Therefore, first there is that part of God that simply IS. We call that part of God, the Father. Yet, it was necessary for Goodness sake to be able to share Himself graciously with us because God is Love. There is that part of God that from the very beginning always looked upon God, appreciating everything about Himself. And that is the part that the Father released when He said, 'Let there be Light'.

"And indeed, no truer, no more faithful witness could we have than that Light from the beginning, being the part of God that always beholds Him and appreciates Him. It is that part which spoke to the Father, and asked to make man in their image. When the Father said we would sin, that Light said 'Prepare me a body and I will go down and redeem man from his sins, by preparing for him a new will, and a tried Spirit. One that has gone through all mortal trials and tribulations for Your namesake and overcome all evil, even death, and I will give that Spirit to all who love the Father and the Son, and I will free them from death'. And that Spirit which Jesus Christ gives is rightfully called the Holy Ghost, having been in a mortal body, but delivered by Goodness to the other side, to life eternal for His Goodness sake and our welfare."

Stephanie stopped, but thousands upon thousands of people that crowded around made not one tiny sound. The people in their homes across the nation at their TV sets also became quiet. And on the faces of many were tears they couldn't quite figure out. Their stillness was broken when she asked, "Dear Judge Mathew, my next question please?"

She's good, I have to admit that. How will I be able to keep her for myself now? Damned bitch called me a 'father to her' in front of everyone. Ha! She thinks that can stop me from taking her? I need to trip her up somehow then the other Judges won't want her. Though if I do that then what good is she to me? Ahhh, I can redeem her later, after we marry, or we marry quickly right after I redeem her. "What did you do to receive the Holy Ghost?"

Lady Stephanie leveled her eyes into the crowd and the cameras focused sharply. "I've suffered, weathered the attacks of evil trying to convince me that evil is me therefore I'm not worth saving. As Jesus said to seek Him as you'd seek hidden treasure, the goodness in me that so desperately wanted to be free from being overcome by evil searched for God. And when I truly believed that this makes total sense that God, being Love, would have it be so, my little goodness was pleased to give itself entirely back to God, being the Greater Goodness. Knowing in true faith only goodness comes from such an act, I was able to give my whole will up to Jesus Christ so that He could give me a new one and rid me of the evil and corruption in me.

"For only when we give all of ourselves, will God give us a new will, for He will *not* force Himself upon us. But the goodness in me knew, for goodness sake, that in order to be free, I had to give myself completely away to Christ, and I did. This was *not* an act of blind faith, dear people, but an act of seeing clearly through understanding and experiencing what goodness is, and what God is. For God is specifically Light, that we may always see and understand and thus our true faith is of such Light."

They waited to see if she was finished and the silence felt sacred. Then someone in the crowd cried out, "Pray for us, Lady Stephanie, pray for us!" And that was soon joined by many others both present and watching on TV.

The judge quickly stepped forward so the people hushed. His face had turned stony but the crowd was pleased for him to test her thoroughly, knowing that Lady Stephanie would only further glorify the true God. *She said nothing about Christ's death and resurrection. What kind of Christian is she? And she seems to be implying she's perfect. No one is perfect. That's why we continually need forgiveness. I should ask her if she's perfect. But what if she says she is? Then we'd have to kill her for blasphemy. My superiors would want that done quickly. No. I can't ask her that question. Let's hope she's smart enough not to volunteer it. She likes to talk too damn much.*

Judge Matthew's voice took on a sharpness, almost an accusing tone. "Do you believe Jesus Christ *died* for your sins?"

She looked straight at him, at the crowd, then into the cameras. "I do *not!*"

Many were disappointed. Some were indignant. But the *faithwalker* then held up her hands, and for some reason, the crowd began to hush, perhaps out of simple curiosity. "Even in my short stay here, I've heard that question repeated over and over until it's asked without thought or feeling. I don't know who started this *ridiculous* question but I believe it's misled many! Jesus Christ did not die for sin, not for evil. How could pure goodness do *anything* for the sake of evil? Jesus Christ died so we could *live*! I don't just believe, I *know* the Lord Jesus Christ died for me so I could live in holiness!"

Cheers erupted, laughter showed relief, and fingers pointed at their TV sets. "She's right!"

She held up her hand, again, and received instant silence. Across the country souls hungered, starved for something new, and hearing the power in her words made them acutely aware of their deepest desires. "Why is it called The *New* Testament? The old one, also God's Holy Word, is a testimony of God's truth and the extent of man's will to keep it by the strength of man's will. In olden times, animals were sacrificed, their life traded to give back the life that our sins took away. Inevitably, we had to accept that evil remained part of our nature and that weakness of will allowed it to be so.

"Today, when many people are asked 'Do you believe Jesus died for your sins?' and they immediately see themselves in the condition of the *Old* Testament, where sin is inextricably a part of their nature, their character, and not so lively lives. They answer 'yes' to that question with the belief that even though they are *still* chained to evil, have evil in their nature, they are saved simply because Jesus died. They believe they will live anyway but that is a *lie!* That belief makes Christ's death be in vain!"

Many of the people gasped again. Some clutched their hearts. Mouths dropped open, and tears swelled some eyes. A few nodded emphatically, and one or two clapped joyfully.

"Why is it called the *New* Testament? Did Jesus suffer for righteousness' sake and die simply to stop the slaying of innocent animals? God the Father got tired of the yearly and monthly sacrifices? Did Christ die simply to make a statement that, well, even though they'll still sin anyway, my death will say that I now count them alive anyway. *without* any change in us from the time of old? Without any change in us to make us *new*? And I'm *not* talking about simply calling a new name for God or holding a new belief. What profit is *that* if our natures would still be no different from that of the old?"

As Lady Stephanie spoke, the golden light that a few thought they saw became bright enough that most perceived it clearly. People began falling on their knees, beginning to understand something for the first time. Now rainbow colors shined from her tears and everyone in the audience, including those watching TV, could feel a spirit of love they'd never felt before.

"Dear people, understand the difference between the Old and New. In the Old, we were commanded by God to keep his ways with all our heart, mind, soul, and strength but that was specifically by our own defective will. The Holy Spirit at that time could only be that, the Spirit of Goodness advising us from the outside in with that goodness. But when the wonderful Light from the beginning that the Lord said He made to be the beginning of His way, the first of His works of old …

"When that Light was joined also to a mortal life to endure all evil, all temptation, to empathize in the *flesh* with all mankind, even suffering the terrible pains of death… when that Light came out the other side of life as the Holy Ghost, it now possessed something *new*. That Holy Ghost retains the *experience* of fighting evil in the flesh. Dearly beloved people for whom the Lord suffered so …"

Many people were now weeping. Most of the crowd was on their knees. Many were holding their TV sets as if to be closer to her words, to her feelings, desiring to be nearer to the goodness they experienced. Judge Matthew did his best to hide his utter surprise, and only the slightest twitch of his jowls betrayed that he no longer felt in control.

"In the Old Testament, the children of God were given a country with borders and told to keep the evil out because if they let it into their land, they were too weak to withstand the temptation. But in the New Testament, the Holy Ghost made them so strong they were sent throughout the whole world two by two. They were so strong because the Holy Ghost contained within itself the experience of fighting evil in the flesh. No longer just a nature of goodness, of holiness removed from human experience, but a new nature fashioned to maintain goodness within the heat of miserable mortal suffering.

"The Lord God was true to His promise. He said 'I will make them a new heart, and a new spirit will I put within them, and they shall no more go out and come in'. Dearly beloved, this is what the Lord Jesus Christ died to give you in your very lifetime."

People wept, some even wailed. *Why didn't we know this sooner? What do we do? How do we gain this, this Holy Ghost?*

Judge Matthew had enough, and couldn't restrain himself any longer. "Excuse me, but this is *my* flock! We've not even decided yet whether you've been truly *Christianized.*"

Mouths gaped as some whispered to others. "He's right!"

"Are you saying we can be perfect? Perfect here? Only God is perfect." *What am I doing? I didn't want to ask her that, not now, not in front of everybody!*

Many in the crowd agreed. "He's right. What *is* she saying?"

"Dear Judge Matthew, are the angels in heaven perfect?" Stephanie asked with a smile.

Matthew stood, still stony-faced though his jowls suddenly seemed droopier. When he saw that she waited for his answer as did the audience, and *'Answer her question!'* was shouted, he cleared his throat. "Well, we know that many of them fell from grace."

A growing number of boos came from the audience, but others scolded the hecklers.

"But the angels that remained loyal to God, yes, they are perfect," he quickly added.

"Dear Judge, they are perfect but they are not God."

"But they're in heaven and…"

"But the Holy Ghost is said to make us even higher than the angels! Dear people, it is not blasphemy to believe we can have a perfect nature. It pleases God for us to be so, and to be perfect obviously does not make us to be God, for only God is all powerful and omniscient. But our Savior told us the Holy Ghost which is the Spirit of Truth will guide us from the inside out into all, *All* Truth. The Spirit will be our teacher and our comforter, give us a pure heart and a made up mind to serve only Him. All we have to do is ask, though to ask for this precious treasure requires a level of seeking and patience that you've read about in both the Old and New Testaments. But remember this: you cannot receive that which you don't believe. If you do not believe you can be perfect in this lifetime, how are you to receive the Holy Ghost that Jesus Christ so graciously died to give you? For when it comes close to you with its perfection and your heart begins to accept it, the lie telling you that you cannot be perfect will *stop* you!"

"*She's right!*" Many across the country proclaimed, "I get it." Others indignantly thought otherwise. *She's crazy. Who does she think she is? She's not even a Christian yet.*

"Dearest people, this is a lot to think about, and think you must. Search, pray, continue in faith of goodness. Everyone receives what they truly ask for." She turned to face the Judge. "Dear Judge Mathew, as I've confessed my understanding that indeed Jesus Christ is God's only begotten Son, and that He did in fact die for us to live, and that I've indeed demonstrated that I have within me his Holy Ghost, is there any further question you wish to ask me to prove that I am true?"

"When did this happen? Your conversion?"

"Dear Judge, I just told you! I've described it clearly."

I know you think you received your supposed spirit before you even got here, before you knew a damned thing about Jesus Christ. You're a phony! But what am I doing? I don't want to ruin her, but… I can't seem to help myself. "Where did it happen?"

"Dear Judge, it happened in my very heart, mind, and soul while experiencing the depths of the meaning of the Holy Spirit. What good is calling on the true name of Jesus without knowing his true meaning? While some may question whether we can do without the true name, none will doubt that we cannot do without true meaning." *OK Judge Mathew, I see you're being tormented and you can't fight it.* "And now, I would like to say a prayer for our good Judge in thanksgiving for his thoroughly testing me. Oh, Lord Jesus, ever gracious, slow to anger, behold this leader of the people and drive away all evil that tries to hinder him from doing Your good work."

Stephanie extended her arm out, spread wide her fingers then all saw bright light move from her hand to surround the good Judge. He shook as an odd, inhuman wail emerged, and the transparent black arm that Stephanie could see extended into Judge Matthew's head disappeared.

She walked up quickly, and whispered, "Don't worry, dear Judge, I won't let you fall. You still have to proclaim me a Christian and marry me!"

"What?" *Is she saying what I think she is?*

"Tell the good people, dear Judge!" she whispered with a smile.

"Dear… ahh, people of United for Christ. I…" Stephanie squeezed his arm tightly, and he felt scared by a strange power coming from her. "I proclaim Lady Stephanie a good Christian."

Many people roared in delight, but others cursed in disgust. Lady Stephanie beamed. "Dear people, I also have another astounding announcement to make. I've been asked by a gallant Christian man for my hand in marriage, and I have accepted."

Many people cheered but Stephanie let it go on for some time.

I can't believe she's actually going to marry me that easily.

"Good Judge Matthew can perform the ceremony."

But how can I perform the ceremony for myself?

"Would you come forward, my dear soon-to-be husband?"

Oh Vaughn, it should be you, but I know you. You can't lie about such things. You'd fail the good Judge's Christian test right now, and we just don't have the time to wait.

Large men from the group of strangers who escaped the North came onstage. When they were squarely before Stephanie, she declared. "You may reveal my future husband."

The crowd of men opened for all to see Captain Joshua dressed in a decorated smart gray uniform. Gasps escaped across the whole country for all had heard of his murder. Judge Matthew began to collapse, but Stephanie's grip held him tightly or perhaps it was her power. Her thoughts appeared in his mind and he knew she somehow sent them. *Alright, you bastard! I'm not done with you, yet! Stand up straight!* Fearfully, the judge stood and Stephanie let him go.

But I thought he was dead!

Stephanie read his thoughts and sent her reply. *Not hardly, you bastard!*

જ

Her eyes were black daggers as she peered through the dirty blue orb. "I thought he was dead! The spy was supposed to *kill* him!"

The Highest Councilor shook his bulbous head in sympathy. "Hmmm, it seems your plans just aren't working out, Queen Karen."

Karen narrowed her eyes at ScrabaGag. "You know, I'm sure there are other demons around that would like to have what I'm offering. Keep your smugness to yourself!"

Amazing! I could consume her right now and she's the gall to talk back like that?

Karen looked sharply at him. "Don't bet on it, Buster!"

His huge Eye widened. "Did you just read *my* mind?"

છ૭

"Ha! Now that *is* an interesting development. But what good will it really do you, Stephanie? The Judge is still going to have you. You may have driven my arm from him today, but don't worry, I'll be back!"

છ૭

"That's interesting! Got to hand it to you, Stephanie. That was *masterfully* done! But I can't have you bring the Judge down. No, no! I need them in control, not the military. No, definitely not the military, and *definitely* not Captain Joshua. Hmmmm, but how am I going to do that, now that you've televised everything. Oh, very clever, my sister… very clever indeed. Seems I may have to go higher up the ladder.

છ૭

He grabbed the phone as quickly as possible and dialed three times because he kept missing the right numbers. *C'mon, damn it! Pick up*

"Yes, Hiram! I saw her."

"What do we do? I've never seen someone so dangerous sprout… out of *nowhere*! "

"You're too quick to react. She may prove to be quite useful, her position and all."

"She's *wooing* all the people!"

"Not to worry. The people are fickle and, it's not like she has our pulpit. I'm surprised, though, how Matthew let *that* one slip through his fingers. She's a real looker."

"Yes, well, I just heard her on TV. Apparently, when the media rushed up to her, and asked whether she would address the nation again, she floated the idea of her *own* Sunday prayer and spiritual show. They seemed to love it!"

"That could be a problem. OK, let's pull resources and find out as much as we can about her and her people. And Hiram, careful using the phone, will you? You wouldn't want to be marching to the beat of a military drum.

༄

In fitting gray uniform, Captain Joshua walked to center stage, and Stephanie stepped aside with a slight bow on cue. He held up his hands and the crowd instantly hushed. They all knew this man as gossip had spread most of the truth of the bad blood between him and Judge Matthew. The Captain was notorious for plucking soon to be condemned souls from the Judge's claws of punishment by using military prerogative to enlist forcibly anyone he deemed useful for national security. Because the military had so much sway from the beginning, the theocrats had to incorporate such privileges into the constitution.

The conflicts between Matthew and Joshua had even reached national news at times because they were some of the most flagrant in the country and helped spur further debate. Their issues opened platforms for political wrangling and though they were all Christians, there'd been bad blood since the inception of the government. Military matters required a level of thought, freedom, and judgment that always didn't seem to coincide with the theocracy's patent view of the world. But mostly, it was the military's semi-independence that ruffled theocratic feathers.

Judge Matthew tried his best to mask his horror as his nemesis began to speak. "My dear people whom I have pledged my life to protect…" Loud cheering was heard across the nation. "I know you thought me dead and I sincerely apologize for my secrecy. My heart continually went out to you as you mourned, as I love you all so dearly." More cheers and tears. There was something about the spirit of this man that drew love from all except the Judges.

"But it was extremely important to keep the attempted murder a secret till now." Another outburst from the listeners was a mixture of anger and sympathy. "I know who was responsible for plunging a knife into my gut, but the investigation is far from over even as we hunt the man down. I was unable to care for, nor protect myself until I had recovered, so it was best to secret me away.

"An innocent man, my Corporal Vaughn, my *best* friend who was responsible for saving my life, voluntarily subjected himself to false accusation, prison, and maltreatment in order to protect me, and our blessed country! All that you have heard about him in the media is a lie!"

The roars of outrage went from coast to coast. Poor Judge Matthew couldn't run or hide, but stood very much appearing pale as a ghost. "At this very moment, my men are releasing Corporal Vaughn under military order, and I'm sure Judge Matthew approves!" He looked squarely at the Judge who nodded meekly just as the cameras focused upon him.

"Corporal Vaughn and his people have been crucial to our national security for some time now but I have kept this also under wraps until now. His people sheltered me, nursed me, and kept my secret faithfully until this time."

There were hushed conversations as everyone mulled over their mixed feelings for the strangers who had settled in their country only a year ago. "Dear people for whom I gladly offer my life to protect each day, I hope I have earned your utmost trust."

The crowd began chanting Joshua's name. When the TV viewers across the nation saw it, they chanted along. Judges across the nation called each other back and forth. Judge Matthew didn't know who to fear more, the other Judges or the military.

The Captain continued his speech. "Your trust in me is paramount as I ask you to honor my declaration that by military decree, Corporal Vaughn's people are now under full military jurisdiction. The bravery they exhibited, risking their very status in this country which is their only safe haven and hope for eternal salvation, have earned them our protection."

Common people, other military and Judges alike, were astounded by this magnificent political move. *He can't do that! He doesn't have that authority. That privilege is only extended to individuals.* Others ruminated, *Can he do that?* Still others raved. *Absolutely brilliant!*

"If I'm contested on my being able to extend a *general* privilege, if I have to, I will personally go to each individual and extend it!"

Balls! The man really has 'em. Others thought, *Damn it, the knife should have been stuck in his heart, not his gut. How'd he recover so quickly anyway?* All over the country, good Christians pondered the miraculous events unfolding in their previously dull lives. It began to occur to many that the Captain and Lady Stephanie are indeed well suited for each other.

Joshua signaled for silence again and the uproar calmed. "The false witnesses have been apprehended and are at this very moment being interrogated by military police. We will of course be happy to share information prudently with the people and the Judges. Now this is all I have to say at this time. From this point on, no longer will there be *any* nonmilitary guards or officials dealing with Corporal Vaughn's people in any official capacity. All problems concerning them will be handled within military jurisdiction and law. Do you have any objections, Judge Matthew?"

There were boos across the country as many suspected that the Judge was the one who had the Captain killed! Captain Joshua stepped away from the microphone, beckoning the beleaguered Matthew to step up. "My good people, let me first say how happy I am that the good Captain is alive and so well. We will also be investigating people within my fold who appear to have taken egregious liberties and broken our dear Lord's law. The penalties shall be severe, I promise you!"

Some of the crowd cheered, some whispered, and others held their peace. The good Judge continued. "The Judges, of course, always yield to the rights of our constitution which clearly defines our responsibilities to you." Many people across the nation pondered. *That seemed vague, wasn't it?*

Matthew stepped away, making to leave but Captain Joshua called him back. "Dear Judge, it would please us, and

I believe the country, if you would marry Lady Stephanie and me before the people right now!"

People from coast to coast cheered, cried, oohed and ahhed. The Captain's rugged handsomeness and character along with Lady Stephanie's utter beauty, and excellent nature made a perfect match in almost everyone's eyes

The Judge stepped forward. *You little bitch. Go ahead, read my mind if you can. You're going to pay dearly for this.* "Good people, it would be my pleasure."

The rest of that day, well, after the very short marriage ceremony, people felt quite elated. That single tender kiss between husband and wife remained imprinted in everyone's memory except Vaughn's. He had been immediately sent on secret official business at his own request even before the ceremony.

CHAPTER 7

A Dream

GrrraGagag studied her intently. "She is definitely the right one," he told one of the underlings before him.

"For what, Master?"

He ignored the question. "Patience is the most important virtue we possess. One in a billion human females perhaps has the necessary ingredients to produce the kind of offspring needed for the ultimate plan.

"What plan, Master?"

He continued to ignore the nuisance. "Now watch what I do with her right *here*." GrrraGagag reached his arm deeply into his dirty blue orb into both her heart and mind. "Drink a little of that drug." And the young blond woman began to drink. "Stop! What are you trying to do to your unborn child?"

"Master? But you just told her..."

"Idiot! Slow, *stupid* underling! Are you really the offspring of the Third High Councilor? I don't want her to give birth to a *moron*. It's all about dosage level. Just enough drug to taint the child and deflect the *glow* just beginning to flourish in her. A tiny little bit can sever *just* the interface in her brain that allows *glow* to reach her in the physical world, but the growing child's genius will still be preserved. Further, you won't believe what severing that infinitesimal piece of brain will do to her appetites."

"Master? Appetites?"

Master GrrraGagag's Eye drooled. "Yes, indeed… without any hindrance from the *glow,* she'll be very much like us in her perfect desires. Though human and even mortal, in time she would make the perfect mate!"

"Mate, Master? You already have a mate for her before she's even born?"

GrrraGagag's Eye twitched excitedly, even though he tried to hide it. "You ask too many *stupid* questions! Consider the difference between Alpha and *them.* When we even just *consider* having offspring, we begin to take the utmost care to produce them perfectly. Which meal should we hunt to use to create it? Which part, if any, of ourselves should we mix with it? Who will take the new underling in? How can we create the best underling who will eventually further our personal cause? But the humans, they have no forethought except for their sex, their orgasm. It doesn't matter what happens after their seed is sown. They only care for the pleasure of sowing it. If they can increase that pleasure with drugs or whatever, so be it, even though those very drugs harm their offspring. They don't give a damn even when they're pregnant. Dear underling, they can be enticed so easily for their pleasure. Stupid, foolish humans let their species be destroyed like that. If we were to be so degraded, the Father would consume us quickly so as not to lower Alpha standards by birthing defective offspring. But instead, do you know what the humans do? Not only do they *not* kill such women right away, but they make sure they are taken care of and their defective children, too! I must say, I really don't delight in consuming any of them. I usually pass them over to the underlings I train, like you."

"Oh Master, you're so gracious. Thank you, thank..."

"*Don't* interrupt. I'm choosing a name for her."

"You're going to name her?"

"Of course, such a child should be named by *me*. She shall be Karen, which is a shortened form of Katherine. I've always been partial to the human royal names. The short version, however, doesn't carry the sense of *glow* in it as does the longer."

Acting a role for so long sometimes messes with one's self-perception, especially if it's a role of how you used to be but aren't any more. That role-playing for the last year might not seem long if a person is like forty years old, but when it happens from seventeen to eighteen years of age, it could seem a lifetime. Also add the conclusive knowledge of your being the sole sober witness to the growing plague that will enslave and destroy humanity. It was almost too much for Trevor. *Well, I guess that knowledge is the only good thing for me, because if nothing else, it keeps me from both going insane or becoming what I used to be. It's just freakin' too scary to crack up now!*

Shut away in his tiny room, the only solace in Trevor's revolting busy day was the memory of Stephanie's compassionate touch, kind voice, and actually everything from the first time she wished him well to when she brought the Holy Spirit to meet his deepest regrets. He recalled that somewhere, somehow, within that mesh of his utter shame and deepest regret that he could've lived better, he found himself recognizing the goodness of that pure Holy Spirit and surrendered quite quickly, quite entirely to it. And when the change had become complete, Stephanie had bestowed a smile he understood then walked away from Vaughn and him, leaving the men together.

Men? Ha, ha, ha! It was times like these when Trevor began to laugh uncontrollably that he wondered if he was losing his mind. But then his now beautiful spirit would show him it was funny, indeed, in an ironic sort of way. Being surrounded by human demons made real men meeting together seem like a rarity. Trevor shook his head over just how much he, a mere teenager, had seen. *I thought I'd seen a lot before this year, but now?* And then he began to weep, not wanting more hideous images to flood his mind once again. Even though Vaughn had helped him become more or less immune to the drug and the Ethereal poison they had placed in it, Trevor simply felt flat out exhausted from all the constant degradation. *But if I fail now, then there's no one to reveal what I've seen.*

It was really more complicated, though, because being undercover required Trevor to be, to do so much more harm than he'd ever anticipated, all for the hope that somehow, someway he could make a difference. *Besides, it's not like all these stupid kids* don't *want these drugs I give, or sell them.* But that reasoning became weaker by the day because the simple fact is, Trevor was once very much like any one of them, and he felt it to be an ever-increasing hypocrisy to act as if they didn't matter when he mattered so very much to himself now.

Trevor broke out into hysterical laughter again, because of his realization. *I matter to myself now.* Except for concern for his younger sister, he really had not cared if he died. *Alyssa, I've got to get you to Vaughn and Stephanie somehow, I just have to but how can I do that without blowing my cover? They watch me all the time, I know.*

Sometimes he really did feel like rubbing his cheek again *hard.* But that quickly passed from him and he only did that to keep in character when around others. Still, lately it seemed that the ever-weeping cut on his cheek was getting longer, but at the same time, he believed the taint that Vaughn had re-introduced into his cheek was the only thing disguising his true identity. *But what if they really know my true nature? But then why not kill me? Ha! Because they can get me to do all this for them anyway! It might even be more enjoyable to them, knowing I'm doing their bidding though it's exactly what I despise so much but I can't afford to break my cover.*

Trevor folded his hands in prayer. *Please Lord God, let my letter reach Vaughn. Make him understand, even if that's all the good I can do, even that little bit might be enough. Besides, how am I ever to escape this mess, anyway?* But then he remembered his own words to Stephanie as to why he would do what he does now. *'It's the only way I can try to eventually set things right. Remember, Stephanie, I wanted to die. As far as I'm concerned, I'm dead already! But this is different for me now. Before, when I didn't care at all about my life, I told Jargono to kill me if he wanted. Now the life I have is to care, and care so much that if I lose my life in caring, I won't have lost anything at all, but truly lived! See? No life left to lose!'*

Trevor didn't know how long he'd been asleep when one of the numerous women from the town rubbed up against him. "I want to feel you inside me," she purred.

Trevor had lost count a long time ago of the many women he'd played with, but ever since these particular women begat the demon's offspring, they'd been quite uninterested in sex at all. "Why now?"

She surprised him with a sober answer. "Because I hear that tomorrow, our God Demi-Fred will visit us so that we may bear him children, too. All of us have come into heat now. I hear he's angry that we gave ourselves to his lesser, Demi-Glen but that he'll forgive us if we also bear children for him." She then tried catching Trevor in her pleading stare. "Trevor, maybe *you* can make me pregnant first please!" But when she saw his eyes widen, she knew she had to explain. "What the hell, I'll tell you. The other day, I cut my finger and my son, who's grown so quickly, he looks three or four instead of one, well, he grabbed my hand and began to suck my finger. He said he wanted to help, but I started feeling faint. Trevor, it felt like he was sucking the life from me! I had to pull my hand hard to get it out of his mouth. He then stood there smiling and asked 'is it better, Mommy? My hand had stopped bleeding but looked like it had been sucked completely *dry*."

Trevor thought before he answered. *This could be a trap. They're testing me. Besides, what the hell did she expect? I remember how ecstatic she was to screw her god.* "It's not for me to blaspheme by taking you before our God does. Besides, even if I did get you pregnant, the God's seed would simply devour our child and use it to grow itself!" *Maybe, because I really don't know what would happen now that my life has been changed by the Holy Spirit… if I even am still changed. God, all I've been doing is so… But even if my child could kill the demon's seed, then they'd know right away about me. Besides, why would I want to have a kid with her?*

"*What?* How do you know?"

"I travel between all the villages of the God. He's given his leaders power to… well, I don't know exactly how, but they put their hands on me, and the next thing I know we're in a different place. All day long, they take me all over the country to spread our sacred drug, or do some special things. In the other villages, anyway, pregnant women whom the God mated with would within minutes, no matter how far along the pregnancy, have the God's seed consume the child and take its place. It was quite painful to watch, but they all rejoiced when the conversion finished."

"Oh, God!" she whispered.

Trevor narrowed his eyes at her. "Yes, I'm sure you'll be screaming that tomorrow!"

"I hear that if King Jargon finds out about us, he'll destroy us all! So the more you spread drugs, won't he be more likely to figure things out?"

"You know, I've actually met him, and spoken with him. He's too arrogant to waste time on a bunch of high teenagers. As far as he's concerned, he doesn't give a damn about any of them except his Queen. Besides, the government itself sells drugs and makes a profit."

She snuggled up tightly to Trevor, just holding him, but he noticed more to her clinging to him than just lust, and he found his arm encircling her, gently caressing her naked shoulder, surprisingly trying to comfort her.

Vaughn, Stephanie… you have to *put an end to all this please … dear Lord, they have to.*

☙

"You're kidding," Barrack blurted out to Matthew as Barrack looked around then behind him as they briskly strode together back to the courthouse, while trying to discern from Matthew's face if what he said was simply a joke, a bad one, at that.

As Mathew's black and Barrack's gray robe flapped in the wind, Matthew spoke frankly, "Hardly. As if we don't have enough to deal with… his timing is just *perfect*! For the past few months, not one of our spies has returned, and the military confided in us, and I actually believe them on this point, that none of their spies have returned, either."

"What's his pretense? I mean… he's the *King* now?"

"That's correct. I didn't believe it myself. He claims the whole government is different now, sort of what France had when they had both a king and a parliament for a while, except…"

Barrack saw the serious concern in Matthew's pause, and despite his utter hatred for the Judge, he knew enough when to respect him. "Let me guess, except his power is increasing and the rest of the government is decreasing?"

"I don't know, but my sense of the momentum is that's most likely happening. Anyway, since we haven't gained any intelligence for some time, the *Court* feels it would be to our advantage to let him visit, but…"

Barrack nodded. "He's shrewd, isn't he?"

After a long pause, Judge Matthew nodded slowly. "I believe that might even be an understatement. He wants to introduce himself to the whole country, and is floating the idea of beginning relations again."

"What *kind* of relations?"

"*That's* a good question, and I don't like him informing the public first instead of dealing with us directly."

Barrack sighed but he had to suggest it. "You know, we have a lot of people right here who know the man. Why don't you start by talking to Lady Stephanie and Corporal Vaughn?"

Mathew noticeably darkened, then whispered, "I'll talk to them in time, but *not* from a position of weakness or need. Send some people out to mingle, engage in idle conversation with the foreigners, and see if they can learn more about this *King* Jargono. What a repugnant name… jargon, like pretentious gibberish."

એ

The Judge had quickly recovered from *officiating* the unexpected wedding, learning of his rival's vitality, and all the political implications of the surprises. Every secret phone call he received got the same quick, consistent response, or rather, threat. "We protect our own, good Judges. We stand together as one or all fall as one!" None of them doubted that Judge Matthew would carry out his threat. They also knew any mysterious fatality would not sit well with the people, and the military would have such a close watch on Matthew that would make it next to impossible for him even to stub his toe. The good judge had unwillingly gone from chief nemesis to a chief asset when he was forced to both solemnize that *wedding* and grant the foreigners *status,* even *hero* status before no less than the *whole* country.

Vaughn knew it was now imperative to find Mandy's sister, Carla, and rescue also Mandy's substitute. It was quite likely the Judges would rid themselves of any incriminating evidence due to the extra scrutiny following Captain Joshua's return.

Intelligence had placed Carla in an unspecified room within Judge Hiram's very compound. The tracking device on Sergeant Hanna, the fake Mandy, had pinpointed her location within Judge Aaron's compound. Using recently discovered surveillance technology, the military also had determined its floor plans.

However, Hiram was fond of old castle design and built his from heavy stone, making spying technology useless. Yet, sure that action was necessary *now*, Vaughn, Mandy, Larson, and four others hid in darkness amid the thick brush outside the castle's western wall.

Mandy studied Vaughn intensely while he seemed pre-occupied in his thoughts. *God, he's every bit as handsome as Joshua… but he's very different from him… though in another way, they're just alike. Oh my God! I can see why Stephanie loves him!* Putting her hand on Vaughn's shoulder, she drew his attention. "I read your poem. It made me cry for a long time."

Vaughn didn't seem all that surprised and simply nodded. When he was about to turn away, Mandy touched him again. "I'm sorry about Stephanie. I know you both are supposed to be together. This is a really screwed up world. What are you going to do?"

He looked deeply into her eyes, surprised at her boldness. "I see why Stephanie cares for you so much!"

Once again Mandy had tears. *I don't understand.* "Vaughn, can you tell me why she does?"

He smiled tenderly, and she suddenly saw a whole other side to him that made her heart skip. "You're just like her! When I first met Lady Stephanie…" the way he said her name, he spoke it as if she were a revered queen, "she was just like you! We were both so lost, and helped one another out of darkness. We saved each other's lives more than once!" The depth of his warm stare and the level of knowledge expressed by his face captured Mandy. She knew at that very moment she had empathized with Vaughn and absorbed… something. *But what is all this? It sorta feels like I know but I don't. Oh God, why do people have to suffer? God, he's so* hot, *and he's… I don't know, but he shouldn't be alone. Someone should* treasure *him.* And when Mandy remembered the meaning of her feelings of truly cherishing another person, she recalled that very special bond she'd had with Carla. Her heart skipped at the possibility of reuniting with her. *And this man is risking his life for* me! *Just like Joshua did. Josh, he told me to call him Josh!*

"I'm so sorry you and Stephanie can't be together." She was sorry, too, she couldn't be with Joshua, but she truly meant them both at the same time. Mandy then looked deeply into Vaughn. "You haven't given up, have you?"

"Those two, Joshua and Lady Stephanie, I both love and respect with all that I am. What will be, will be."

But he didn't answer my question. Why? Mandy leaned over and kissed Vaughn on the cheek, and he chuckled as his eyes asked why. "You're risking your life for my sister and me though I don't even know you."

Larson smiled at what he overheard. "Little lady, you don't know even the half about King Vaughn!"

When Mandy saw Vaughn wince at the title, she knew he really was a King. *Oh, my God!* "King?" she whispered, "Who *are* your people?"

He spoke with a faraway look. "Strangers… in a strange land."

Larson echoed the word. "Strangers, ain't that the truth?"

They then fell silent, and lost track of time.

Finally, the other watchers returned with their reports of guard locations and a new shift change, as well as the successful interception of the people they'd be replacing. A certain level of unmitigated gall combined with a surgical plan of attack using only a few highly skilled troops seemed to be the best approach.

There had been some discussion over the risk of being held up and investigated when trying to enter. They doubted they could pass unchecked through any of the castle gates. However, considering that people always fall into a routine, it seemed quite likely that once inside, anyone else they encountered wouldn't be very suspicious, believing that the gatekeepers already allowed them entrance. Barrack confirmed such a hope, adding that if they did meet any resistance, none of the castle regulars were exceptional or at least not like the military in their fighting skills. He suggested that resistance be dealt with quickly, and to hide the bodies somewhere so they wouldn't be found in the next hour.

The other point of concern had been whether fatalities were acceptable, and everyone agreed that no matter what, excessive force would be a *very* bad idea. No matter how justified they were, actually killing any of the opposition would still seem like murder to the rest of the country, and they didn't need to start another civil war. So disarm and neutralize became the strategy of choice.

Vaughn turned to Mandy, smiling a tease. "Well, here we go. You want to climb onto my back and hold on, or go up the rope yourself?" As he said that, it brought back memories of when Stephanie had clung to him for dear life as they went down the ladder from the bathroom window. It also reminded him of climbing up and down the tree of freedom over the border fence. *Hmm, this is getting to be all too regular.*

Mandy noted how casual he seemed. *Like he's done this before.* "I don't know. I think I'd like to try to climb the rope myself."

Interesting choice. She's a go-getter. Vaughn nodded to Larson who threw the padded grappling hooks which then soundlessly grabbed hold on the western wall. This was their way in to avoid being discovered by the gatekeepers.

"King Vaughn, let me go first, please." Larson pleaded.

God, he called him King again. Ha, ha! Look at Vaughn's sour face. He really hates to be called King. Oh my God! Vaughn's so… adorable.

Vaughn was about to ask Larson *again* to quit calling him *King,* but he grudgingly focused on how a King would act upon the suggestion. "I hope you're right that this spot is really blind from the cameras now."

Larson gave his reassurance. "Since I was knee-high to a quarter horse, I loved squirt guns. My favorite sport was paintball before I became a ranger. The tricky part here was firing such a tiny pellet that blocks only a portion of the camera's view while not enough to make them want to run out and fix it right away. But just enough to make it safe for us."

"You sure they haven't come out to clean it? They've had all day."

"I'm sure. We've kept watch."

Mandy became so engrossed in how much went into this rescue that she couldn't help interjecting. "But why didn't you just, ahh, squirt them now, then there'd be no worry about it?"

Larson smiled, but Vaughn answered. "We actually discussed every detail of your sister's rescue. We felt it would be too suspicious to do that at night and so close to shift change. We did it at first light when the birds become active."

Mandy broke into laughter at realizing the impression they were trying to create. When she eased up, Larson continued. "We did it about a half hour before the night shift would leave. Well, little lady, I don't know if you know much about working people and their shifts, but the last thing a late shifter wants is to go outside right before they're expecting to go home to bed, and climb a ladder to clean messy bird poop off some little lens that will probably smear and…"

Mandy broke into laughter again and Vaughn picked up where Larson left off. "When the new shift sees the mess, they'll be pissed as hell, quite sure the last shift passed the chore onto them. That'll make them want to put off cleaning it till later." Vaughn made a yuck face to match Mandy's, and concluded their reasoning with a question. "Do you know how hard it is clean up dried bird poop?"

"Oh, my God… Stop! It's ridiculous you guys are making me laugh! This is a *very* serious matter."

Vaughn nodded. "We know, dear Mandy. Precisely why we're being humorous, because being too high-strung is when you screw-up. We need to ease tension so we can focus the sharpest now."

Larson asked, "Did you tell her?"

Seeing Vaughn turn red, Mandy poked him in his side, making him flinch. "Tell me what, King Vaughn?"

Larson had started to enjoy the situation, and had no problem fessing up. "After we're all over the wall, we can't all just come into plain sight nor do we want them to see us coming into view in succession. Either would still look suspicious so I came up with this idea."

Vaughn nodded but with serious dissatisfaction. "It's his idea."

"We need a distraction, something that will make them actually break protocol and follow someone with the rest of their cameras for a bit."

Mandy scrunched her forehead and it very much reminded Vaughn of Stephanie. "Ok, what?"

"You and King Vaughn are going to come out of the shadows into view first. We need you two to… give them something to watch, so they follow you as you walk away. Something that will explain…"

Mandy quickly understood. "Why we came out of the shadows. No problem, I know just what to do." And she gave Vaughn a wink.

Trying to sound unhappy, Vaughn declared, "Let's get on with it."

Larson grabbed the rope and seemed almost to float all the way up with effortless climbing. Vaughn nodded to Mandy who recalled how she'd done something similar in gym class. As a kid, she'd actually spent a good bit of time way up in the local trees, but her climb this time was far from effortless. Yet, she made it over then down the other side with another rope Larson had secured. Vaughn and then four military followed, so seven went over the wall while another four remained outside to watch each gate at the center of the four walls.

After climbing over the western wall, the group took stock of their appearance. Mandy was dressed up as a maid, Vaughn as a novice apprentice Judge, and Larson as an attendant to the castle. The other four had donned uniforms with two as guards, one as a grounds keeper, and one as a freshly appointed apprentice judge whose robes were a couple shades lighter gray than a full apprentice.

"I think the gray robe suits you!" Mandy teased Vaughn, but added, "Well, maybe not the color but definitely the robe."

She really is like Stephanie. Gorgeous too, but in a different way and even bolder. Vaughn shook his head.

Larson spoke in a mock heavy tone. "Well, King Vaughn, are you ready to do your *duty?*"

Mandy chimed in, taking Vaughn's hand. "Don't worry, just follow my lead!" She pulled him out of the shadows by his robe then yanked him tight against her and held him in place with her hands around his buttocks. She had positioned them for a profile shot to give the viewers their best eyeful of all the action.

Vaughn awkwardly took hold of her, but Mandy whispered, "That's perfect. You're acting just like a young judge would act, but you need to warm up a little."

Even through all their clothing, Vaughn felt her vitality, her real need that went far beyond the physical. Suddenly, Vaughn felt a deep love for Mandy, love through understanding her nobility in spite of her recent history. *She really is* a lot *like Stephanie.* And his hands began to cherish her as they slowly ran up her back, firmly making contact with her flesh through her dress. As he kissed her, he took patience that allowed the meaning of love, cherish, and respect to join their sensations. Mandy felt herself being drawn into the kiss in ways part of her seemed to know though she never experienced it before. When they finally ended the kiss, she couldn't help a gasp and a tear as she held him by his back, staring into his eyes. "Oh God, no wonder Stephanie loves you so much… I never…"

He smiled warmly at her, reminding her. "Don't forget to keep acting!"

Coming back to her senses, she smacked him on his backside and pulled him down the narrow stone walkway then stopped again. This time she kissed him from feelings she'd never had before.

Oh no! God, I can't help but treasure her. Now if she can just treasure herself. Vaughn remembered how he'd tried to do the very same thing with Tracy. *I think I'm a lot better at it now, though. I'm* not *letting Mandy be murdered nor abused anymore.*

Larson nodded, whispering to everyone else who was also nodding. "She's good, isn't she?" After checking that the camera had moved, Larson pointed and whispered, "Go." One headed in one direction, another in another direction. Vaughn and Mandy continued their walk down the path and now other cameras as well began to search for them.

Before they'd all split up, they checked their communication devices. The only way they were going to find Carla was a lot of luck, patience, and diligence. Vaughn reasoned there would be some direct access from the Judge's bedchamber, but no possibility could be ignored. Fortunately, the halls were virtually empty this late at night, and the occasional cameras posted inside all had built up a considerable dust layer.

After one last kiss, Vaughn sent Mandy to the maid's general station where he hoped she could coerce information from other staff. For his part, he took a deep breath then confidently went into the security room where they monitored all the cameras.

"We've all been watching you," the young man, obviously in charge, greeted him with several meanings packed into his words. "But we don't recognize you… although the girl reminds us of… someone." Vaughn appraised the others who were also trying to hide their snickers while they nodded, but also unable to place why or from where Mandy seemed familiar.

Vaughn counted. *Only six.*

The chief spoke again. "Actually, I think I *have* seen you before… somewhere." To which the others took a closer look.

As the chief and a security officer went to confront him, half from a routine but also half from a growing sense of concern, Vaughn smiled and hung his head as if a bit embarrassed, then waited for them to get closer and block the others' view, then rapidly hit them in the solar plexus with right and left punches. The strikes took their breath away but left them standing for an instant before they doubled over.

An instant was all the time Vaughn needed to cross silently over to two other men sitting side-by-side before two monitors. The pair couldn't rise fast enough before he chopped each in the throat, one with his right hand and the other with the left. One fell back into his chair as the other choked and fell into a monitor. As the other two sitting at another set of monitors began to stand up, Vaughn front kicked one in the face, which impaled his head within a shattered viewing screen. He grabbed the other by the throat, and asked, "Do you know what I am?"

The terrified man shook his head, saying, "I've *never* seen anyone move like that." The security officer felt he was peering at death itself as Vaughn's dark eyes bore into him. But Vaughn offered the next worse possibility, "Military intelligence."

That almost made the man pass out but Vaughn squeezed his throat. "You only get one chance at this. If you help me, we'll see about a military pardon. We can protect you, ya know?"

The man nodded, trying to take a breath through his squeezed neck and fear. He also realized Vaughn seemed so young and it just felt, well, … wrong to be bested by one this age.

"Show me the secret passage the Judge disappears through."

"Which one?" The man rasped.

Damn! "The one he uses late at night."

The man shook his head. "I've never seen him use one late at night."

"Show me the ones you do know."

The man adjusted the monitor cameras, and indeed the quality of the images appeared as if looking through years of dust. "Two in the halls and one in this study. Turn the wall lamp clockwise, and the wall can be pushed open. That's it."

"What about the Judge's bedroom?"

"We don't have cameras there."

Vaughn nodded. "Does the Judge seem to eat a lot?"

The man half chuckled. "Don't know where he puts it all."

"Where's he keeping his secret mistress?"

"Which one? They come and go, but can't tell no one and no one to tell. Who'd believe it? Branded as a devil and burned alive if anyone told."

"Show me the Judge's bedroom door."

The man brought it up and showed Vaughn how to get there. "But the way it's guarded, here, here, and here… ahhh, but that shouldn't be a problem for you."

"Show me the maids' quarters."

The young man became embarrassed but pulled up the views of the live-in maids' private rooms and communal areas. Mandy was sitting at a round table with six or so other young women gossiping away. Vaughn then instructed the young man to pull up the other locations where he might find the other troops. Watching the extent of the operation disconcerted the security officer, but seeing one of the troops dragging an unconscious man into a storeroom made him shake even harder. Vaughn pulled out his communication device and pressed once on a button, causing all the other devices to vibrate just once. In succession five other replies made their way to everyone, informing all that things were secure for now.

"Oh God! Oh dear God!… forgive me, God!" The young man began to blubber.

Everyone always seems to ask God's forgiveness after *getting caught. I wonder… does God even respect that?* Then he remembered Trevor. *I suppose so!* Vaughn gazed at the young man, wondering about his soul's fate. "Thank you. What's your name?"

"Christopher, Sir."

"I'll see to it you're reviewed for pardon, but sorry I have to do this." And Vaughn punched, knocking him out.

After tying the officers up with electric cords from the equipment, and locking the door, Vaughn headed for the Judge's door. Along the way, he gave very official nods and gestures to the few people he passed, looking every bit as if he knew where he was going and had to get there so no one stopped him or did anything more than return his same gesticulations. At the bedroom door, Vaughn knew it would be locked, but he had a hunch. He knocked loudly… but no answer came. Looking up and down the hall, he went to one end then the other and seeing nobody around the corners, he came back to stand before the door again. He held out his hands in prayer. "Lord God, for Justice and Mercy."

Deep blackness fell over Vaughn as he stepped back then kicked the heavy oak door whose lock splintered with an explosive sound. Calmly, he stepped into an outer room and closed the broken door. After listening a few moments to the utter quite, he walked into a large hexagonal central room dimly lit by soft wall lights. Shadows fell upon lavish furniture. An antique desk, cabinets with shelves full of books, and a dark round table all conveyed an official feeling. The thick carpeting felt odd beneath his shoes. Each wall had a doorless opening so Vaughn started at his left to inspect each room. The first was a study, the second a plain bedroom most likely for guests. The one directly across from the entry hall seemed to be an official meeting room, but the fourth only had a table, chair, and a phone. *This has got to be where his secret conversations occur. No place to hide surveillance here.* And finally, the fifth doorway led to the master bedroom.

The ornate bed had dark wooden posts that supported a white, lacey canopy with a distinctly feminine feel. *Of course the bastard is married… Damn! He could simply be with his wife, wherever her bedroom is.*

Vaughn searched around a while, tugging on lampposts, pulling on various books from various shelves until he shook his head then finally began to leave, but with each step, he felt he was doing something wrong until he had to stop just before the door out.

Something doesn't feel right. He turned back around, feeling he was supposed to stay, and while recognizing that feeling, he felt his eyes darken. *This is the same feeling I had when I went to rescue Stephanie.*

Two full years ago, Stephanie had locked herself in a bathroom in Gary's house where her former gang prepared to rape her. She was to be drugged and passed around, but she never drank it. Vaughn, having heard rumor of the party and sensing a great evil, couldn't keep from investigating. Climbing up a ladder to the bathroom, he heard Stephanie pray, wanting to die, but also to live.

Vaughn sat down in a chair in the corner of the guest bedroom and his feelings intensified. He kept nodding his head. *She's here! I know it. I can feel her. Oh God! I can feel her cry!* Minutes passed into an hour, and Vaughn kept trying to rise but the chair seemed to hold him in place. The other troops had signaled several times that everything was still OK but they all knew one hour had been the decided safe limit. *How long do we have before we're discovered?* He kept repeating, *God, I can feel her* as tears crept into his eyes. Mandy's descriptions of Carla and how she had sacrificed her education to work in the shoe factory to support Mandy kept haunting Vaughn. Through Mandy, he could feel Carla's love, her goodness. *It sure feels like I also can feel her directly for myself, not just from what Mandy told me.*

Precious seconds ticked by that seemed like minutes that felt like hours. Seemingly paralyzed, unable to rise, nor quell his growing sense of danger and failure, Vaughn didn't notice the bookcase silently swinging open just a few feet away from him. But he suddenly sensed another's presence entering the room. Judge Hiram was dumbfounded as they stared into each other's eyes.

Middle-aged, but with a full head of black curly hair, Hiram was wearing only his undershorts. Vaughn noted the judge took good care of himself, appearing to be in excellent physical shape. Vaughn also realized that his gray robe was confusing Hiram. He bowed his head to the Judge, rising slowly. "Begging your pardon Judge Hiram, but someone kicked your door in!"

"*What!* Who are you? What are you doing in *here?* No one is allowed…"

Now standing fully upright, Vaughn wagged his index finger back and forth. "Na, na, na! Dear Judge, why don't you show me where you just came from!"

Judge Hiram narrowed his eyes at him. "You're not one of us!"

Vaughn shook his head.

"Military." the Judge spat out.

"More than even that. How do you want to do this? Easy or hard?"

Hiram made the realization. "You wouldn't be here if I had any guards left."

Vaughn shook his head again, and pointed to the secret entrance indicating the Judge should lead the way.

"You don't know what you're doing." He said half in anger, half in plea, attempting to sound reasonable. "If you bring us down, this whole country will collapse."

"If a tree has a diseased branch, you cut it off so the rest of the tree can live. The people themselves are the roots. Government is nothing more than branches at best!"

"*Matthew* told you, didn't he?" There was distinctly focused anger in his words. Vaughn merely listened. "If that's the way it's going to be, I can tell you some things about *him*."

"You'll have your chance in military court, now *shut up* and lead me to Carla!"

The judge whispered, "Carla! That's her name! I'd for-gotten."

Vaughn fought to restrain the urge to kill him on the spot, but felt pretty sure that before they left, the Judge would be dead. The secret passage seemed to travel between the sone walls of other rooms, then down very narrow stairs. Then they went down even lower as he turned left to descend another narrow flight of stone stairs. Only an occasional low wattage electric bulb gloomily lit the way until, finally, a heavy, narrow wooden door marked the end to the passage. All along their secret route, nothing branched off from it, making it quite clear that this secret passage had only a single private function.

Vaughn spoke softly, almost a whisper. "Go ahead, open it."

The judge opened the door a crack then hesitated and turned to Vaughn. "Look. You're a man. Really, this is every man's dream. You have to under…"

Vaughn leapt and kicked the good judge dead center in the chest and the heavy oak door flew open and crashed against the wall, while the Judge burst through the entryway, tumbling upon the floor.

The room was far more spacious than Vaughn ever expected, and surprisingly heated to a comfortable temperature for being down so far under the castle. The furniture must have been disassembled and reassembled, or had been placed there first then the walls built around them! Elegant, dark wooden cabinets, dressers, refrigerator, and an open bathroom with shower formed a completely self-serving unit. But sitting straight up on a bed very similar to the one upstairs was a stunning, naked young woman with wavy dark brown hair.

A long, heavy iron chain fastened to an eye-ring to the center of the stone floor was also attached around her right ankle.

Hearing the door crash, seeing the Judge hurtling to the floor, and Vaughn walking in while staring at her, left Carla thunderstruck. Being totally absorbed at the sight of Vaughn, it seemed several minutes went by before she realized her naked breasts and slowly reached for a cover to hold over herself. She whispered with tears in her eyes. "I know you!"

God, her eyes say so much. Vaughn spoke softly. "I don't think so. You disappeared before I even entered this country."

But Carla shook her head in disagreement, beginning to cry. "Oh, God… dearest Jesus! You came to me in my dreams, told me you would come. I know you! I do! "

Tears clouded Vaughn's eye, knowing she spoke truly. He had become quite acquainted with mysteries over the last two years. But out of the corner of his eye, he saw Hiram try to crawl away. "I wouldn't if I were you. Unchain her, and I'm not going to tell you again."

"I… I can't! There's no lock. The chain's been welded shut. She was never supposed to leave."

Carla kept weeping, saying over and over, "I know you! I know you…"

Vaughn turned to the doorway when he heard footsteps, but Carla just kept her head bowed. Mandy came in but froze then cried out her sister's name. Larson entered just as Mandy ran over to her sister and Carla picked up her head.

The sisters were arm in arm, both in tears of joy, then Carla pointed at Vaughn. "I know him, Mandy! He came to me in my dreams and told me he would come!"

Tears still pouring, Mandy looked from her sister to Vaughn and back again, feeling a presence she'd never felt before, something good, something greater than herself. *God is real!* She began to say over and over within herself.

"Larson, do you believe the bastard welded the chain shut?"

Larson went over to inspect it, shaking his head. "The only way he intended this to come off was to cut her leg off! We don't have anything to break this. Perhaps if I had a pick, I could…"

Hiram managed to laugh! "That bolt goes a foot deep. You got time for that? By the time you get her out, they'll be a hundred of my people here in the morning."

"Mandy, find her some clothes," whispered Vaughn.

Hiram laughed again, feeling more confident by the minute. "Aren't any. Told you this is every man's dream."

Vaughn shot a particular look at Larson who knew he had to do something or Hiram would die right there. Larson remembered the story of the former elder who bitterly chided Vaughn for believing his people could be rescued from Jargono. Ranger Vaughn had him chained to a post, and left to be burned up from Jargono's fire. Larson went over and grabbed the Judge by the hair, standing him up. "I'd be *very* quiet if I were you."

Vaughn went over to pick up the chain that extended from under her bed covers. "May I?" As she nodded, he uncovered her ankle. *Damn! Too tight!*

"Break my ankle!"

Mandy wouldn't hear of it. "No!"

Carla put her hand upon her cheek. "It's the only way. I've thought many times to do it myself but every time I tugged, it hurt so badly but nothing seemed to move."

Vaughn looked closer and saw all the scars. He shook his head again.

Larson shook his head, too. "What we need is a large bolt cutter." He took Hiram by the throat. "I know you've got a tool hall here."

Hiram smiled arrogantly. "By now, it'll be busy with early morning grounds keepers. They rise *early*."

"Bolt cutter… bolt cutter…" Vaughn kept mumbling.

"Please break my ankle. Or if you have to, cut it off! One of you has got to have a knife"

Mandy screamed. "NO! You'll bleed to death."

"Then leave me! At least I know now, dear Mandy, that you're safe."

"No." Vaughn said. "We can't leave you. They'd kill you for sure."

"You don't know. I'm already dead!"

Larson turned away, thinking of his departed wife and of the kids he's raising alone. *No, Carla, you're alive!* He thought of his little daughter, Rebekah, and the next thing he knew, he had grabbed and rammed Hiram against the wall, rendering him unconscious.

Vaughn placed a hand upon Carla's cheek, and she looked up to see a golden glow in his eyes. His gentle touch and his special words blended together. "You're a long way from being dead. Besides, in your dreams didn't I say I would free you?"

Carla gripped his hand and kissed it. "Yes."

Mandy spoke sharply at Vaughn. "Do something!"

After a pause, Vaughn ordered them. "Get off the bed!" Both girls looked at him. "*Now!*"

Carla rose without her covers, used to being naked, and Vaughn noticed she rivaled Stephanie in beauty and form. He pulled off a bed sheet and handed it with a knife to Mandy. "Make her a covering. She'll need it when we leave!"

Vaughn stripped off the bed canopy then unscrewed its posts. Farmers he'd worked for even before he'd met Stephanie had taught him to be resourceful beyond most people's imagination. And what he needed now was to imagine a doorway to freedom. He tossed off the mattresses revealing a metal frame which he took apart. Grabbing two of the metal rails, he shoved them through the eye-ring which was large enough to allow the chain to swing freely. Larson understood immediately and took hold of the other end of the rails.

With Vaughn at one end and Larson at the other, they began to push counterclockwise to literally unscrew the foot long bolt. Mandy raced over to help Vaughn while Carla, now wearing the crude robe Mandy had cut out from the sheet, went over to Larson.

Vaughn bowed his head. "Lord God of my forefathers Abraham, Isaac and Jacob, whom I have only recently read about, You helped me before, help us now to free this girl as You promised her in her dreams!"

And with a demonic sounding screech, the bolt began to turn round and round. It was indeed a foot long but eventually came loose. Vaughn wrapped the iron chain, which was a good twenty-five feet in length, over and over his right shoulder. Larson approached to take it but Vaughn shook his head. "Get us out of here, Larson."

Nodding, Larson pointed to Hiram who was waking up. "What about him?"

In utter disbelief, Hiram saw the chain wrapped around Vaughn with the bolt hanging free. "How? That's impossible! Oh, God!"

Vaughn dropped the full weight of the chain onto Hiram's lap, and commanded. "You should carry the chain, Hiram, so everyone can see *every man's dream!* We won't have to run with you carrying the evidence! "Put it over *your* shoulder!"

Saddled by the heavy chain, imagining himself walking out into the light of day, Hiram's breathing became labored. "I can't."

Larson reached down to stand him up, but Hiram seemed to choke, clutched his chest then slumped over dead. Vaughn took the chain and rewound it around himself.

CHAPTER 8

Fate of the World

Paul's display of discomfort and his remark confirmed to Peter that Paul could read his mind. "Peter, you think I was wrong for chastising you in front of everyone."

Peter folded his arms across his chest, sighing. "Do you know what you've done? You haven't been doing this nearly as long as I have so you haven't had the opportunity to learn… certain wisdom."

Paul softened, but spoke his mind. "Look, you walked out on the gentile converts. What was I supposed to do? Those damned gray arms appeared in their heads almost immediately. I could hear what those demons were telling them, that they were no good being here, that Jesus Christ is only for the Jews, just *their* God, and how foolish they were for thinking otherwise. If I hadn't scolded you…"

"Do you really think I was wrong?"

Paul narrowed his eyes at him. "No! You were doing the exact same thing I was! Except you could see and hear what the demons were telling your Jewish converts."

Peter nodded. "Yes. They were saying this was nothing but a new religion disconnected from God's word, and at worst, throwing away God's word because the *Jews* are the only chosen people. Therefore Jesus couldn't be..."

Paul finished for him. "Jesus couldn't be the true Messiah. I know what you were thinking, doing, and why. Look, we both wanted to give our charges time to learn better. We both needed to adjust our appearances in the present so there could be a chance for them in the future."

Peter echoed Paul's word, "Appearances."

"Appearances." Paul reiterated.

But Peter looked at him gravely. "I fear, though, that we have committed a great error in wisdom, for by trying to save the immediate, we have sacrificed those further in the future."

"How so?" Paul objected.

Because when the people in the future read about all this, without the benefit of our context, their leaders will use our *apparent* disagreement as proof that since even I sinned, then we all still sin even though we're saved."

"That's ridiculous. Read about *this?*" Paul laughed.

"As I said, I've been doing this longer than you. Are you going to tell him to stop recording? And how would you explain that request to the young man?" Peter pointed at a young scribe furiously writing, reflecting... though not privy to the current conversation between Peter and Paul.

"Still ridiculous! So what? He writes, I write, too! A lot of letters I just whip up are going nowhere but eventually into the trash."

Peter shook his head. "You underestimate what we fight, my friend."

"Very well, I'll make sure that in my future writings, it's clear about the purity we now have through the Holy Ghost, that it brings *every* thought and imagination of our hearts into oneness with Christ. That sounds plain enough."

Peter shook his head again. "You still don't grasp what you can't take back. Those gray arms reaching inside people's heads are going to *explain* the meaning to people when they read it. They will *prove* their evil unmoved internal reality to people, that they cannot help but to keep sinning, and then they will interpret the words you've written to support *their* meaning and the people will believe it."

"But I just told you, I'll write clearly that…"

Peter smiled. "But the people will have accepted that, of course, of course, *eventually*… given enough time, all our thoughts and imaginations are captured by Christ. Why? It's a lifelong process. They'll say 'Look at Peter, he even walked with Christ. He's the rock, and he was saved but he still sinned because Paul said so, and, anyway, the process only *approaches* perfection but everyone knows we can never *be* perfect.'"

Paul scowled. "You just twisted everything up. That's *not* what I meant and you know…"

"Of course I know, and so do you, and I'm no master at twisting the truth, but the demons are."

Paul shook his head. "This is *impossible*. How are we supposed to not sin *and* also adjust our appearances perfectly so that such misunderstandings won't happen?"

Peter put his hands upon Paul's shoulders. "My dear friend, Jesus, whom I walked with every day for those years, said the Holy Ghost would lead us into all Truth, give us a pure heart, and teach us all things, but he never ever said he could show us how to present appearances that couldn't be misunderstood or misinterpreted. Just look at what so many said about him when he was here!"

Paul frowned, remembering how twisted his thoughts had once been and how he had murdered because of that. He still felt the utter guilt of his travesties, even though he'd been fully forgiven.

Peter gently shook him. "Paul, we're not God. We're not the Holy Ghost. Perfect as we may be, there's a limit even for us. That's why Jesus made it plain that only the Holy Ghost would be people's leader from the inside out. Not me, not you, and certainly not some words we scribbled down in the midst of scurrying here and there, or in the midst of any number of other sundry things."

But Paul just kept shaking his head, for now the future picture of the consequences of what he'd done descended upon his understanding. "Oh, Lord! They're going to make a damned religion out of me! You too, Peter! Dear God, no!" And then he whispered the next part of his prophecy… or perhaps mere understanding. "And their damned religion won't be anything like what Jesus died for. It's going to be the opposite!"

Joshua watched Stephanie's every move as she came out of her bathroom naked. His first time beholding her full beauty made him love her so much more. Her breasts and her hips swaying, her firmness yet softness and vulnerability pained him with the urge to protect her, hold, and cherish her. He saw his wife take something from around her neck and place it into a little drawer in a nightstand then take something out which she hid behind her as she walked slowly up to him. The only thing upon her that was not tender flesh hung between her breasts. Joshua asked about it even though he didn't want anything to come between their lovemaking. He wanted her so badly right now. "What's that necklace? I've never seen…"

Patiently, she leveled her eyes into Joshua in a way he'd never seen before. For the first time, he felt that she truly stood naked before him in a far greater way than just flesh. "There are many things you don't know about me yet, my husband, but there's one thing I have to tell you before we make love. This around my neck is the Seed to the Tree of Life. Besides Vaughn, Lynnara, my adopted daughter, and now you, no one else is to know and you need to understand why."

She pulled back the covers, revealing her husband's nakedness, then sat down on the bed across from him. She placed a piece of ancient-looking paper face down between them. "I'm going to tell you the whole story of my life, of Vaughn, of demons, and battles you wouldn't believe had you not known me. I speak truth without exaggeration. We sit here naked together because we're husband and wife, and I want our nakedness together to be a testimony of the truth that shall openly pass from me to you."

Stephanie began with her earliest memories of her parents, their mistreatment, her father's brutality and how it affected her, of how she degraded herself not thinking women had value nor meaning to men beyond sex. She told him of her lewd behavior, her slovenliness, drug use, and pettiness, her provoking girls to jealousy. She told him how Vaughn rescued her, of their conversations, their problems with her former gang, and how the Appendaho, which Joshua secretly knew through his father though he never knew about the Tree of Life, had adopted her.

"I spiritually bonded with Arlupo's father so he could help me understand. His daughter became more than a sister to me, and they entrusted to me their secret of the Tree of Life. Through that spiritual tree of direct meaning of goodness, I gained a new will by what I now understand to be called the Holy Ghost of Jesus Christ. In fact, the Tree of Life *is* the Lord Jesus' Tree! It always has been! I became a *faithwalker,* traveled in the spiritual corridor to heal Vaughn, and got caught by a demon."

The whole time, Joshua felt torn as she sat naked in front of him, because his sight kept roaming back and forth from her flesh to the inner visions her words created, and his love and desire increased their burning for her on all accounts. "You… you fought a real demon? He wrapped you up in his coil?"

"Yes!" And her stories continued long into the night: How Arlupo cleverly rescued her, how the Appendaho, people who turned out later to be hers, taught her, knowing beforehand that they would die for helping her. When she got to the point just after her best friend Arlupo's death, when the sacred box that hadn't been opened for thousands of years called her to open it, she said, "That is how I came to possess this letter which was inside the sacred box!"

And she turned over the paper, knowing that even though only a few special people were able to see the words, Joshua would be able to read them.

Dear Stephanie,

Long ago I came upon the two most precious things in this world, besides the Light from which I was born. The Tree of Life and my true mate who became my Queen. I found the Tree alone on top of a dead mountain. The Tree of Life, standing asleep on top of a poison mountain, like a prisoner, as I and my future wife were. As I wept upon the Tree, it sprouted, as did your Tree for you, as you wept the true tears of true grief. The day I married my Queen, we went to the top of the mountain, and the Tree had born a single fruit that glowed to us. We ate from the fruit, and as we ate, the Tree died, and crumbled to ash.

Inside the fruit was a single, beautiful seed, shiny like a black pearl. That same day, we took the seed, and with the whole town, constructed the inner basin of the sacred brass receptacle where the current Tree resides now. That same day we were married, we planted that seed together. On our first night, we slept together in the sacred room you are now in. It was the first time we had been together that way. When we awoke in the morning, the Tree of Life had spouted. Nine months to the day, our first of many children was born to the Tree of Life.

On the day of my beloved's passing away, I wept before the Tree, and it bore another fruit. As I looked upon the Tree, the leaves began to fall off, and the Tree began to sleep, even as my heart felt from my beloved's passing. But we were just the tiniest twig on that Tree, and I did not know the meaning of these things that were happening to the Tree, even though I had been taught a long time and deeply by it. I was again as a helpless child, not knowing, not understanding. Then the fruit began to glow, and the Tree became a vision. The vision I saw was you, dear Stephanie, with red hair, true tears, scars not a few, and true love and faith, my daughter, and I understood that this fruit was to be put away for you. But I knew the fruit would perish. So knowing through wisdom that the spirit of feminine goodness passes from mother to daughter, I took all the fruit and placed it with my wife's body with a prayer that the spirit of goodness would be passed down to you.

One of our children, a red haired girl, the only one to be born such, had long ago disappeared from us when she was just thirteen. We never knew what happened to her. We were stricken with grief, as we felt for each child as if each was our only child. But I know that you are her descendent.

When the Tree showed me your vision, I understood that this was the way the Tree of Life was to return to us that which was lost, so I wept again to the Tree, to God, and to my departed wife, that all had been put at peace, and that our child's life had not been in vain. Then I understood that I should place this seed in the box, and tell you of your ancient history. But as to *what* you are, that will always be your choice, my beloved daughter.

You must guard this seed with all your being. I have fastened it to a gold chain, which my wife assures me will be fashionable in your time. Wear it my daughter, next to your heart, where also your beloved mate rests. At the time that both of you know is right, do what you know is right with the seed. My daughter, there is no other seed like the one that you now protect. Protect it with your faith. This is not the time of the end for you, my daughter, it is your beginning. Queen Yinauqua, your mother, used the ribbon I tied to the scroll, to tie our lost child's hair. You and your mate shall always be with us through our prayers.

Your *beloved father* for eternity,

King Mafferan

Overwhelmed by sharing a special knowledge, they both shed tears. Joshua whispered, "This is thousands of years old." Stephanie nodded, and he added, barely able to make his voice audible. "You are a very, *very* special woman!"

With pain in her eyes that she tried to hide, and scrunched up shoulders, she grimaced then burst out with racking sobs. He delicately placed the letter aside on a bed stand, took her in his arms, and pulled the covers over for more warmth.

The Tree of Life. The Tree of Life, he kept repeating to himself as he tried to calm the depths of her torment. *So much pain. I never knew she hurt so much. I never knew the terrible responsibility. The Tree of Life. But I thought it… well, I didn't know what I thought except that it had to be on Earth, somewhere. God made it grow fruit for her ancestors, so to live forever one would have to eat from it regularly, but God doesn't have it fruit regularly. She's the protector now. I'm… At the time that is right. What does that mean? Oh, dear Jesus, what have you blessed me with? I'm so ignorant. How does this all fit together?*

His caress felt long awaited, but for another's touch, not his. Still her body responded, leaning her back with ever slightly more pressure into his chest as his hand stroked her head, shoulder, and arm.

How could she not love Joshua? He had earned her respect on so many levels. She knew she couldn't withhold herself from him. Her feeling that wouldn't be right made her pains even worse. *But I thought… Oh Light… I thought… How, dear Jesus, who suffered in this mortal lifetime, how does all this fit together? What will Vaughn do without me? I thought… God, what good are my thoughts? Oh my God, I love him so much, I can't let go of that, either. I love Vaughn so much.*

Through all the traps that had previously swallowed the *faithwalker*, through all her misery, even when Jargono had trapped her, she had never felt so torn apart. When she had decided to sacrifice herself and marry Jargono to protect Vaughn and learn how to defeat Jargono, she still had known she would always love Vaughn and not Jargono. *But I can't do that to Joshua. He's a good man and he really does love me.*

When trapped in the Dead Forest, Stephanie had to choose between Lynnara or her own life plus the Seed of the Tree of Life, and she couldn't choose. But even as unimaginably painful as that was, it wasn't like this. *I can't be untrue to Joshua, but I can't stop loving Vaughn, either, and I can't be both. Oh my God, dear Jesus…*

After Stephanie fell asleep in his arms, Joshua couldn't rest because pictures of his wife's life kept playing in his head, his heart. He eased out of bed to go to the bathroom but stopped by the little stand with the single drawer. He looked back at his sleeping wife, sighed, stared at the drawer then quietly slid it open. Perhaps it was his intelligence training, his desire to investigate, perhaps intuition, or plain curiosity, but he just had to look.

She hadn't finished telling him about her whole life yet, and somehow he knew that what he found inside the drawer… *My God… I've seen this somewhere before!* Lying on top of a beautiful ribbon and an envelope was a simple cord strung through a very ancient looking wedding ring that had distinctive engravings. He held it up to the light, rubbed and inspected it more closely. *I know I've seen this before!*

Joshua took the ring over to where Stephanie laid and stood before her. Somehow he knew she'd woken and dangling the ring before her face, he waited. When she opened her eyes, he said, "I've seen this before, Stephanie, but I can't remember where."

Her head still on the pillow, her eyes went up to his in the dim light. "Then you must have seen it around Vaughn's neck."

He paused then nodded as his memory drifted back. "Yes." He looked off as he remembered the time and place. "When I awoke from his prayer that saved my life, it was hanging there. I gave it no thought then because my mind was so much engaged elsewhere. And I only saw it briefly as he knelt over me then it was gone." He looked at her with all seriousness, with no anger but a calm that was nonetheless intense. "You're married to Vaughn!"

"Well, not really! It was never consummated!" She turned her face slightly into the pillow.

Usually, Joshua wasn't surprised by anything. *Why? Why didn't I see this?*

When she fully faced him again, tears were rolling from her eyes. "My dear husband, I have to tell you about the rest of my life, but I don't think I can bear it right now. Still, I can tell you this. I'm your wife and you needn't fear about any other."

Joshua leaned over to stroke her head over and over, watching her pain and found tears rolling from his own eyes. "I'm so sorry, Stephanie. I'm so very sorry."

Leaning her head into his comforting hand, she said, "Don't be. You truly love me and there's *nothing* to be sorry about for that. I'm very fortunate."

"What does it mean, in your letter, when the time is right?"

Her eyes suddenly kept shifting in focus. She seemed to be looking into ages gone by and into the future at the same time. "Among the Appendaho, there are certain questions that we don't answer for someone else because they can only be truly answered from the inside out."

❧

"Well, I see things aren't quite working out down here for you."

Vaughn wondered at Mafferan's ability to understate as he sneaked quietly away from his camp where Carla and the others were sleeping. They'd managed to make it safely out of

Hiram's castle before sunrise as his story of lots of people being around in the predawn morning was a bit exaggerated. But having been up all night, they could only drive a few hours before it became necessary to stop.

All the major roads went through all the major cities, but about one-hundred years ago when the Great Religious War's plague and poisoned water turned those cities into dead zones, new roads were built around them. Using those connecting roads to the small towns that had survived made for rather awkward travel.

Vaughn didn't feel it wise to stop too near to any people in this particular state which had a much smaller military population because of being further inland. They veered off the road and made camp, reminding him of when he and Stephanie camped while searching for their escape to this country. He whispered to Mafferan. "I can't go far, I'm keeping watch."

"Well, far is exactly where you *must* go, in a manner of speaking. I finally have your pass!" Mafferan waved his hand and a subtle glow surrounded the camp. "They're now protected until you return. It's an ancient blessing, actually one familiar to *your* forefathers who wandered the desert. This is your pass."

He dropped a leather pouch embroidered in black and gold into Vaughn's hands. Immediately, the pouch inundated him with deeply conflicting feelings.

Mafferan ignored his intense stare. "Open it, dear boy."

Vaughn found two bottles inside. One filled with cursed Black Oil and the other with golden Light Oil. He recognized the Black from encounters with Jargono, and the Light from when Stephanie's faithwalking power had turned Black into glowing Light Oil. "But I thought the Light Oil was destroyed when Stephanie cast it into the Black River?"

"Like the Black River, there's also a river of this Golden Oil. This is from the River of Peace."

"River of Peace." he echoed. "Stephanie believed the Black River came from the decaying bodies of all the souls gone to hell. From where does the River of Peace come from? I don't think there are enough…"

"You're correct in your assumption. There's a special grove of spiritual Olive trees, and they drop their fruit which releases their oils to form the River."

He put his hand upon Vaughn's shoulder. "I'm very sorry about you and Stephanie, but you must concentrate on the task at hand, otherwise there'll be no future at all."

"Future!" Vaughn heard himself whisper bitterly, kicking at the ground.

Mafferan knew his thoughts and gripped Vaughn's shoulder more tightly, "Yes, King Vaughn!" he said sternly, "You're responsible for the future of your people!"

"My people!" Vaughn nodded his head. "Yes, they *are* my people and I still haven't gotten used to it. How can these bottles be my pass?"

"Take a small bit of Light Oil first and put it upon your right cheek. Then, take a bit of the Black Oil on your left. Focus your mind on the demon you came in contact with in your dream with your … with Stephanie, when you…

were together. That memory of his presence will lead you to his ethereal room. It's up to you from then on. I don't think they'll try to eat you, my boy, but just in case, the Light Oil will protect you."

He knows about that *dream? Is there anything he doesn't know!* "But… but I'm not a faithwalker! I can't travel like Stephanie."

Smiling, Mafferan placed both his hands on Vaughn's shoulders. "The Lord Jesus blesses you to travel, since you do us service. Oh, and one more thing." He put his finger to Vaughn's forehead. "The Lord Jesus gives you orb knowledge."

Something disturbed Vaughn, and Mafferan's stare told him to speak his mind. "That's the first time I've heard you use, ahh, call the Lord by the name of Jesus. Why haven't you used it before?"

Mafferan nodded with understanding. "I wasn't supposed to use it before. Your understanding wasn't there to receive the name, though for all intents and purposes you certainly lived by its meaning, the goodness it represents. And as you'll find out more deeply, much more may be done through meaning than through a name but even more may be done through both together!"

"Well, I still haven't figured out how to gain that new will."

"Ahh, you might want to hold off on that awhile! In order for you to be 'neutral' you must possess both sides. If you fully convert, you can no longer represent me."

Vaughn shook his head at the increasing ridiculousness of his situation. "Great!" But then a thought came to him. "This

Light Oil's very powerful. Stephanie told me so. But it's OK for me to have this? I mean, downstairs must have agreed to it. It's mine, right?"

Mafferan knew when Vaughn's mind was traveling in directions that were a mystery to him. For some reason, he couldn't always read Vaughn's thoughts or guess them. "That's correct. Why?"

"Just thinking aloud!"

"Well, that's it, I'm afraid. This investigation is your idea. Have fun."

"Oh, I will. You can count on it!"

After Mafferan popped away, Vaughn looked at the bottles. *He wants me to put the Light Oil on first so that the counter to the Black Oil is already in place. But I've already battled this Black Oil so I know I can resist it. I'll put the Black on first, this way the Light Oil will be fighting the Black Oil to dislodge it and I'll learn more of such battles that way, rather than simply having the Black Oil blocked from reaching me!*

Vaughn stared deeply into the pouch, considering the ability to travel spiritually, to pop in and out of physical reality just like Stephanie… and Jargono. Memories of how Jargono avoided Vaughn by simply vanishing flashed by. *I wonder if I can chase him now, when he tries that. Well, actually, Mafferan only expected me to travel downstairs, but the blessing is simply to travel. Hmm, I wonder if he knew I'd use it in other ways. I mean, I believe I can.*

So absorbed in thought, Vaughn only faintly registered the morning sun warming him and making him drowsier. His days and nights being mixed up also conspired to veil from him his next surprise. All he really wanted to do now was sleep, but motion made him vaguely aware of Carla standing in front of him. His eyes came into focus upon the iron chain still attached to her ankle that now was all coiled around her neck! How she was able to bear all that weight was a mystery to Vaughn.

Vaughn scolded himself for being caught unaware. *How did she manage that without any noise? How did she manage it at all? If I don't pay better attention, I'm going to end up dead!* The look on Carla's face also told him she'd been watching for some time. *I'd best wait for her reaction to see what she actually heard.*

Carla stood silently. *Who are you, really? Or maybe the better question is, what are you?* "Interesting friend you *had* there!"

Vaughn masked his knowledge, blandly speaking. "He is that."

"Does he always pop in and out of reality like that?"

When Vaughn nodded, Carla turned him to face squarely with passion in her eyes. "Who are you?"

Gazing into her expression, Vaughn recalled the first words Carla spoke upon his entering her prison, *I know you!* "You already know! I'm the one God sent to rescue you, the same way I was sent to rescue Lady Stephanie almost two years ago. You'll shortly meet her 'cause she's actually primarily responsible for your rescue!"

Lady Stephanie. But why did his friend say he was sorry about her? "May we talk? Alone?" Carla darted her eyes around so Vaughn knew she was speaking of friends popping in and out of reality.

"Certainly!" Vaughn took her chain upon his shoulder, and guided her by the arm to a small patch of grass where they sat across each other. "I'm sure when we get back, Lady Stephanie will take care of you. Don't worry."

Carla rubbed her painful shoulders, smiling her thank you. "Mandy's been telling me all about her during the drive home. Thank you for letting us ride by ourselves."

"Ha! My wi… Stephanie's express order was, 'Take an extra vehicle so they can be alone. It's important!'"

The engrained patterns of hopelessness and torment from what seemed an eternal captivity were not yet reconciled with the love and kindness Carla was now hearing and seeing. She burst into tears then stared into the distance as she spoke. "I don't know how I'm going to live. I can hardly face Mandy… can hardly stand myself!"

Vaughn remembered the night he rescued a weeping, praying Stephanie in a similar condition, though this, now, was far worse. *I wish I could have saved Carla before all that happened.* Pains streaked across his chest and he found himself rubbing it.

Carla looked deeply into Vaughn's eyes. "What did you mean when you told me I'm a long way from being dead?"

Vaughn looked away as his own past and the present brought an overflow of emotions. He waited for the right words to come, then said, "When I lived in the Northern Country, those *idiots* still haven't named her, it seemed every woman wanted sex with me and everyone else. Really not like here, sex is thrown around like a local sport up there. In my former high school of over a thousand girls, well, I doubt there are any virgins over fifteen years old, nor even fourteen! And none of them married. Unlike here, they wait a long time to marry, well into their twenties."

Carla's amazement morphed partly into disgust, scorn, and confusion. "I don't understand."

Reading her reactions, he challenged her. "Actually, you do! I just told you all this so you could see that you do. Your understanding, which is your anger and your disgust, reacted accordingly to what I just described. There's really nothing to understand about their wretched behavior up North, except that they're hollow even at such an early age, that they fill their empty meaningless lives with the only intensity they can find, that being sex and drugs." Vaughn waited for what he expected next.

Carla turned away in self-reflection. *I was forced… but they willingly, actively degrade themselves. But actually, I…*

Vaughn saw the pain come up in her face and continued. "You do understand, that's why you feel pain."

"Are you reading my mind?"

"No. I don't have that gift. Just reading your face."

Carla sighed deeply, and her voice came out strained. "But you don't understand. Actually, I'm not much different. I gave myself away when I was fifteen, just for a *stupid* job in a factory."

Vaughn shook his head. "From what I was told, you lost your parents and had to take care of Mandy. That's somehow an excuse."

Carla shook her head, the pain deepening. "But I didn't realize what it would do to me. Every time I felt a little less, and less like a person." She looked Vaughn straight in the eye. "Truth be told, when Judge Hiram took me, I don't think there was much left of me. It's just that Mandy was my life. At least I could protect her from what I had to go through."

Vaughn clasped her hand. *If I didn't love Stephanie so much, I know I could love you, dear soul.* Carla felt love pour into her through his hands. Part of her wanted to jerk her hand away, but another part…

"God sent me to you for a reason. You're important, and you're no good to Mandy if you're no good to yourself. She'll pick up on the double standard and likely follow your example. Is that what you want?"

"No!"

"Your love for goodness far outweighs the bad choices you made. The evil in your choices, if indeed there was, only partly contributed to your dead feelings now. Having to submit yourself over and over again to those bastards, their evil claimed more and more of you, and you couldn't help it because evil told you that you had to accept it. How could you not? You were mating and that's an open door. You could feel everything about them inside of you. Evil used that door to force you to accept ever more evil. Even now it still permeates you, raping you!"

She broke down with miserable wails, not expecting that assault of truth but he gently continued to press on. "Not only that, after you reach such a low, evil asks you what's the difference, what does it matter, you might as well enjoy it! But that's a half truth, because once convinced that you have no integrity, then you have nothing to block the natural reaction of your body being stimulated. The body is dumb and follows its natural course. Then evil faults you further for the pleasure and you can't stop the downward spiral. You might as well go further and further and…"

Carla clamped her hands over her ears, turning away, wailing with ever more pain. *How does he know?* Her gut cramped violently. *I can't live. I can't stand it.* Feeling her heart pounding so hard, she thought it might give out. *Yes. Let me die! Please, just die!*

Even though she tried shutting out his words, Vaughn knew she heard every single one. Even though he knew she wanted to die, he also knew that another part of Carla, a part buried in untold depths screamed in feeling, unable to form the words, but meaning: *Oh Jesus, take it away, take it away, take it away… so I can live.*

But Vaughn wasn't done. "And finally, after convincing you that you've willingly decided to enjoy it, and willingly enjoyed evil men, then you're no better."

She sprawled herself on the earth, unable to bear any more, pounding her fists into the grass. "Stop it! Oh, please, no more… *please!*"

Vaughn pulled her helpless form into his arms, knowing she felt she was dying from shame.

"Please, no more. God, let me die!"

It had been a very long time since Vaughn had held any woman. She reminded him so much of Stephanie, but differently from how Mandy did. Holding her, stroking her head gently, patting her back and squeezing her shoulders, he rocked back and forth and prayed silently. *Lord God. Let Your Love touch her. Bring life back to her.*

"But there was something else, too, Carla. God began sending you dreams. But there was no way you could hold hope and real life feelings at the same time you were being degraded, so you did the only thing you could. You partitioned yourself. Only in the deepest part of your night, you called the hope of those prophetic dreams into your heart, to cherish, to keep the real you alive somehow. And every time you had to endure insult, each time you fell down that spiral, you buried your hope deep inside, out of reach of destruction. But now, you don't know yet, how to let it bloom."

Through her sobs, as he cradled her into his chest, she confessed. "I'm still being raped. Dear Jesus, help me… please help me. Forgive me for what I've done, what I've become."

Vaughn's tears dropped upon her as he continued to rock her, back and forth as he used to do when he was younger, rocking to forget the world. He rocked for Carla now, entering into his unique form of meditation. The rocking had evolved through his grief, allowing him to release the physical world, soaring into the depths of goodness. He carried her with him now. After some time she calmed and he resumed.

"Evil tells you since you deferred to it, that you belong to it. You've already made up your mind to be it. But what does goodness say? Your reaction to what's up North proves to you the kind of life you truly love and what you truly despise. But evil knows this, too, and uses even that against you through your guilt."

Vaughn picked her out of his lap and sat her in front of him. He cupped her cheeks into his hands, and stared through her eyes into the depths of her being. Feeling the utter depth of his empathy, she felt as if her whole being was drawn into his hands and suspended there. "Dear Carla, understand what guilt and shame are. Understand what their purpose is. They are good in as much as they are the reaction of good to what harms it, that which hurts it. Guilt and shame are types of pain that let you know to back away from evil. They are *not* meant to enslave you!"

And he tapped his finger on the chain still attached to Carla's ankle, which suddenly made the picture come clear, inundating her with the deepest desire to be free of such chains. "Just like when you get burned and you jerk your hand away, tear yourself away from all that raging evil and delve back into goodness, just as you would plunge your burnt hand into ice-water. You wouldn't let the burn's pain keep you from the ice so neither should you allow guilt or shame to keep you from reclaiming goodness and going ever deeper."

She took his hands, kissing them over and over. "I knew you when you came to rescue me. Though you're young, you're more a man than many who're older. God showed me the man you are and I knew you'd come!"

Vaughn laughed. "I'm only seventeen, and not long at even that!"

"Maturity and nobility is not always related to age, Vaughn. You're far more a true man than many who've grown old and *died.*"

Vaughn led Carla back to camp, then laid her down on a blanket. He stayed by her for some time, petting her head until she fell asleep. Then he walked off into the woods again, desperately wanting sleep but knowing he still had other things to do.

So, now I can travel. I believe Mafferan, but he never said my travel was restricted. Vaughn uncorked the Light Oil. *I only want to use the tiniest bit. This is far too valuable.* He barely placed a drop in the palm of his right hand and immediately felt the Oil's power. He smiled at what he would do with it. *Let's see, I remember how Stephanie told me all about this. Ha! Now I'm glad I took such an interest in it. My questions have paid off… err, at least I hope so. I don't want to just pop right in on her. I don't know what she might be doing, but I can concentrate on the corridor parallel to her.*

The next thing Vaughn knew, he was there. He remembered how Stephanie told him that it takes a while to adjust, but he actually gained sight very quickly. *Probably, because I knew what to expect.* He looked down upon Stephanie as she showered and she instantly jerked her head up, sensing him. But she shook her head, not believing herself.

"Stephanie!" He called to her, in utter concentration.

She jerked her head up again, but shook her head more strongly. *I'm going crazy. Oh, God. How am I to do this? How can I be wife to both? I'm sorry, Vaughn.*

"Stephie! Come up for a second!"

What is going on with me? Then she heard Joshua's voice. "Dear, I have to go! I do run the military, after all."

"Alright, Joshua. And I have to visit my people. When do you think Mandy gets back?"

"We're running silent, dear. This is too important to screw up. They'll get here when they get here. At least we know they were successful."

Vaughn followed Joshua to make sure he wouldn't double back then popped into Stephanie's bathroom just when she was stepping out of the shower. He couldn't take his eyes off her, fought every nerve in his body from holding her, knowing she was now married to Joshua. *Oh, God!* He turned away thinking how stupid he was for popping in like that.

"Vaughn! Vaughn? But, but…" She fought every urge to take him in her arms.

With his back still to her, he rushed his words. "I don't have time to explain, but, ahh, Mafferan blessed me to travel… ahh, I have to defend him."

Her hand went to her mouth. *Oh, God!* She remembered her disturbing prophetic vision of a very dark room with giant demons and Vaughn appearing to defend King Mafferan. "But… but… I should…"

"No, Stephanie. This one you can't be in, but I need you to do something right now for me. Remember the bottle of Light Oil?"

"Yes, but…"

"Can you use your powers to make another bottle?"

"I, I can't create *that* Oil out of nothing."

"Can you make an empty bottle? Just the empty bottle?

"Yes, but…"

"Just do it now, please, for me. Right now, without any questions."

Without any questions! That was probably the hardest thing anyone could ask her to do. No questions. She bowed her head, held out her hand, and the empty bottle appeared in it. His back still turned, she handed it over his shoulder.

Stephanie hadn't covered with a towel yet, and though part of her told her to, she didn't. Part of her wanted Vaughn to turn around, part of her didn't. After he took the bottle, she could see his arms moving, handling something, but couldn't see what.

"Stephanie, I love you so much! I'm so sorry I'm not able to make the home for you here that we'd hoped for but you've got to live and be happy. I love Joshua, too." He paused for what seemed like a long while. Stephanie didn't know why but it was because Vaughn had trouble finding the right words. His voice rasped and he cursed it for not being as clear as he wanted. "I want you two to be very happy together." He vanished, but upon a little shelf on the bathroom wall sat the bottle she had created, now half full of Light Oil. She raced forward, instantly recognizing it. She clutched it to her breast, where the Seed to the Tree of Life also hung. "Oh, Vaughn… Vaughn."

His voice came from the corridor. "It's a wedding gift, dear Stephie. We should be back tomorrow morning. Carla's rescued and needs you very badly!"

As Stephanie came out of the bathroom, Lynnara stood rubbing her little eyes, clearly just waking up. "I heard Daddy in the bathroom." She smiled noticing her Mommy. "Was Daddy naked, too?"

Stephanie put her hand on Lynnara's head, guiding her to the kitchen for breakfast. "No, dear, Vaughn wasn't naked. He just popped in and out, just like Mommy does sometimes. You can't say anything about him being here. It's our secret."

"But my other Daddy knows about your secrets."

Stephanie sighed. "Not all of them yet, dear one. You must let Mommy tell Captain Joshua when she wants to. If you tell him, you might hurt his feelings."

"I'll keep our secret, Mommy."

Stephanie picked her up and hugged her passionately, still clearly remembering how she had mysteriously rescued her. Jargono' fire was falling upon all the children so Stephanie had reached out with all her being, all her faith, to try to pull the children out from under the fire through the spiritual corridor and into the real world again beside Stephanie.

But only Lynnara had faith enough for Stephanie's power to take hold, and then Jargono tried to burn them up, too. They escaped to the ethereal Dead Forest where the demon threatened to eat Lynnara. And then Stephanie had passed away, but Lynnara returned her life with a child's sincere prayer.

"I don't know what I would do without you, Lynnara. You're my little angel and I love you so dearly." Stephanie looked into her daughter's eyes while she held her in her arms, and once again recognized within the little girl, the same heart Stephanie had when she was five.

CHAPTER 9

Downstairs

John sat at his desk running his fingers through his hair again, wondering about spending his last years in prison instead of helping people. All this power I've been given … now wasted. Paul, you really don't know how badly you've screwed things up! If you only knew what they've done with your words, your letters, and try as we might, we just can't seem to stop people from copying and recopying them. The only saving grace is that such a process by mere mortal hands can only produce a limited quantity. God help us if one day someone figures out how to do it more efficiently.

How am I to try to resolve this mess we're in? What can I write? We have so many mere believers now – not holy but simply believers. If I write what needs to be written to fix your poorly written words and address your somewhat thoughtless actions, then I'll surely cause many mere believers to fall away, though I'm sure those left holy among us will certainly feel better.

Very well, I must at least attempt to remedy this. I'll first state that Jesus our Lord is quick to forgive when we fall. The mere believers, who cannot help but fall every day, they shall take heart in that and hopefully press on to that prize you,

Paul, so beautifully described, but buried *in so many other of your lengthy messages. But I* must *rectify the confusion you've wrought and explain that holy prize we all know and love, even through our being murdered, tortured or whatever. So here goes my best attempt to let people also know of the holiness that Jesus Christ died to give us:*

"… And every man that hath this hope in him purifieth himself, even as He is pure. Whoever abideth in Him sinneth not; whosoever sinneth hath not seen Him, nor known Him… Whosoever is born of God doth not commit sin; for His seed remaineth in Him; and he cannot sin, because he is born of God. He that loveth not knoweth not God; for God is Love…

Hereby know we that we dwell in Him, and He in us, because He has given us of His Spirit. Herein is our love made perfect, because as He is, so are we in this world. There is no fear in love; but perfect love casteth out fear, because fear has torment. He that feareth is not made perfect in love."

MASTER SCRABAGAG instantly turned around. "Oh, it's you!" The next thing he knew, a smiling Vaughn was shaking his demon sort-of-hand.

"Pleased to meet you, Mr. ScrabaGag, Sir." *The bastard looks just like the cave pictures!*

So flummoxed was the Highest Councilor that it took him a moment to notice his appendage burning. He jerked it away as Vaughn immediately said, "Oh, forgive me. I forgot I had some of *that* on my hands." He fished around in his pouch, then dumped most of the bottle of Black Oil onto the Highest Councilor's appendage.

Master ScrabaGag shook his bulbous head. There was something familiar about this routine but he couldn't quite place it. "You idiot! You're going to need that Oil. I didn't need that much."

He floated over to the orb, fished around in a compartment that Vaughn noted and retrieved a rather large jug. The Highest Councilor got Vaughn's bottle and filled it again for him. *I should find a way to charge Mafferan for this, especially now that our Oil is in limited supply.*

"Thank you, your Blackness! Now I must be about my business." Vaughn pushed by the Highest Councilor, readjusted the orb's focus to finer detail and began looking through files. Then he turned to an astonished ScrabaGag who was looking over his shoulder, and Vaughn, appearing at a loss for words, said, "Ahhh… ahhh … your Grace…" ScrabaGag growled and Vaughn quickly made correction. "I mean, your Blackness … ahhh, I really need to be alone right now!"

The Highest Councilor's Eye began to bulge a bit. He tried very hard not to let his anger show. "You want me to leave my room?"

"Yes. This investigation must be impartial. Those are the rules!"

ScrabaGag quickly popped out of sight, and went to visit HrorrarrAggrang. Upon popping in on the other demon's room, he was surprised to find the orb there tuned to watch the Highest Councilor's room. He was even more surprised to find him laughing quite heartily for an old demon. So absorbed in the spectacle he had just witnessed, and having been sensing the presence of the Highest Councilor through the orb, HrorrarrAggrang didn't notice when his Master popped in.

ScrabaGag floated up directly behind him. "I'm glad you're amused!"

HrorrarrAggrang spun around with what could only be described by using a human expression like egg on his demon face. For all his clever wisdom and ancient knowledge, he had never been in such an awkward situation. In fact, he had always managed to avoid them. "Ahh…"

"Well, save your intelligent retorts! Mind telling me why you're watching me so closely?" He peered deeply into HrorrarrAggrang's Eye. When only silence was the answer, ScrabaGag sharply followed up. "Never mind, I'll check your orb myself, and find out. Besides, since you've got it tuned so sharply into my business, I think I'll just watch my friend in my room awhile. You may leave!"

HrorrarrAggrang thought about asking if ScrabaGag really wanted him to leave his own room, but then thought the better of it. *I'm not going to fall into his trap and repeat the humiliation he just went through.* He simply left, but his Master called him back. "HrorrarrAggrang!"

ScrabaGag put his arm around HrorrarrAggrang who'd popped back in, and said, "I'm glad you thought better about asking if I really wanted you to leave. I really do!"

A very angry HrorrarrAggrang popped away after the Highest Councilor turned back to study the orb to try to figure out what Vaughn was doing and why. He could see that the boy had called up the Dead Forest within his own orb, and had gone back into the record to the very first row that consisted of only two trees.

Vaughn remembered. *In the beginning, God…*

What in heaven is he looking there for? That has nothing *to do with what he's sent here for.* In disgust, Master ScrabaGag flipped the orb to recent files and began searching through HrorrarrAggrang's records. *Fascinating! Oh, too bad on that one! Ha!* He saw how the old Demon had been cultivating a young woman held captive, how utterly delicious she would become over the long term but now a risky investment since she'd escaped. He also saw how artfully HrorrarrAggrang had boxed up all her glow but left just enough to season her with almost unbearable suffering. *She's very tasty, indeed. Her travails have brought much power into her, but she doesn't know it.* Her ethereal tree had looked almost perfect, but now infectious glow brightened throughout the trunk. ScrabaGag knew it was only a matter of time before the infection could spread to roots and branches. *This one could become a problem, too.*

He remembered how out of control Stephanie and Vaughn had become. "Neutral," he muttered. *But meeting him in person, he seems far less impressive for sure. Hmm, it's rare to meet them in person. I wonder if our orb technology exaggerates the* glow. ScrabaGag searched more records to see if HrorrarrAggrang had any provisions in place to counter these unfortunate circumstances, but found none. *How could he be so lax? At least with mine, I have several backup plans. I have them wonderfully boxed in so the* glow *won't do them any good at all now. I've even used them to bring down heaven itself. Fortunately, I boxed Vaughn in before he became Mafferan's arbiter.*

But then ScrabaGag was irritated again at Vaughn poking around in his very own ethereal room. *Still, it'll give me a chance to work on this boy directly. Hmmm, no demon has ever had that opportunity before, at least not here. It ought to prove quite amusing.*

The Highest Councilor flipped to another set of files marked '*Highest Councilor*'. He pressed the marker and waited… nothing happened. He tried several other access avenues but still nothing. *Hmm, I could demand he open these, but then I run the risk of him tripping a failsafe and deleting them all.* Then ScrabaGag found another section titled '*The Father's Tribe*'. He felt his ripples begin to prickle; his shimmering began to dazzle as he knew he'd found something he wasn't supposed to know anything about. *Who are you, HrorrarrAggrang?* He tried to access the file but couldn't get into it either.

Without a moment to spare, Highest Councilor ScrabaGag waved his powerful, massive arm and Grinchback appeared next to him. "Master, you summoned me?" *I've never seen Master look so… excited!*

"I have a hunch, my faithful offspring. I'm excellent at orb technology, but no one is better than you are. I want you to crack open HrorrarrAggrang's secret files, do it without him knowing, and I want copies of everything downloaded to our orb but in a place where our nosey *friend* will never find them."

Grinchback loved the way his Master talked. *Our orb, our orb, yes! Our orb… not his orb… Ours!* Master ScrabaGag grabbed his underling and shook him, something he'd never done before. "Pay attention, Grinchback. There's no room for messing this up."

The underling looked into his Master's Eye. *He's not shaking me to be sadistic, nor out of whim. He means emphasis. This is important!*

"And listen to me. You can't be cute with any of this. Take my Alpha word, we're dealing with something … ancient, way before our time. If you screw up, we could both end up on the wrong side of the Eye!"

"I understand, Master. I will do *exactly* as you've asked."

Master ScrabaGag could see that he meant it. "I'm going to find HrorrarrAggrang, and have a long private talk in my secret room. We'll pop directly in there so he'll have no idea where it actually is. How much time do you think you need?"

The Highest Councilor's offspring went to the orb and began tentatively examining files. He opened a window his Master had never seen before, and another at a deeper level.

"My word, Grinchback, but you *are* good! I never knew those existed."

"I need to concentrate, Master. I believe you're right. HrorrarrAggrang must go back a long way. Some of these encryptions I only remember as footnotes of ancient orb programming. Their cleverness is … hidden."

Grinchback snickered, a rare demon event, and his Master's eyelid lifted a little higher. "Because you're the truest Master ever, and there's none like you, nor has been… I'm *not* flattering." Grinchback knew how uncomfortable his Master was with flattery, since his Master had employed it quite cleverly to manipulate his former Master GrrraGagag before eating him. "I'll tell you a secret. I've invented a program like the worm that we put into the ethereal trees, but this is an orb worm. I've infected every orb there is with it! It synchronizes them all to your orb and allows us to manipulate from there. It's designed to force any orb to reveal its deepest encoding and that's where all the safety precautions would be. I'll only need a short time here, just to make sure there's no odd partitioning that escapes my worm. Then I can do the rest from home!" *Besides, it doesn't matter that I tell Master, the Father has expressly forbid me to eat him.*

That was true, his punishment for his part in allowing Stephanie to turn the Black River into Black Stone. *We'll soon see about that at the trial. I just hope Mafferan is wise enough not to bring full records. He seemed to understand.*

☙

HrorrarrAggrang peered around, amused. It wasn't as dark as the Father's room, had a few oddities about it he'd never seen… something struck his face! It shocked him, having not been treated that way since… he couldn't remember that far back.

The Highest Councilor laughed to himself as his tail whipped HrorrarrAggrang. *I bet he hasn't been treated like that in a very long time.* "I didn't bring you here to study my room." Seeing the old Chief Alpha was poised to consume him, ScrabaGag grinned. "Go ahead, it will make my job that much easier if I beat you!"

HrorrarrAggrang held himself back. He was not used to having so much anger direct his actions. *There has never been a demon like this one! No wonder the Father is so fond of him*

"What about the Father, HrorrarrAggrang?"

"I see you have a bit of mind reading, too. I'll have to watch that!"

ScrabaGag pulled HrorrarrAggrang Eye to Eye. "You do that. And while you're at it, would you mind telling me why Carla's tree all of the sudden has so much infectious glow?" He waved his massive arm and a small orb lighted within the secret dark room, showing Carla's ethereal tree. The infection had already begun to spread into branches and roots, meaning that her mind and heart were opening to glow.

HrorrarrAggrang sneered at him and waved his arm to turn the tree into the vision of Carla's person. He flipped it back in time a bit then angrily pointed out, "Well, Highest Councilor, if you'd simply done your job and not let your charges escape your country, then they wouldn't have come to mine and spoiled my wonderfully cultivated meal!"

Having been so preoccupied with the coming trial and matters far greater than a few petty Earth souls, both ScrabaGag and Grinchback hadn't followed Stephanie and Vaughn as closely as they normally did. There was so much to do with hiding so many different files. *Besides, my plans are so perfect, there's really little if anything at all they can do to escape.* Yet even though he was sure Vaughn didn't know what he was doing, and he would soon work on him directly, he knew Mafferan was involved, too, so Vaughn deserved closer attention.

ScrabaGag watched the unfolding recent history. Through Carla's tree, he saw Vaughn rescue her. "I know you!" she said, "You came to me in a dream." *This could be trouble. There's more going on here than I realized!* Anger began to creep into the Highest Councilor at this unforeseen element. He didn't know if it was a threat, but that was just it, one couldn't figure out all the odd angles the *glow* took in defending itself. And Master

ScrabaGag felt he needed to know *everything*. Too much was at stake, and it was obvious the glow was doing *something*.

Grabbing HrorrarrAggrang by the throat, ScrabaGag, who was larger and full of confidence, immediately realized the disproportionately greater power within the old Chief who had immediately tried to mask it. Peering deeply into HrorrarrAggrang's Eye, ScrabaGag asked, "Who are you?" The old demon remained silent and no thoughts were there to be read. "There's something going on here I need to know about, HrorrarrAggrang. From now on, I want you to follow Carla *closely*. We're poised to change history for *all* of us. We don't need in-fighting to hinder us from our great destiny now.

"Yes, Master." HrorrarrAggrang replied with the slightest edge of confidence that unnerved ScrabaGag. *Now I know there's much more going on here. I need to know who he* really *is.*

❧

As ethereal seconds turned into… well, actually, time was quite irrelevant to eternal beings, but needless to say, Highest Councilor ScrabaGag became increasingly irritated with how long the human was occupying his ethereal room. He needed to meet with Karen as well as to check her progress, and as irritating as she was to him, too, at least she loved being brief.

"How is your investigation proceeding?"

Vaughn upped the brightness of the Highest Councilor's orb to mask his work and continued without turning to face the demon. If ScrabaGag didn't know any better, he could swear the boy was being intentionally rude.

"Would you mind?"

"Oh, sorry! I needed a bit more light to see. You know, staring into this orb for all hours is hard on the eye. Ha, ha, get it? Hard on the Eye!" And he pointed at ScrabaGag's huge Eye.

The Highest Councilor began tapping his tail in his arm, and repeated his request a little more strongly. "Would you *mind?*"

"Oh, right… sorry!" Vaughn turned the brightness of the orb back to ethereal normal and closed out the program he was running. Seeing the Highest Councilor still tapping, he remembered his question. "Oh… slowly, very slowly, but don't worry, I'll get to the bottom of it all!" Vaughn stared at ScrabaGag to see if he understood his joke but realized he had it backwards. "Oh, I mean I'll get to the top of it all."

Highest Councilor ScrabaGag let out what is akin to a demon sigh, sort of a gurgle concomitant with a dulling of his shimmering and a slowing of his rippling. "Tell me something. You love Stephanie, don't you?"

I wondered when you'd get around to this! "Well, what do you mean by love?"

The question sent a sharp pain across the Councilor's bulbous head. *This boy is… odd. I don't remember ever seeing anyone like him.* "You want her so badly for yourself. She's as important to you as your own self. I understand the concept young man, even if I think it foolish. So doesn't it anger you that by your own human selves, you screw things up quite badly? I mean, I'm not even involved in much of that. I don't have to be. And they've made it so you can't be together. And worse, your best friend, another concept I understand but think foolish, is sexing with her instead of you. Well, I don't mean to be rude or overly nosey…" Letting out a demon laugh, he jabbed Vaughn in the chest a few times with his tail-tip, and then pointed to his bulbous head where only slots were instead of a nose. "Get it? Overly nosey?"

Vaughn burst out laughing. He did get it and being there, you had to be there, made it hilarious! The Highest Councilor, realizing Vaughn truly laughed at his joke, suddenly felt strange. *He really thinks I'm funny! How 'bout that? Oh, let's not get sidetracked.* "Anyway, the point is you're rightfully angry about not being with the love of your life, and your best friend is having so much fun with her. Am I right?"

Of course you're right, you bastard! I can't help that! And you know it! "Well, maybe I'll come back later. Right now I just don't feel like doing this anymore!" With head hung, Vaughn began to dematerialize.

Heaven, I don't want the boy to go. He needs to finish *this investigation.* "Wait! I do apologize for being rude."

"It's alright. Fair question! You know, part of this entire problem between upstairs and down is, I believe, just a problem of understanding one another! You each have different feelings, even if you're able to share some common conceptual knowledge. Maybe what we need to do is find a better way to communicate, to better understand each other's feelings!"

What kind of ethereal dung… wait, there's no ethereal dung! We don't waste anything. This is the same kind of drivel those boring Earth diplomats used to spout. And this boy is going to defend Mafferan? The Highest Councilor strained to keep from seriously laughing. "You might be on to something there, my boy. For instance, I don't think Mafferan understands how we were very hurt by his directly interfering so many times, especially turning the Sacred Black River into stone. Let me try to explain what that means to us. We use the river for reproduction which provides an exquisite ecstatic experience I could only describe as a thousand of your best earth orgasms. Now think how we all feel, being deprived of *that*! You know how you feel! Is it fair for one spirit man to have deprived so many, just because my underling disobeyed me, and went after your love? Sorry about that, I really told him to let her alone. I'm actually quite fond of you two!"

Vaughn burst out laughing again, and slapped the Highest Councilor on the chest a few times, leaving slight glow prints that quickly began to fade. "You're fond of us! That really *is* funny. 'Cause I know it means you want to eat us!"

"Well… true, but nevertheless, it *is* the highest compliment we offer to anyone! Besides, you *are* off limits to us all, and your wife, I know she really is your wife, well, she's a bit too powerful for us to easily consume. Of course, I have to constantly monitor others who are already talking revenge if this trial doesn't give us a fair tail."

Vaughn seriously asked, "You think they might go after Stephanie?"

"I'll do what I can to prevent it, if your findings turn out to be, shall we say, less than desirable. But what *are* you going to do with all that anger? You said it was a fair question."

"I don't know! It's very hard to contain, as you well know! Any suggestions?"

Truly surprised at the question, ScrabaGag paused then said, "Hmm, I'm not sure, myself. When we Alpha have *that* much anger, we usually plan, and plot to consume the provocateur. Unfortunately, you've so many enemies and even your friend's doing you great harm! I guess your answer doesn't rest on Earth at all! But I really can't speak of this anymore till your investigation is complete. Wouldn't be appropriate."

"You know, Highest Councilor. I like you already! Thank you for the insight. I believe you're correct! Unfortunately, I now have to be going to tend my Earthly duties."

"Good Earth day to you then, and if you need anything else, just call me."

Vaughn nodded then disappeared into the corridor.

Well, that was certainly interesting! He was quick to pick up on my wit and feed it back to me. He wants this investigation to go quickly. But nothing I can do about my anger. Damn, it is so hard to control! And something doesn't feel quite right. I don't think the Light Oil prevents everything they can do. I'll have to meditate on this further. Ah! If you only knew what I'm learning about you Alphas! Don't give me that innocent Eye when I confront you! Before I'm done, I should have enough to blackmail your whole damn lot! Thing is, I'm not sure if all this I'm finding is real. It could be just a ruse that you want me to find!

"Grinchback, did you see how I split the tiniest portion of my tail off?"

"Indeed, Master, but I had trouble following what you were doing. Usually we do that within the orb."

"Well, there was a time before their *Christ* when we used to work on them directly. When you mature more, if you encounter an actual person, you'll be able to see into them, then simply work on them as you would in the orb. Once

Mafferan showed me where our root was buried, even though so much *glow* was around it, I knew exactly where to go into his heart. It was uncomfortable for sure, but not beyond my capacities. I merely fertilized that root a bit more. Not enough to make him aware of any sudden changes, but enough to make it grow in time. You see, my conversation with him was only one part of my work on him. The other part's the infiltration of his heart on a direct feeling and manipulative level. When I insert my tail, I'm touching certain parts of his heart that have weaker relationships to each other to encourage those connections further. I encouraged his latent anger and the scars of his past to come alive more strongly when his current injustice bothers him, which is continual!"

"But what if he does something through his anger that gets him killed or in more trouble on Earth?

"Well, like I told him, he *is* quite tasty, and he's only off limits while mortal! Once he dies, he's mine! And if he does die, poor Mafferan will just have to find another defender!"

❧

"You're kidding me?" Judge Matthew asked his acolyte.

"I wish I was. He's coming right here, twelve noon sharp, and it's also to be nationally televised!"

"And this comes from the *highest* of our Judges?"

"From the top, Sir!"

"Have they lost their minds?"

"What are you going to do?"

"I guess I'll have to play host. What can I do? How many others are coming with him?"

"I'm not sure, Sir."

"What is it about my parish that all of a sudden everything has to be national?"

"I don't know, Sir."

"Well, let's see if we can't make this awkward situation even more so. Invite all our immigrants to this little gathering. Give them front row seats, but don't tell them anything about it. Tell them we want to honor them, tell them whatever can get them here. I'm going to enjoy this."

"Excuse me, Sir, but didn't he vow to destroy them all?"

"Indeed! But I've been hearing rumors from… well, I've heard he's a good King… a gracious King. Why, he might even be the Son of God incarnate!"

The point of Judge Matthew's mockery was not lost on his understudy, but he didn't need to be told of rumors, for he'd heard them first hand. "I look forward to seeing what will happen, Sir!" Then he left to do his master's bidding.

ↁ

Lady Stephanie was given a seat onstage and front row seats to her people expecting their Queen to be honored. *After the last time, how could they not honor her?* At King Jargon's request, a small colorful tent had been set up at the backside of the stage. No one saw the harm, neither did anyone understand why he would want it, unless he needed privacy to change clothes from one scene to the other.

At eleven fifty-nine, everyone began fidgeting at the seeming lack of preparation or forthcoming movement. Since the only odd thing around was the sole closed tent, the camera men found it amusing to all focus on it. As one asked what might pop out, King Jargon, dressed in his usual

Appendaho brown tunic and pants, walked out of the tent as if on cue.

Having her back to the tent, and engrossed in waving to various people, Stephanie was quite oblivious to Jargono walking up directly behind her to whisper in her ear. "Good to see you again, sister! I have to hand it to you, your moves have been simply ingenious!"

Cold chills ran through her as she tried to reconcile the scene in front of her with the voice in her ear. *It sounds like he's here in person.* She immediately threw up a block to prevent Jargono from entering her mind.

Jargono squeezed her shoulder and Stephanie reflexively turned her head upwards and found herself face to face. He murdered her the last time he had laid a hand upon her. After that, he'd tried to burn her and Lynnara up. Through her thoughts though, he tried to reassure her now. "I'm not yet here for you, nor for your vermin. I'm here on a diplomatic mission, Ambassador Stephanie. I've been invited by the Supreme Judge of this land. Send your thoughts to your people, and tell them to behave or it will go badly for them!"

Stephanie smiled at him, and knowing he meant every word, she bowed her head and did exactly as he told her. She projected her thoughts into all her people, not even knowing she could but doing so out of necessity. *Besides, he wouldn't tell me to do this if it couldn't be done. Dear people, do nothing concerning him. I'm not sure what's going on, but he'll not harm you. I won't let him!*

Wide-eyed, the audience all nodded to their Queen then Jargono's thoughts entered her mind. *Very good! Thank you. Do you really think you can stop me if I choose to act?*

She answered in his thoughts. *What will you do, kill me? When a person knows he has nothing, or everything to lose, he tends to do the miraculous, don't you agree? I'm not green anymore, unlike when we last met.*

Jargono did note the ease with which she performed his request and also the refinement of her faithwalking posture, a particular sight privy only to him. *You just get more beautiful every time I see you!* Walking up to the stand, he picked up the microphone and moved it away from the front of center-stage.

♋

The Highest Councilor tapped his tail-tip gingerly on Karen's shoulder. "You just get more beautiful every time I see you!" And he snickered, which was really more like a repetitive snorting.

Karen definitely turned several shades darker as she slowly turned away from the orb vision of her husband. "I'll tell you what. How 'bout I throw that bitch in, body and soul, with the deal? I'll deliver her to you myself, in addition to what I've already promised."

ScrabaGag remained silent, knowing there was more, always more with this one.

"All I want for this little addition is a power upgrade."

"Power upgrade? Like what?"

"I'm tired of depending on you to summon me. I want to be able to move around freely, pop in and out like *she* does, like my husband does."

She's already powerful enough. "What makes you think I need your help in consuming her?"

"Oh, just a hunch, that's all."

There's definitely more to her. She could be playing me at her husband's direction but I'm not sure.

Smiling sweetly, she then said, "Kindly remove that tiny piece of tail from under my dress please. I've had quite enough, thank you!"

Surprised Karen was aware of his subtle act, he complied.

She's not supposed to be aware of that! "I'll think about your request… for power, that is. You do know I'm the *Highest* Councilor, don't you?"

"Of course, I only deal with top dogs." And she beamed again her sweet smile, but the Master had quite enough of it.

"I'll summon you later to let you know." ScrabaGag waved his arm, and she vanished. "Grinchback!"

His underling came out of their secret room. "Yes, Master. Is she what the humans would appropriately call a bitch?"

Highest Councilor ScrabaGag nodded. "I think that meaning would apply here as well! And something's not right with her. I want you to comb through all her files, and if anything even slightly odd shows up, then find out why. She's playing me some kind of way and so confident I can't do anything about it. Things are so crucial now… too many odd things going on. I don't like it at all. Have you found anything about Carla?"

"No, Master, nothing yet, but HrorrarrAggrang is actually watching her as you requested. And who do I prioritize, Carla or Karen?"

"Definitely the bitch, Karen!"

"Very well, Master." Grinchback kept slightly jerking his bulbous head that it finally caught his Master's Great Eye.

"What's wrong with your head, Grinchback?"

His underling slightly frowned as if his Master was the most stupid Alpha in the ethereal, and his tail-tip briefly pointed to the secret room. The Highest Councilor finally understood, waved his great arm then they rematerialized in his very private chamber.

"Master, I don't think you're going to like this at all! But I've cracked open the secret file about you…"

❦

Jargono smiled broadly at the audience who all felt some special warmth radiate from him, except for those who knew him and many of the military who've been trained not to be beguiled easily. Stephanie realized that she could clearly see the difference between those affected by his charms and those affected oppositely. And then she noticed scattered through the large crowd, those that didn't fall into either group. *Why? They're not charmed, but they're not repulsed. They look like they're hiding familiarity.* She nodded her head ever so slightly. *Got you!* And right then the *faithwalker* began noting each one of the infiltrators. There were so many more than she'd expected. *I need a way to mark them all so Joshua and Vaughn will know them.* The faithwalker bowed her head, concentrating on the bottom of their left shoes.

Finally King Jargon began to speak. "Good people, we all know that we were once united."

Most of the audience started to look perplexedly at each other. Also a number of people nodded vigorously in under-standing and approval. Stephanie came to realize the game Jargono was setting up. *Damned spies!* She also noticed that others were beginning to react by nodding with the infiltrators.

"Now I am fully aware of the differences that used to separate us, but I intend to bring back the understanding of God to the North."

At hearing that, the spies began to clap and cheer, making the others clap and cheer, too. After a while, Jargono requested silence but one among Stephanie's people shouted. "He's a phony! Don't listen to him!" Others around the shouter, surprised of the disregard for the Queen's orders, hushed the man who just yelled again. "Phony! Devil!" Stephanie sent her people the understanding that the agitator was a spy, and the next one to shout insults should be immediately incapacitated. She also began telling them who the spies were, their left shoes leaving a black print beneath them.

But it was too late as other infiltrators who were far from Stephanie's people yelled back in response. "You're the phony! This is the best thing that could've ever happened to our great country. Jesus will rule up North again!"

Another spy among Stephanie's people who shouted 'He's the anti-Christ!' was promptly hit in the gut and forced down to the ground. But other agitators began to boo, and soon many in the crowd also booed against all the immigrants until King Jargon raised his hand again for peace.

Laughing, Judge Matthew leaned over to his understudy. "I'm liking this man more and more!"

The acolyte nodded then turned to hear Jargono.

"Dear citizens of the United for Christ, I know these people here in front of me. They have good reason to be angry at the former government. Do not be *too* hard on them! I'm sure in time even *they* will come to understand. Now on to the business

I have with your great country. I propose we open trade negotiations. A lot of changes up North have happened so we can help you raise your standard of living. From this point on, those of you who are in need of medical care that you cannot find here, please come to my country and we will treat you for free!"

Damned idiot who let this man speak to the whole country! As everyone cheered, Matthew decided he had heard enough, and rose to grab the microphone that King Jargon didn't seem to need. "Dear people, we wanted to let the gracious King Jargon tell you first, to introduce the *possibility* of such new relations."

But before he could continue, one of the spies shouted. "Let's do it, let's do it, let's do it now!"

And that chant spread all through the crowd, all across the nation in front of every TV set. "Let's do it now!"

Finally Judge Matthew reined them in. "As I said, we are embarking on new relations. Those of you who wish to take advantage of the King's kind offer will need to report to your local judge to arrange visa and other requirements. I'm sure the King understands the need for orderly implementation."

Jargono grinned broadly again. "Let us start then, dear United for Christ, with good Judge Matthew's request. We shall await your provisions for such matters and we stand ready to help you. Perhaps in time, we will indeed become one country again. As a sign that God is truly with me, I shall walk back into that tent from where I had appeared and will disappear from you. As easily as this kindness I offer is granted, so it'll be as easily possible to slip through your fingers and that would be a terrible shame."

King Jargon bowed to all the people, many of whom bowed in return. He sneaked a peek at Stephanie, made a subtle kissy face, and walked back to the tent. Many in the military mumbled. *He'll use some magician's trick, probably some secret door under the tent. We'll find it when he's gone.*

All cameras were glued to the tent but moments after he entered, Jargono and the tent itself disappeared. Across the nation, many fell to their knees while numerous secret phone calls were exchanged between the Judges. No secret door was found by the military, and Lady Stephanie requested their audience to discuss with them the grave matters that had befallen the country, knowing it was time to reveal the knowledge Stephanie, Vaughn, and their people had hidden. *Were we right to hide it? God, it's too late now. Jargono has already poisoned them. I've never considered anything like what he just did. Joshua, where are you? I need you. Your country needs you. I know I can convince the military, at least those here who know me... well, they all saw me across the country. Oh. my God! I need to speak to the nation again. But how will Jargono react if I do that? We're so vulnerable! It's hard enough fighting the Judges, and now... the highest Judge is letting Jargono speak!*

CHAPTER 10
Cheese

Master GrrraGagag found it difficult but not impossible to follow them. It was about as difficult as getting inside a bird's little brain and figuring out how to control it, but that's exactly what he needed to do. He knew the prophecy that she would bear a son who would rule the world. *But it isn't clear as to what kind of rule, and I'm simply going to nail that down a bit.*

Opening his most secret file on the Appendaho, he brought up her glowing tree and then quickly turned it into her person. *Very good … very, very good. I love routines!*

Every day at eleven in the morning, she brought her pot, vegetables, and fruits to make her famous stew which her husband never tired of eating. For some reason he couldn't figure out, and his wife would never tell him, the stew always tasted different from day to day though the same ingredients were always used. Under the same apple tree every day, they ate together as the pot simmered under the same branch. These particular people loved consistency. *I do, too!* GrrraGagag laughed as he found the crow he'd been training and sent him to fetch a piece of the corpse of a thief who'd been shot but escaped to die in the woods. That too, had been the Master's doing.

A piece of rotting, maggot infested human flesh. Just perfect for your stew, for the child you now carry. The bird lit upon the branch above the pot. *Not yet my feathered friend, wait for their morning kiss and hug. Good little bird. Now, drop it!* And into the pot the rotten meat splashed amid the bubbles, and already severely decayed, it quickly disintegrated and dispersed throughout the stew.

She served him in his special bowl. He served her in hers. Together they blew on their spoonfuls and gulped down as they went about tasting for yet another new flavor. Each immediately made faces of concern, each agreeing that for the first time something was … odd about the flavor, difficult to describe, and both began to feel nauseous.

Master GrrraGagag slapped his tail up and down upon the ethereal floor, laughing for utter joy, shouting into the orb even though they couldn't hear him. "Go ahead, vomit if you want, it's *too late*! You know you weren't even supposed to *touch* a dead human, let alone eat their rotting flesh!"

The couple did throw up, but the Master was exactly correct that the taint of the profane had entered her, shattering the holy bond between mother and child. The baby immediately felt disconnected, alone, and abandoned. To offset its perception of being held prisoner in some odd world, it focused on its growing feelings of self, turning deeply inward. When his mother, after a whole week of being ill, finally regained her strength, the holy bond naturally attempted to reassert itself in her womb but the child rejected it.

Master GrrraGagag used the unborn child's grayness to gain better vision and understanding of his mother while she carried him. It was all locked away in his secret file on the Appendaho in a subfolder named Jargono. *Who says prophecy can't be shaped?*

Rushing down the street past the old shops to Joshua's compound, Lady Stephanie put yesterday's events behind her. *What will be will be, but today is today and I have to deal with the now. Besides, I haven't a freakin' clue what to do. I think it's time to consult Vaughn's Book of Wisdom, but for now I have other really important matters.*

She simply couldn't wait to see Mandy, but entering the large common room with the long tables and their many standard chairs, she saw Carla in front of the first table with the heavy iron chain still attached to her ankle. When their eyes met and a special connection instantly formed, each sensed their knowledge of deepest suffering. Pulling her eyes away from Carla's, Stephanie commanded the chain with an angry voice. "In the name of our Lord Jesus, release her!" It instantly cracked off her ankle, but Stephanie was so mad she sent a blinding light-beam from her finger that turned the chain into white ash. "So be it. So be your ordeal."

Lady Stephanie ignored their gaping stares as she had told them yesterday that she was gifted, a *faithwalker,* with similar powers as King Jargon. Many doubted and some wanted to ask her to prove her powers but everyone felt that testing her would be flat out rude. Now they had their proof and the word of it quickly spread as did their deepest love for Lady Stephanie, their Captain's perfect wife.

She walked straight up to Carla and took her hand. "Come on, you're coming home with me. You too, Mandy." She instructed Joshua. "You can question them later."

When Joshua looked at Vaughn whom he was sure knew a lot more about his wife than he did, Vaughn merely smiled. The Captain then motioned everyone to join him in his office. There was much to discuss. He'd only just heard of King Jargon's visit, making Vaughn a little distressed, and Joshua's skin crawl. *Vaughn doesn't get distressed like that for nothing.* Also besides these new events, they still had to implement their next moves toward the Judges.

☙

As they approached her door, Stephanie spoke to the guards. "My good Jonathon and Samuel, from now on you will also guard these two ladies. I've given them my guest quarters next door."

Stephanie opened her door and beckoned her guests. "All of your things are already next door, Mandy." She took Carla's hand in hers. "Please, I've run a hot bath, let me indulge you. First bathe, and let the past *be* past. Think only of the goodness you've cherished and kept deep within you."

Carla wanted to hug Stephanie, but felt too filthy even to touch a strange but obviously holy woman. But she did manage to speak amid her tears. "I know him! He came to me in my dream and told me he would come for me."

Mandy touched Stephanie's arm and whispered. "She knew Vaughn when he first walked in to rescue her."

Goose bumps ran up and down the length of Stephanie's body as she pulled the two further into the living room.

"Mysteries are being worked here that I don't know anything about. But I do know this, we're brought together for purpose. Go bathe, Carla."

As Carla walked to the bathroom, Stephanie noticed the deep scars that ran full circle around her ankle. Tears clouded her vision as pains shot through her chest. *Dear Jesus, so much to do.* Little did Stephanie know that her best friend Arlupo often said those same words over her.

Once inside the bathroom, it finally dawned on Carla that she was finally free but she wondered about Mandy. They had talked very little of themselves since reuniting, both afraid to ask each other about their lives. Carla then wailed aloud. "*Life! Dear sweet Jesus, Life…*"

Stephanie held Mandy back who was about to race to Carla. "I know about such things. Please let her be for now."

Oh dear God, what kind of life has she had to know of this, too?

"One day Mandy, I hope to share that knowledge with you."

Carla looked at the steaming tub of water scented with mild lavender and speckled with little gold floating droplets of some kind of oil that almost seemed to be glowing. Stepping in, the temperature felt perfect, and as she immersed herself, she began weeping uncontrollably as she realized the meaning of cleansing herself' After she had soaked a long time, she felt the need to immerse fully, praying from under the water. "Help me, Lord Jesus, take away my filth, my sin, my wretchedness. Let me feel life, goodness again."

When she finally came up for air, she felt more relaxed and made a game of trying to unite the oil droplets on the water's surface. When she'd succeeded in gathering a good bit, she noticed the oil really did glow. She placed as much as she could in her palm then rubbed the oil into her hair, and she began to weep different tears. *That's peace I feel. Dear Jesus, if only I always could have peace …*

There was a door that connected Stephanie's living room with the guest quarters. As they went through, Mandy was shocked at the luxury, and the thought that this was now her new home. She faced Stephanie and implored her, "Forgive me."

"For what?"

"Because when we first met, and the things you did, I hated you! I was jealous… and I thought you, being rich… well, I don't know. And I, I… spied on you. I mean, an agent paid me to spy on you, and I… I told him about some of your life, but nothing that would harm you. God, please forgive me. I've been such an ass."

"And you love Joshua, Mandy. I don't hold anything against you. I only wish I had a sister like you or Carla."

Mandy rushed into Stephanie's arms. "You… you're responsible for saving my sister. You set a watch over me when I didn't even know what the heck I was doing and I'd have hated you for it if I'd known." She eased back from Stephanie looking her straight in the eye. "You're my sister, Carla is yours, too. I know it already. I know her, you know… Oh my God, she's gonna kill me!"

Stephanie just smiled, opened a closet full of beautiful dresses and pulled out drawers of underwear built in beside the closet then glanced at Mandy who blushed.

"I'll wear them from now on."

"They're all yours, and that's your sister's closet."

Mandy saw it was also filled with clothes. "But… but she's taller than you."

"I got a lot of gifts. They weren't returnable."

Mandy eyed her, not believing a word of it, but also knowing Stephanie didn't lie. *So what is she really saying?* "Let me guess, they'll all fit Carla perfectly."

Stephanie nodded then both noticed a soft glow as Carla walked into the room. The faithwalker welcomed her. "This is your new home."

Carla looked into Stephanie's eyes and they lingered in this gaze, the deepest levels of their lives communicating as only those who have suffered terribly can. They hugged as Mandy watched with delight amidst her tears. "We're a family. Well, we are in a way."

Breaking off the embrace, Carla announced, "I'll try to get my old job back at the shoe factory." She pointed at Mandy. "You need to go back to school." She knew there was no way Mandy could have been going, and ached to know what had happened to her while she was gone. If it hadn't been for her dreams, and the hope of seeing Mandy again, she knew she would have died.

Mandy turned pale as Carla gave her the older-sister look that said fess up. Mandy had let slip to her co-workers how she got her job in a kind of proud way. Eventually, that had been the cause of her manager leaving her alone. "I have your old job, and I wish there was a way we could both go to school so we …"

Carla turned dark, knowing what she had to do to get that job to support Mandy. "What do you mean you have my old job?"

There was so much implied in Carla's words. It suddenly dawned on Mandy. *Oh, no! Not Carla. God, no! She didn't do that for me. That bastard!* Mandy couldn't speak, but she knew the color of her face told all.

Stephanie opened her arms, and both of them came into her embrace. "Sometimes, though we hate it, we just can't keep from getting dirty. But one of my people taught me about cheese."

They both backed up from her, wrinkling their faces in confusion. Stephanie tried to impersonate the voice of the older Appendaho cheese-lady. "Cheese is a peculiar product, dear. It can only come about after the milk has been spoiled. The work applied to the spoiled milk gives us a product that is far more nutritious, lasts a lot longer and is easily transported. Frankly, I also think it tastes far superior."

Mandy looked shocked. "You know, I think I finally understand something you've said." The serious look on Mandy's face sent both Carla and Stephanie to laughing. Mandy became incredulous. "No, really! She's always saying these mysterious things that I'm *never* understanding, but now I think I got this one."

That sent them into hysterics, the waking up of youthful ignorance. But Mandy felt the need to prove she understood. "OK, look. It means that we've been spoiled, but we can make ourselves into something even better because…" Now she had to think for the right words. "Because now we can appreciate more deeply what's right, and… we understand it better."

Both Stephanie and Carla nodded in unison, but Mandy wasn't done. "But to make cheese the milk is spoiled on purpose… so maybe, I hate to say it, but maybe we've been spoiled for some greater purpose?"

Stephanie broke off the embrace, smiled knowingly at Mandy, and pulled a bankbook from a drawer. It was in the same kind of stand as the one in her room. She looked at them with a grave expression that almost scared Mandy.

"My best friend Arlupo was a prophetess, but she never told me what she knew. I figured out that she knew after it all happened. Knowing that all the Appendaho including her were giving their lives for me, she left me all their inheritance. I'm sharing a small bit of that wealth with you! I think she would be very glad." She handed the book to Carla who just held it.

"Open it, Carla!"

"I don't need to. There's more than enough there for us both to go to school and to live for some time." Carla handed the book to her sister.

Mandy peeked at the bankbook. "Oh, my God! You're right!"

☙

He'd planned on meeting with his troop but as soon as they entered his office, he was called away to Judge Matthew for a *conference*. Having nothing more pressing to do than meet with the commander, everyone waited for his return. An hour later, their Captain glumly entered the room. "We've been beaten to the punch!"

Their collective sighs followed by their respectful silence begged Joshua to continue. "Somehow Judge Luke found out about everything. I don't exactly know how, he couldn't just call up and ask anyone whether his judges were kidnapping and raping young girls. Perhaps the Judges spy on each other as well! He's addressing the nation tonight with apologies for Hiram and Aaron. He vows that any other Judge caught in such crimes will be publicly executed. He has *thanked* the military for our help."

"Damn it! Larson, get hold of Harris and find out how we got burned." Vaughn suddenly blushed when he caught Joshua's raised eyebrows. "I'm sorry. I can call him back…"

"No, that's alright. I see you're used to being in command. We'll work together." Captain Joshua addressed the others in the room. "This is King Vaughn, the ruler of his people and our secret ally. As you know, he saved my life, and before this is over, perhaps even our whole country. I swear you all to military oath. He is Corporal Vaughn to all of us."

They all saluted but Captain Joshua turned more somber. "I'm afraid there's more. Barrack has been found dead with a suicide note confessing him to be responsible for Mandy's abduction and for my attempted murder. Judge Matthew has made his apologies and he'll be appointed to Aaron's office, but he'll reside here!"

Corporal Daniel shook his blonde head, and grumbled. "That's two steps up the ladder, makes him much more powerful."

Joshua sighed in agreement. "I'm afraid so, but everyone was impressed with Judge Matthew's two national appearances. They liked the way he carried himself with both Lady Stephanie and *King* Jargono."

Vaughn took Joshua's arm, and asked softly. "Does Stephanie know?"

"Not yet."

❧

Stephanie gently roused Carla from sleep at four-thirty in the morning. "I want to take you and Mandy somewhere special. Joshua will come, too! Wake Mandy. You three will be the first outsiders to join me. I know it's a bit early, but I haven't done this for a while and I need to. We leave in twenty minutes if you'd like to come."

Carla stared at Stephanie's beautiful royal blue dress with red and gold Appendaho embroidery. It was the one Stephanie wore when she'd been placed under the water for her final prayer, the holy dress in which she'd received the Holy Ghost. Carla remembered Stephanie showing it to her just the other night when the girls decided to have Stephanie sleep over leaving Joshua alone. All through that night, the girls swapped many stories of their lives and one of them was how Arlupo had made that dress special for Stephanie, for her quest to become a holy woman.

Getting quickly up, Carla went to her own closet that now had many similar dresses, along with more regular clothing. Stephanie had encouraged her and Mandy to go shopping and for the last week, they broke down and let loose. But for this morning, Carla chose a dark purple Appendaho dress with red embroidery.

"Mandy, wake up! Our sister wants to take us someplace special."

Mandy smiled, stretched, and sat up. She loved being a family together. She's the one that started calling Stephanie her sister and Carla adopted it right away.

The night before that sleepover, in the privacy of their new apartment, Mandy had wept and confessed to her big sister all that she'd done. When she finished, she laid at Carla's feet weeping for her to forgive her, apologizing for letting her down. Carla had told her 'the more you understand, the more it'll hurt, but the more you accept that understanding, the more you'll heal'. But Mandy couldn't bring herself to ask Carla of her ordeals. She suspected her and Stephanie spoke privately of them. Mandy was still the baby sister, but she loved it.

After Mandy finished dressing up quickly, she raced to the adjoining door but her older sister pulled her back with a deadly serious look. "What, Carla? What is it?"

"I've been dreaming. Not normal dreams but like when I dreamt Vaughn came to rescue me." Carla suddenly embraced her sister then whispered, "She's going to need us, Mandy. Perhaps even more than we need her so strengthen yourself! You're about to grow up fast."

Mandy had always had a special respect for Carla, and looking at the steadfastness in her sister's eyes, she knew she spoke the truth. *I don't understand.* She rubbed her arms, suddenly feeling chilled. "Have you told…?"

"I don't think I'm supposed to! I want to, but every time I try, I just can't. Maybe… maybe that's the way it's meant to be."

"Well, what did you dream?"

"I don't know whether I can tell you either! I'm not used to it yet, but I think the Lord has given me a gift. It wasn't just for my… time away."

"We're *sisters*." The finality of Mandy's statement was more than devotion, respect, or even love. It almost possessed a warning against any evil that dare try to undo what they now had as sisters. When they joined the others, Mandy still couldn't help fawning over Joshua. *But I can't be jealous. That's just too selfish.*

"Well ladies, may I have the pleasure of escorting you all to… where are we going, Stephanie?"

"Follow me." And out the door she went with a sister on each arm with Joshua behind them.

They entered through the iron gate that was now manned by military watchers rather than the Judge's guards. Curfews for the strangers had been lifted, although everyone still voluntarily kept them. Dawn was barely breaking the horizon when they reached the first giant circular tent. Upon entering, Joshua halted in surprise at seeing another circular tent within, just about seven feet shorter in diameter than the one they just passed through.

"I have to go to the podium. There are three seats already reserved for you in the front middle, but Rebekah said she wants to sit next to the Captain and Lynnara will be sitting next to her and I said you would keep an eye on them." Stephanie then disappeared through the next doorway.

Opening the flap, they stood in awe at meeting the entire population of the village. Joshua searched for certain faces, the spies Stephanie and Vaughn had warned him of, and he noted where they sat and with whom. He looked around some more, trying to guess who Vaughn's secret service would be. Larson he knew of, but no one else because he never looked at that part of the documents Vaughn had given him.

Mandy and Carla had clasped hands, thinking silently the same thing. *The feelings in here … Oh, Jesus … it's so spiritual, so much greater a presence.* When they noticed Stephanie and Vaughn on a little platform together, waiting for them, they hurried to their seats.

"I'm pleased to have Lady Stephanie join us this morning. We've all missed you dearly." Everyone silently nodded at Vaughn's sentiment. "To our honored guests, we all welcome you. These are Captain Joshua, Mandy, and her sister Carla." Everyone bid them welcome.

"Our people were given a name from ancient times. Jews. Joshua has advised that we keep this identity secret. So be it, but as my studies of Scripture finally proceed along, I will say that not Abraham, nor Isaac, nor Jacob, nor those that quickly followed their heritage, none of them thought themselves to be anything special beyond seeking real goodness, simply being a human being seeking a way that has true meaning. It was never about them as an ethnic nor national identity, knowing full well the weaknesses and evil they fought continually. The only thing special to them was not themselves, but the Goodness and Meaning they could receive from God. They understood that greatness is by virtue of that goodness and that the moment they would praise themselves, they immediately disengage from that heart of Goodness. The branch not connected to the tree dies. To that end, before we go further, I ask you all to consider your inner state of affairs at this moment and address it between you and the Lord God.

"For why do we meet here? Remember, we are strangers in a strange land, but we are merely human beings along with everyone else. We ought not to think ourselves as a group of distinction, but rather goodness within anyone has distinction and it is our love, our desire, our hope and prayer to help further it. We don't need a group distinction to prop up weakness as so many do. If the goodness in us is real, then it is our strength. And when I say goodness, I don't mean anything that's forced on another, but something by its very nature inspires others to appreciate Life. God Himself never forces, so neither should we."

Stephanie simply beamed, turning to Vaughn. "Dear God, how long I've longed to hear your voice, to hear you speak again."

The people breathed a collective sigh. *It doesn't matter to us that she's married to the Captain. We all know who our King and Queen are!*

"Let's do as Vaughn suggests and take time to look within. As you know from the start with us, anything worth being, worth knowing, must be from the inside out. The Holy Spirit, to be truly appreciated, must be so with us. We'll all know when it's time to break silence, if indeed we shall."

It was indeed sometime before silence broke. In the meantime, Mandy couldn't help herself, turning around to look at so many different people. She seemed to pick up immediately on the feelings of each one she studied. After a while, almost as if a new language translated within her, she thought she began to make sense of some of what she felt. After a while, she stopped looking around and began to look within.

Carla had tears from the start. *Dear sweet Jesus, this has been so long awaited, so long awaited.* She peered at Vaughn. *I knew him, Dear Lord, I knew him.* She looked at the little girl who for some reason immediately had moved to sit next to her, and they smiled at each other. Lynnara wasn't quite sure whether to make Mandy and Carla her sisters or simply add them to the Mommy list.

Carla's heart pounded as she studied Lynnara's eyes. *Oh God! No, I can't tell her! It can't be avoided.* She took the little child's hand, then bowed her head. Lynnara just watched as tears dropped from Carla's eyes. *Dear Lord Jesus, keep this little child. Give her the courage as you gave the Prophet Samuel from the time he was small. Make her fearless.*

Carla was unaware of the special bonding between Stephanie and Lynnara, how when Stephanie was dying in the Dead Forest, she had passed on to Lynnara a special knowledge of the Tree of Life and also told Lynnara to save herself. The little girl had refused to do as told and would not remove the Seed to the Tree of Life from around Stephanie's neck because she didn't want to lose another Mommy. Lynnara's utter determination, and love for her third Mom, Stephanie, translated into a prayer that transported them both out of the demon's clutches into the sacred cave, but not before Stephanie had passed on.

Carla looked next at six-year-old Rebekah, Lynnara's best friend who was just a year older. Rebekah immediately sensed the attention and stared at Carla who reminded her of her

Mommy who'd gotten blown up by the mine but lived in a better place now. Vaughn had helped her understand what it means to be a person and that good persons, when they can't live in their body anymore, go to live in a beautiful place.

Dear Jesus, bless that *child. The fate of the world may very well rest on her little shoulders.* Neither was Carla aware of Vaughn's vision of Rebekah and a voice that had told him, 'Save the child, save the world.'

Carla kept having dreams over and over again, but there always was a bright light around Rebekah and a deep darkness around Lynnara. It was the same darkness that had surrounded Carla when in prison. She also kept seeing fierce animals, some part-bear-part-lion and others of other vile combinations, all gathered around Lady Stephanie, slashing so her blood ran through her torn, holy dress. Desperately, Carla finally looked within.

Rebekah felt as if she might see her Mommy appear at any moment. *This place feels like … like one big person!* The memory of Ranger Vaughn's rescuing her a year ago played again in her vision. He had put his hand to her little cheek so she'd face him. "When very good people like your Mommy die, the person that is your Mommy leaves the dead body and goes to a beautiful place for good persons, who don't have their bodies anymore."

"Do you still feel how good your Mommy is?" She nodded. "Do you feel the love here, for your Mommy?" He had pointed at her heart, where all human beings feel their emotions. She nodded.

Still pointing at her heart, he continued. "You see, that feeling is from the person *you* are." He took her hand. "Do you feel me holding your hand?" She nodded as Vaughn looked deeply into her eyes. He gently squeezed her hand, holding it up to her. "That feeling is from your body." Then, pointing again to her heart, he reaffirmed. "The feelings in your heart are from the person you are."

Seeing this again within herself, for herself, Rebekah studied that knowledge further. *My feelings don't come from my body. My feelings and my thoughts are me, my person. Let's see. Five fingers, five …* She tried to remember what Vaughn had called them. *Yes, senses. There's taste and smell and touch and my eyes and ears. But those don't think or love. They're from my body. They don't know anything. Only my person knows something, like love. My body doesn't know that. I do.* She tapped her chest. *That's the feeling of touch.* Then she looked into her heart. *That's love. They're not the same. My body can only feel touch but my person feels feelings. My person knows things.*

She also remembered her wonderful realization after understanding Vaughn's explanation. When she and Vaughn had buried her Mommy, Vaughn had said, "This is so her body can go quietly back into the Earth from where it came from. Our bodies come from here." He had held out a handful of earth and let it drop to the grave. "But our persons inside the body come from Life. Life is like the feelings here." He had pointed to their hearts. "You can't see your feelings with your eyes, can't hear them with your ears, can't taste, or smell them, or feel them with your fingers, but you know they're real. We call Life a Spirit. People become spirits after their bodies die."

Rebekah peered around the great tent again to see if she could see her Mommy. *I feel a lot of spirit here so I think my*

Mommy lives in this. She still struggled with the where of it all. She wasn't sure if her Mommy might be sitting in one of the chairs or floating above everyone. *But I know she's in this big Spirit somewhere...* "Hi, Mommy!" And she waved as if there was someone standing in front of her.

Joshua watched as his wife and Vaughn, his best friend, stood together at the podium, their heads bowed, their hearts and minds delving deeply. *Never in any of Judge Matthew's services have I felt like* this! *Oh, dear Jesus, what's the meaning of all this?*

And a voice spoke from within him, from everywhere around. *"What do you see?"*

So shocked, Joshua immediately looked around at everyone to see who else was startled, but no one seemed to have heard anything. With tears clouding his battle-hardened eyes, he buried his face into his hands to hide. *What do I see?* He let his feelings range out and immediately felt many souls searching deeper into goodness. He also felt a Greater Goodness wafting around everyone. *Dear Jesus, what should I do?*

And the answer came back to him. *"What is in your heart to do?"*

God, there's so much in my heart!

"Then do much!"

Joshua felt a rush of emotion but when he peeked to see if anyone noticed him, he found everyone as equally absorbed from within. Rebekah leaned against Joshua's arm then pulled him to whisper in his ear. "Dying isn't so bad. You just get to live here," she pointed to her chest, but then waved her hand about, indicating the whole room and perhaps beyond. "But everywhere else!"

Joshua couldn't take his eyes from the little child's beautiful, open face and recalled. *And a little child shall lead them.*

Both Stephanie's and Vaughn's heads lifted at the same time. They smiled at each other, lingered for an eternal moment before Stephanie nodded to him.

Vaughn broke the silence. "Dear souls, it seems we've needed a great deal of silence this morning and our time is almost up. But I want each of you to remember that we are never here for formality or for tradition. We are here because we know that the Spirit of God lives always in the present. To that end, we don't hinder or constrain the Holy Spirit as others have so structured in their services. We know that the Holy Spirit is always here to provide each of us with whatever is good at the moment, whether that be words or song or silence. When we, on one accord, seek His will each time we meet together, the Lord God brings us harmony. Harmony, that special branch on the Tree of Life grows from the junction between Wisdom, Understanding, Love and Peace."

Stephanie stepped forward as Vaughn stepped back. "As you all know, the Lord gives gifts. We often try to hide them, not wanting other's to make big of us, or to look upon us rather than the Lord." She paused, looking into the distance. "But there's a limit to what we can constrain. Inevitably, we'll be brought into conflict with the world when they don't understand or they hold to the tree of death instead of the Tree of Life.

"Both Vaughn and I have shared with you on two avenues. We've shared what the Holy Spirit teaches us from within and we've shared with you, as you also read for yourselves, the Holy Scriptures that we are now so fortunate to have access to in this country. It's becoming increasingly clear that what we read, what we see many in this country do, what we are told by their Judges and what we know to be true in our own hearts and minds, all these things do not always match up. It's incumbent upon us to let the Holy Spirit sort all these things out from inside you. We must pay attention to this deeply. It means our lives, for no person may live truly who's divided against himself. The Holy Scriptures, The Holy Spirit, and the goodness you hold and do, must all agree. If there's contradiction or conflict between any of those, seek the Holy Spirit to resolve them, that *way* we won't follow lies.

"You've all seen how I've confessed Jesus Christ as the Lord God. This revelation, His unity, sameness with the Holy Spirit has been delivered to me through the natural understanding of Goodness that flows from the nature of God, from His Tree of Life. But I do *not* ask any of you to adopt Jesus' name! No! That is *not* for another human being to request of another! Although the Judges of this land impose and in subtle ways demand it, I despise such manipulations!

"Goodness never forces nor coerces. I caution each of you not to let their unholy forcefulness drive you away from considering Jesus Christ. Early on, back in the athe-istic country from where we came, the day my mother was murdered, Vaughn pointed out to me not to judge the things of Almighty God by what people may do with anything that belongs to God, such as life, freedom, or name. Indeed, on a deeper level, many religions may actually exist to drive us *away* from the truth, rather than inspire us towards it. Determine the nature of God by the nature of the pure goodness that you may find in your hearts. And when the tree of death fights you, declaring that there's no pure goodness, it's up to you whether you will accept this death sentence or go deeper and find that all your hope and true desire is exactly for goodness that will not fail, that will be ever true. Realize that if you can recognize the reality of pure goodness, there must be something in you, in your heart of like quality that is doing the recognizing!

"To be true, you must seek the question of *what* God is and answer from within you. Goodness from the Spirit of God will bring each of you along the true course via the goodness out of which He made you. I only ask that you seek goodness and its meaning with all your hearts, souls, minds and strength. All truth will flow to you from there, from the inside out."

One young lady in the third row earnestly raised her hand and Stephanie nodded. "Won't we have time for discussion? I've run up against something I don't understand. I... can't get passed it."

Stephanie looked at Vaughn. Some meetings even began with such discussions, people voicing their troubles, their problems, their insights. At first glance one might think it to be a chaotic gathering, but upon staying to the conclusion of their meeting, the Holy Spirit simultaneously found ways to answer the issues of the day.

Vaughn stepped forward as Stephanie stepped back. "We can't hinder. Go on."

Looking embarrassed, she started to sob. "I know God is real… but so often I can't feel it. I try to pray, but the prayers feel empty. I don't know what to do."

Vaughn nodded. "There's a trick that evil plays. It surrounds a person all the way around with its dead spirit and asks, 'What God? Do you see any God?' And evil seems to be telling the truth, 'there is no God' but it's a half-truth that there is no God. When you look all around you and all you can see and feel is evil that's because there really is no God in that evil spirit, then you feel empty because you're tricked into believing this to be the total of reality. No hope.

"Look inside you. Find any branch or even twig or leaf from the Tree of Life. It may be just a general desire to help, love for your child, your husband, or friend, awe at the grandness of life in nature. Once you find goodness somewhere, look deeper into it. What does it mean? Every leaf connects to that which is greater than itself, to a twig, to a branch, to a tree. The feelings of goodness will rush back within you and then ask for their deeper meaning. What feeling came to you when I said it was the truth that there is no God?"

The young lady looked up into his golden-glowing eyes. "Pain. It hurt my heart."

"Start there! Why pain? What's hurting?"

She looked inside while the feeling clawed more severely at her heart and mind. "I don't want to be empty. It just hurts and it scares me to think I'd only be like that."

"What's hurting? Focus on the pain, *not* the emptiness seemingly causing the pain."

The girl in third row looked deeper into the pain that she'd tried to evade. *Focus on the pain,* not *the emptiness,* she guided herself. Suddenly there was something more to the pain than just pain. "I can feel something definitely hating this emptiness. I want to be loving, to do good, to feel alive."

"Why? What says so?"

Strange questions! Let me see. "Because … the feeling just feels like that."

Vaughn grew stern. It almost sounded as if he were scolding her, mocking her answer! "What *feeling?*"

Stephanie watched in awe. *How does he know to do this? It's the same thing Arlupo's father did to me to help me understand. God, how I love him!*

The young woman completely ignored Vaughn's tone. "I… don't know! The feeling's just there. It *is* loving! It *is* alive! God, it's just there!"

Vaughn calmed and smiled. "That's because it's always been there from the beginning. The essence of reality itself is made out of that sense of being, that sense of living! There's nothing more primary than that, nothing before it. *That* is God within you! Take hold of that feeling, what you're feeling now, and look deeper into it."

The feeling felt almost childish at first, just a little girl wanting to be good, to do good, to be appreciated for good. *Why?* The young lady asked herself. "Why not?" A whisper came into her from no discernable direction! *That's right! Why not?* "Which would you rather be, ever torn apart or ever reaching for deeper meaning? Being deeper meaning!" It was another whisper. *Oh, my God. Finding meaning. But how do I do that from just a feeling?* "Just feel it for now, deeper and deeper. Learn from it, but start by simply feeling." *Sometimes we have to start by simply feeling,* she repeated to herself still not fully aware that it was the Spirit of God who had been talking with her and not just her own thoughts.

Stephanie watched the battle, seeing light and darkness swirl in and out of the young woman. She bowed her head, remembering her own battles and the pain of them. Vaughn broke the silence. "How do you feel now?"

Placing one hand to her mouth then the other to her heart, as if feeling with her hand what was there now, she tried to get the words out between sobs. "I... I..."

"Do you still feel empty?" asked Vaughn.

She shook her head. "I... still feel it clawing at me, but it's more on the outside trying to get in." She paused and then tapped at her heart. "I feel love here, now... I feel like..."

Little Rebekah couldn't help it, and called out. "A person!"

The young woman then blurted out. "Yes! I do!"

Vaughn responded with a fervent prayer. "The Lord bless you to continue your search for goodness and understanding. Please come and find us later, or to someone else the Lord would lead you, to talk further. You'll undoubtedly fight this battle over and over again, but now you're a little different, because you know it can be won. Reserve your love more deeply for the feelings you now have."

"What is all this?" asked an angry voice from the back. Several judiciary guards pushed Vaughn's watchers into the tent behind Judge Matthew.

Stephanie saw a shimmering blackness come over both Vaughn and Joshua so she quickly stepped forward. "Come up, Judge Matthew! It's good that you've honored us with your presence."

"Don't kid me! And keep your voice out of my head. There will be *no* such meetings as this. Do you understand? Only Judges, sanctified by Jesus Christ are allowed to conduct religious meetings. If you're caught again, we'll revoke your military protection under our Judges Authority of Sanctity. Do you hear that, *Captain Joshua*?"

The Captain stood up then faced the Judge. "What harm are they doing to meet and study together about Jesus Christ? They're not preaching any other doctrine."

"What right do you have to challenge my authority, *Captain*? Are you now part of the clergy, the government? I shall report your challenge, and we'll see how long you remain Captain of anything!"

Judge Matthew began to leave, but then turned back around. "Every Sunday, after I finish services at our communal church, I'll expect everyone here to be right here. I will conduct your services from now on. You're disbanded *now!*"

Vaughn nodded and everyone got up to leave. Judge Matthew fumed, noticing that no one moved until King Vaughn gave the signal. *I'll have your head, too, before this is over.* Matthew then instructed, "Lady Stephanie, I expect to see you in my chambers this evening at six."

CHAPTER 11

Whose Deadly Wound was Healed

"My dear fellow countrymen, while in the midst of a civil war, it's hard to find any semblance of reason or security of heart, but through these last fifteen years, we've all fought for what we know is right. We are willing to *die* for what is right. The goodness given to us by our Lord and Savior Jesus Christ ought *not* to be assaulted, outlawed, denigrated or mocked. It is not right that our children are forced to learn pretentious hypothesis purported as facts stating that there is no God, and that obscene and immoral behavior are not only expected but *normalized.*"

Not only the present crowd but also everyone at home in front of their TV sets cheered their new president.

"To this end, for goodness sake, we are hereby suggesting a permanent change to our government's structure. Across this land, pick out the most honorable, the most impeccable of character, those who have faced death routinely in defense of the goodness we cherish, and appoint them to be your judges.

After this is concluded, send them all to our new capital, and we will establish a hierarchy for expedience sake. My dear people, in times past our former countrymen who were Christians never had to face death in defense of their faith. There is something that happens to the quality of faith when people are willing to die for what they know is right. The people you appoint as your judges will know this all too well and they shall continue to love the people with that same strength by which they defended you for all these years. These judges you appoint shall be better able to minister to all our new country's needs."

The people cheered and cried together. It made so much perfect sense.

"I know that when those up north hear of our changes that they will further liken us to the very terrorists, the very religious zealots who destroyed the United States. I hope that at some point in the future they will come to understand that this is simply not so. We do *not* wish to kill anybody. We do *not* wish to conquer or convert, and are *appalled* by use of force to further *any* religious conviction. Our actions have been strictly in defense, after being attacked by the forces arrayed against us. Dear people, the power of conversion is not ours, but belongs to the love in our hearts that Jesus Christ has so graciously bestowed upon us. In time it is my hope that by being of such love, we will win the respect from others that will lead to their understanding. Our children will grow up appreciating the decency of morality, knowing the joys of their virginity, and keeping their integrity so that when they marry they'll have the deepest love and respect for each other. The children born of them will see and know truly loving homes, and we will restore the fundamental dignity and joy of being the human beings God so graciously meant us to be."

The people wept even more, many down on their knees in front of their TV sets. Many remembered how grossly distorted their education had become while still in the United States. All of them endured increasing ridicule for their faith in Christ. And all remembered that in the time of their dire need, after the terrorists had destroyed loved ones, cities, and so much more, they all remembered the terrible insult dealt to them by their northern countrymen comparing them to the very terrorists who hurt them so badly. Caught between these two extremes, the United for Christ became *exactly* that, *United* in their generation of the first generation of the Judges for the United for Christ. And so the official scribe began recording their new country's history:

"In the first year, the *first* generation of the Judges for the United for Christ ..."

Vaughn was sitting alone on the little stage when he heard a tapping on the polished wooden floor. Mr. Alder's cane tapped as he shuffled down an empty aisle with six men and four women in tow. Vaughn suddenly thought about the floor, and the many rough and fine carpenters among his people. As soon as this land and cutting rights to the woods around were given to them, their first task was to build the floor of the common meeting place while the women set to work making the great tents. *Poor though we are, we're certainly industrious.*

Mr. Alder and two other men were the village's administrators, taking care of most of the practical needs of the people and reporting the results to Vaughn. Before he had met these people, each village had three administrators but now everyone also had a wonderful King and Queen.

"Mr. Alder, I'm sorry, I've been neglecting you."

He waved it off with his bony hand. "Nothing could be better."

Vaughn shook his head and laughed. "That's a perspective I need to be acquainted with."

"Look, King…err, what the hell! Everyone knows you're our King. These ten people here waylaid me. *Their* idea and they wanted me to put it to you."

"When I was in prison, our dear Judge Matthew let me know how much he thought of my Kingship. Still, we need not rub it in his face. Speak your mind."

"The people won't tolerate our meetings being cancelled. They'll all fight to defend them if they have to. They will die to keep that right!" He paused to let his words sink in.

I guess I knew that, but I just didn't think about it. Vaughn nodded and Mr. Alder continued. "But I have a better idea, and these ten may make it possible."

The old man had aged patience and wanted Vaughn to take time and think through the idea. Vaughn did, then urged him. "Yes, Mr. Alder. Please go on."

"I remember stories told to me when I was but a small child by my Grandfather who lived in the United States before the country split up, before the North and South were controlled by different kinds of *bastards!* My Grandfather had the knowledge of our people, of our history but I was too small to pay it any mind. Still I recall some stories and apparently this isn't the first time the Jews have faced what we face now!"

Vaughn raised his eyebrows, fully focused now. "Is this in the Scriptures? I haven't got to those yet."

"No. Maybe. I don't believe so, although I haven't read them all either. But I do remember asking if the stories my Grandfather told me were in the Bible and he said that the Bible was only a small part of our history, that much more had been passed down by word of mouth!"

"Word of mouth?" Vaughn shook his head. "Then I'm afraid it's lost."

"Perhaps, but he also said that someone recorded that, too, out of fear it would be lost. I don't know the name of such a book, though. Anyway, one of the stories goes like this:

"Our people had been taken over by a hostile enemy and commanded not to study God's words. Anyone caught doing so would be put to death but to get around this, the people invented a game to give them excuse to meet together. They spun a sort of top that I remember playing with, but can't remember the name. They bet on which side would show up but underneath the table they played upon, there were their Bibles and other materials from which they discussed God."

Vaughn had that feeling again of past and present colliding, and goose bumps raised his hairs on end. "You want to do the same thing?"

"No! They do! I'm too old and not quick enough to react if a spy comes close. But there's more, these ten souls want to be baptized! We all heard how Lady Stephanie, while with the

Appendaho, had herself immersed in water even before she knew about the baptism spoken of in the Bible. She figured out the necessity through pure meaning of goodness. As she'd said, 'There's a prayer you can't make anywhere else but under the water. You can't breathe and can give your whole life back under there. But not if you fear and not if you haven't searched as deeply as possible.' She's told us that the baptism written about in the Holy Bible is in essence *exactly* the same thing, but that it's meaningless without going under the water with true meaning. These ten souls here feel with all their hearts that they *have* that meaning, the will to give themselves completely up to Jesus Christ, to release their wills completely to gain that new will of which Lady Stephanie spoke that Jesus Christ died to give us."

Dear Lord God, so much goodness in the midst of this mess. "What can I say? What would you have me to do? I …" Vaughn hesitated. He'd told the people before, over and over, that though he'd been gifted to teach them, indeed, they'd pressed him to do so, he didn't have that new will that Stephanie had. Now, being faced with others also surpassing him, he was at a loss for words.

But Mr. Alder understood. "Young man," he pointed his bony finger at Vaughn. "I'm old, but I know I'm not ready yet. They want Lady Stephanie to baptize them! They'll accept *no* other. They know you wouldn't feel worthy to do so. But of course, if you feel ready, they'd rejoice for you to join them. After that, they feel with Christ's blessing, they'll be led to help you teach the people! They'll be able to divide the people up into smaller groups and do as our ancient forefathers did during their oppression! *They* will be able to share your burdens!"

Damn! I think I very well might be ready! Or, at least, I'm finally getting the feeling I'm really close, particularly since the Highest Councilor has been messing with me. He made it more obvious for me to deal with! But … I can't! If I do, I can't defend Mafferan and my plan will never work. Damn it! "I'm not ready yet. We'll have to do this very secretly. Use Larson or Zachary to get the message to her. I like what you've said."

Vaughn looked at the ten souls and opened up his arms. "You're fulfilling my deepest desires in seeing you come to goodness the way you are. The Lord God bless you. I look forward to all your help. And remember that you'll all teach me things I've never known. Don't doubt that we walk *together* and that the Lord gives a unique treasure to each specific individual which they can share with others. And I'll need you not to hold yourselves back from me. You're about to surpass me in these matters, and I rejoice for you!"

They all put their hands to their hearts, the common salute of respect his people had developed. Craig, a young man with short, curly brown hair, sincerely spoke. "We love you, King Vaughn. Our receiving the Holy Ghost will only increase our love further, if that is indeed possible!"

Vaughn bowed his head to them, and Mr. Alder and the ten all departed.

Larson, Rebekah's father, came down the aisle. He'd been talking a long time with Carla at the back of the tent. He first met Vaughn a year ago as part of the test for Vaughn to become a Ranger for life. His two partners had been killed fighting Vaughn while Larson had been spared and only wounded. Rebekah was rescued by Vaughn who had no idea Larson was the girl's father.

"Ranger Vaughn!"

"Ranger Larson, it's good to see you!" Of all the Rangers, Vaughn held Larson with the deepest regard.

"I've only one thing to report, how Judge Luke found out our plans and bested us. He confided in other Judges that God warned him."

"God warned him!"

"Yes! That's what he truly believes."

Deep into the woods they came, each from a different direction, all sure that Judge Matthew would be furious if he knew. They converged at the bend where a clear brook slowed and one could wade out from the inside part of the curve to where the water went waist deep. The drought had lowered the water level considerably, exposing a good deal of the bank, but it also made for a weaker current. Summertime came early here and stayed long, but the trend had been harsher weather every year for the last five.

Only the ten were there, Lady Stephanie was not. Patiently waiting, they felt the sun beating down from directly overhead through the trees that were already straining to find adequate water. This was the time agreed upon but none was ready to start worrying. This was God's time and everyone knew it. Deciding to form a circle, they joined hands to begin a common prayer when suddenly Lady Stephanie appeared in her holy dress in the midst of them with no little surprise.

"Dear God!" Was the common expression and Stephanie smiled mischievously. "Well, we're all about to gain secrets so I thought I should demonstrate one of mine. Besides, dear Judge Matthew is watching me closer than ever. He believes me to be taking a nap." She paused a moment then chuckled. "Oh, did I tell anyone I can travel spiritually to anywhere?"

Dumbfounded, they just shook their heads.

Lady Stephanie held out her arms, bowing her head. "Dear Lord Jesus, you've blessed us to be here to fulfill the reason for your beloved sacrifice. Grant that we may all walk only in true meaning. Guide me in baptizing these in Your holy name. You've blessed me with many gifts. Healing, faithwalking, spiritual travel, and even a touch of prophecy, but one thing only You can do, only You Lord Jesus can give us true life, a pure holy life forever."

As she called off the various gifts, the people nodded as they'd seen firsthand many miraculous deeds done by her, but to hear her name all those gifts brought home the depth and power that God had bestowed upon her. Their collective Amen rang clear with their understanding.

"I wish Vaughn could be here. I really do, but it's not possible. They watch him even closer now, too. Who'll be first?"

Craig stepped forward. "Lady Stephanie, it doesn't matter to us who's first, only that it be done. You choose for us, please."

"Very well, Craig. You're first!"

She took him by the arm and led him into the water. When they stopped at the correct spot, he turned to face her but she spoke sternly. "I'm not here! All of you, do you understand? Don't think of me when you're under the water.

I'm merely the means for you to submerge. This is all between you, the Father, the Son, and the Holy Ghost. The meaning of the Tree of Life has recorded within it all of what Jesus Christ is. He *is* that Tree of Life, but sent in human form to do what could not be done in tree form. That meaning, let it be all that is with you, and know that somewhere on that tree is a little twig that *is* you, and that he wants you to partake fully of all the blessings that Tree has to offer."

Stephanie looked at Craig and smiled. "In the name of the Father, of His only begotten Son, that Light from the beginning who promised not to leave us destitute. And in the name of the Holy Ghost that He died to create anew for us and through which He redeems us by giving us a new will, in the name of Jesus Christ, I place you under the water to make your final prayer. For anyone who goes under truly, does so with finality. For their life ends under the water, that it may be born again onto that Tree of Life, becoming an everlasting branch." She placed one hand on his back and the other holding his arm and eased him into the water.

Stephanie paid no attention to how long to hold Craig under. It would take as long as it would take. That's what she'd told Arlupo's father who'd wondered how long he needed to keep her submerged. She'd told him simply to have faith that he'd know. She laughed to herself at his worry about drowning her.

Just then Stephanie felt the Holy Ghost appear within the young man. She saw the bright light and his broad smile so she knew what he would say upon rising from the water. Still smiling as the water ran off, his words sounded songlike. "Dear Jesus, oh, dear Jesus … I didn't want to come up!"

Stephanie laughed. "How I know it! How I *know* it."

Then the young man walked off raising his voice unintentionally, "How peaceful, dear Lord! Oh God! I understand just being …" And he walked off, unable to keep from praising God as rather than easing up, his desire grew steadily deeper.

As Craig walked away, Stephanie smiled again. "Next please!"

A young woman stepped forward, and Stephanie saw her heart paining. "The Lord knows all about you, dear. He's good, that's why he forgives, for goodness sake. That's where His pleasure is so remember that when you go under. You're not the evil in you, but you're the good crying to be saved. Let go and trust, Melissa." And after Lady Stephanie called on the name of the Lord, somewhat differently than the previous for Craig, the girl was submerged, too.

Under the water, Stephanie saw a terrible battle take place as the gray transparent arm writhed but a blacker arm also tried entering her head then her heart. *Trust, dear Melissa. Let go!* At first, all Melissa could feel was her innate failure, but then out came the deepest cry *not* to be that. *I'd rather die than go on like that.* And in response, the Holy Spirit lighted beside her as a friend might sit down in an easy chair next to their host. Melissa felt the Lord's presence, His Meaning, and how sensible He is.

"Don't you want to *be* this?" the Spirit asked.

"Oh yes, I do!" Melissa's heart pounded her reply, as the Holy Spirit became like a mirror that reflected her person back to her. She saw exactly what Lady Stephanie had said at the meeting earlier, 'This desire to really be that goodness of God is me.' *The* real *me, but … but it's also the Spirit of God!* And when Melissa perceived this perfect agreement, then nothing else was real to her anymore, and all the arguments evil was making to her didn't make sense. She let her will completely go for the Holy Ghost to do whatever it came to do. It was the deepest way that she understood to ask for forgiveness, to totally not be that old person anymore, but be only the goodness that agreed with the Holy Spirit beside her, and now moving to be one with her…

Lady Stephanie saw her relax. *I didn't realize she was so close to receiving. She was so distraught this morning.* A huge ball of fire lingered under the water in conversation with Melissa who was in the very center of that glory. When she finally came up before Stephanie even had time to put in the effort, she shouted and stretched out her arms. "Yes! Oh Lord, yes! I'm Yours! I feel so clean, pure, so much life!" She kept weeping for joy and thankfulness, wondering at the flood of newness that quite overwhelmed her senses, and yet feeling so peaceful.

Melissa also went away speaking many things, some of which Stephanie believed to be prophetic, but couldn't follow for the task at hand. And each soul had words uniquely said to them by Stephanie, and each received the Holy Ghost in a unique fashion, and each ended up with something unique to declare.

There was one young man with whom Stephanie actually had to keep herself from laughing while holding him under the water, because for some reason she became privy to the discussion between him and the Spirit. The man felt he needed to keep repeating his request for forgiveness, so when the Holy Spirit sat down beside him to talk, the Spirit opened with "I'm not deaf!"

The young man immediately shut up, momentarily at a loss for what to do next. The Spirit asked, "You feel pretty bad about the way you've been, the way you've acted, huh?"

The reply was a shy nod.

"And you want to keep asking for forgiveness … for how long?"

The young man still could not find words, surprised at the conversation. Stephanie had to concentrate fairly hard to control laughter since it might be a distraction.

"In all your asking for forgiveness," the Holy Spirit asked, "are you trying to say you just want righteousness?"

"*Yes!*" A picture of himself became instantly crystal-clear and while his reply was being uttered with all his heart and mind in one, Righteousness was exactly what he got as the Holy Ghost appeared smack dab in the midst of his mind and heart with no argument, no disagreement, and no more asking for forgiveness.

There was one young soul, a young lady, whom the Holy Ghost came to, briefly entered, but didn't stay, yet left a glowing blessing within her. Stephanie wondered deeply at this, but the Lord said to Stephanie, where only she could hear. "This one was ready to give her all, but it's wiser for her not to receive all, yet. Yet she will serve me and I will fully come to her at the appointed time."

After they had all been baptized, Stephanie said her closing prayer. "To this end, dear Lord, Vaughn and I have labored. We thank You that You have made our labor meaningful.

Now dear sisters and brothers, in addition to the bonds we have together, we're now bonded in that very power you now know and live by. We'll help each other in ways we were never able to do before. Our leader is inside of us, the Holy Ghost who'll lead us how we shall all work together without us even having to worry about it. Amen."

❧

Feeling more than on top of the world, Lady Stephanie sang Appendaho tunes in her apartment. Their haunting melodies celebrated the beautiful complexity, and paradoxical simplicity of life. Their scale wasn't quite major, but not minor either, put together to search out the depths of anyone's heart whether for joy or sorrow. She had both.

Her deepening friendships, marriage to Joshua, the joyful baptisms, her aching for Vaughn, and growing apprehension about Judge Matthew all played into her music as if trying to work it all out. And interspersed amidst her floating melodies was her anticipation of springing a surprise for Mandy, Carla, and Lynnara who had gone nature exploring.

As soon as the girls entered, Stephanie descended upon them before they could even greet her. "OK, now you might not believe this, but I'm taking you underground to show you something. And since they watch me all the time, I have to *pop* us all there."

The sisters didn't know what to expect but both noted her peculiar exuberance. Lynnara clapped her hands, and exclaimed, "Oh, goody! I love when we do that!" She turned to Mandy and Carla. "I actually saved Mommy's life doing that. But I didn't know what I was doing, it just happened."

Stephanie explained her traveling gift, part of her *faith-walking* abilities, several times until she decided to preempt further clarification by placing her arms around the three girls and popping them all into the spiritual corridor. "If you close your eyes, you won't get dizzy. I think I've finally found a safe place to enter."

Mandy's memory flashed back. *My God! I was too drunk to know that I actually* did *see right!* She grabbed Stephanie's arm. "That night we met, you did just pop right in front of me, didn't you?"

"Can't you remember?"

Carla got the picture of Stephanie just popping in front of a really drunk Mandy, and burst out laughing.

"What?" Mandy asked, her embarrassment growing.

Carla reached over and pulled her sister close, kissing her on the side of her head. "I love you, sis. But the look on your face right now, just cracks me up!"

And then they were suddenly in a dimly lit basement with sounds of deep passion filling their ears. Some ten feet away, lying on top of a pile of clothes, a naked young man moaned as a naked young woman in long blond hair bounced up and down upon him, also moaning.

Stephanie whispered. "Damn! Not again!"

But Lynnara lacked tact and loudly asked, "Mommy, are they making love? It looks like fun! Is the woman always on top? How do men hide such big things?"

The woman, upon hearing the voice of a little child, immediately tried jumping off, but the man grabbed her hips, holding her in place. Stephanie decided to make the best of it. "Well, the lessons might as well start now. No, Lynnara, they're *not* making love. They're doing sex."

"But you told me when a man and woman love each other, they make babies that way. That's making love, except you didn't tell me the girl's supposed to be on top."

Carla and Mandy were enjoying watching Stephanie squirm in this predicament. "Well, you wanted to know where you came from. Your first Mommy and Daddy made love. Ahh, either one can be on top. The, ahh, man is only big when he mates."

"Oh! That's probably a good thing. I don't think they could hide that very well all the time. What's sex? It looks like fun!"

Stephanie wondered how long that couple would stay in place, but everyone seemed to be under five-year-old Lynnara's spell. Now all eyes were upon Stephanie again.

"It's fun, but there's a big difference between love and sex. Making love is enjoyable to our bodies and the persons inside the bodies. Doing sex is when the persons inside those bodies don't really *care* about each other." Stephanie stared deeply at the couple. "Their persons don't enjoy it, so in order to have fun with their bodies, they sorta stop being a person to have *just* sex."

Stop being a person? It didn't sound right to Lynnara. "How can they do that? I wouldn't want to do that."

"Some get drunk or high on bad drugs so they forget or can't feel the person inside their bodies. Others try real hard not to think, or else think their bodies are just toys to play with like your dolls.

Lynnara remembered her best friend Rebecca explained about a person inside the body and pointed to her Mommy's person floating around all happy at the meeting. Lynnara waved at Rebekah's mom who waved back. Lynnara couldn't imagine what it would be like *not* to be a person or to forget being one. Her deep gaze met the eyes of the naked woman who tried twice more to dismount, but was held fast by the man.

The woman didn't want to struggle in front of everyone, but she couldn't seem to pull her eyes out of this child's so she did the next best thing. "You just wait till you get to be a woman, kid. You'll change your mind!"

The little girl emphatically shook her head. "I don't think so. I'm gonna stay a person all the time." Then Lynnara pointed between her legs. "Besides, it's too special down there to let in someone who doesn't love you."

Seeing that this was probably the utmost interruption the couple would tolerate, Stephanie steered Lynnara out of the basement.

"*Shit!* Who the hell *are* those people?" the young man snapped.

"I don't know. It's like they just popped in out of nowhere."

Once up the stairs and quietly closing the door, Stephanie breathed a sigh of relief. "Well, I really screwed that up."

"It's alright, Mommy! I think it was a good lesson!"

Mandy studied Lynnara. "So you think you learned something down there?"

"Oh no, not me! *Them!*"

Carla burst out laughing. She'd been doing a lot of that lately. *I can't believe I've been so wonderfully blessed with such high-quality people.*

When they turned the corner, many eyes fell upon them. Unlike before, Stephanie, aka Red, no longer wore make-up, nor her underground garments. In fact, none of them fit in, with Stephanie still in her holy dress, and the rest of the girls in their brown nature exploring garb, but it was especially awkward appearing to have a little girl along. Stephanie's purpose was twofold: lessons for the child from the adult, and lessons *from* the child to the adult's conscience.

Stephanie guided everyone over to a table just being vacated then went up to the bartender who recognized her.

"Hi, Red! Just orange juice again?"

Stephanie actually found herself considering something stronger but brushed away any thought of indulging. "Yep, straight," she said with a twinkle in her eye, "and two more for my sisters over there plus a glass of milk!"

The bar tender, a slim middle-aged man, black hair, and good humor, put on a serious face. "What makes you think we would have *milk* in a place like this?"

"For heartburn?" Stephanie fished with raised eyebrows.

He couldn't keep a smile from breaking onto his face. "Milk it is." But then he eyed her more closely. "Red, you all don't look like you belong down here. But you look familiar, I mean, I swear I've seen you in real life."

"You've always seen me in real life. You just didn't know it." The loving but serious look she gave him with the tone in her voice sent shivers up and down his back. *I know her from somewhere. I recognize this feeling but I can't place it.*

Stephanie paid the bill plus tip although he never expected to be tipped for orange juice and now milk. Coming back to the table, drinks in hand, it was clear to all that they were out of place though some young gentlemen couldn't resist their beauty.

Unfortunately, when the men got to the table, they also encountered Lynnara, but then again, from time to time other women had brought their little brats. *What's the difference?* they thought, and decided to ignore the kid.

"Hey girls, I've never seen so many really *hot* women all together. Fortunately, there are three of us, too. What a coincidence!" One of the men actually opened with those lines.

Lynnara studied them briefly then offered her observation to the table. "I think they wanna have sex with you!" As all eyes bulged a bit, she turned to the gentlemen. "They don't want to have sex with you." And seeing that the men needed a little more information, she added. "Because they're all persons and they're gonna stay that way."

The young men stared at her in disbelief. *Isn't she a bit old for her age?*

Lynnara dismissed the three men. "You can go now!"

She sounds like a damn princess, ordering us around like that.

Stephanie echoed the dismissal. "You heard the little Princess. You can go now!"

The men walked away speechless, and Lynnara tugged her Mommy's arm. "I didn't like them. There wasn't much person in them. I could see that!"

All the girls nodded and Stephanie simply beamed. *My plan is working beautifully.*

One young woman in shorter straight black hair kept peeking over at Stephanie so much until it began to annoy her suitor. When he became sufficiently irritating to her as well, she simply got up and approached Stephanie. "I know you."

"I'm Red. I come here a lot."

The woman knelt down by Stephanie's chair. "Your hair may be red, but *you* are Lady Stephanie. I saw you on TV."

After several minutes, two more young women came over, leaving their men. The general male population picked up on the competition and started to migrate over, too. The young woman who had been kneeling looked up at them, and said softly, "This is Lady Stephanie."

Of the five men who had gathered around, only one left in disgust. The faces of the other four changed as their eyes shifted back and forth as if searching, but when they focused again, there were persons in all their faces.

Lynnara studied every detail of what was happening, but sat in silence. Mandy felt goose bumps creep up her arms while Carla had wet eyes as she thought, *Dear Jesus, I can't believe I'm seeing such beautiful spiritual work!*

Stephanie was very warm to them all. "Dear people, what can I do for you?"

They looked at each other as being in her presence was their first goal. They hadn't thought beyond it. The kneeling woman spoke up. "I think I speak for all of us when I thank you for speaking up the way you did on TV, for telling us those things. It made us feel like there's hope. And we've never been treated that way before."

A chorus of *yes* sounded in the large bar room that had fallen almost completely silent. Squeezing between everyone, the bartender placed the money Stephanie had given him on the table. "I knew I know you. The drinks are on me." He pointed to the woman who'd just spoken. "She's right. No one has ever made us feel like we mattered or that we were loved until you spoke up."

Now I have them, dear Light. Stephanie motioned with her hands for the crowd to part. After they did so, she peered through the human corridor to a man still sitting at the bar. "Uriah, you're one of the higher Judge's apprentices, come over to explain why these souls haven't felt loved!"

Everyone's eyes turned to a man with reddish-brown wavy hair and blue eyes. If anyone else had used a person's real name down here, he'd immediately have been booed, harassed or worse. *He's with the Judges,* many thought, as they suspected they were frequent visitors but only a few knew them by sight since the classes of people were mostly separated.

With all eyes expectantly upon him, he eased off his stool and walked over. Stephanie motioned for Lynnara to get up. "Mommy, I'm gonna sit up there." She pointed to the high stools and got Stephanie's approval.

Uriah sat down at the table then cleared his throat. "You all may not believe this, but I'm probably one of the few Judges who actually enjoyed Lady Stephanie's speech."

He was right that no one believed him, and the crowd's scoffs gave him enough answer. Lady Stephanie looked warmly at the crowd. "Please hear him out."

Uriah studied each and every face he could lay eyes upon, causing the people to hold their peace. He looked down at the floor for a moment then said, "When I just looked into myself, I asked a question. Why all of a sudden do I now have all these true feelings? I realized that I've had many of them for a long time that somehow got pushed to the background and my work as a Judge has suffered accordingly. Then I asked myself why I feel the way I do now." He paused, his face also posing the question to everyone else. When the results of the crowd's self-reflection became evident, he continued. "It's because ever since I heard Lady Stephanie speak, these feelings have steadily pushed themselves up by degrees out of the mire and into fuller participation. I actually came here tonight, feeling more comfortable here than at my station with my comrades."

The consensus on Uriah's truthfulness was reflected in his audience's subtle communications with each other. They held their peace, waiting for him to continue.

"I think that for some time now, we all have needed new life breathed into us. I think that rivalries between classes, jealousies, arrogance, and pomposity of the Judges have inflamed a sense of *injustice* in all of you. But sensing your disapproval, the Judges fear a slide into anarchy, causing them to clamp down even harder, and further widening the divide."

More nods in response but the bartender, still skeptical of Uriah, didn't soften his tone. "How come you speak this way to us only now and why only you?"

Uriah nodded his approval of the question, of even the tone. "If you recall, it wasn't always so."

"It is for me!" A young woman chimed in, then an older man. "Me, too!"

Uriah held up his hand. "I know. I'm sorry. I was speaking historically. After the Civil War, when we first formed the United for Christ, all of us rich or poor celebrated together. We all worked together, sacrificed, comforted, and prayed together."

There were many blank looks then everyone glanced at his neighbor. One middle-age man with sharp blue eyes spoke from behind the crowd which parted so all could see him. "My grandfather used to tell us stories about that. Back when everyone had high ideals and hopes that this country would become God's paradise. We finally got Christ into our government, morality back into our schools, destroyed a lot of evil that had been bringing society down. I even heard tell that in the beginning, the Judges visited all neighborhoods to ask about problems and finding solutions, from job training to outright giving away money!"

"You're kidding!" Many in the crowd were astonished. Uriah shook his head adamantly. "He's not. I've particularly noted that the Judges do keep accurate and extensive historical accounts."

Stephanie's pleading eyes begged Uriah for an answer to her next questions. "Then what happened? How could so much be lost so quickly?"

"I guess the new Judges didn't have the same feelings as the ones they replaced. The original Judges were men who fought side by side with everyone else in the war. They came from all walks of life, but when we set up their children to follow in their places, those children had gained privileged lives. I don't know. Something began to change. And when the regular people began to see a privileged class developing, it began the downward cycle I described."

Uriah lamented further. "As I read the history of our beginning, I wept." The crowd saw tears in his eyes and began to find some in theirs, too. "Because I could feel how great we were, and I don't mean military might, but I mean a lot of goodness." He shook his head again, running his hand through his wavy hair. "But I don't know what to do now. I don't know how to fix things."

All eyes turned to Lady Stephanie who thought, *Oh God, what have You suddenly brought into my hands? Lord Jesus, what do I do? What do I say? I think this part is more for Vaughn, or Joshua.*

"You heard the words I spoke on TV to the whole country. Beyond my deepest hopes, I see the Holy Spirit that gave me those words has deeply touched all your lives. I'm beginning to believe the Spirit has touched people all across this great country. There's a wonderful new feeling now, a feeling of goodness that we need to cultivate. 'Everyone and his neighbor' as the Scripture says, needs to reinforce it. When we do, those feelings of goodness will deepen further and bring strength, tolerance, better ideas. If we, the regular people…"

The young lady who had knelt at Stephanie's feet couldn't help interrupt and chuckle. "Regular people? You're not regular, Lady Stephanie!"

Seeing the crowd's agreement about her distinction and feeling their love for her, yet, hardly believing what was now transpiring but knowing the truth, Stephanie shook her head. "But I *am* really regular! You don't know from where I came, not the country, but I mean the terrible evil in my life, the terrible suffering."

Suddenly, they all found tears in their eyes and Stephanie realized she had them, too. "We need to reverse the resentment amongst the regular people. We need to kill the Judges...with kindness! They need to learn from *us* how to regain their virtue." Then she looked into everyone else's eyes deeply. "We need to stop degrading ourselves! All of you here know why you come here. You mean to tell me that of all the men and women here, that instead of using one another you can't find it in your hearts to love one another?"

It was a question from pure love, both hers and the Holy Ghost, a plea to the best in them. And now they saw Stephanie begin to glow with fire in her eyes. Sobs from women and men alike broke out while many heads hung in shame. "This young lady here," she pointed to Mandy, "many of you *know* her." She paused to make sure they all got the fullness of her meaning. "But did any of you know what a wonderful person she really is? The terrible pains she's gone through? Did anyone help or even ask? And yet she and I are sisters now, so before you continue in your anger at the Judges, you look inside and shape up first!"

The Holy Spirit, its power, love, and conviction, was now apparent from the weeping and tears inside the bar as Stephanie continued. "Love, truly love each other and I bet right now, there are many single men and women who could be matched together well, if each only took the time to know and help each other. Those of you who are married, if you are allowed another wife, why not! Isn't it better than just using each other?"

There were nods of agreement while a few had even gone to their knees. Still, a sound kept nagging at Stephanie from the background, but being so caught up in spirit, she hadn't been able to pay it any mind. She opened up her arms, and all felt the Spirit of deep Love come around them. "Dear people, we can change things in this country by starting right here. If we start with the underground bar here then go to every other in turn, with the same good spirit and message, with the same power, I believe we can again make right this wonderful country! You asked me what can be done. It's for you to take on the awesome responsibility of being human *beings!*"

The sound of raucous children's laughter finally reached Stephanie who managed to see over the crowd that Lynnara was standing up on a stool laughing at a little boy, perhaps a year older. The child was jumping from one stool to another but then missed, hit his head on the edge of the bar, and went down cold. Lynnara stared for a second, saw blood gushing then shouted, *"Mommy!"*

Her scream split the peace of the room. The bartender rushed up to the boy. "Brad!" He nudged the boy who didn't move as the pool of blood grew. "Someone find his mother." They only looked at each other but a young blonde said, "I'll be right back. I know where she's at."

The bartender shook his head as the seconds dragged on. The boy began to twitch every so often with Lynnara crying, *'Mommy!'* by his side. A young woman finally pushed through the crowd, looking as if she'd just thrown on her clothes and gotten out of bed. Stephanie made her way through the other side of the crowd. "Excuse me. Excuse me." The two women arrived beside the child at the same time.

The mother let out a wail as guilt had clearly pummeled her. "God, please somebody help me." She pleaded, looking up into the crowd, hoping for a doctor.

The bartender replied. "I could carry him…"

Another man shook his head. "I think he's bleeding too badly. See how he begins to twitch? I don't think you'd make it to a doctor in time."

"Oh, God! No! My baby, no…" She looked up again, frantic with desperation, and her eyes fell on Stephanie. There seemed to be an eternal moment as she processed her memory and guilt, and shame suddenly exponentially multiplied. She buried her face into her hands and collapsed to her knees beside her child. "What have I done? Oh God, my baby!"

As soon as Lynnara saw Stephanie, she knew everything would be all right. Still on a high stool, she kneeled down and put her little hand on the woman's shoulder. "Don't worry! Mommy can heal him."

The boy's mother looked up at Lynnara and remembered as the child's same soft brown eyes stared into her soul again, then she followed where the young child pointed. Once again, guilt savaged her, but she couldn't take her eyes out of Stephanie's this time.

The blond woman who fetched the mother spoke. "Susan, this is Lady Stephanie." Another moment of processing her exposure in the basement, of understanding that this was *indeed* Lady Stephanie, and recalling her mixed emotions when she'd heard her on the TV. She remembered the rainbow light that had radiated from Stephanie's tears and thinking that she just may be someone special. When her eyes snapped back into focus, she whispered. "Can you please help my baby?"

All eyes turned back to Stephanie but the bartender urged everyone else. "Move back, people! Move back!"

Stephanie knelt down on the other side of the child, placing her hand upon the child's chest. *Not yet, dear one, but the Lord holds you here.* Stephanie looked into the mother's eyes. "Do you know who the father is?"

Abashed, Susan's mouth dropped open. Part of her fired up in anger, part of her instantly rebuked it , but another part went to the memory of the boy's father, knowing she couldn't say anything.

Stephanie read her mind then turned to the crowd. "Do any of you know who the father is?"

Everyone looked at the others, shaking their heads. Some of the men declined more emphatically than the others did. Somehow, Lady Stephanie took them all in with her gaze. "This is a Judge's child!"

Susan's hand went to her mouth with fright on her face. *Dear Jesus, how could she know?* "Who… what are you?"

The crowd, seeing Susan's reaction, knew it was true, and was addressed by Stephanie. "Some of you may know this from before that whenever the Lord has done something special through me, I've asked you to keep it secret, but now I ask you *not!* I would like all of you to spread what you see. Tell everyone that a Judge's child has been miraculously healed!"

Susan's quandary twisted her face with hope, fear, anticipation, and confusion. *What will happen?* That wasn't only her thoughts, but everyone's deep concern. The Judges had not been exposed in such a fashion before.

Stephanie explained to the crowd. "You all sought my audience, in your hearts I know you asked my help. This child is a bridge between you and the Judges. I know there are many more out there, children who may be your future! They're able to become Judges as your first ones were."

Stephanie's eyes began tear as she placed both her hands upon the child. Lynnara leaned close to Susan. "Mommy's gonna heal him now!"

"Dear Lord Jesus, this country's so messed up. This child is a sign of a people broken and left for prey. Heal this child, Lord God, in the name of Your true savior Jesus Christ."

When the child began to glow, gasps moved in waves back and forth through the crowd. Brad then took a deep breath, sighed then moments later opened his eyes and smiled. A weeping Susan hugged him then Lynnara scooted off the stool to pat his shoulder. "I knew if Mommy got to you soon enough, you'd be OK. Mommy, can Brad come over to play? He's my boyfriend! I think we'll get married someday!

Stephanie stood up and placed her hand on Susan's shoulder. "Rise."

Feeling energy vibrate in her, Susan seemed to be standing without her volition but it wasn't disagreeable at all. Once again, their eyes met and Susan whispered. "Thank you."

"I'm nothing without the Lord God." Stephanie looked serious then suddenly smiled, and shook Susan's hand profusely. "Hi, I'm Stephanie. My daughter wants Brad to come over and play. Can he?"

The crowd went hysterical, slapping each other on the back, some laughing so hard they couldn't remain standing. Susan's perplexed look cracked them all up and she burst into laughter and tears of joy, too. Mandy confidently whispered into Carla's ear. "See, I told you there's nothing to worry about. Nobody's a match for Stephie."

Carla sighed then whispered back, "Just be ready, like I told you."

CHAPTER 12

Orb Games and Other Stuff

Shut away in their little shop, Chiam grew irritated with his friend. "All that's happening and you sit there simply *carving?*"

Shalum kept working patiently as he replied, "I think Judah would approve when he understands. It'll take time for him to muster the forces needed to beat King Antiochus, maybe years as well as a miracle or two. In the meantime, should we sit idly by while our children are forced into ignorance and worse, forced to learn of and even worship their cursed gods?"

"We should be organizing resistance *now*, start making them *pay* for making us suffer. I've been talking to others who agree. Their military barracks are guarded well but their women and children and their sympathizers are not. How long do you think they could withstand if their women and children started dying?"

Shalum kept carving though he found it difficult to control his anger while asking, "It would do us well to be known in all the lands as murderers of women and children? Then how long do you suppose it would take until the people in those lands all agree to wipe us out? Frankly, if I were them, and you did what you're proposing, I would most definitely slaughter us all … if I were them. No kingdom can survive if they tolerate such offenses against humanity, and so even if they're wrong to kill some innocent Jews, it would seem far more right for them to kill purposeful murderers of women and children. And no kingdom can survive yielding to blackmail, which would give them even more reason to kill us."

"You're *wrong!* If we do this secretly, and the other Jews come forward begging the rulers not to harm them because they had nothing to do with it, the rulers will listen because they already have them cowed anyway."

Shalum grew even angrier. "So you would hide behind the innocent … or would our people even be innocent at that point, or would they also be complicit in being murderers of women and children? The more you talk, the more you convince me that if I was Antiochus, I'd wipe us all out! The way you talk you begin to make this Greek seem *civilized!*"

"Shalum! What *is* that you're carving?"

"I call it a dreidel, and the letters stand for 'a great miracle will happen here'. It's a new game I've created. "

"You sit there making a *game* when we face such dire circumstances?" Chiam got up to storm away but his friend called him back.

"My dear friend, when did you lose faith in me? This game will give our children the excuse they need to meet regularly together, whereupon they may continue to study Torah in secret and have fun when our enemies watch us too closely. What greater victory can we have over our enemies than to both preserve our integrity and enjoy ourselves *in spite of them."* And he meant it as a statement of fact, rather than a question.

Floating just a few feet above and behind Vaughn in his usual position, Grinchback seemed bothered as he watched Vaughn wondrously manipulate the blue orb. Sensing his discomfort, Vaughn finally turned his head around.

"You're rippling quite loudly! Is something on your mind?"

Rippling loudly? My ripples make sound? "Ahh yes, in fact there is. Why won't you let Master stay in the room with you but allow me to watch everything?"

Vaughn smiled as he answered. "Well, we're a lot alike in a way! I like you!"

He likes me! It was a strange sensation, one Grinchback couldn't figure out easily. It gave him a pain behind the eye, yet also fascinated him with a strange sort of longing. *It's somewhat similar to my changing feelings for Master when he says 'we' instead of just him.* "How are you and I alike?"

Vaughn turned around fully, and seriously stared into the underling demon's large black Eye. "We're both pawns, in a way, because we're caught between powers far greater than we are. I'm between Mafferan, Jargono, the Judges, your Master, and other Alpha. You're caught between Mafferan, your Master, and other Alpha who want to use you, HrorrarrAggrang in particular. There are others who've intimidated you but none watches you as closely!"

Grinchback's Eye widened. "How would you know of such things?" Then it occurred to him. "HrorrarrAggrang watches me? Closely?"

"Very closely! He feels your Master would find a way to mask himself for important things but wouldn't mask you as well."

Something didn't make sense so Grinchback studied Vaughn who simply waited. Narrowing his Great Eye at him, the underling couldn't help but ask, "But how would you *know* of such things?"

Vaughn smiled again. "Would you mind, ahh, coming down a little bit? Looking up is giving me neck pain."

"Pardon me." Grinchback floated down to his eye level.

"You're quite good, technologically, you know. That's another thing we have in common. We should be friends!"

Grinchback's Eye appeared as if it had gotten caught in a bright light. There was a moment for him bordering on stillness. *Friends?* "You and I?" *Alphas have no friends. I understand the concept I think, but do I?* "Why? What would make us … friends?"

Vaughn studied him. "Well, one thing I've already pointed out, we've a lot in common. We both know deeply what it feels like to be trapped between powers greater than us, and we share common technological talents. That secret program you created has helped my job immensely!"

Grinchback's rippling froze. *Impossible! He couldn't have found out!*

Vaughn read his demon face. "Not impossible, but only because, as I've pointed out, we're alike. I'm sure no one else could find it, but I found your access point."

"But… you're trying to trick me! You're trying to get me to reveal…"

Vaughn turned away from him back to the orb. "It's right here!"

Grinchback's Eye bulged. *My Blackness! Master will eat me for sure. He has access to* everything, *but I haven't even had chance to examine everything.* "But there's nothing… no button there!" The young demon's voice had quite a bit of strain in its raspiness.

"And that's exactly why I looked! Where else could you have so effectively hidden it? I've been using your program for some time now. That's how I know what I know. And don't worry, I've created a program against HrorrarrAggrang's programs so as long as you're with me, he only sees what I want him to see."

Grinchback took several moments to think things over. "You discovered HrorrarrAggrang watching me through…"

"Of course! You mean you didn't know? The only thing HrorrarrAggrang can't figure out *is* this very program you created. He hasn't a clue what you did, in part because he can't find your access point, but also because you were wise enough to octuple encrypt it while you created it. So even when he intercepts certain *oddities,* he hasn't a clue as to what they are." Vaughn motioned Grinchback to the orb alongside him. He tested a theory by putting a friendly arm around the demon. *Just as I thought! It doesn't feel great, but I think by wearing both the Black Oil and the Light Oil I'm somewhat immune.*

He's got an arm around me but he's not repulsed. Friends? Grinchback picked up his tail and hung the tip over Vaughn's shoulder.

The boy smiled at the demon's gesture of affection and turned back to the orb. "Look here!" He accessed Grinchback's program and immediately delved into window after window.

"Here's HrorrarrAggrang's spy program, and here's *his* encryption. By using your *stealth discover,* I cracked it open…"

"You know, I've been so busy working for Master I never even thought to think about myself lately. And you also are quite good technologically" Grinchback had grown prouder of both himself and Vaughn by the moment.

"Thank you, Grinchback. Oh, by the way, I've masked your access point even further. If you want to use it, from now on, you must push your button that's not there twelve times! *I* didn't need to do that because I've tuned it to my fingerprint but you don't have any. By the way, you know for a long time on Earth, I've been made fun of as kind of a freak, nerd…"

"I know. *I know!* I've studied you…" There was a pause in Grinchback's enthusiastic response. "Sorry to say but I never thought you were going to amount to much. I mean, with all those weird things you used to do like screeching, hurting yourself, and being so conflicted. I thought for sure that *glow* would undo you."

He's sorry! Good! "I know what you mean, but the important thing is consistency. I realized life is important. It *is* important for both *you* and *me.*" Vaughn turned to face the young demon again. "Look, I know we have different kinds of life. I know if you could, you'd eat me in an ethereal second, but that's your nature. How can I fault you for your nature? And at one time, you've tried to eat my wife and daughter, I know. But that's all just Black Oil down the river… ahhh, at least it used to flow down the river."

Amazed, Grinchback stuttered. "You, you mean… you don't hold it against me?"

"Of course not… times change! You were just being true to your nature, as any good Alpha should do. I understand that. But now you're not allowed to eat me and that changes everything. It's not as if you're an animal, like something that can't use its mind to control its impulses. Like I've said, we should be friends!"

Grinchback had all kinds of new feelings he never knew possible. They began to form a whole new world for him that he now longed to explore. *Friends! True, I can't eat him, like I'm not allowed to eat Master. Friends? Friends!*

Vaughn saw what he waited for. "Look, friends help each other so I'm helping you now. Look here!" He opened the replay of HrorrarrAggrang's spying then moved aside for Grinchback to continue the examination.

After some time, the demon mumbled. "What's he up to? Hmmm … You see, he's watched me all these times, but this is just general work…"

"Look, help me understand something about orb manipulation. I've been given standard knowledge, but so much has changed recently, I fear the blessing is not up to date! I know how to get what I want but the steps are far too lengthy and cumbersome. Right here we can see which scenes HrorrarrAg-grang is watching but we can't see what he's doing with his orb at the same time. To see that I have to exit this file, and…"

"I know just what you mean, Vaughn. Watch!" Grinchback split the orb vision, opened up two new screens on one side, activated a few buttons then dragged the two screens into the other half. The orb flickered, went blank for a moment, and then split again with one screen back to the original, the other synchronized to show HrorrarrAggrang's orb manipulations.

After a moment, Vaughn alerted his *friend*. "Do you see what he's doing?"

Grinchback shook his bulbous head. "Not really. He's off focus from watching me. He must have floated away from the orb and it simply drifted away."

"You're still thinking one-dimensionally. What *is* he focusing on?"

Grinchback scrolled the huge image down to try to find the center of focus. "He's studying my control panel!"

"Precisely! He's trying to learn from *you*, wants your technological know-how."

"Oh, no! That means he might…"

"No, I checked. The problem with his spyware is it's not really made to watch the control panel but only the view within others' orbs. He did his best to adapt it, but every time you move in front of his focus, his vision is blocked. Ahh, you like to sing and bounce a lot while at your orb! It makes it very difficult for him so he watches you so much to try to put together the missing pieces."

The underling chuckled. "I inherited my love for singing and bouncing from my Master. He used to do it to infuriate the High Council before he ate them all."

Vaughn burst out laughing and slapped Grinchback on the back with a powerful blow, knocking the demon halfway into the orb. The bright blueness stung Grinchback a bit before he could be pulled back, and Vaughn apologized. "Sorry, got carried away, but I didn't realize your Master had such a sense of humor! I always pictured him as kind of a stodgy demon."

Grinchback enthusiastically corrected Vaughn. "Oh, no! Far from it. Master is quite funny most of the time. There has never been an Alpha like him before." The underling thought for a moment. "You've brought to my awareness many new things. In an odd sort of way, I think you would like my Master!"

"Perhaps. Now you taught me something about orb technology and I showed you about HrorrarrAggrang's spying. We're helping each other because we're friends."

"Friends!" Grinchback felt an odd bumpiness mix into his ripples. His shimmering added a new color that had been nonexistent in the Alpha. It was hard to say what color it actually was but not quite gray, and just a bit dirty brown.

"Ahh, you'd better do something about hiding your goose-bumps. They're producing a noticeable color that might not do well with your fellow Alpha."

"Goose-bumps? Yes, I can mask it. Thank you! You know, except for my Master, all the other Alpha generally abuse and make fun of me, thinking I'm stupid."

Vaughn shook his head in sympathy. "That goes with being the best. Those who cannot excel are either envious, or too stupid to appreciate."

Grinchback nodded in understanding and Vaughn turned serious. "Look, there's something else of grave concern, but I don't know if I'm supposed to share this knowledge with you because it deals directly with my investigation."

Grinchback quickly responded. "We're friends, but if you'd rather not, I understand. I often hesitate to share with my Master, though oddly, he has my best interest at heart, and he looks at his Rule more as *our* Rule."

Vaughn nodded then went to HrorrarrAggrang's file marked *Father's Tribe*. "Here! Look at this!"

Grinchback's shimmering immediately intensified. "That file is of particular interest to us. Master senses something odd about HrorrarrAggrang, and has asked me to uncover it. Unfortunately, as good as I am, I've not been able to crack that file. I don't understand the ancient language well enough."

"But I do!" Vaughn waited.

Grinchback's rippling stopped in mid-ether. His shimmering became more vibrant than ever as he whispered. "You understand this?"

"Yes, and I think you don't because it's in the original orb language."

"But, but it's nothing like what we have. How could it be the original? I thought it was some odd offshoot."

Vaughn looked as if understanding had just found him. "I see. You don't know!"

"Know what?"

"The orbs weren't originally yours. They weren't made by *your* Father. They were made by…" Vaughn pointed above his head. "Him, upstairs!"

"But… but…"

"I know. I understand how you feel. I know when we learn the truth about history, sometimes it's a shock. But listen to what I'm about to tell you, or ask you. How could

HrorrarrAggrang know *that* language? Answer that question and it proves my point"

After considering, Grinchback shrugged. "I don't know."

"I'll show you." Vaughn opened the file with a few commands unfamiliar to Grinchback then both peered at it together.

"It looks like a genealogy." The young demon was intrigued.

"More to the point, it's the reverse of genealogy. It's a record of *consumption*!"

Grinchback watched as the columns at the top of the page began to grow fewer and fewer as he scrolled down. He realized the many names at the top were unknown to him, but a syllable or two within other Alpha names further down were recognizable. "You're right! The names above have been consumed by the names below." He kept scrolling on, noticing all the names were in deep black but two names at the very bottom were in *red!* Since it was the first time ever that Grinchback had seen any ethereal color outside shades of gray, his Eye bulged out, and his new dirty-brown shimmer came back even stronger.

"Grinchback, hide your goose-bumps!"

"Sorry! But why do HrorrarrAggrang's name and the Father's appear here in *red?*"

"Come on, you know the answer, Grinchback! What's the name of the file?"

Grinchback could barely speak the words. "He's one of the original tribe. The *only* one left besides … We thought the Father consumed them all long ago. But…"

"And the Father, ahh, your Father has to know!"

Grinchback looked around uncomfortably, feeling suddenly quite endangered. "But…"

"Don't worry. I've thoroughly debugged your Master's room. I had to have this knowledge from on High in order to make my investigation impartial. You can trust the blessing to be true. You know that."

"I suppose I actually do! So the Father knows Hrorrar-rAggrang is the last one to have vision into heaven. He would know the original orb language … from heaven." And his demon voice trailed off.

Grinchback dropped to the ethereal floor, clearly shaken. "I've always thought we had something original. That *after* we came here we created the orbs."

"Sorry, my friend, I suppose if you thought hard enough, you could come up with a theory that would support your original belief. But anyway, are there any demons in history like you or your Master? *You two* are original!"

Grinchback's astonishment mixed with pride now. *Yes! We're original. Yes, we are.*

"Come on, Grinchback, get off the floor. Float like a respectable Alpha should float!" Vaughn lifted him up and placed him back into mid-ether.

"Thank you."

As they went back to the orb, Grinchback placed his tail tip on Vaughn's shoulder while the boy wrapped his arm around the demon. When Vaughn closed the file, he did something Grinchback couldn't quite make out. "Sorry, I had to lock you back out of this one. This record has to remain sealed for my investigation, but it might be wise for you to … ahh, leak this particular knowledge to your Master."

Astounded again, Grinchback stammered. "But, but I thought you just said…"

"Oh, all good investigations always have leaks. They won't necessarily be able to pin it on me. I can always deny it and claim the leak must have come from elsewhere. Besides, leaking this is *part* of my investigation as I'll be watching what transpires from it. Tell your Master first. You two are clever enough to figure out what to do next and to understand the implications of this new knowledge. I think you two may be pawns as well. The question is how you're going to survive!"

"Pawns? In what? And to whose advantage?"

"That's what you need to find out. Why has your Father spared HrorrarrAggrang all these years? Why isn't *he* Highest Councilor? He *knows* the original truce between upstairs and downstairs because he was *there* as an underling! That file I showed you has all of HrorrarrAggrang's history if you click on his name, but I can't let you see it because it's too much to reveal. And the point is that although your Master and Mafferan appear to be at the center of this upstairs/downstairs conflict, HrorrarrAggrang's really got more knowledge of the particulars than you or your Master. In reality, he's the one who knows Mafferan better, and was there for all the discussions… I don't know. Yet he seems particularly non-existent in this conflict. Does that seem right to you?"

Grinchback turned blacker. "No, not at all! Hrorrarr-Aggrang was also about to challenge Master recently, but he held back, not because he knew he'd necessarily lose, but for some other reason." The underling mused a bit longer then changed the subject. "So, does being able to watch the original truce proceedings help your investigation?"

"Well, let's just say it helps me focus on my goal."

Grinchback Eyed him, thinking there was more to the boy's words. Vaughn saw the young demon studying him, and said, "Come on, we're a lot alike! My goal is *me!* I'm caught in the middle of a big mess, and so are you. We're friends and ought to be able to figure out what's best for *us!* You know what? There's a lot of souls and bodies on Earth I wouldn't mind delivering to you *personally!* What's best for *us,* Grinchback?"

For us! Yes! The demon began imagining consuming souls and bodies whole. A delicacy. His Master was kind to him, sometimes luring lower demons and giving occasional Earth souls that passed on so he could consume them. But to consume the live souls in the live bodies of some people he thought Vaughn might offer was a thrill. He began to bounce a bit, developing a tune in his mind. *For us, for us, we go the way for us…*

A voice from behind startled them. "Very, very cozy! If I hadn't seen it with my own Great Eye, I wouldn't have believed it." Master ScrabaGag's expression vacillated between humor, anger, and astonishment. "Shall I let this be the talk of the ether, Grinchback?"

"Master!" Grinchback whirled around, removing his tail from Vaughn's shoulder. "Ahh, we were… ahh… I need to talk to you in private."

Vaughn walked up to the Highest Councilor. "Pleased to see you again, Sir. Grinchback's right. You *are* funny!" He offered him his hand.

Master ScrabaGag's Eye narrowed at him. "I'll pass on the handshake."

Vaughn turned back to the orb, quickly closing out everything. "I must be on my way. You have a wonderful offspring there!"

ↄ

ScrabaGag hauled his underling into his very dark black secret room. "What in heaven's name were you doing?"

Grinchback told him everything, even his strange new feelings and color changes. He hid nothing from his Master, and on second demon thought, this seemed odd to him. But there was something about the concept of *friends* that had stuck with him and grown. He finished off his account with an observation. "And you and I, Master, we're also like *friends!*"

"Friends!" ScrabaGag couldn't contain *something*, but he wasn't sure what. This was all new to him. True, he favored Grinchback highly, even defended him from the Father. But *friends?* He'd never thought of it that way.

"Yes, Master, and I believe it to be important to our survival, because HrorrarrAggrang's knowledge and power must indeed surpass us. There has to be a reason he's hidden them for so long. To beat him, we must reach for something new, unexpected. We must have *friends!* They'll combine with our power."

ScrabaGag Eyed his underling, his anger growing. His Great deep black Eye lowered on his offspring, "We consume others and take their power. I can't believe you're…"

299

"Master, I don't know how to convince you that this is the only way we have a chance to survive. Perhaps it's just a feeling, but it's a *bad* feeling. I've seen HrorrarrAggrang's file showing all the power HrorrarrAggrang has. He wouldn't just sit on it and do nothing. We also know his propensity to cultivate for a *very* long time. You're far better than me at strategy. You *must* figure this out. Friends are able to combine their power but act *independently*. Consuming them does not allow for this advantage"

Highest Councilor ScrabaGag's hesitation still betrayed his reluctance to believe his underling so Grinchback spoke the unthinkable. "Master, eat me!"

"What?" This was truly unheard of.

"Eat me, take all my knowledge! It's the only way you can understand. Then you can vomit me back out afterward, just like the Father made you do before, once you see I *am* telling you the truth."

My word! ScrabaGag remembered how he had consumed Grinchback just after the Black River turned to stone but the Father made him vomit him back out to hear the story straight from the young demon's mouth. It was the worst experience of his Alpha life. *I'd not like to ever vomit again. It's so… un-Alpha.*

ScrabaGag's Eye rolled around, his mind, his demon heart going places they've never gone before. *But Grinchback is right. I actually have brushed up against these thoughts. We* are *like friends… Friends! Hmmm.* "I may eat you later! For now, I'll see how this new idea, *friendship*, tastes."

Grinchback began forming another song. *Friends, friends, you gotta have…* The words seemed familiar but he had trouble recollecting from where. When he noticed his Master about to leave their secret room, he placed his tail upon the Highest Councilor to restrain him, a gesture not lightly taken by his Master. "Sorry, Master! There's one other concern. That *bitch,* Karen. If we let her proceed with her plans, as they *appear* to be, then we may run straight into conflict with Vaughn." Grinchback hesitated then looked doubtful. "He may not take that well. It may cause Vaughn to turn against us somehow. Remember, he's out for himself."

ScrabaGag's tail began tapping in his arm as he mulled over the conundrum. "What she offers is too important to lose, but I fear you're right. Let's try to forestall her until we get from Vaughn what we need and figure a way to best HrorrarrAggrang. You don't like her, do you, Grinchback?"

"Master, I tell you the truth, she may be more dangerous to us than even the Father himself!"

The Highest Councilor's surprise amazed Grinchback so the underling elaborated. "Master, you've given her powers, knowledge, and access to our orb. She seems particularly bold with us and even *smug,* if you will. I also sense something about her hidden in the background, some kind of power. I don't know, but it's *not* anything you gave her, I don't believe. There's more than meets the Eye. What if she's betraying us with HrorrarrAggrang or with something devious from Jargono, or even both? For a human, she seems very, very *Alpha.* Please don't let the fact that she lets you slip your tail up her skirt cloud your Great Eye."

The Highest Councilor mused with fondness. "That she does! That she does!"

Grinchback eased back from his Master not believing his Eye. *Truly there has never been an Alpha like my Master. But we might end up on the wrong side of the Eye because of it.*

☙

A gentle knock on her door set Stephanie to wondering. *What a nice knock. It has, hmmm, a happy sound. I wonder who it is this time. This morning is just full of surprises.* She flung the door open with a happy greeting that went dull halfway through it. "Hi, how … are you?"

Judge Matthew, grinning peacefully, stood waiting to be invited into her apartment. Joshua had been gone for some time, being sent on some special mission to a whole different city. Lynnara stood staring at the Judge from behind her Mommy. Stephanie felt stymied actually. She couldn't remember feeling so disjointed, and a bit unnerved, which caused her to wonder. *What's going on? I'm* never *supposed to feel this way now.* "Do come in, Judge. Welcome into our home."

As Matthew strolled in, the memory of Fred, her father, flashed into Stephanie's vision, not a good feeling at all. That misogynist had caused Stephanie to sink to lows no one should have to endure. And Fred, that demented man, who had been high up in the government up north, was responsible for murdering the Appendaho after being manipulated by Jargono to destroy the protectors of the Tree of Life. Hoping the Appendaho's sacred treasure possessed some power, Jargono had coveted it, but never found out what it was. Stephanie arrived first to the treasure, the Seed to the Tree of Life, which was handed down to be protected solely by her.

Why am I thinking of my father and Jargono now? These memories troubled Stephanie deeply, not only for the harm Fred had done to those she loved, but also because Stephanie had erred in dealing with him. The Lord had sent her and Vaughn to confront him and the men who had destroyed the holy Appendaho people. Through God's power, they were supposed to destroy every last one of them, but in a moment of personal vengeance that Stephanie felt she could get away with, she had prayed for her father to live.

Her prayer didn't reek of vengeance, after all, life is a good thing, but Fred had poured a whole bottle of cursed Black Oil on his head which drove him into unspeakable torment. When Vaughn saw what she prayed for, he scolded her but it was too late because the Lord had given to faithful Stephanie automatic respect so she received anything she prayed for. They had left the tormented man lying on the ground, intending to come back after washing off the blood of battle and then to place him in an institution for the rest of his wretched days. But when they returned, Fred had disappeared back in the Northern country.

Lost in thought, Stephanie had no idea how long Lynnara had been holding her hand. Her daughter's tighter grip brought Stephanie back to awareness. It was the pressure of fear, though Judge Matthew looked uncharacteristically amiable.

Once again, Stephanie had a deep feeling of incongruity unsettle her further. "I'm sorry, Judge Matthew. My mind just wandered. Can I offer you something to drink or eat?"

To her surprise, he nodded, and had Lady Stephanie waiting on him with food and drink for the better part of an hour before he actually spoke. Matthew seemed to be delighting in life but Lynnara kept so close to her Mommy, she had to keep avoiding tripping over her.

A whole week had passed since Stephanie healed Brad. Word of the miracle had been publicized that very same day with pictures of the boy still bloodied but without injury. Of course, left out in the story was the exact nature of the setting but what added much credence to the event was an enthusiastic Apprentice Judge Uriah describing how Lady Stephanie called on the Lord Jesus to heal the boy. Unfortunately, when the media sought her, Stephanie had mysteriously disappeared with her sisters and daughter.

Nonetheless, there seemed no end to eyewitness accounts showing true conviction. News of Stephanie's other miracles also began to surface, along with the heartwarming stories behind them.

All across the country people wept, feeling the holy presence of the Spirit of God come closer as never before. Calls inundated media networks asking for Lady Stephanie to make an appearance but were all refused. "This isn't about me. This is about healing the country," she told them.

In passionate, artful words, Uriah relayed the sermon Stephanie had spoken to them at the time of Brad's accident. He also added his own thoughts concerning the country's history and direction, emphasizing that the boy's healing was a sign that the country also can heal. Suddenly, there was less anger, less resentment, and many pensive expressions all across the country. Economic conditions had yet to change, but the spark for that to follow had been ignited in the people's hearts. The Judges' quarters received many requests for Uriah to speak, and there wasn't a day that went by when he wasn't featured on at least two media channels. Seeing his passion, honesty, and true love in his eyes, the people began to speak well of the Judges again.

Stephanie didn't want anything misconstrued. The miracle wasn't about challenging the Judges, nor any bid for her to gain power. But it was meant to be more than saving a boy, it was intended to reunite the classes of people in ideal Christian love. It was meant to destroy the arrogance of the Judges, the jealousy of the common people, and more. Only the best of intentions. However, tons of mail, calls, and requests for visits had inundated Lady Stephanie since the healing was performed.

Naturally, curiosity turned to the identity of Brad's father, whether the claim he was a Judge was indeed true. A cover up had been attempted by the local people but it only fueled the desire to know. After a bit of investigation, the news media broke the story that Brad was indeed a Judge's offspring, although the identity still needed to be verified. Reports began to surface that there were many other such children. The media intensified their search for the truth and called on the military to investigate since the Judges could not be trusted to reveal their dark secrets willingly.

According to Stephanie's vision, Uriah had begun laying the foundation for the Judge's abandoned children to gain admission into the Judges' quarters. However, they were to be housed outside their actual establishment, not because they were pariah, but far from that, because they needed to be raised in both worlds to make them empathetic to all.

Every morning last week, Stephanie woke up to the news, astonished at seeing how fast her plan was progressing. *I can't believe I've finally made a difference ... a real difference to so many.* Yet she longed to talk with Vaughn, the one with the superior strategic mind. All Joshua did was sit and listen in amazement and admiration, not feeling worthy to comment. She wished Joshua could be here right now, though, because the happier Judge Matthew seemed to be, the more her discomfort increased.

But there was *one* unfortunate development, one unforeseen twist that Stephanie hadn't considered. The conflict between the Judges and the military got entangled in her plan and drew media attention like a sewer draws flies.

"Is it true that God now favors the military over the Judges since Lady Stephanie is married to one of the top Captains and the military is now taking charge of the investigation into the Judges' bastard children?" One exceptionally foresighted reporter asked but many of the military officials had sense enough to deny emphatically the suggested conclusion. Nevertheless, the media did turn up several fundamentalist military folk who touted their new superiority, so the reporters were ecstatic with their newsworthy find. These latest stories enflamed and polarized the people, many common people suggesting that at the very least, the military ought to have a greater role in government. Some even thought, since the military was impartial, they ought to run the whole country.

Yesterday morning, when such stories broke, Stephanie cursed the media. "You selfish, narrow-minded idiots! What the hell are you doing? You're supposed to be helping bring the country together, not create another civil war. All you care about is … *what?*"

She had half a mind to call them up and ream them out, but had no faith that the story would be framed properly. Besides, the media was also serving its purpose, because everything else had proceeded in the right direction though also posing a dilemma. *Will this conflict being inflamed between the Judges and the Military undermine everything else being accomplished?*

Finally, after wiping his mouth, Judge Mathew interrupted Stephanie's many thoughts. "This has been a delightful meal. I look forward to more. You are hereby invited to join me today at noon at the town's main podium. Your long awaited audience with the people has been granted."

Stephanie looked almost ashamed and in an apologetic voice, she said, "But I never asked for that. I told them I wasn't interested."

"Come now. You've never been shy before. I've already told the media you'll be there. You're to speak on your vision of peace for our country." Matthew flashed the most agreeably pleasing smile Stephanie could have imagined on any pure saint, then stood up from the table and excused himself to her bathroom. "No need to show me out. See you in an hour!"

"Mommy, I *don't* like him. His smile really isn't a smile."

❦

The throng at the public square chanted soon as she appeared. "Lady Stephanie, Lady Stephanie …"

She felt the love, the deep sincerity, and should have been happy, but each time they cheered she shrunk a little more inside. *Why am I getting these* awful *feelings? I wish I could talk to Vaughn.* A smiling Judge Matthew, already onstage, looked very much like the happiest man on Earth.

Clothed in her holy royal blue dress, her three traditional red braids now down to her waist, Stephanie seemed to effortlessly flow through the crowd as they joyfully parted for her. As she mounted the stage, the cheering rose, peaking as she joined Judge Matthew. She searched for Vaughn but didn't see him or any of her people. *That's odd. They should be here!* Judge Matthew held up his hand and the silence was instantaneous.

"People of the United for Christ, it's my pleasure to present our newest addition to our clergy, honorary Judge Lady Stephanie!"

The crowd went wild while Stephanie looked dumbstruck. *Member of the clergy? Honorary Judge? What does that mean? There are no women judges!* Judge Matthew let the crowd cheer for some time. Finally, with his official looking jowls looking positively jovial, he raised a hand then spoke. "Dear people." Stephanie looked at him, *Dear people? He's never called them that before.* I *started that!* "The Judges thought well to give Lady Stephanie honorary Judgeship in honor of all her good works. We shall continue to monitor her progress as a new Christian and offer guidance. Unforeseen evils in this world are many, and it takes experience to know them all."

There was more cheering, albeit far less intense and with an almost hesitant quality to it. "We're looking into this matter of illegitimate children. We shall test them for paternity so all of us have offered to give blood samples. After paternity is established, those guilty of infraction shall be disrobed!"

Stephanie's heart sank. *No! That's not what I wanted. Then their children have no inheritance into the clergy. This will simply maintain the split between the Judges and the people.*

"I'm sure Lady Stephanie would appreciate these wretched Judges being punished. It's our responsibility to keep your Judges pure and the God-given office sanctified."

He turned the page and continued. "Apprentice Uriah is to be commended for his compassion to the people. All of the illegitimate children shall receive a small stipend to help make their way in life."

You bastard! No wonder you've been smiling so much.

"We thank the military for their offer to help but with simple medical testing, this problem is easily solved. Their time is far better spent protecting our borders."

The palpable hush from the crowd blew a contrary wind that the Judge braved without any concern at all, resolving that by sheer force of will he would have it all his way, the right way, God's way. *Besides, the Bible is filled with examples of when we must ignore the people in order to lead them in righteousness.*

"Lady Stephanie, you are the first outsider to ever be admitted into the Judges' quarters. Entry is usually by inheritance only, my commendations to you." And he stepped aside and behind her to allow her his spot at the podium.

Before Stephanie could begin any kind of response, she felt a presence then saw from out of the crowd a balding man with glowing red eyes stroll up and begin climbing onstage. *No! It can't be. God, what do I do?* Fire burned all through her, bringing an instant response of self-control. *I can't let everyone see* that *kind of power in me, can I? Oh dear Jesus, what should I do?* Her hand went to her chest, where underneath her dress hung the Seed to the Tree of Life, the sacred treasure she vowed on her very life to protect, and for which she had given her life once already.

As the man approached her, her lament intensified. *Oh God, his eyes! Vaughn was right. What have I done? I should have destroyed you when I had the chance.* Her prayer sparing him supposedly to an Earthly existence full of torment echoed in her soul, but now condemned her. *What is he going to do?*

Reaching out his arm, he hugged her. "My daughter, congratulations!" The crowd oohed and ahhed, but his evil began smothering her senses. Her usual foresight only increased the helplessness now mingling with her growing sense of failure, because she never saw any of this coming. *Just when things had been going just right.*

A voice whispered in her mind. "Won't you acknowledge your father in front of the people? What will they think?"

She heard the word uttered but didn't remember her own volition putting it on her lips. "Father!"

The crowd hushed upon hearing her endearment, but from behind Stephanie, a voice roared. "No, Lord Jesus! It can't be!" Judge Matthew's voice carried a rage that shook through the crowd, sending many a heart racing. "Reveal yourself, demon!"

Fred, with his arm still around his daughter, backed away a bit, pulling her with him. Judge Matthew's finger pointed at him. "In the name of our Lord Jesus, I command you to reveal yourself."

The demon began to transform! The crowd gasped. Stephanie finally came to some of her senses, and jerked away. A sickly gray began to shimmer around Fred and his face elongated. His arms began to lengthen as well as his shirt burst open at his growing stature; talons grew out of his enlarging fingers The crowd shrieked in horror but still holding them in place was the drama unfolding onstage and the hope that their savior was up there.

Knowing that all her hopes for this country had just crashed and crumbled to dust, anger finally snapped the faithwalker fully back into reality. Lady Stephanie threw her hand out, sending fire streaking towards Fred. It engulfed him but he stood unharmed after the flames dissipated! *Dear Jesus, Why?* Peering more closely through the remnants of his charred garments, she could see the cursed Black Oil. She remembered fighting with Jargono who used the Black Oil to nullify the effects of her faithwalking. *But I didn't know then, like I do now. I can* fix *you! I'll turn that Black Oil into Light Oil first, or I'll just call Christ to deal with you directly.*

Fred, half human, half demon, cursed by the Black Oil that Jargono had given him to use in case he got into trouble, smiled. "You still love me, I can tell! You can't hurt me."

Judge Matthew raced forward with outstretched hand. "In the name of our Lord, Jesus Christ, I command you to be gone."

Fred howled in pain and Stephanie's mouth dropped open. Demon Fred shrank away from Mathew's hand, shrieked, and cowered each time the Judge's palm was directed at him. As Stephanie gaped she suddenly became aware of herself looking stupid. *But there's nothing coming from his hand, nor from Christ. I can tell!*

Judge Matthew boldly strode over to a fearful demon Fred, thrusting out both hands. "I command you to banish yourself, in the name of our Lord Jesus."

Demon Fred howled in anguish then disappeared. Stephanie, clearly perplexed and upset, kept repeating to herself. *But … but there was no power coming from Matthew* at all. *None at all!*

Clearly terrified then clearly saved, the crowd fell to their knees repeatedly crying out the Judge's name. He in turn, marched up to the microphone and scornfully asked Stephanie. "Was that your father?"

The crowd hushed then murmured, having heard her say he was. Stephanie viewed a crowd of people that only minutes before had been cheering her name with love. Now she saw confusion, doubt, and anger as if she had somehow betrayed them. Upon defocusing from their expressions, she saw transparent black arms en masse maneuvering over many of the people's heads. *Dear Jesus, I've never seen so many demons all at once … I've never seen this. I've been an* idiot *for not considering how the ethereal would react to what I've been doing.* Frozen, Lady Stephanie completely forgot Judge Matthew had asked her a question.

"I take it from your silence *that* was indeed your father. I think that in light of this, your appointment to the clergy," she knew he would revoke it now, "… should be under review!"

Under review? I wish he would've just taken it away! Under review!

How do you like that, bitch? *I'm going to keep you on the edge of* everything *from now on.* "Now, all of you may go home in peace. I think we don't need to hear from … Stephanie, today."

Many in the crowd nodded, grunted, or even vocally agreed. But Stephanie felt something burning inside her, asking her, *Where are you? What are you?*

She quickly answered the questions. Oh dear God, I am Yours! I know that.

Stephanie received a response. *Then act like it! Speak!*

Finally, the fog seemed to lift. She needed no microphone, though she knew she wouldn't be received well now, but words flowed anyway. "Excuse me, but I *do* have something to say!"

Many in the crowd waved Stephanie away in disgust while some began hurling insults. Some stopped still, and others with tears in their eyes began to nod. A few cried out. "It's about time!"

Mandy wept in Carla's arms. "I don't care what I saw. I don't believe it. I don't."

"You're right not to doubt dear Stephanie, my sister, but *that* was her father. This is only the beginning!" Carla warned while Lynnara watched everything.

Matthew stepped in front of a tearful Stephanie. "I won't have you speak at this time!"

She stepped around the Judge to the very front of the podium then fell on her knees. *I could ask Jesus to show the people a sign that I'm true, that I speak true, but I don't understand what's going on. What if the sign is somehow countered or if something else happens which I can't answer. What do I do?*

She heard an answer. *What is in your heart?*

Lifting up her head to the people, Stephanie expressed her love. "No matter what you've seen, no matter what you may think or feel now, I want you all to know, I do love you. Please don't judge me by that traitorous man who has sold his soul to be a demon. He has robbed me of most that's been dear in my life and tried to destroy the rest." With that said, she bowed herself low with mournful sobs. *The people! Dear Jesus, the people don't know, don't understand … I don't understand. Why?* Most of her audience felt greatly conflicted, but those who had been in Lady Stephanie's actual presence at the bar remembered her words. *'You don't know from where I came. I don't mean the country. I mean the terrible evil in my life, the terrible suffering.'*

Mandy ran up the stage to Stephanie's side, weeping. "I don't care, Stephanie, I don't care! I know you're true. We're *sisters.*"

Carla stood in front of the Judge, and softly spoke, "Tell me, Judge Matthew, so I may understand. You didn't seem surprised at all by Stephanie's father. How did you know he was a demon?"

The official looking jowls took on an air of importance. "My dear young lady, you've suffered much so I shall answer you. God came to me one night, told me these things would happen and that I must banish the demon then He blessed my faith. How else could I have done what I just did?"

Carla nodded her head slowly. "When God spoke to you, it was in a cloud that glowed over your bed!"

Judge Matthew's eyes focused on her. "That is true. How do you know this?"

Carla met his eyes with warmth. "How do you know what you know?" *He wouldn't believe me if I told him the truth.*

Lynnara wanted to hug her Mommy, but something angered her to the point that she had to stand with Carla, staring into the Judge's eyes. Something of the blessing that Stephanie had placed within her while in the Dead Forest suddenly came alive. *He hurt my Mommy* real *bad.* He didn't even notice her until she spoke, pointing her little finger up at him. "You lie! But you don't know it. God didn't speak to you because you can't even hear Him!" To her five-year-old understanding, it wasn't Stephanie's father who was to blame for her Mommy crying.

Judge Matthew dismissively guffawed as he pointed at Stephanie. "Get her up! We're going to service at her village. All her people have been waiting. I'm conducting their first *true* Christian meeting."

CHAPTER 13
The Right Meeting

They ground their teeth as he banged the gavel down, dismissing their proceedings, and with that, another attempt at reform became defeated. "What are we going to do? He's the damned last one and he *still* feels he has to rule over *everything.*"

And it was true because Judge Zachariah was the last of the original Judges, having ruled in that first generation for sixty-three years. And now being a full ninety, he still showed no sign of ebbing at all. His eyes were still sharp and his gait almost as quick as any healthy sixty. As soon as he *died,* they all looked forward to the next historical entry which would read – In the first year, in the *second* generation of the Judges for the United for Christ …

"I don't think he'll be around much longer. It's frankly unjust that he keeps blocking our legislations."

His brother gazed at him, hearing more in that *opinion* than mere opinion should allow, but he had no desire to delve deeper. "Well, you best be getting to his quarters. Our father gets grumpy without his oldest son bringing him his shot of whiskey. You're next in line to take over, you know."

"I know it."

Upon entering his father's chambers with a bottle of whiskey in hand, he tried one last time. "Father, I really think we ought to build separate judges quarters. The people need to know we're special so that they'll respect us."

"You think respect is earned by having official quarters? And how will you pay for such a project?"

"Well, of course the people would have to do as they have always done in the Bible, but that's what's required of them."

"Son, as I recall my Scriptures, the original Judges over Israel had no such facilities, but even beyond that point, you think you'll earn the people's respect by taxing them to death, extracting their labors … would you even pay them fairly? And where would we acquire the money to do that?"

"Again Father, they're required to provide it."

Judge Zachariah sighed, shaking his head. "It's my fault, actually all the first generation's fault. We've sheltered you all too much. None of you have had to work for your living. Don't forget the people have supported you."

"But that's their duty, Father."

"Son, all first generation Judges, we knew what it was like to work for a living, to scrimp and suffer. We never ever saw ourselves as different from the rest of the people. Do you even *know* what the people think, what they feel about the second generation of judges? It's not good son, not good at all, and I'm the last of the first generation and probably the only Judge left with any sense. Please, can't you see what your generation has become? You all are only entitled to the people's offerings if you are *worthy.* Are you worthy my son, to take my place?"

"I'm your eldest, Father."

"Yes, well, I see you're skilled at words. Tomorrow I shall order new legislation. We shall pick a new set of upper level Judges directly from the people as we did at first!"

"You would do that to your own son, Father, and to all the other sons of Judges?"

With loving eyes he stared into his son. "I do this for everyone's best interest, *especially* your soul. I fear the wrath you would incur from the Lord if you take over."

"Father, as you wish. You *are* my father, and I love you."

His son poured him his usual evening shot of whiskey and his father gulped it down. Seconds passed as his son stared into his father's eyes until he saw what he wanted to see, the recognition of death coming for him. But it wasn't as he'd expected. He thought his father would be either angry or scared."

But he looked into his first-born's eyes with love and a tear. "Forgive me my son, for failing you!" The father then collapsed back into his desk chair with a tear rolling off his face.

By order of judge Matthew, everyone needed to be in the village meeting tent at noon sharp. Two hours past twelve, the people began to wonder.

Vaughn sat on the platform's edge listening to an older man's questions about whether it was really possible to be inundated with so much new life when you're old and set in your ways. The ten baptized souls had already made quite a stir among everyone but many wondered whether only special or certain people could be so blessed.

Indeed, for the better part of two hours, Vaughn fielded many questions and returned answers as the Holy Spirit guided him. Marveling that so much flowed through him though he hadn't even received the new will yet, he recalled the Holy Scriptures: "I dwell with you and shall be in you." *Lord, I feel You so strongly, but I understand. Until I give that last little root up, You're not really in me but You're* definitely *with me. I* know *what to do Lord, but I can't yet.* Vaughn groaned inside. *You know, Lord, it's not really* neutral. *That's a lot of garbage. How does mixing evil with good produce neutral? That's a bunch of crap! Ehh, reality is what reality is.*

Vaughn had actually brought vision of his own ethereal tree into the blue orb and studied it. Every time he touched a part of his tree, he felt it directly inside of him, identifying which part of his tree corresponded to which aspect of his person. Actually, the more he did, the more the position and relationship of every tree part to each other and to the whole tree made sense. That last dead root, a remnant of his own anger confused with righteous anger and twisted by his desire to control, just barely maintained the tree of death within him.

As soon as he'd uncovered that root through the orb, reached out his finger and touched it, he felt the corresponding place within his heart and he instantly understood. Being mistreated from an early age, his automatic anger to perceived injustice was buried deeper than he'd been aware, that is, until he touched the dead root. Immediately, he felt understanding naturally ridding him of his last bit of the tree of death and the Holy Spirit responding to fill the void, to fill him completely up.

Desperately, Vaughn reached out to try to hold onto that dead root to maintain his *neutrality.* That proved to be quite difficult because true understanding naturally has a life of its own and continued its natural course of healing. Finally, by taking his mind and heart off the subject, he stopped the progress. It had been a tense moment as Grinchback had witnessed *glow* begin to destroy the dark root, though actually having the demon so close at hand was what Vaughn needed. Focusing on the demon enabled him to halt the dead root's destruction. "Had you worried there for a moment, didn't I, my friend?"

The elder cleared his throat, bringing Vaughn back to the present. "Sorry, my mind's kinda traveling in different directions all at once. But I heard all your questions. Have you ever seen an old tree?"

The man nodded of course which then elicited Vaughn's smile. "Does being old keep the tree from being filled with new life every season?"

The old man's eyes widened as a smile slowly broke out across his tired face.

An angry voice scraped through the stillness of the meeting. "What did I tell you about conducting any more meetings, *Corporal* Vaughn?"

Vaughn smiled calmly, already prepared for him. "Dear Judge, you misjudge the situation and me. I'm not standing at the podium, but merely sitting on the stage talking with my people. The discussions are mutual. I'm not in charge. We've eagerly been waiting for *two hours...*" Vaughn stopped in mid-sentence squinting at Stephanie and the two apprentice judges flanking her. *Something is* very *wrong*. The pit of his stomach seemed to drop. *But what?*

As the Judges and Stephanie came down the aisle, Vaughn watched in disbelief but not knowing exactly what it was he disbelieved. As they ascended the stage and Stephanie sat to the side but a bit behind the Good Judge, Judge Matthew ordered Vaughn. "You may take a seat *down there,*" He pointed his head toward the floor below.

"Thank you, Judge Matthew, for your direction." Vaughn wasn't sarcastic at all but actually loving.

All the people looked to one another remembering Vaughn's urgent advice. *Under no circumstances should you let that bastard provoke you. Keep focused on God's goodness inside you.* They all knew what he'd tried to do to Mandy besides all the other treachery they'd witnessed from the beginning of entering this country.

Judge Matthew's grave demeanor tunneled into every face causing quite a few to readjust their sitting positions in their wooden folding chairs. The noise from their shifting spread like a wave throughout the great tent then receded into calm. The Judge's tone added to the gravity of the now dramatically changed atmosphere. "This was to be a very happy occasion, our first official Christian service together and the announcement of Lady Stephanie's appointment to the clergy as an honorary Judge. However, due to the current developments, I must at least hold that appointment under review."

Everyone looked at each other shaking their bewildered heads.

Realizing they didn't understand, he informed them. "I forgot you weren't there. But I suppose it's no shock to you that Stephanie's father showed up. You know, the half human, half demon." The Judge stared hard checking for confirmation, challenging everyone with his indomitable glare to own up then rechecking even harder for *any* reaction at all. *They think they can deceive me. I see right through them.* He decided to impress Vaughn's people. "I had to banish that foul demon *myself,* as she didn't have the heart for it."

The people sat stone silent. Not a peep, not a word, but many bowed their heads. Vaughn hid his face in his hands. *Oh God, I was right. Fred did become a demon. Stephanie, what have you done? I knew I should have killed him right then. But how could I, you'd just prayed for him to live. Why's he here? Why now?* Then Vaughn realized the incongruity, and his head snapped up to glare at Judge Matthew. *Banished him? You?*

It took every ounce of strength and probably prayers from everyone else to keep Vaughn in his seat with his mouth shut. He buried his head in his hands again, but this time to hide his fury at knowing that somehow Fred and Matthew were working together, that somehow these two different forms of evil had now combined their efforts.

All Vaughn could see was marching up to the good Judge and ripping his throat out. He felt the dead root strengthen within his heart and at this time it felt quite right. He wondered if the Highest Councilor was helping to further the cause, or perhaps even his *friend.*

Vaughn looked up into Stephanie's eyes. They were fearful, pleading, and staring just above his head, a stare that penetrated through his rage, giving him further pause, a deeper moment of self-reflection. He knew what she was focusing on, and nodding to her slightly, returned his head into his hands. When he re-adjusted his perception, he could feel the demon's presence stoking his dead root. *But I don't understand! He wants me to kill the Judge? What's going on?* Pains streaked across his temples as he rubbed them futilely.

Seeing absolutely no display of emotion except tacit acceptance of him as Judge where he should have seen cowering in denial or biting back, Matthew angered. "You people are *all* under review!" Still not a single reaction from anyone infuriated him more, so he challenged them further. "Tell me none of you knew her father was a demon. I mean a *real* demon."

Mr. Alder, going on eighty years of age, hobbled his way to the podium. One of the younger men rose to help him, but he brusquely waved him off. "For what I have to say, I will climb this stage under my *own* power." And climb he did, as he came beside the Judge who still hadn't moved away. "Is it also part of your Christian custom to begrudge an old man's giving an answer to your accusations?"

Alder's knife-like stare confronted every bit of Judge Matthew's righteous indignation yet Alder had a special air of the aged, a demeanor commanding respect that trumped the Judge's. Even his tired old stature with his head held painfully high in opposition to the hulking Judge carried a sense of power beyond Matthew. Alder had dealt with many Judge Matthews in his days. *True, different titles but the same damned man!*

The Judge reluctantly eased back and the people eased up as well. Further surprising all was Mr. Alder's voice, its power and clarity belied his feeble frame. "I speak for all, *yes?*"

Everyone nodded. Then Alder turned to the Judge, pointing his bony finger at him. "Thou shalt *not* hold a child guilty for their father's sin! Am I speaking correctly, Judge Matthew?"

Silence. Alder motioned for the Judge to give him the Bible in his hand. "Would you like me to show you where it's written in *several* places?"

Judge Matthew remained quiet. *Old man, I don't give a damn what you say. Your fates are all sealed.*

"Did you know *Good* Judge Matthew that Stephanie's father murdered all her ancestral people on her mother's side? Did you know that her people hid her from her father to protect her?" Alder's anger rang out through the meeting so sharply that it seemed to still every soul in mid-breath.

Seeing news media had crept in, now televising live, Alder knew Judge Matthew had asked them here. *But this will not play your tune, Judge Matthew.* "Are you news people getting this clearly?

They all nodded so Alder pointed to Lady Stephanie. "This young lady pulled herself up and out from the very bottom because she refused to let goodness die."

No one in the tent, except Judge Matthew, knew the extent of the media coverage. Just after he and Stephanie had left the noonday meeting in the town square, an apprentice had made the announcement of the first official Christian service among the newcomers being covered live nationally, and of an inquiry into Stephanie's lineage.

Sensing a wrong turn, Matthew stepped forward expecting the old man to give way but was ignored. *You'll have to push me out of the way and how good will that look, Good Judge?* "From the first day I saw you, I've watched you, Judge Matthew. And my years have given me certain knowledge about people."

Careful, old man.

"When I saw your black robe and fierce appraisal of us, I wondered whether we'd fled the North from one evil tyrant to another oppressor of the people. Do you know what your northern neighbor did to us? Just after the civil war, the new government fully outlawed God. No mention of Jesus Christ was allowed, no mention of God at all except through their phony government sponsored religion which more or less made a nameless god a prop to support them. Their first commandment was 'pay your taxes'. But in all their schools they taught strict atheism along with their nationalist indoctrination. When they discovered one of *our* towns secretly worshipping God, the government burnt it with all its people to the ground, but only *after* they had made a spectacle of torturing the women and children there! They then proceeded to show the video of the torture to little school children for almost a hundred years and *still* counting."

No one had ever heard this story in the United for Christ. No one in the meetings had talked of it, having chosen to banish it from memory. Upon hearing the story again, many broke into tears while cameras panned them. Across the country, gasps escaped as people realized the brutality of their northern neighbor.

"Do you know what that does to a people when they're shown, *shown,* not just told, from an early age that anyone believing in God beyond the government sanctioned god will be *obliterated?*"

Alder paused to let the people contemplate then he turned to Lady Stephanie again. "Yet *she* and Corporal Vaughn through sheer courage, introspection and love discovered the Holy Spirit and under threat of death came to us with that spiritual knowledge while we all were back up North, before we even came here. Now many of us have found Jesus Christ to be the Lord God because of *them*. And I tell you this, Judge Matthew, you can review us until your official looking jowls drop to the floor. What difference does that make to us, having developed a faith in God, a faith hard earned and *well* tested?"

The people who heard the old man characterize the Judge's facial features burst into laughter. The camera crews struggled to hold their equipment still, and a few even dared to do close-ups of the Judge's face. No one else could have gotten away with such a comment except Mr. Alder, but placed in the middle of so much passion and a clearer picture of tried faith, the people's laughter also carried more than just humor.

"Can you imagine the difference in faith between a people sorely tested and a people who only have to worry about their shoes getting muddy on their way to church, Good Judge Matthew? Mr. Alder spread out his arms to the people before him. "How many of you would die today, this *very* hour, suffer torture to uphold the living God, and even to defend *this* country which has given us a glimmer of freedom, to be true to your faith?"

The crowd roared to their feet, raising their hands, shouting as one. Finally, Mr. Alder raised a hand and the crowd instantly hushed, amazing further the people at their

TV sets. "You may review us, Judge Matthew, but never forget it is Christ who is Judge of all." With that, Mr. Alder walked off the stage, a young man rushing to help him down, the cameras shooting the old man's face, its sternness, bravery, and glistening single tear.

All across the nation, people sat wiping their eyes. Many felt God was moving in their great country but still didn't know in what direction.

Finally, Judge Matthew stepped back up to the microphone and stood very erect. *Damn! I can't do what I want right now. Doesn't matter, though, I have time, and still have a Christian service to conduct.*

Finally back in control, he scanned his audience, quickly noting the prettier, livelier faces and anyone else who might appear useful. It was hard to tell which direction events would turn, who would survive, but everything would be far better in the end. Someone once said a revolution every hundred years or so is a good thing. *Well, the masses have far too long enjoyed too much freedom in their wicked ways, and don't show proper respect anymore. No wonder God is angry. Now they even turn to strangers. I don't know where the military ever got the idea that they know better than we do about how to protect this country from evil. How is it they protect strangers but try to bring us down? Lord Jesus, everything is upside down, but I trust in you.*

He waited, expecting the voice of God in his head to guide him again but none sounded. Never quite sure when God would speak to him, he was sure that when He didn't meant his own decisions were blessed, that anything he'd do would be right because the Lord is pleased in him. After all, who is so righteous as to have the Lord speak directly to them on a regular, well, somewhat regular basis? Nothing matched that wonderful, no, magnificent feeling of approval. *Jesus only needs to speak to me when I may be veering a bit, or for something unforeseen.*

Judge Matthew had been surprised though, when a second voice showed up, a female voice. And then there was also that *bitch* Stephanie, who somehow, at times, managed to put *her* voice into his head. At one point, the question as to how to verify the identity of these voices posed a brief dilemma. But no one spoke as God, no doubt about that. God's voice always made perfect sense. *All I have to do is simply depend on my sense of righteousness. Anything that disagrees is wrong.* When he questioned the female voice, she merely said she'd been sent to help. He liked her plan quite a lot, and because of that, he knew it to be right.

Everyone sat silently waiting on Judge Matthew as he seemed to be transfixed. When their expectancy intruded upon his little interlude, he refocused his eyes and cleared his throat, bringing his mind to bear upon the present. "Now that we have all that behind us, I have a service to conduct. Forget about how you did things before. This is the *right* way to do it. I will begin by leading everyone in prayer. You may repeat after me. Our Father in heaven, who gave us true Judges."

They echoed the words, looking from one to the other.

"That they should lead the people in righteousness."

"That they should lead the people in righteousness." They followed the Judge.

"Hallowed be thy glorious name."

They repeated Matthew's exact words.

"Christian."

Someone raised a hand, and because of it, no one repeated after the Judge.

He grimaced then said the word again with extra emphasis, "*Christian!*"

Everyone still looked around as the young lady waved her hand more urgently, her long wavy dark black hair jostling as she flailed her arm. Vaughn finally spoke up, "Excuse me, Judge…"

But Matthew fired back. "The holy prayer is *not* supposed to be interrupted."

Vaughn turned calmly to everyone. "I know our custom was to answer questions as they come up so as not to leave anyone behind, and that the Holy Spirit flows with us in this way, but Judge Matthew would like to do it *his* way." Vaughn turned back to the Judge, and repeated. "Christian."

And everyone followed. "Christian."

But the young woman interrupted, rather annoyed. "I'm not compromising the Lord's truth for anyone. And this is *not* the Lord's Prayer. You have added to it, Sir!"

Vaughn hung his head, not sure if he should laugh or cry while Stephanie both smiled and groaned inside. The newsmen all focused their cameras tightly on the young lady whose black hair spread naturally down past her shoulders. Just before Matthew had graced Stephanie with his hungry presence today, Marissa had visited and passionately asked to be baptized. Stephanie had agreed as soon as another group could be gathered together. *I understand. You won't compromise. So be it, Lord.*

Judge Matthew reddened. "And how would *you* know that?"

"I read it, Sir, in the gospel of Saint Matthew, sixth chapter. There is no mention of Judges there, and the name hallowed is simply *thy* name, particularly the name of God the Father since Jesus was praying to *Him*, not the name *Christian*."

"Young lady," Judge Matthew seemed to find just a bit of patience as the cameras swung back to him, "I have the Scriptures right here and I'm reading it exactly."

"So am I!" Marissa got up, gathered her long brown dress, then excused herself past several people to carry the Holy Bible to the Judge.

As he held a bible in each hand, his eyebrows rose. "This is *not* the proper version. Where did you get this and how did you even know…"

"King … ahh, Ranger Vaughn got his from you! You gave it to him just after you *falsely* imprisoned him. We've compared your version," she tapped her fingernail on his bible, the clicks sounding more sharply than expected, "to the more original version you gave Ranger Vaughn." And she clicked it even harder for more emphasis. "The King James version makes a lot more sense, seems far righter. So we sent word throughout your city to buy the original version and many people sold us their extra copies! Check the dates, *Judge*. King James is more original. Besides, does it make sense for Jesus to be hallowing Judges or the Father in Heaven?"

Matthew smiled. "Thank you. You may take your seat."

He waited for her to comply, but Marissa waited a moment for a response, and realizing none would come, stretched out her hand for him to return her Holy Bible. Matthew grinned then gave it back to her as if giving up a mere token to a child. None of this finesse was lost on the zooming cameras. People across the country ran to their bookcases, their desk drawers, their basements to search out their old copies, spreading both open to Saint Matthew, chapter six.

The Judge, not losing a beat, tried to endear the audience. "Dear people," he turned briefly to Stephanie and smiled. *I know that irks her.* "You don't have to repeat after me, just listen. Eventually, with patience and due diligence, you may come around."

And Matthew started the prayer at the beginning. There were other liturgies and more repetitions to which everyone eventually yielded just to keep awake. Heads began to bob and elbows shot into sides, but no antidote surfaced for the coma-inducing spell of the Judge's words.

At the conclusion, Judge Matthew's exhilaration beamed. "I know true Christianity is difficult to understand at first, especially because you're heathen, but repetition eventually brings understanding. Lately, some Christian youth groups have been springing up at services filled with young people's music, lots of emotions, and tears. Perhaps some of you may prefer such a service and I may arrange for a younger Judge to provide it. Some people need to be emotionally charged, I suppose, but I myself am leery about the youth movement. Simply producing a state of emotionality is no true substitute for living continuously by the Holy Spirit."

The Judge smiled again and Stephanie shook her head. *Oh, my God! How does he do that? How can he be so phony and yet speak such deep truth?* She had already visited several of those youth services, having been told how deeply Christ moved there, but it was *exactly* as the Judge described. They whipped each other up into a state of emotional frenzy week after week. That emotional state became their goal, it seemed, rather than the solid continual presence of the Holy Spirit which brings a blend of peace, deep emotions, and intellectual gratification whether in church or not. These youth groups seemed to need their Sunday fix. *In a way, it's just like when I used to do drugs.* When Stephanie attempted to question their leaders under the guise of wanting to understand, they became suspicious of her, and a cold wind suddenly seemed to blow. Yet, the youth groups were sure they were more right than the older generation, pointing to their dry and dull services.

So much confusion. Pointing out another group's fault doesn't make you right even if you're right about their fault. I don't know which is worse, the Judge Matthews or the youth movement. They both dominate, just differently. And who will give the people the real truth that seems so hard to face? Stephanie felt a burning in her chest as tears blurred her vision. Her hand went to the Seed to the Tree of Life hanging underneath her dress, and felt it glowing against her.

Judge Matthew packed up his drinking cup and motioned to his apprentices, then addressed Stephanie, "I expect you in my office." When she didn't respond, he grabbed her arm.

"I'll be along later. I have duties." She pulled away, noticed Marissa with a newsman, and caught Vaughn's eye. He knew then they needed to *really* talk as they used to before.

CHAPTER 14
Lower Lows

"Heil Hitler!" Snapping his heels together with a loud crack, the SS officer's attendant saluted then stood at attention, knowing not to do anything unless directed.

The officer retrieved some costly brandy from his glass cabinet then sat down at his desk. "Do you know why we put the Jews through so much?"

"No, Sir. But I presume to gain scientific knowledge that may further our cause?"

"Yes, that too, but much of it goes deeper. I have a demonstration for you. See if you can figure out the point of it. Bring them in!" Two soldiers brought in a family of a husband, a wife, and two little boys.

The SS officer smiled then asked the adults. "You love each other?"

The couple grew suspicious of the question, but nodded.

And the SS patiently nodded back. "That's good, very good! You love your children?"

Again they assented, growing even more apprehensive.

The SS repeated. "That's good, *very* good!" He spoke in a dear tone to the children who were around eight and ten years old. "You love your Mommy and Daddy?"

And they also nodded to which the SS responded. "That's good, *very* good! Only two of you will be allowed to leave here alive and if your Mommy or Daddy say anything from now on, then none of you will leave here alive. Do you all understand?"

Feeling their hearts pounding and barely able to bear it, the adults could only nod their heads. The SS officer emptied the bullets, slowly replaced two and gave his pistol to the youngest. "You choose, young man, decide whom you will save. Shoot your Mommy, your Daddy, or your brother. And oh, if you shoot yourself, they all die."

Crying, the child could barely hold the gun in his hand. He was shaking so terribly and the whole family was quaking. The SS officer leaned in closely and suddenly screamed in the boy's ear. *"Shoot!"*

And the lad closed his eyes and shot the arm of his father who fell to the floor. "You're a *terrible* shot." The SS officer grabbed the boy, brought him close and made him lower the gun to his father's head. *"Shoot!"*

The boy closed his eyes then shot, killing his father. "OK! That's very good! Now, I'll give you a day to think it over whom you'll shoot next. Take them all to separate rooms and feed them well."

After they were gone, he turned to his attendant. "Well?"

The young man was at a loss for words but suddenly spoke wisely. "Sir, I am but a mere attendant and too stupid to understand." It was the correct answer.

"This is a study in what some call the human spirit. I will watch them all very closely now, to see how empty they become inside. I want to know if I can make any of them die simply from the emotional and psychological pain. The question is can the human spirit simply stop, simply stop living because it no longer wills to live. The answer may determine how to conquer whole countries simply by sufficiently demoralizing them!"

Vaughn had seemed careless with a satchel full of military plans and, as expected, infiltrators had photographed them then returned home. Joshua wanted to know whom they'd meet and their next orders. Stephanie's descriptions of Jargono's manipulations and desires, the kind of psychology he had, all made acquiring intelligence reports more urgent. Deep in Joshua's gut, he knew time was marked.

Captain Joshua now hid behind a boulder, waiting for his spies to return across the border, and mused. *Whether being a Judge or a Captain, we're all under Christ. Though it seems different duties breed different characters, I really don't feel ungodly for being military, even if the Judges imply it.* Since their first night together when Stephanie related her life, he'd been feeling small, very small. When he thought of all she'd suffered, when he thought of how deeply she'd been blessed, Joshua hardly felt worthy to be in the same room with her. *Yet, she's so easy to be with, and all I want to do is hold her in my arms and make love to her.* She'd promised to tell him the rest of her life, but the timing never seemed right and Joshua didn't feel he could ask.

The Seed to the Tree of Life. I still don't know what to make of it. Such a mystery held in secret for so long. But I guess it had to be on Earth, somewhere. I just always thought ... I don't know what I thought. I guess in heaven, the tree would fruit all the time, if there's one in heaven.

Captain Joshua's thoughts were disturbed by rapid movement that didn't sound natural in the forest. His extra training made him ultra-sensitive to the extra subtle and out of the ordinary, whether it be an odd vibration felt through the ground, or a sound too subdued to register as anything but a feeling. He whirled around, propping his marksman rifle on the boulder, peering through the telescopic sight. Scanning through the fence from one direction to the next he paused then quickly swung back.

Joshua spotted Vaughn's man, Harris, running through the brush at top speed. This had been a joint operation since his previous spies weren't making it back anymore, but Vaughn had no trouble with his operatives coming or going. Either they were better at it, or Jargono just didn't care, or had other reasons for allowing them in and out. However, something had obviously gone wrong now. There was no sign of Joshua's two men, but several were in hot pursuit of Harris. Squeezing his trigger twice with muffled hiccups, two pursuers toppled over themselves, but the others kept chasing, unaware their comrades went down.

Knowing Harris wouldn't slow for the electric fence, Joshua grabbed his remote controller from his vest pocket. When they'd first met, he remembered each arrived at the same conclusion: they could trust each other with their lives.

It was odd how such deep conviction results from even the briefest of exchanges. Their firm handshake had sealed the pact and from then on they'd worked together perfectly, and more than once, they'd dined at the other's home. Harris' children, two boys and a girl, the youngest, took immediate liking to Joshua, stoking his own desire to have children. As he watched Harris's desperate run, with memories playing in his heart, he tried to take out another enemy but missed. The bullets probably deflected by an errant, swaying branch whipping around from the increased wind.

A few feet before Harris made the fence, Joshua hit the button cutting off the fence's power. Not even breaking stride, Harris grabbed the horizontal middle fence rail, slung himself between it and the one above, then rolled as he hit the ground. Joshua's heart skipped a beat when he heard shots, but saw Harris continue to roll. *Dear Jesus, let him be OK.* Panning his scope toward the shots' location, with four more hiccups, two more men toppled head over heels.

Harris sprinted through the thorny wild raspberry, trying to make it to a tree, feeling Joshua's presence. *Dear Lord, let me live long enough to at least tell him what they need to know.*

Two more pursuers came out of the forest and suddenly gained the fence. *Damn, they want Harris this badly! Why?* Joshua hit the green button and electrocuted the men, their shrieks sending birds into flight. Crackles and pops resounded through the now calm forest as their cooking flesh released gas then became charred.

A sense of guilt struck Joshua with the ease in which he began to dismiss six deaths because he didn't even know them.

What am I becoming? Dear Lord Jesus, forgive me. Perhaps the Judges are right. But what am I to do? Should I not protect my wife, my country, and the helpless innocents? Oh God, I don't want to have to kill, but if I don't defend, then am I killing the innocent by inaction? Thou shalt not kill. I know, but what if the world only leaves you with that choice? Either I kill them when it's in my power, or they kill the innocent. Oh, dear Jesus.

Joshua scanned the woods again, but no more enemies were apparent. *If I go to Harris and snipers are hiding … Damn! I have to wait for him in case he needs cover. What if he's wounded?*

෨

That night, Stephanie couldn't shake her guilt for allowing her personal vengeance to convince her to let her father live in what *she'd* thought would be a fitting punishment. God had granted her request since He had granted her the respect of an open prayer door. At least that was Vaughn's opinion when they'd discussed it a whole year ago, but now her foolishness was causing her much grief. *Oh Light, many are my sufferings. Because of my father, they don't know what to think, and because of me…* As she wept quite uncontrollably, Lynnara quietly crawled into her bed then placed her little arm around her. "Mommy, don't cry. Please don't! Remember our secret."

Stephanie opened her eyes, while the child pulled on the chain around her Mommy's neck attached to the Seed of the Tree of Life. When they'd been trapped a long time in the ethereal Dead Forest, the place had drained most of Stephanie's life, but had no effect on Lynnara, probably because she was a child. Knowing she would die, not having enough strength left to transport them out, Stephanie had performed a special abbreviated bonding with her adopted daughter. She transferred into her some of the knowledge of the Seed to the Tree of Life and charged the little girl to protect its secret. Stephanie also had placed seeds of knowledge that would sprout as Lynnara grew up. Now, one of those seeds apparently had sprouted as the child did her best to refocus her third and best Mommy.

"You're so precious, Lynnara! You've made my life so much better. I love you so much." Stephanie gazed deeply into the child and once again saw her own self when she was that age. Their striking similarities in hearts, pains, attitudes, deep love, and faith in goodness had become an instant bond between them even before Stephanie had passed on her secret knowledge. *If anything happens to me, I know you'll continue on for the Tree of Life.*

Lynnara recalled the demons closing in to eat them. Having made up her little heart that she wouldn't take the Seed that belonged to Mommy, that she wouldn't leave her alone, she somehow found the right combination of her little prayers, holding the Seed and the pretty ribbon, and transported them both out of the Dead forest and into the sacred Cave.

Now, having pulled the Seed out from under her Mommy's nightgown, Lynnara played with it between her fingers. The Seed began speaking in soft feelings to the child, which comforted Stephanie by seeing how the Seed related to her daughter. She breathed a sigh of relief and let her thoughts wander to her conversations with Vaughn.

Jargono, they knew, created the Earth demons. Vaughn had destroyed demon Glen, who'd confessed that Jargono sent him to kill Vaughn and capture Stephanie before they could come to this country. Though no direct proof, Stephanie was sure Jargono controlled her demon father. *Oh God, I hope so! If not, there's no telling how many he's impregnated.* Vaughn and she had briefly entertained the ugly scenario of her father escaping like Glen, and impregnating another town. But it was simply too much to consider, now, and they tabled any further discussion.

What was hard to figure was Matthew's supposed banishment of demon Fred. Based on Stephanie's perceptions and Vaughn's insight, they both agreed he couldn't have done it but neither of them could believe Matthew would work with Jargono. Remembering what Carla had told her about God appearing in a cloud and blessing Matthew, Stephanie had shrugged it off as his delusions of grandeur, and jokingly mentioned the detail to Vaughn.

Yet upon hearing it, he asked for everything she knew about the experience. He then told her about his intelligence report concerning other Judges receiving forewarning from *God* about Joshua's plans. He reminded Stephanie how Jargono had come to him several times posing as God, trying to get Vaughn to accept the Blackness that followed the cursed Oil that turned people into demons.

Stephanie laughed at the absurdity. "You think Matthew believes Jargono is God?"

"Not like that. He doesn't know it's Jargono, just like we don't know for sure either. But Matthew listens to a voice, a glowing cloud that comes to tell him what he wants to hear. Because he believes he's righteous, really right, then the voice that encourages him, well, that *must* be God! Remember, a person's sense of what and who God is comes directly from and through their perceptions of what's right."

"Dear Jesus!" Stephanie hung her head. "What are we to do?"

Vaughn replied, "I think Jargono doesn't want the military running anything. He's trying to undermine them in preparation to invasion … but at the same time, he's also leaving the opportunity open simply to win the popular vote! Free health care!"

He shook his head with heavy seriousness, and whispered in Stephanie's ear. His closeness made her ache, but his words made her hurt. "Be careful with the Seed. You know Jargono always has multiple levels to his plans. He may have found out about the Seed by now. The demons already know."

As Lynnara's little fingers wiped her mother's tears away, Stephanie lingered in the memory of Vaughn's closeness. The child, holding the Seed in one hand and her Mommy's cheek in the other suddenly picked her head up. After turning her head around to see if anyone was in the room, Lynnara pulled the covers over her and her Mommy's heads, then whispered in her mother's ear.

∽

Judge Matthew spoke coldly. "You're late. You were supposed to be here yesterday."

"Well, I had other business." Stephanie had an odd thought. *I wonder if he wears that black robe to bed. I've never seen him without it.*

"I'll make this short and to the point. I expect you in my bed. You can visit me willingly, or I will make you!"

Stephanie's mouth dropped open. "You're joking!"

He came around from his desk then backed Stephanie up against the wall, and leaned down only inches away from her. "You think you're so clever. You're no Christian! I don't know what you are but you're obviously sent by the devil to undermine our great country. Go ahead, use some witchcraft on me! I have two guards with orders to rush in here and shoot if they hear anything amiss. And if by some means you get by them, can you protect everyone else? I have a letter to be opened upon my death condemning your seditious people as my murderers and sentencing them to die."

"Well, if I'm a *witch,* then why do you want me in your bed?"

"You're a heathen. I have a right to you. You're created only for our pleasure."

Stephanie reminded Judge Matthew. "I'm married."

"I didn't say you couldn't be married to the good Captain. Matthew snickered then ordered her. "Now, get out! I don't want you right now!"

"What will you do if I…"

"I don't give a damn what you do! Tell your Captain! As soon as he makes a move on me, I'll kill him! I don't need you anymore. I'm already advanced in the government. Get *out!*" He grabbed her arm, opened the door, and threw her out. As she flew through the doorway, one of the guards stuck out his foot and Stephanie splayed forward and had to use her power to keep from smashing her face on the floor. Matthew's guards eyed her maliciously. *Maybe we can get some, too.*

❧

The rest of the day Stephanie spent alone in her apartment, having asked Carla and Mandy to take her daughter shopping. The three walked through the town, peeking in store windows with Mandy and Lynnara excitedly gibbering about clothes and what would look good. Carla seemed quite subdued, and her feelings finally penetrated Mandy. "What is it, Carla? What's wrong?"

"Everything!" Mandy's distraught sister cried.

Just then Larson strode up with Rebekah. "Ladies." But he focused on Carla who quickly wiped away her tears.

Lynnara pulled her best friend a little away for them to whisper. While Larson and Carla were too shy for anything like a formal date, they kept managing to run into each other. Seeing their rapt attention, Mandy quietly moved to focus on the kids.

❧

Around ten o'clock at night Haniel, Barrack's replacement, summoned Stephanie with a sharp knock at her door. "Judge Matthew needs to see you *now!*"

She wondered at the timing and the rudeness. Joshua hadn't returned and she didn't want Lynnara woken up. "I have to see to my daughter first. I'll be…"

He put his foot in the door even as Stephanie tried to hold off the power that had come up in her eyes. Haniel smiled upon seeing it. "I wouldn't if I were you! This compound isn't a nursery. Neither does it belong to the military, nor to *witches!*"

Her stomach lurched when she heard the accusation. Stephanie pushed past him to look for Joshua's guards but they were gone. "I'll be with you in a moment."

She stepped back in, and went into the bedroom next door. "Wake up, Carla! I'm being summoned to the Judge's chambers. Will you look after Lynnara?"

Seeing Carla's nod, Stephanie whispered into her ear. "Wait ten minutes then get Mandy and Lynnara over to Joshua's compound right away. If he's not back yet, find Vaughn. Ask him to keep you safe, he'll understand."

Carla grabbed Stephanie's arm, then looked her in the eye. "I understand."

℘

Dear Lord Jesus, please watch over everyone. Forgive me for failing you. I don't see a way out of this. Stephanie entered the Judge's chambers but couldn't bring herself to look him in the face. Smiling ear to ear, he wasted no time confessing. "I've had my eye on you from the first time I saw you. You know it's too bad you didn't choose me. I would've given you a good life and made you important along with me." He went to his bookcase, reached behind a few books and the whole case swung open. "Come in. Don't be shy."

The Judge descended a narrow, dimly lit stone stairway. Stephanie had to follow, and sickened more with each step down. She started sobbing but was sure the good Judge wouldn't care about her tears. *What am I doing? What else can I do?* She thought about how her virginity had been mysteriously restored after her baptism, how special making love is, and how she'd explained to many its true meaning. She was proud of Mandy for now turning away many men, proud of so many others like her, too. Stephanie felt worse thinking of them, and it didn't help that the room below was immaculately decorated with a large plush bed with four wrought iron posts and a lacey canopy.

"C'mon. Strip!" *What fun! I love the look on her face. Not so high and mighty now, are you?*

Staring at the Judge, she tested him. "You know, if I wanted to, I could incinerate you where you stand, or do half a dozen other quite undesirable things to you."

"Go ahead! You know the score." *I'll wait and let her think it over.*

Part of Stephanie began building power to inflict *something*, but another part of her halted it so she only stared at him.

"Well, what's taking you so long? Oh, you're worried about their survival. So, where's your power now? *Strip* already!"

Stephanie remembered when Jargono had made her do the very same thing. As he groped her, she was able to make him consider actually having her willingly as his wife by truly winning her love. *Oh, my God! Even Jargono is better than this … this monster.*

Taking off her brown dress with Appendaho embroidery, the sight of its traditional design increased her embarrassment. *Oh, dear Jesus! King Mafferan's letter implied that my progeny are supposed to protect the Tree of Life. Please Lord Jesus, though I be defiled and no longer worthy, don't let me bear children unto this beast.*

Now she recalled how badly she'd desired Vaughn and had pressed him to make love but he refused, saying the time wasn't right, that he couldn't take care of her yet. And Vaughn wanted to honor her fully so when he made love to her, it would truly be love. When finally he could take care of her, they married with the proviso that until they could provide the sanctuary wherein the Seed to the Tree of Life could be planted, they would not mate.

She barely got out the words to Matthew. "Give me a moment." Dressed only in her undergarments, she knelt down weeping, not caring that the Judge saw. *Dear Jesus, let Lynnara take my place to carry the Seed to the Tree of Life. I'm no longer worthy. Forgive me. I know You appointed me its caretaker so I wasn't supposed to mate until the exact right time for the Tree of Life. Your Seed won't be in danger if Lynnara is to wear it and in time she'll grow up to be far better than me. My sacrifice will buy her the time to do so. I know that You will grant my prayer.*

She then resolutely stood up and dropped off the rest of her garments. The Judge's mouth fell open and his heart pounded. Nothing could have prepared him for her powerful vibrancy. *But not yet, you're not quite* broken *yet.* "Go and wash well. I don't want to come in contact with any of the good Captain's filth. Take that off too! I want you completely naked." He'd pointed at the Seed to the Tree of Life.

Recalling she was told not to take off the Seed for anything until it was time to plant, Stephanie fingered the shiny black pearl-like object. She knew there would be no sense arguing, and if he even just sensed her objection, he might even try to take the Seed away. She took off the chain and placed it on the nightstand beside the bed where she thought she could keep an eye on it. As directed by Matthew, who stood in front of the open shower stall, she then washed in certain ways, then he rewashed certain parts of her himself.

Stephanie bit her lip, remembering how she used to deal with all the vermin from when she was just a gang member. Long forgotten parts of her resurfaced and asked her where she'd been for so long while her holy life now seemed more like a distant memory. An odd thought came to her that the demons were probably watching and throwing a party, then her holy feelings reasserted. Back and forth her sensibilities went from a past life's hardness to a current holiness, each shift in the tide paining her even more.

Finally washed to the Judge's liking, she reached for a towel, but Matthew got it first. "I'll dry you."

He took his time, permeating every grope with his lust and vileness, humiliating her further and further. After a while, he spoke almost lovingly. "You know, you'd better start enjoying this or it's is going to hurt."

She quickly approached her limit as if gripped by a type of insanity. "You'd better shut up because I don't know how much more I can take." She looked him in the eye and he knew she was at her breaking point.

Right where I want you. "You know, I've changed my mind for tonight. Think about our having a more amiable relationship. I want you to at least tolerate me." He stepped back from her and held his hand out to the stairway. "You may go!"

She stood staring in disbelief, at first relieved, then despairing that she would have to relive this all again. It would be different if he simply took her now then came back again and again. But to repeat the first awful time, the agony of initial destruction, seemed unbearable. While away from him, she knew her conscience would rebuild itself, only to be torn down as it just had been. She considered giving herself to him right then and there. He couldn't resist and would definitely change his mind.

She's thinking of giving herself to me right now! Too easy! Where's your faith now, bitch? *I knew it, you're no Christian.*

Not knowing what guided her, Stephanie moved to the nightstand to put back her necklace. "No!" She searched under the bed, frantically pulled open the stand's drawer and dumped the contents on the floor and knelt to inspect them. She turned to the Judge while still kneeling beside the bed. "Where is it?"

Still in his righteous black robe, he smiled. "Where's what?"

Naked, Stephanie scrambled to her feet, and grabbed his robe. "The… my necklace! It's a gift."

The Judge carefully removed her hands. "I don't know. There are mice scampering around. Perhaps one of them took it to its nest. Or maybe one ate it! But I don't think they like pearls." He walked out and up the stairs, expecting her to follow.

As Stephanie half-mindedly threw her clothes back on, her thoughts raced. *Oh, NO! It's a seed. Mice* eat *seeds! But, but … that's ridiculous!* Again it occurred to her how much fun the demons must be having over her right now.

When she finally returned to the Judge's chambers, he smiled again. "If you like, I'll buy you a far prettier necklace. There's no good reason why we can't make the best of things." With that he extended his arm to the door, relishing in what he perceived to be her emptiest feeling he'd witnessed so far. *Oh, my dear. It gets even better shortly.*

When Stephanie returned home, Vaughn was with Carla and Mandy who were still weeping in her apartment. It was midnight so Stephanie worried their cries would bother Lynnara, and without understanding why they wept, went to check Lynnara's room. *She's the heir to the Tree of Life now. Nothing's more important.* A moment later, she ran back into her living room. "Where's Lynnara?"

They all just looked at her so she asked almost in a scream. "Where is she?"

Vaughn stood up, and grabbed Stephanie's shoulders. "You were set up. They anticipated your sending the girls out to me. Someone has taken our daughter!" He caught her as she collapsed, and carried her to her bedroom.

Mandy met Carla's look that reminded her, *I told you to be prepared.* Recalling that Stephanie had watched out for her, saved Carla, and so much more, Mandy grew angry. *This isn't right. Stephanie doesn't deserve this!* She marched into the bedroom, whirled Vaughn around, and yelled, "What are you doing here? Find those bastards! Find Joshua, too! I'll take care of her."

Vaughn nodded, pulled out a glowing bottle from its leather pouch, put a little Oil on Stephanie's forehead then vanished right before Mandy's eyes! Though she saw it, his vanishing simply couldn't be considered at the moment. Mandy had a sister to take care of.

Larson and Rebekah showed up at the door just after Vaughn left, and Carla told him all that transpired. He took her in his arms, comforting her. "We'll get her back!"

The child listened to everything, and recalled what Lynnara had asked her to do when they find out where she is. Rebekah never thought how odd it was that her best friend had told her something that hadn't happened yet, but she did know about keeping it a secret because adults never let six-year-olds do such things. But she believed in her best friend and Lynnara believed in her.

"Did you do as I've asked you?" Carla prayed Larson had.

I believed you, so we had the kidnappers followed. But we didn't interdict. I don't know why not."

With tears in her eyes, Carla begged him. "Please trust me. There's so much more going on here than appears. This is the best and only way to proceed that gives us even a chance. I don't know what's going to happen. My dreams don't tell me everything. But the light only shined on this way, everything else was in *darkness*."

Larson looked into deep brown pleading eyes and felt himself surrounded by her character. He'd loved his former wife, mourned her a whole year after a mine blew her up, but he now truly loved Carla. He took her in his arms again. "I never thought I would say this to another woman, but I think even my dearly departed wife would approve. I love you, Carla, and trust you. You tell me what to do, and even if it costs me my life, I'll do it."

She buried her face into his broad chest. "I love you, too, Larson. I love you so much, and I hardly believe my life now."

"Why didn't you want me to tell Vaughn, Carla?"

"Because there's more going on here than meets the eye, and he'll go where none of us can to hopefully uncover the deeper truth. Without that, even if we rescue Lynnara, we'll lose."

CHAPTER 15

Out of the Depths of Darkness

'And I will give power unto my two witnesses, and they shall prophesy one thousand … these are the two olive trees that stand before … and I will give power unto them, to shut the heavens, that it rain not in the days of their prophesy … and that they should smite the Earth with all manner of plagues, as often as they will …'

"John, why are you writing all of that?" He tried remaining silent while he read the first draft over his shoulder. "You've always focused on love, but what's *this?*"

John turned around in his seat, pointing his quill at him. "You ever known love to stay as love without justice? People now think Jesus is some different God than *the* God. They mistake God's patience as an open pass to be lewd, and His forgiveness as an excuse to sin again and again, instead of the means to be free of it. After all Jesus and we have suffered, *this* is what the world has fallen to. God has shown me the end so they should know it."

His friend felt like pulling his beard out. "John, I can't make heads or tails out of what you're writing, so what good is it? Do *you* even understand it? No one is going to understand *anything* from this little book you're writing. So somewhere in the future, the longer into it they go, the more foolish stories they'll spin. It takes their mind off from serving the Lord. They're either going to be looking for these prophets each day of their lives, or use this to scare people, or laugh at it as being a joke. You're talking about them traveling the whole world in a very short time! It's just preposterous!"

John smiled mischievously. "Oh, it gets worse! When they look for these prophets I write about, they'll be expecting the wrong thing! They'll never guess or understand who they are until too late! Do you know the world is going to celebrate killing them?" John was laughing now and his friend wondered if he had finally gone mad from all the stress.

"Why are you laughing? You think that's *funny?*"

"As a matter of fact I do! I write about the time when the Lord's patience finally runs out. God allows man to take his best shot at all of what he thinks is real power, even to kill his prophets, and even celebrate that until three days later when God raises those prophets back on their feet and the world finally gets to see how lame their power really is. Yes! I think the irony's kinda amusing!"

"How can *that* be love?" John's friend asked, shaking his head.

"Because God allowed them their best shot! He allowed them to achieve their goal, their ultimate pleasure, their *choice* to reject as fully and completely as possible any real understanding of goodness until the truth is finally revealed, and they know without any doubt they're wrong but it's *too late!*"

"Too late? And you still think that's funny? What's wrong with you? Do you still claim to love?"

"As a matter of fact I *do*! But only because I can rejoice in knowing what truly works and that their boast will eventually fail. They made their choice, decided what was good for them, and enjoyed it fully in their season. Don't the evil people rejoice and revel in their wickedness? Then why do you fault me for rejoicing in goodness and justice?"

When John saw he still disapproved, he became more serious. "Look, my friend, it's like this. The time to choose good or evil is always in this mortal life when the 'powers' of God, I mean all the fancy miracles and all that stuff, *aren't* apparent! This way all people deal with are the very qualities of good and evil in themselves. No fancy tricks to blind the eyes, no fire falling from heaven, no rods turning to serpents. What good did all that do anyway! Just dealing with what they are inside then they decide what's good for them. So if they managed to drive away all reasoning and understanding of the goodness they were born with or that comes to them, delightfully choosing evil to *be* their good, *then* God will finally decide to seal their fates *they* have chosen. He will reward them on the outside with what they desire to be inside. Only thing about that is when they experience that manifestation it'll be hell! Why shouldn't I rejoice at the victory that goodness has over evil? It's not like those prophets didn't tell the world the truth! In fact, they even backed it up with signs and wonders. But if you only knew how they suffer so *terribly* before they are given their final task, then, my dear friend, you would rejoice with me!"

Now his friend began to soften a bit. "The Lord showed you their lives?"

"Neither you, I, Paul, Peter, nor anyone we know, nor I dare say Elijah himself, nor *anyone* who has ever been, could have gone through what they will go through *before* they become those prophets I have just written about." And he leveled his eyes deeply into his friend. "If the Lord was able to give me a choice about being born to be them, and showed me all they would suffer, I would have declined! Even me!"

"But how do they succeed?"

"Love, my friend, and the most tenacious display of spirit that says *no matter what.*

As proper etiquette decreed, Vaughn needed to announce his arrival. Either call into the ethereal for the Highest Councilor or even Grinchback, but his desire to accommodate civilities had waned recently. *Besides, soon it won't make any difference whether they like me or not, just a few more little tweaks.*

As soon as he popped into the Highest Councilor's ethereal room, Grinchback sensed him and immediately dematerialized then rematerialized in front of Vaughn, blocking his vision. The others in the room couldn't see him either. Yet in that brief moment of arrival, Vaughn couldn't believe what he glimpsed.

ScrabaGag quickly turned around, sensing someone coming and going and only realized that his underling had just shifted in and out. "Grinchback, what are you doing? Can't you see we're busy?"

"Sorry, Master. I meant to pop into our ... ahh, I need to do some orb work."

ScrabaGag understood that his loyal offspring didn't want to mention anything about their secret room in front of Karen. It was *their* secret room now. Grinchback had rejoiced over it for days. When he winked his Eye, his Master turned back to the orb with Karen. Without turning around, Grinchback rapped his tail around Vaughn and they disappeared.

Vaughn had grown a bit more used to Grinchback's touch but was still glad when he let go. They were in the darkest room he'd ever been into so far. It took a moment for him to adjust to both the pitch blackness and having been so tightly enwrapped by the demon's tail.

Grinchback activated the orb and it cast its blue light upon them. "This is my, our secret room. I had to bring you here to keep you from *her.*"

He could see Vaughn's anger. It kept building until even Grinchback began to feel uncomfortable, and felt the need to explain. "Alright, we're friends so I'll tell you. You weren't supposed to know, but now you do... That's Karen."

"I know who the hell she is. What's that *bitch* doing here?"

Waves of very black energy vibrated from Vaughn so Grinchback cautioned him. "Look, you warned me about my color changes. Now I'll tell you. You'd better control yourself quickly. I don't know if this room can mask that kind of power you're emanating. You don't want to be found out."

Vaughn tried to calm himself. "And why's that?"

Grinchback came as close to sighing as any demon could. It was sort of a rumble with a strange sequence of rippling and shimmering. "It's… complicated, but I don't know what Master would do if you and Karen came to blows here. Besides, I don't think you want to tangle with her now. She's… got powers!"

"Powers?" His anger began to escalate again.

Grinchback found he actually had demon love for Vaughn, his only friend ever next to his Master. It was amazing what kinds of feelings a demon could have when he knows he's not allowed to eat someone. Placing the tip of his tail on Vaughn's shoulder, he begged. "Please! You must control yourself. She's been granted certain powers by Master. But I believe she's playing us and also acquired powers elsewhere, probably from her husband but my suspicion is from another Alpha as well."

Vaughn studied Grinchback. "You don't like her, do you?"

"No. I don't trust her and I don't mean it in just a general Alpha way. I know trust isn't really a quality here, but this goes way beyond that. It's just… a feeling, but Master is quite enamored with her. I think he even believes she'll mate willingly with him!"

"I don't doubt she would!" Then Vaughn refocused, stepped up to the orb then manipulated it. He watched Karen and ScrabaGag as well as what they were watching in their orb. Grinchback, thoroughly impressed with Vaughn's ease with orb functions, wondered if he had excelled even him in orb ability.

They had Stephanie's tree in their orb, but the view had been turned to the actual vision of her. She laid on her bed, looking even worse than when Vaughn left her. Once again, Grinchback placed his tail upon his friend. "I've studied you so I'm warning you now, you're not going to like any of this.

It's going be the worst experience of your life, but if you want to help her, you must *keep calm.*"

Vaughn looked at the demon wryly. "Excuse me, but why do you care? You were in on *this.*"

"It's in my nature, true, but you already told me you don't fault me for it. But now I'm convinced this is the *wrong* plan. I believe, in the end, it will destroy Master and me."

Dubious, Vaughn asked, "Why?"

"For now, just watch. You need to understand, and then we'll think of a solution if there is one."

Karen leaned into the orb then looked at ScrabaGag. "I'll show you how well I've learned." She extended her hand into the orb, then spoke in her cloying voice, *"Stephanie, it's time to wake up!"*

The faithwalker laid on her bed, still unresponsive.

"Listen, you bitch. If you don't wake up, I'll start chopping fingers and toes off your daughter, and send them to you piece by piece."

Mandy squeezed Stephanie's hand when she saw her head shaking.

Karen continued. *"I'm going to tell you what to do and you're going to do it. And I'm watching your every move, so you can't hide from me. You can't find me and you can't beat me anyway. Right now your hand is being held."*

Stephanie looked over at Mandy, fearful for her, but Mandy saw her fright. "What is it, Stephanie?"

Karen mocked. *"What is it, Stephanie?"*

Stephanie rubbed her temples. "Karen… in my head."

Mandy didn't understand. "Karen? Who's Karen?"

"Shut up!" Karen commanded.

Mandy's own fright began to build as she watched Stephanie. *Dear sweet Jesus, what's going* on?

Karen regained her sweet tone. *"From now on, you're not to tell anyone about me. Now here's what you'll do, or I'll start sending your little whelp's fingers and toes. You're going to take the whole day tomorrow into putting yourself in the right frame of mind then you're going to good Judge Matthew and ride his old bones all night."*

Mandy watched Stephanie who seemed to be listening to a voice. "Carla!"

The urgent tone in Mandy's voice brought her sister running into the room. Carla sat on the bed with Mandy and watched Stephanie, too. Larson and Rebekah stood at the doorway.

Stephanie replied to Karen through her mind so no one else could here. *"How do I know you won't…"*

"Shut up, bitch. You don't know, but you have no choice because you do know I'll carry out my threat if you don't do exactly as I say."

"You know, it's not necessary to do all this. Matthew has control of me anyway."

Karen's delight was obvious. *"Ha! How do you think he got it! I told him what to do. You know, he was actually scared of you? Besides, your little daughter ensures you don't come up with anything cute. Matthew knows about your heathen daughter, too. He thinks I'm helping rid his country of heathen. He thinks I'm God's helper and all this is God's will."*

Karen laughed and the Highest Councilor couldn't help laughing, too. He placed his tail tip ever so lightly on Karen's shoulder and she seemed to enjoy it. Stephanie heard the demon's laugh, and understanding began to dawn on her. *Oh dear Jesus. She's got to be watching me through the orb!"*

Vaughn could hear everything through *his* orb. Grinchback had to tap him on the back, quite hard at times, using actual physical pain to try to counter his rage.

Karen realized she'd never enjoyed herself quite like this. *"That's right,* slut*! I'm in the ethereal. Would you like to come here so they can eat you now or later?"* When she got no response, she continued. *"This is what you're going to do. What I mean by the right frame of mind is that when you do everything with the old Judge, I want you to enjoy it!"* She waited for Stephanie's reaction but saw none. *"You'd better have a whole lot more reaction with the Judge than what you're giving now. When you ride that delicious hunk of a righteous man, I'll be watching very closely, and I want you to really enjoy it. I'm a woman so I'll be able to tell if you're really enjoying yourself or not. If you don't, I'll cut off her thumbs and send them to you. So I suggest that maybe you find some good drugs somewhere, but oh, wait. You're in a Christian country. No drugs! But remember,* enjoy *it!"*

"Then what?"

"Don't worry about the future, dear. You have none. When I get through with you, my husband won't want you anymore, not Joshua, nor Vaughn. Then we'll see. I may not want you anymore either. You'll be free." And Karen couldn't help the most ironic, self-satisfied laugh possible when the clearest picture came to her of what Stephanie was going to become on the inside, from the *inside out.*

"What about Lynnara?"

"Don't question me. All you know is that if you don't do as I say, you'll be the cause of her suffering. Oh, one more thing… If you somehow manage to find where she's at and you're thinking of popping in to rescue her, or even getting close through the corridor, help yourself." Karen then turned to the demon. "Now turn the view back into her tree and see what it looks like!"

The Highest Councilor waved his arm and peered in amazement. Stephanie's tree, which for so long had been so bright that he couldn't even look at it, had only a faint glow throughout. Many branches were on the ethereal ground, broken off. The only strange thing was, though they should have been dead and gray, the branches still had that dull glow albeit no longer connected to her tree. This manifestation was not recorded in *The Forest,* the manual for proper tree pruning. Her roots looked similar, only there was a frantic mixture of blackness, odd grayness, and very dull glow. The Highest Councilor pointed to the gray in her roots. "Impressive. This gray shows her heart has accepted us. Gray belongs to us."

Feeling it all, Vaughn wept bitterly, but then extended his hand out into the orb. Grinchback's arm quickly snatched it back. "If you do that, they'll sense you're watching."

As the Highest Councilor's admiration for Karen shimmered all over him, and his tail tip vibrated on her shoulder, she looked at him brazenly. "You're very good with that tail of yours!"

Once again ScrabaGag's Eye widened as he felt her deeper thoughts. But he wasn't Highest Councilor for nothing, and shook off the moment to address more relevant concerns.

"I've studied her extensively. Not only can she pop in and out, she can…"

Karen lost her mood. "I know what she can do! I was there when she rescued that brat before. But my husband, well, let's just say he's shown me a few tricks. You know the glowing netting he uses to keep our pet demon locked away?"

ScrabaGag frowned at her, but nodded. *Pet? You little bitch!*

"Well, it keeps him from escaping. He can't pop out either. Well, I had Jargono… ahhh, let's just say he showed me a trick or two. Same kind of netting around the brat except in reverse. Nothing can get in! *Nothing!*"

Vaughn shook his head then looked at Grinchback, and actually sensed something akin to real friendship, or at least a common cause. "I still don't understand. Why do you care?"

Grinchback readjusted the orb and played back Stephanie's encounter with the Judge in his secret basement room. Vaughn backed away from the orb and fell to his knees, hardly able to watch, but knowing he had to. Grinchback studied him. *Love. I don't know if I really want to understand something so painful. But then what am I doing trying to protect Master? Hmmm.*

Vaughn didn't understand until the end of the encounter when the Seed to the Tree of Life disappeared. This picture suddenly became a much wider puzzle than just their own welfare. His oath to protect the Seed burned in him.

Grinchback tuned the orb to Karen talking to ScrabaGag. "You see? You couldn't bring her down. The more you did to her, the more *glow* she got, but *I* brought her down. You couldn't get your hands on the sacred treasure, but *I* have it now. Give me the rest of my power!" It was a command, not a request.

The Highest Councilor laughed, clearly smitten. "A deal is a deal. Half before, half after. When I have the cursed object in my grasp, you'll get the rest of the power I promised you. And there's another concern. Your *husband* wants the treasure as well."

"He still doesn't even know what it is. He doesn't know anything about what I'm doing." She gave the demon a coy look. "Some things he knows and some he doesn't!"

Vaughn still didn't understand. "This still doesn't tell me why you care. You all seem to have won everything."

Grinchback shook his bulbous head. "Master isn't thinking with his Great Eye but with his great… desire. It's too easy. I don't believe Karen will deliver the object to him. She's out for power, and there's someone here more powerful than my Master besides the Father."

"HrorrarrAggrang."

"Yes, and I feel he's got to be deeply involved, and I believe this even ties into your investigation because he couldn't care less about Karen but *much* about those above! Which means, that *Seed* must give HrorrarrAggrang some kind of advantage. Also, something on *this* scale takes *very* long term planning. It's HrorrarrAggrang's work, and that means Master is somehow ending up on the wrong side of the Eye because something on *this* scale always needs a fall-demon to sacrifice. Not that there is any *love* between HrorrarrAggrang and my Master."

Vaughn watched him, and said, "And that means you, too."

"Precisely. HrorrarrAggrang will gain the cursed object… ahhh, your sacred object, but Master will never allow it.

As we discovered before, somehow the Father is backing HrorrarrAggrang since he can't afford to lose his last Eye into Heaven. This can only end up badly for us, *all of us*, except for HrorrarrAggrang and the Father. They will acquire the object, but I believe, to cover their tracks or to make amends in the current trial, they will sacrifice my Master and me. They'll eat us but *also* your glowing friend Mafferan in the name of restoring the balance!"

Vaughn appeared doubtful of the last part of his *friend's* conclusion but Grinchback knew his thoughts and shook his bulbous head, saying, "The proof against your *glowing* friend is fairly solid, I think. On further orb investigation, I discovered that when your wife … ahhh, Stephanie, turned the Black River into stone, she had help! In the very corner of the orb's scope of vision is a glowing hand, masterfully masked but I unmasked it. I blew it up, and compared the prints to Mafferan's, which I retrieved from when he manipulated our orb. Also, the reappearance of the Seed to the Tree of Life is in question.

"You can verify this if you want by going through HrorrarrAggrang's file which I'm sure has a complete record of heavenly events. I'm sure Mafferan brought another Seed down from the Tree of Life in heaven which is a *clear* violation of the truce. What stays above and below *must* stay above and below except if somehow procured by man alone. My Master's former Master GrrraGagag was very clever, and used Jargono to introduce the Black Oil into the Earth and thereby had human demons created, but Mafferan *directly* brought that second Seed out of heaven."

Vaughn stared deeply into Grinchback's Great Eye, "Let's say you're right… then you ought to be happy about all that. What's your problem? I'm sure you can figure out how to avoid being consumed."

"This might sound odd, perhaps surprising, but I trust Mafferan far more than HrorrarrAggrang! We're going to need Mafferan's help! I believe he has the power to come against HrorrarrAggrang, saving Master and me. But I haven't the faintest idea how to bring any of this about, and as soon as the Seed arrives here in the ethereal, it'll be too late. Hrorrar-rAggrang will claim it then identify it as being Heavenly, not Earthly. Mafferan will be condemned but HrorrarrAggrang will also accuse Master of hiding its knowledge from the Father all along, which both of us certainly did hide, and other things as well. In the spirit of *justice*, both ours and yours, the Father will demand that HrorrarrAggrang eat my Master for his part in the deception, but also for the provocations on Earth, and eat me because I was actually the catalyst that caused Stephanie to turn the Black River to stone! In essence, they will sacrifice my Master and me so that Mafferan can be *consumed!* In the name of restoring the balance. Actually, I really don't see how this *isn't* the most just solution because we have all equally offended, even if our side can claim certain petty nuances of remaining within the rules. "

Grinchback studied Vaughn a moment to see if he was following everything but all Vaughn did was simply nod slowly. That's all! So Grinchback continued, "I also sent Mafferan a hidden message within his summons that I meant to try to help him. But honestly, I don't know what to do now.

Things are far more complex than I first thought because I didn't understand about HrorrarrAggrang." Grinchback paused, Eyeing his only true friend with something akin to a plea for help. "Mafferan has placed his trust in you for some reason. That can only mean that you're very special, indeed. Don't take this the wrong way because it's a compliment. If I had my choice of eating anyone, it would be you."

Vaughn actually laughed, slapping the young demon hard on the back and into the stinging blue orb again. He grabbed him before Grinchback could fully disappear into it. "Sorry!"

"I think you do that on purpose!"

Vaughn smiled. "Thinking is good!"

Grinchback had to ask. "Well, you have any idea what to do, any kind of plan?"

Vaughn smiled wickedly. "It'll take further adjusting due to the new circumstances, but as a matter of fact, I do, at least for all this upstairs, downstairs stuff. But in order to make it in time, you're gonna have to help me. And if we succeed, I'm going to feed you someone!"

The underling's Eye dramatically drooled. "You would do that for me?"

Vaughn's grin looked truly evil. "Oh yes! Now, this is what we have to do." Vaughn brought up Grinchback's schematic of all the orbs and their connections. "I need you to make the following adjustments here, here, and here, like this!"

The young demon didn't understand. *He* has *surpassed me!* "What will this do?"

"I'm sorry, but for your own good, I can't tell you. Listen, Grinchback." Vaughn grabbed the demon by a ripple, pulling him close, ignoring the pain. The gesture, though not hostile, nonetheless surprised the demon by its raw intensity. Vaughn's stare into his Great Eye seemed to reach to his very depths! "You don't want to know *anything* about what I do. Because every demon will want to eat you, even if they only suspect you know, so they can gain your knowledge. Do you hear me, Grinchback?"

This reminded him of his Master's similar warning when dealing with HrorrarrAggrang. He bowed his Great Eye to Vaughn. "Yes Sir! And I'll do as you've told me!"

"We have less than a day to pull this all off. We have to do this before the Seed arrives and before…" Vaughn couldn't bring himself to say it, but Grinchback understood he meant before Stephanie could go through with Karen's order.

"But how will you stop Karen? I believe she's more powerful than you, my friend. And even if you harm her, you'll also have Jargono to fight. You won't make it."

Vaughn leveled his eye into the demon's. "If I have to die, I will. I swore an oath to protect her. Do you understand?"

"Perhaps. And that's asking a lot from an Alpha."

☙

Rebekah refused to eat and even her older brothers couldn't persuade her. Her father knew where Lynnara was being held captive, some small building at the north end of the Judge's compound, but she didn't know how to get there. Her dad grew suspicious of her questions and wouldn't say any more. Time was running out. This was the second day. Lynnara told her she had to do something *this* second day. She was already so hungry from not eating yesterday.

Eleven years old and blond hair like his father, the oldest brother, Bruce, grew fretful. Ever since their mother died, his love for his sister had grown stronger. She reminded him so much of their mother, whom he'd never got to see often because it had to be a secret that he belonged to his mother's people. He told their brother Michael, nine-years-old, that, "Rebekah is simply special. We have to make sure she grows up strong and safe."

Rebekah tried to make a deal with Bruce. "Show me where Lynnara is and I'll eat." Being pretty smart, Bruce went out early in the morning to the mail station. He began asking how people there knew how to deliver the mail to everyone. Slowly, he worked his way to asking how the Judges got their mail, seeing as how they had so many buildings. They showed him the addresses on a large postal map of the compound. Every building was labeled. From the station, Bruce walked across town searching for the building he knew some of his father's men were watching. His unsuspecting father had earlier told him how he hid his men, explaining a bit of the art of spying. By mid-morning, Bruce had returned, told everyone he and Rebekah were going for a walk, and out the door they went. "You promise you'll eat if I just show you?" he asked her. "You always keep your word, Rebekah."

"I always keep my word. I'll eat over at Lady Stephanie's after you show me."

But once on their way, Rebekah made him stop first at Stephanie's before going to the building, telling Bruce it wouldn't be polite to come for lunch unannounced, so they needed to tell her they'd come later to eat. But really, Rebekah needed to know the way from Stephanie's house to Lynnara. *Oh, my brother's gonna kill me but I gave my word to Lynnara first. I always keep my word.*

Lady Stephanie didn't look well. All she did was lay in bed and stare at nothing. Her face and eyes were all red and she wore a regular black dress, nothing like the beautiful embroidered Appendaho dresses that Rebekah loved so much. Neither was her hair neat and pretty like always.

Rebekah grew really worried and wanted to tell Lady Stephanie that she'd get Lynnara back but her friend told her not to tell anybody because no adults would understand. She pulled on Stephanie's arm, got no response, but told her anyway. "I love you like you're my own Mommy. I'll be back for lunch."

True to their agreement, Bruce guided her down several streets, carefully sneaked through some yards, and pointed out their father's spies and the little brick building with a guard standing at each side of the door. Rebekah never watched anything so closely as she studied the route that led to her best friend. Satisfied, she told her brother, "I'm hungry."

Carla, who was not looking much better than Lady Stephanie, took them to the kitchen and made lunch. Rebekah felt her little heart hurting since she loved Carla, too. She inquired about Mandy and was told that she was at the military compound trying to stir up more help.

After the meal, the little girl thanked Carla but looked very sleepy. "I wanna lay down with Lady Stephanie for a bit."

Even as Carla disagreed, Rebekah had already excused herself and went into Stephanie's bedroom. She climbed onto the bed, and tried to console Stephanie who was weeping on her pillow, unable to find a way to twist herself into someone who could obey Karen's command. "Please don't cry, Stephie."

Not long after she lay down, both Carla and Bruce peeked in. Thinking Rebekah was asleep, her brother said, "I'll come back in a couple hours. She's been real upset so I think she'll sleep a good while."

Rebekah had petted Stephanie's head until Stephanie fell asleep, although against her will. She studied her face to make sure she was definitely asleep then kissed Stephie on her cheek. "Don't worry. Remember that you taught us about faith?"

Little Rebekah opened the bedroom door a crack, saw Carla weeping on her knees, then crept down the hall into the study. Seeing the little stand that Lynnara had told her about where her Mommy kept her special things, Rachael opened its drawer. There seemed to be so many interesting things inside but she didn't have time to investigate now. She crept back down the hall, stopped by Lynnara's room to pick up her favorite stuffed black and white doggy, then tiptoed out and down the back stairs. Remembering clearly how Ranger Vaughn had told her a whole year ago how to pray, how you just talk to God inside, she began, *Dear God, help me do what Lynnara told me. She's the best friend I ever have so help us. We need to be person's inside our bodies for a long time, because we got things to do. Lots of things. Because Stephanie and Carla and Mandy need us. Because they're so sad… Oh, and all the things we got to do, they're all good things God. You'd like them.*

Down the street she went, not too fast and not too slow. No one seemed to notice the little girl who talked and played with her stuffed animal, and appeared to know exactly where she was going. Rebekah studied each turn she made, replaying in her mind where her brother had led her earlier. When she got to where she could see the building, she knew her father's men would see her if she came out into the open.

I got to do this quick or they'll stop me. She sighed. *I wish grownups would understand better. OK, here we go, Doggy.* She ran straight across the street and straight up to the guards at the door who wore regular work clothing, but had a hardened look about them. Larson's spies froze.

"Go 'way, kid. What you doin' here?" Seeing a little girl come out of nowhere just didn't make sense. But it was about to get even more surprising.

"I came to play with Lynnara!" The little child waited, staring both men in the eyes.

They didn't know how to respond so Rebekah knew she had to say more, but Lynnara hadn't told her what else to say. Pointing at the door, she added in her normal little voice like she knew exactly what she was doing, "She's in there, and needs someone to play with. I'm supposed to play with her."

The two men looked at each other, then at the little girl in her white, frilly dress, squeezing a stuffed toy. "This is Doggy. Do you like dogs? I can make her do tricks. Watch." Rebekah began giving commands like 'sit' and 'shake'.

Obviously not a fan of little ones and in no mood to play, one of them complained. "Damn it! Why don't they tell us? Do this, don't ask questions. Kill anyone who gets close. Now they send a kid to play with her?" One guard eyed Rebekah closely as the other unlocked the door, let her in, and then quickly locked it again. Larson's men watched in a mixture of horror and amazement, creating various explanations for Rebekah being there, but of course not getting the truth. This was strictly the plan of two small children.

It worked! I knew they didn't want to play. Two more men just as ugly as the first two immediately towered over her. Two large hands grabbed her by the arms and lifted her up to eye level.

Her heart beating fast, and close to crying, Rebekah knew she looked scared. Being so close to the ugly man's face, she could feel all his evil, and smell his bad breath, too. It reminded her of another time she felt totally surrounded by evil. Her Mommy had led her through the minefield, and she had asked her, "Are *you* scared, Mommy?"

Her mommy told her the truth. "Yes, of course. But doing what I have to do is more important. I love you, Rebekah."

She had thought a lot about that since. *I love you, Lynnara, my bestest friend.* Rebekah wondered if her Mommy was floating nearby, watching her. *I'll be just like you, Mommy. Do what I have to do.*

The Man's hands were hurting her arms and her shoulders began to ache, but Rebekah wasn't scared any more. *Because I'm a person and I'm gonna float with Mommy one day.* Her heart knew being afraid of bad people was wrong because they really couldn't hurt her person as long as she was good. She pushed the stuffed doggy into the man's face. "This is Doggy. She won't make a mess. I'm here to play with Lynnara."

The burly man jerked his head out of the toy's way, looking at his partner, who said, "Must be OK else they wouldn't have let her in."

In a harsh voice, the man tried speaking around the doggy. "How'd you know to come here?"

Rebekah didn't know where her words came from. "I was told to." *Now would be a good time to cry, I feel like crying anyway.* She buried her face into Doggy, letting out shrill wails. "I want to play! I was told to be here. You're hurting me!"

The intensity of her cries seemed to shock the two grown men. One backed up a bit, putting his hand to an ear, trying to blunt the sudden pain. The other quickly put her down, saying to his buddy, "That's why I never go home, damn it! I *hate* kids!" He glared at Rebekah. "OK, brat. Go down the hall, then turn that way. Go to the end and knock on the last door. Get going!"

Rebekah glared at the man. *I'm gonna remember your face. I'm gonna tell Ranger Vaughn. You're gonna be* sorry! And down the hall she went, but knowing what to expect. *More bad men. Mommy died getting away from bad men to save me. I'll die trying to save Lynnara if I have to.* She knocked on the door. No answer so she knocked louder. Still no answer so she reached up to try the handle but it wouldn't turn. She then stepped back and began kicking at the door.

Finally, she heard a latch turn. The door cracked open then swung wide. A fat, droopy-eyed man, looking very much as if he'd just woken up, shouted at her for disturbing his rest. "*What?*"

Rebekah would have none of it. *I'm not scared of you, you big, fat, ugly man.* "I'm here to play with Lynnara. And if you hurt me, someone's gonna be *real* mad."

"Thank God! I thought that brat would never shut up! And I can't get to her to wring her little neck!" He turned his head back toward the room, mocking Lynnara's words, trying to sound like her, "The demons are going to eat you. I've seen them, you know." He turned back to Rebekah. "I don't know where a little girl gets all that crap, but don't you go listening to it. Find something little girls talk about."

Finally, the big oaf stepped aside and Rebekah could see into the room. "C'mon, c'mon, I'm not supposed to unlock this door except when absolutely necessary."

Rebekah's heart felt the coldness of the small, dank, cinderblock room with its bare concrete floor, single hanging light bulb, with only a wooden chair beside the door and a metal cage barely tall enough for her friend to stand in. She had seen such cages in a pet store, except the wire mesh faintly glowed with an odd greenish light that every so often flickered with blue, yellow and black sparks.

Lynnara, still in her blue jean jumpers slowly got to her feet, pushing objects aside: a large red pillow, a doggy bowl, a raggedy gray blanket, and a small bucket.

As Rebekah drew closer, the man cautioned her. "You'll have to play on the outside because you can't get in and if you touch that cage, it'll hurt."

Standing just inches from the cage, the children's eyes met and everything else seemed to disappear as their thoughts mingled together as one. *Oh God, you're in a doggy cage. I knew you would come. How we gonna get out? Don't worry, everything will be OK.*

Lynnara whined to the man. "I have to go potty."

"You just went," he quipped.

Reaching under the blanket, she pulled out a roll of paper. "I have to go *again*." Her tone was somewhere between whining and ordering. "I can't go if you're *here*."

The man shook his head. "Fine! I have to go, too." On his way out, he slammed the door then locked it.

Rebekah grabbed the cage without thinking, shrieked, and fell quickly backward to the floor.

"Over here!" Lynnara pointed to a one foot by one foot opening in the cage. "Over here. Put your hands through here."

Her best friend crawled over then stuck her hands through the hole.

"Don't cry, Rebekah! I know what to do. I've seen Mommy do it." Little Lynnara rubbed at her chest a moment as if feeling for something. She took her friend's hands and bowed her little head. *Dear Lord, please help Rebekah from hurting.* Never having done anything like this, Lynnara had no forethought, only the present feeling that it should be. Her hands began to glow brightly.

Rebekah's crying softened then stopped. "How'd you do that?

Lynnara smiled. "I didn't. I asked God. He did it."

"Thanks. And we got important things to do. That's why we're still persons in our bodies."

Lynnara nodded. "I know. Did you bring it?"

Rebekah nodded, patting at her waist. "I brought Doggy, too, because I couldn't bring Spot." Vaughn's real dog had been crucial in his escape from Jargono and rescue of Rebekah but Spot was still up North now. Vaughn felt the dog could be more useful helping others escape

"I miss Spot. He'd bite this man if he was here."

Nodding, the six-year-old began to pull up her dress to get to what she had brought.

"Not yet, Rebekah. It's not time yet."

"How d'ya know?"

She shrugged her little shoulders. "I just know." Lynnara took down her jumpers and squatted over the bucket. "I hate going like this but that fat man hates taking it out even more." Lynnara made a yucky face, and Rebekah burst out laughing.

As if on cue, the man came back and Lynnara commanded him, shoving the little bucket through the opening. "I'm done! Take this out!"

He glared at her while Rebekah turned away, trying to hold her laughter in. After the guard left again, she said with glee, "When he comes back, I'll go next!"

Both girls rolled on the floor in laughter. "Make it a real stinky one."

The fat guard returned and just as he carefully began to put the pan through the opening, Rebekah announced, "I have to go, too!"

He stood up quickly, and glared at her. "I don't have to let you play together, you know."

"Yes you do! Because if you don't, you'll get in trouble."

"*Two* little bitches." He dropped the plastic pan then began to leave but Rebekah called after him.

"I take a long time. Don't come back too soon. I think I have to go *a lot*."

The door slammed again, but with even more force.

"I don't even know really how I did it when I saved Mommy, but she does it easy. But I can't do it at all like her because she doesn't even use the ribbon anymore."

Rebekah pulled up her dress then squatted over the bucket, revealing Stephanie's blue and gold hair ribbon tied around her waist. She took one end of the ribbon in her free hand. "It feels so special."

"It is, but we have to both pray real hard for it to work. And we both hold on."

"But how you gonna get out? I don't think anything can get out of that." She pointed at the cage.

Lynnara shook her head. "No, watch!" She placed her hands smartly against the cage.

Rebekah gasped but nothing happened. "See? Nothing can get in, but I think I can get out if I could get through the bars. The ribbon will get me through and take us away from here."

Rebekah finished with the bucket and tissue, and walked back up to the cage. She tested a theory. Carefully sticking her index finger into a space between the wire mesh but not touching any of the wires still made the black and blue sparks shoot out, and she jerked her finger back, rubbing it.

Lynnara shook her head again. "The same thing happens to me if I stick my finger through, then pull it back. It really hurts."

The door unlocked and a very unhappy man was directed by two demanding little girls to take the bucket away. He eyed

Rebekah to the point that she found herself backing away. "I can't get to her inside that cage but I can get to you. Maybe I don't care about the trouble I'll get into!"

After he left, the girls turned to each other, speaking the same words. "We better get out of here."

"Take the ribbon off and pass me an end through here. It's real hard to do and I almost got eaten by the demon before it worked, but this is what I did." Lynnara sat down and held the ribbon up to her cheek and began to rock back and forth then she looked at Rebekah. "I'm praying real hard. Mommy says there's special Oil in this ribbon and that's what does it. But we have to want to leave real, *real* bad for a good reason or I don't think it'll work. Because right before the demon got to us, I *really* wanted to save Mommy, and then *poof!*"

"Where'd you go?" Rebekah asked.

"That's another thing. I don't know… a beautiful cave. But Mommy got us out. Maybe, if I just think hard enough about being with Mommy, we'll go to *her*."

Rebekah held the long blue and gold ribbon to her face, too, rocking, thinking only of Stephanie and saving Lynnara who thought only of her Mommy and saving Rebekah.

The guard returned, and eyed the strange play. "What in God's name?" He shook his head, sat down on his chair, and went to sleep.

After a while, Lynnara stopped. "This isn't working. Can you think of another way out?"

CHAPTER 16

More Than Meets the Eye

The difficulty presented by everything being bathed in eternal light arises when secrecy serves every good meaning's best interest, and further difficulty manifests when the only saint able to hold this secret has a wife who's special gift is unveiling the truth no matter how well hidden.

The Lord whispered to Mafferan to appear within His brightest chamber, a place reserved only for special creatures. The Holy Father and the Lord Jesus meet there to discuss certain aspects of what appears to be mysteries to us, a place where no one could see into, and no saint or anyone else had ever entered until now.

Upon popping in, Mafferan went on single knee, fully overwhelmed by the honor and glory but also already beginning to receive foreknowledge. He nodded his head as the truth in him began more deeply to agree with the greater truth being revealed. A certain amount of time went by, but upstairs one could never be sure of how much really passed, then Mafferan raised his head.

The Holy Father concluded. "That's what we have to deal with. Do you have any thoughts as to how we might proceed?"

The Lord Jesus, who'd just recently ascended, spoke next. "We are always true to our nature, and light cannot hide nor deceive. The black light of our Light, which is the Light of Justice, is not the blackness of evil. We must create a solution this week."

Still on one knee, Mafferan replied. "Parables."

"Explain," Both Spirits spoke as one.

"On Earth you spoke in parables. They were light, but their meaning was always hidden from darkness because they have no ability to see into them."

The Son of God responded with an amused smile. "A truce cannot be drawn in parables."

"True, but the words can be such that each side will see *their* truth within the same words, even though those *truths* are vastly different."

"Then make it so Mafferan, and let our secret be ours and ours alone until the day when you must seek *him* out. Behold…" They spoke as one again, showing him an image of a young man yet to be born some two-thousand years into the future. "Your wife Yinauqua has our gift to uncover the truth, no matter what, and you cannot withstand it. But if she discovers the truth, all will be lost, for then the ethereal sight into heaven will see it. The Lord blesses you to hide it from the ethereal, but cannot bless you to hide it from her. What will you do?"

"When the time comes, the only thing I can do which is the hardest thing for me to do… I shall run from her!" Mafferan laughed, and added. "She can only discover the truth if she can catch me!"

"We've made her to always be able to find, and *catch* you."

Is that a hint of a smile on the Lord's face? Mafferan stood up and held his hands out, asking for the obvious.

"Very well, the Lord blesses you to be able to outrun your wife… regarding *this* matter."

Stephanie kept seeing Lynnara's bloody fingers and toes being sent to her. *But if this didn't involve Lynnara, just my people's safety, would I still be going through with this? Probably. I was already doing it… but not feeling like* this *though.* She realized it would be impossible to 'make herself enjoy it.' Karen ordered that part to put her through the torture of trying. Hours of twisting her thoughts and feelings simply couldn't produce anything that lasted to allow her to take any pleasure. The Holy Spirit and her love for it kept rejecting such changes, no matter how badly a part of her tried to hold them. *I'll fake it as best I can. Oh dear Jesus, let this shame pass from me one day. One day? How am I to escape this?* However, the complications far exceeded Karen's personal revenge and any escape from it.

Stephanie now realized that from the start, this was about stealing the Seed to the Tree of Life, though she couldn't figure out how Matthew knew. When Matthew said he'd force her into his bed, the plan for the theft had already begun. *But why take Lynnara? Is that really just for her sadistic pleasure? And who has the Seed now? I'm* its *sworn protector! Oh dear God, what have I done? I should've* never *taken it off.*

As she slowly walked down the darkening street to the Judge's quarters, she couldn't believe how hopeless she felt.

The facility and quickness with which she changed from feeling full of worth to feeling worthless left her wondering. *Lord Jesus, why? I don't understand.*

She reached for her chest, but didn't feel the Seed to the Tree of Life between her breasts. *Oh, how I miss you. Where are you? If it wasn't for Lynnara being involved…* then it dawned on her.

That bitch! *She's the one who must have stolen the Seed. Lynnara's the only thing that could keep me from going after it.* Stephanie stopped in mid-stride. The only reason she hadn't considered this sooner was that the Seed was stolen a whole day before Karen appeared in her head and all the focus had been on her *love* affair with the good judge.

Karen was actually quite amazed at Stephanie's stupidity. *You should keep walking to the Judge's quarters! Do you want to test my patience?*

Stephanie knew she couldn't take the chance, so her feet decided for her, though her mind considered tracking Karen into the ethereal.

Yet Karen could read her every thought through the orb, just as if Stephanie spoke them clearly, so she answered within Stephanie's mind again. *Come on up! I'll guide you if you like! But your brat is hidden away and you won't like what will happen to her even if you could beat me, and you can't!*

Why have you taken it?

Now you're referring to the brat as 'it'?

You know very well what I mean.

Perhaps I do, but that doesn't make any difference to you right now, does it? You know what I will do if you don't do as I've told you. Do you know that your tree was too bright for the demons to read? But not too bright for me! All your glow *doesn't affect me like it does them. They've been delighted with all I could tell them about you.*

Why are you doing this to me? I've never…

Shut up! I don't have to explain myself to you.

Stephanie felt Karen's hatred, not just through the tone of voice in her head, but as if actually touched by it. *Why does she hate me so much? Not even being able to ask her… like I'm* less *than nothing.* But even more disconcerting was having no privacy on any level at all. *I've always considered, at least, that my thoughts were private. Even Jargono couldn't get into my head.*

Karen laughed and spoke in her mind. *You're so much fun. I'm going to enjoy watching you fuck the good old Judge. I can't wait to see all the stuff you're going to do together. You'd better do your best to enjoy it. I'll know what you're thinking!*

Stephanie remembered the barrier she'd automatically erected to keep Jargono out of her consciousness but this was different. This was the blue orb enabling Karen to hear her every thought, see her every feeling. Hmmm. *Can the orb translate feelings?* Stephanie remembered how Jargono misread the blackness in her tree.

Stop it!

Stop what?

You know very well.

Dear Jesus, I think certain feelings block her, or rather, if I can just think in feelings…

Ha! Think in feelings? The only feeling *you're going to do is with the jowly, sexy Judge between your legs.* Karen laughed so joyfully Stephanie couldn't help but stop walking again, her anger overpowering her.

Come on up! Follow my feeling, and you'll be here in a flash, I know. Come on!

Stephanie wanted to, but didn't understand why she didn't, or why her feet carried her to knock on the Judge's door.

"Come in, my dear Stephanie. Right on time! I hope we truly enjoy this time. And why not since it's inevitable?"

No sooner had she closed the door than the Judge disappeared down the secret passageway knowing she had to follow. Stephanie, like even the most faithful on rare occasions, couldn't avoid feeling abandoned. It wasn't that she didn't know abandonment, since her father had left her when she was seven. Yet upon maturing and resolving her father issues, she had traded in the wounds of a seemingly distant past for a deep appreciation, a profound knowing of God's goodness. But now the apparent disappearance of mercy staggered any mental or emotional attempt to reach for... *What's there to reach for?*

Even being strangled by a real demon, his pure vileness squeezing her to death as his all-consuming Great Black Eye began to taste her essence, couldn't compare to this. She beat that demon by surrendering to the Spirit of God's Love. *But what is there to surrender to now? Why have You fors...* She stopped the words in her heart, and recalled instead that after she'd received the Holy Ghost, a demon had demanded Stephanie surrender with the Seed to the Tree of Life in exchange for Lynnara, and she had angrily accused God of bringing her to such impasse. *That ended up working out for the better though. I didn't know then, but how can any of* this *work for the better? Lynnara is a hostage. My people are hostages…* And every step descending to his lower chambers replayed the corrosive turmoil from the last time, except this time, *I know this time he won't send me away.*

And Karen's voice stretched the limits of her sanity. *You really are a mess now, aren't you? Where's your lofty nobility now? Where's all that phony high-minded* faith *you always used to* drip? *You need me to cut off one of your daughter's little fingers just to* inspire *you to enjoy it?*

Once again the question came back to Stephanie. *Lord, why have You…* She cut off the question yet again.

That's right, go ahead and ask. Why has God forsaken *you? Don't worry. I won't!*

Stephanie's innards convulsed on the edge of a break down, but she couldn't for everyone else's sake. *But to what end? Does my sacrifice do anything but prolong…*

Say it, dear, The inevitable. *You don't have a choice. God has disappeared and you're mine now,* all *mine.*

On the one hand, Stephanie became highly self-conscious of her previous error in accusing God. At the same time, Karen's invasion of her mind scrambled her senses so that she felt she was walking on broken pieces of floating ice, and each time she was forced to focus on the present, on the good Judge, she lost her footing. She couldn't tell what kept her from falling but knew she had to keep jumping from one piece of ice to another.

Not even realizing she stood before the Judge's bed, she finally gazed upon him without his righteous black robe or any covering at all, and saw him aroused. Nothing could have prepared her for this sight, for this physical manifestation of reality that carved a gaping wound in her heart and a bottomless pit into her stomach.

And then there was Karen's voice again. *Yummy! Get to it. Climb aboard!*

"Disrobe slowly for me. We have all night."

Karen's voice appeared in the Judge's head and he responded. "Hmm, that would be delicious."

Stephanie's eyes opened wide, realizing the Judge wasn't speaking to her. She asked him, "Talking to yourself?"

"No, to the angel who's given me victory."

As Stephanie heard Karen laugh, it was a clear admission to her that she was his angel. Suddenly, Stephanie blazed red fire all around her.

Abruptly startled, the Judge shrank but Karen's warning sliced through Stephanie's heart. *Lose the fire or Lynnara loses some toes!*

Just as quickly, the fire vanished and Matthew's ardor revived with even more confidence. "I think, after we're finished, we ought to talk about what to do with all that power you have. But right now, I can only think of what you can give me here. My angel tells me you have the power to increase my pleasure immensely."

Stephanie remembered how Jargono had used his faith-walking abilities to intensely ramp up her physical desire, throwing her to the edge of being overpowered from within. "I'd have to study on that a bit. I've never…"

"Take your time. We have all night. Now slowly remove your underclothes."

From the moment after Stephanie dropped her last undergarment, everything became a blur. Even Karen's taunts seemed to lose their effect though she didn't seem too perturbed by it. The Judge began guiding Stephanie from one prolonged act to the next, anxiously desiring to know her, thinking that these intimate actions would give him her power. "Take me in slowly. I want to savor every moment."

❧

After a while, Lynnara stopped. "This isn't working. Can you think of another way out?"

"What are we going to do?" Rebekah's heart began to pound. "You said we have to leave by tonight." She looked over at the fat man sleeping against the door. She just knew if they didn't escape, really bad things would happen.

"Don't cry, Rebekah. I think it always gets bad like this first. Remember I told you I thought I was going to get burned up but Mommy rescued me. Remember you said your Mommy got blowed up and you thought you were going to die, too, but Vaughn rescued you."

It was beginning to feel a lot like then for Rebekah, only this time her best friend might die, too. And she knew that Lynnara being away was killing Stephanie who kept repeating her daughter's name. Rebekah shook off her tears and upset and looked at her best friend with steel in her little eyes. "We have to save your Mommy. She's dying without you. I can tell."

They rocked and rocked, and prayed but still nothing happened. Both girls began to cry, feeling the reality of failure. The man woke up abruptly, his sleep being disturbed *again*.

His face contorted, and the angry man rose, then kicked his chair away from the door so hard that it shattered. Rebekah froze as he scowled at her. "I'll teach you." He grabbed the child by the hair then mashed her face against the cage. "How you like that, little *bitch?*" Rebekah dropped the ribbon, barely able to draw breath, then her little lungs filled with more air than seemed possible and she screeched and squirmed in utter agony.

Little Lynnara could feel all her best friend's pains and she wailed, putting her hand to her own pounding chest, and rubbed it real hard. "*Rebekah! … Rebekah!*" Lynnara screamed louder and louder, peering into Rebekah's eyes that were frozen in abject fear and torment, barely looking like Rebekah at all!

Without any more hesitation, Lynnara slammed herself against the cage, and pressed the ribbon against Rebekah's face, forcing her little fingers through the spaces of the cage to press it as tightly as she could. The pain in her little fingers from the cage's energy made her shriek in agony, too, but she wouldn't let go. "Mommy!" she cried. The pain kept telling her to pull her hand away, but she kept pressing the ribbon harder. "*Mommy!*" Until feeling so much pain and knowing she couldn't possibly continue on, she wailed with all she had left, deciding she would die in this last act. "*MOMMY!*"

As the children disappeared, their last cries echoed in the room. The fat, ugly man looked around in disbelief, and wondered if he could escape, but everyone knew he was ordered not to leave.

Rebekah and Lynnara kept screaming, not yet realizing the source of their torment no longer existed, nor knowing where they were. Hearing their horrendous cries momentarily froze Matthew and Stephanie in position, but she twisted to look over and found there in the middle of the floor sat both young girls.

Livid, Karen still determinedly told the Judge. *This changes nothing. You still have control over her.*

"That's right!" So aroused from anticipation, he reached up and grabbed Stephanie by the hips to force himself inside her.

Oh, God! I can't let the children see this.

But Karen warned Stephanie. *You'd better or I'll have the good Judge destroy…* But suddenly, not only her voice, but even the feeling of her presence were cut off.

Stephanie finally noticed Matthew's feverish attempts to gain her, and her red fire became as clearly evident as the deadly coldness in her tone. "Remember I told you I have limits. Not tonight, *not* with the children here. I don't give a damn anymore. You choose. Die now, or have me later!"

Judge Matthew knew it was no bluff, and he nodded as he immediately lost his affection to his fear. Stephanie bounded off him, stretched forth her hand, and was clothed in a flash. The children, just beginning to realize they were no longer against the cage, felt Lady Stephanie's arms around them. "I'm here," she softly said then the three of them disappeared.

↩

Vaughn knew he was late, but not having slept in more than a day did little to improve his mood, and fear for Stephanie competed with concern for the fate of all humanity. No one knew the changes he had in mind, changes that would alter the course of history. *Damn it! If we've been forced into this God-forsaken position, then I'm damn well going to do* exactly *as I want.*

He had summoned King Mafferan and the Highest Councilor to meet as quickly as possible. Not knowing that Yinauqua had to be placed under Cloud Walker's guard, Vaughn didn't understand why Mafferan had been delayed.

To place anyone under guard was unheard of in heaven, but the gravity in Mafferan's eyes almost "forced" *Cloud* to comply to keep Yinauqua from again attempting to interfere with the events unfolding upon Stephanie. Try as she may, Mafferan's wife had for the first time failed to uncover the truth of what entangled her husband. It made her all the more unwilling to abide by the King's or his best friend's bidding. But Cloud Walker, remembering similar instances from long ago, lost his usual humor and started operating on instinct so he followed Mafferan's "suggestions" to the letter.

Grinchback, in course of time, came along shortly, having been trusted to tie up some last loose ends. He couldn't believe the admiration he felt for Vaughn, and wondered if it was developing into some unknown sickness. However, he was sure that Vaughn was his and his Master's only hope.

ScrabaGag glared at Mafferan. "You're late, as usual."

Suddenly, they then all disappeared and reappeared within the Father's extremely dark ethereal room, the blackest Vaughn had ever seen. Everyone, except Vaughn, seemed surprised at the sudden uprooting. He remembered Stephanie's vision of him pleading the case of all humanity in just such a room.

The Father spoke in good humor. "Well, young lad. Your efforts have been quite the talk of the Ethereal. Now, let's hear what you've uncovered."

HrorrarrAggrang, already there when everyone popped in, surprisingly floated up to join in the circle with a new boldness quite atypical for him. He shimmered and rippled with an unusual red glow, his silence speaking quite loudly as he tapped his tail tip on his tentacled arm.

Vaughn smiled at him, but the old demon only squinted back, having not previously paid him any attention. Vaughn turned to Mafferan. "I need your services. There's a small orb that Grinchback knows of. I need it in here *now*."

Grinchback went to offer guidance but Mafferan declined. "I know the one!"

Both Master ScrabaGag and Grinchback looked at each other with surprise. Mafferan waved his hand and the orb appeared in the Father's ethereal room. The Father's ripples stopped as his Greatest Eye bore down upon Grinchback. "How do you know of *this?* It looks remarkably similar to *mine,* the one that vanished so *long* ago!"

Embarrassed, Grinchback immediately realized what he hadn't thought of before. *Heaven! Every room is only supposed to have one. But we had two… but, but…*

Vaughn interjected. "After we're done, I don't think it'll matter much!"

The certainty of his statement caused every Eye and eye to fall upon him, and Mafferan's eyebrows rose. *I wonder what the boy is going to do.* Vaughn mumbled 'excuse me' then pushed by the extremely large tail of the Father who narrowed his Greatest Eye at him. Mafferan shrugged his shoulders, while Grinchback stared at his best friend, wondering if he'd gone mad. Vaughn manipulated the orb then pulled up the record of Mafferan's glowing hand obviously helping to turn the Black river into Black Stone. "Apparently, Mafferan is guilty!"

All of them were shocked. No one expected such an opening line. *What's this boy doing?*

Highest Councilor ScrabaGag decided to beat the others and floated toward Mafferan. "Then it's time I consumed him for justice sake."

HrorrarrAggrang was none too pleased, having already planned a very long time to consume both, but not wanting Mafferan's power to belong to ScrabaGag first. "Not so fast. There are *other* circumstances to consider."

Vaughn pulled up HrorrarrAggrang's file on the Father's tribe and concurred. "Indeed! You're the last of the ancient ones and have *your* tail in all this up to your torso!"

Now Vaughn finally got HrorrarrAggrang's attention. The demon's Great Eye twitched a little more as Vaughn delved deeply into the file and HrorrarrAggrang decided it was time to end Vaughn's participation. "I think you've fulfilled your usefulness. Why don't you run along, and…"

"It seems that Master HrorrarrAggrang has been dealing with a human called Karen, wife to Jargono, and plotting to overthrow the ethereal with them!"

HrorrarrAggrang was truly astonished by the accusation, "Preposterous! I…"

But Vaughn cut him off again. "Here's the record." Amazed, all watched the three plotting to steal the Seed to the Tree of Life, use its power through Jargono to destroy the Father, and create a joint rule between them.

The Father drew close to HrorrarrAggrang, ripples of rage emanating very black waves of power through the room.

I have to think fast. That's a forgery. But why? What would it gain him? That still won't save his friends. "I can prove that's a fake. If the Seed was meant for Jargono to use, then I wouldn't possess it! Everyone knows Jargono would never allow it to come to me first. Besides, I know that once he has the Seed, he wouldn't be interested in any deal with us. The whole thing is preposterous!" HrorrarrAggrang eyed Mafferan who again shrugged his shoulders.

Highest Councilor ScrabaGag decided to assert his authority, and smacked HrorrarrAggrang across the head with his tail to humiliate him. "Then prove it!"

HrorrarrAggrang could taste the Highest Councilor, knowing he had the power to best him. "I'll be right back."

Vaughn held up his hand. "No need!" He disappeared, and popped into HrorrarrAggrang's ethereal room where Karen was intently focused upon Stephanie in the blue orb. Vaughn's glance into its vision turned him so deeply black that it stifled even Karen whose arm he then grabbed and they both reappeared in the Father's blackest room.

Vaughn glared at Karen. "You're a witness! You may not leave until dismissed!"

She was about say something, but between Vaughn's angry power, HrorrarrAggrang being intent on her proving his innocence, and the Father's surprise that an unknown human could be so deeply involved, Karen decided to remain silent. She also stayed for her own amusement, for she probably could have transported herself out, using a combination of powers nobody knew about.

The Father drew close enough to divine Karen's constitution. "Well, well, you would be tasty, indeed. You know I have a right to consume you here and now!"

"Don't bet on it!" Karen stood defiant thinking she could call Jargono. Between the two of them, they could win, but she really didn't want him to know what she had done.

Vaughn replayed the scene in the orb but she only laughed. "That's a forgery."

The Father drew closer. "Prove it!"

Damn it! He knows I must have the Seed up here and that if I do, that proves Jargono isn't involved. I don't want to give it to him… though on second thought, the Father has more power than HrorrarrAggrang. "My deal was that in exchange for the Seed to the Tree of Life…" she thought a moment, "Master ScrabaGag would give me power!" *I want HrorrarrAggrang to survive this so he can make good on his deal, or else I'll tell the truth.*

ScrabaGag shrunk a bit as the Father eased over to him. "Behind my back? Highest Councilor, didn't I specifically instruct you and your offspring to tell me *everything*? I'm sure the defilement of the Black River, the cursed object, and all this," he waved his tail at everyone in anger, "are all related and *you* are responsible."

Master ScrabaGag, quite used to thinking in mid float, decided, *I'm not having this turned back on me.* "Yes, I hid this, but as you can see, things are quite complicated and I didn't want to report until I had the *full* truth. I was… using that promise of power as a ploy, because I felt Karen must have already made that deal you see in the orb with HrorrarrAggrang. I was trying to ascertain the validity of her claims and the extent of her manipulations."

The Father floated back to HrorrarrAggrang, once again rippling in a threatening manner. "What do you have to say about that?"

Why is he rippling at me this way? "Father, you knew…" he cut himself off, seeing his leader wince. Everyone's eyes turned on the Father.

Vaughn smiled then jolted everyone with his sarcastic tone. "You, Father, are also guilty in this. You allowed Master ScrabaGag to ascend to a throne he was quite unworthy to inherit." The Highest Councilor scoffed at the insult but Vaughn continued. "Your plot needed him to make certain changes. You started out using his former Master GrrraGagag to introduce the Black Oil into the Earth to produce Earth demons. But you needed Scraback to cover your tracks so you allowed him to eat his Master, as well as the three High Councilors who also had various tails in the plot. This covered all your manipulations to produce the Earth demons, but you needed the Seed to the Tree of Life out of the way to ensure your earthly offsprings' survival. You feign ignorance but you know *almost* everything that goes on here! In reality, *you* are responsible for causing the turn of events that turned your *precious* Black River to stone."

The Father's wry look confessed the truth. "My, my, but aren't you clever? Nevertheless, I stayed within the truce guidelines. And my *subjects* acted of their own volition." He turned away from Vaughn, and hovered over Karen. "Produce the *Seed*. It's… still evidence in relevant matters."

Still defiant, Karen increased her smugness. "I don't think so! You're obviously losing this case and have *nothing* to offer. You don't need the Seed to prove anything."

"Yes, I do." The Father glared at HrorrarrAggrang.

As if on cue, the old demon, the last of the original tribe besides the Father, explained, "That Seed doesn't come from the Earth. If you just let me access the orb…" He went over to it, used that orb to connect to his, but minutes passed as his labored search increased.

"I don't understand. My private file is gone!" HrorrarrAggrang turned to the Father. "But no matter, because she has the Heavenly Seed upon herself. She was supposed to give it to me just before the trial so I can prove Mafferan's guilt."

The Father insisted. "If this is true, then this circumstance destroys the balance. Produce the *Seed!*" And he glared at Karen.

Karen felt the Father's terrible power, but shook under its pressure rather than reveal her own power. She reached under the neckline of her black dress and pulled out the Seed, still on its chain. She could feel power within it, but as she was handing the Seed over, Vaughn quickly snatched it. "Excuse me, but *I* am the official arbitrator. *I'll* examine it first!"

Everyone couldn't believe Vaughn intercepted the Seed but he knew he was obliged to make a truthful assay, the results of which would be checked later. But it only took Vaughn a brief moment, since he had held the Seed to the Tree of Life many times while he was with Stephanie before they went into exile. Vaughn could easily discern the truth.

Vaughn announced his assessment. "This is a fake!"

Karen was unable to comprehend. "*Liar!* I could feel its power!"

Mafferan scrunched up his shoulders again, actually looking quite stupid. HrorrarrAggrang's Great Eye almost popped out while the Father's ripples stiffened. Vaughn shook his head then addressed Karen. "I am *intimately* acquainted with that object. *You* are not! This is *not* the Seed to the Tree of Life!"

Vaughn requested Mafferan. "Hammer and pedestal, please."

Mafferan waved his hand and they appeared.

"I hope you all understand that the *real* Seed to the Tree of Life could not be smashed, burned, or destroyed by *any* physical means, and I dare say, by virtually anything at all." Vaughn glared his intention, and all assented.

He placed the Seed upon the stone pedestal, and smashed it with the hammer. The shell flattened, revealing a white splotch where the starch of a normal seed had squished out. Vaughn turned to everyone. "As I said, the true Seed to the Tree of Life cannot be destroyed by any means. This is a fake… or *was* a fake!"

Mafferan nodded and finally spoke. "I'll vouch for the truth of that. Only in its natural cycle may the Tree go to ash and be reborn, or its Seed go to ash, if it so chooses to give its life up. But it cannot be destroyed like that, or by any other means." He touched the flattened seed and smiled at Karen. "Pear, I think!"

Karen glared at Mafferan. *Who the hell is* he? *How could it not be the real Seed? That* bitch *kept weeping over it. She wanted to die when she lost it... I know because I watched her very closely. I read her mind, her heart. How did this fake get power in it?*

The Father Eyed Vaughn then Mafferan. "I think your *arbitrator* has *not* been impartial. There are definitely forgeries in the files. We all thought the Seed to be real but it's a *FAKE!* That means Jargono was *not* in on some conspiracy. That means HrorrarrAggrang is *not* guilty of treason or some such. All these allegations against me are not easily verified. Jargono took the Black Oil of his own volition."

The Father glared at Vaughn. "Unless you've tampered with that record, too, but it can be easily proven." The Father wondered how a nobody had managed to interfere in a perfect plan.

"However, this arbitrator *has* verified Mafferan's guilt and Master ScrabaGag's guilt is clear to me. He ate the three High Councilors becoming One, and that *is* prohibited by our truce. He also provoked the Earth demons to mate. And while it's true we're not involved in the Earth demons' creation, I think I'm being more than fair in punishing the *Highest* Councilor. To avoid a breakdown of the truce, there is only one solution. Mafferan must submit to be consumed by Highest Councilor ScrabaGag and the Councilor must then be consumed by HrorrarrAggrang. Frankly, I won't accept anything else. That *is* a fair punishment for both sides."

Grinchback looked over at Vaughn. *It's either now or never, my friend.* While he wondered where the real Seed was, he knew that none of what Vaughn had done was good enough to save his Master, him, or Mafferan for that matter. *I don't understand this. What did he hope to accomplish by all that? Even if the forgery is his, it's still not enough.*

Vaughn walked over to the blue orb and addressed the Father. "You're right, you *bastard!* Fair indeed, but I don't give a damn! In fact, I placed the forgery merely to further draw out the truth so everyone would know that what I do next *is* fair by *my* judgment!" He plunged his arm halfway into the orb, did something no one could see that made the orb flutter, hiss, grow very bright, then go out, becoming completely hard, black, and lifeless!

There was silence in the Ethereal, *all* throughout the Ethereal. Mafferan created a dull glow to see everyone gaping at Vaughn as The Father scoffed. "What do you think you're doing? If you destroy my orb, you'll nullify your neutrality and I'll *personally* eat you."

"I didn't destroy *your* orb."

The Father finally had enough as it had been quite painful enduring this human for so long. He started to extend over Vaughn who held out his hand to stop any action Mafferan might take. "If you consume me, you'll lose far more than you bargain for!"

"And what could that possibly be?"

"I've told you, I didn't destroy *your* orb. I destroyed them all!"

Shaking with disbelief, the Father actually froze in mid-ripple, as did all the other Alphas there. The orbs were the very center of Alpha culture, their means of communication, coordination, and *especially* entertainment. Without the orbs, all reconnaissance would have to be done in the field one on one, very dangerous indeed. There could be no more review of anyone's life and no safe spying on each other would be possible. There would be widespread panic, and chaos. "You're joking!" the Father said of a certainty.

Vaughn began tapping his foot and sure enough, several demons burst unannounced into the Father's private ethereal room. They momentarily gawked at the assorted company but then yielded to more pressing matters. "Father, the orbs are all *dead!*"

Alpha fear as never before in history erupted as the Father never felt a fiercer rage before. Vaughn hadn't considered the possibility for the top demon to lose control and do the very thing that could be self-destructive. Seeing the Father on the verge of consuming the boy, Mafferan glowed brightly as he stepped in between. "I take it you have a plan, a deal to make, Vaughn?"

The question, plus the glow he'd have to fight through, stayed the Father but Vaughn held his peace, and waited for begging to begin!

The Alpha's voice lowered. "I'll ask but once. What is this about?"

"I've told you, I don't give a *damn* about your truce, your sense of justice, or *anything* about you. I'm neutral in the truest sense because I'm thinking about *myself,* what *I* love and care about." Vaughn pointed his finger at the Father's huge, ebony Eye. "You're going to do exactly as I tell you or you can eat me. But you'll never make these orbs work again if you do. Only I can do that, and I have to be around year after year, *forever,* or they'll stop working!"

"You're bluffing."

Karen shook her head, and confirmed. "I couldn't have done it better myself! He's not bluffing, but go ahead and eat him."

Grinchback narrowed his Eye at her. *I really* can't stand her.

But Master ScrabaGag almost seemed to drool after her. *She is so Alpha!*

The Father turned on Karen. "How about after I eat you? You're not supposed to have Alpha powers floating around inside you."

Karen replied with a smirk. "Power is power. It's not Alpha, angel, or human. And *really,* I must be going." Karen began to fade away, but Vaughn called her back.

"I think you'll want to stay for the end of this."

Karen appeared again, clearly now having the power to fade in and out. "Get on with it then. I have things to do."

Vaughn thought about killing her right there and then, but as he looked into her eyes, he knew she knew his thoughts. He turned to the Father. "Here's the way it's going to be with *my* sense of justice. If you want your precious orbs to work again, your truce starts anew now. All former infractions are to be disregarded. In reality, I know my assessment as arbiter is true that you're *all* guilty in some way, and *frankly,* just because you've been clever doesn't absolve you of guilt. But *now* that's all in the past because you can all start with a clean slate. And by the way, I've so entangled your orb system that if you even attempt to meddle with what I've done, everything will shut down permanently! This little orb here controls it all."

Vaughn rapped his knuckles on the orb then a faint glow slowly grew at its edges then suddenly raced to its center, then exploded outward. "All the orbs are working again. And this orb is attuned to my spirit and mine only. Once a year, I must come to it, reset something or your whole orb system crashes!"

He reached his arm halfway in again, then the orb grew so bright the Alphas had to turn away, but it faded back to normal. Vaughn looked at Mafferan. "I've now begun the first yearly cycle. I've picked out the perfect place for this orb to be guarded upstairs. Read my mind and send it there… now, please!"

Mafferan seemed to beg the Father's pardon, and then waved his hand, making the orb vanish. He reassured the Father. "Don't look at me that way. Even though the orbs are actually *mine* to begin with, we really don't need them upstairs."

The Father asked Vaughn. "What do we do after you *die?*"

Vaughn smiled, hoping he would ask that. In fact, it had been a very long time since he had smiled this way. "I suggest you pray that I live forever!"

Mafferan couldn't help bursting out laughing. Grinchback knew better but also got caught up in the irony, and slapped Mafferan hard on the back with his tail in mutual revelry. Even though it stung quite a bit, with good humor the King accepted the payback for having once severed the demon's arm. The other Alpha Eyed Grinchback, but seeing the shot at Mafferan, dismissed his laughter.

It was strange seeing both the demon and the saint laughing together at the same thing, each from his own perspective. Grinchback also finally understood that Vaughn had somehow modified his special program that infected all the orbs. Neither he, nor his Master would end up on the wrong side of the Eye. *That is, if a clean slate applies to us as well.*

Highest Councilor ScrabaGag mused. *I never thought that boy would amount to anything so useful.*

Karen didn't seem at all amused, knowing she wasn't getting any more power around here. Vaughn turned to her. "I've attuned all the orbs to your spirit. If you even so much as set foot within the same room as any orb, you will crash that orb." He addressed the Father. "I advise you to make this known to *all* your Alpha."

The Father finally seemed to grin. "With pleasure."

Vaughn eyed Karen further. "How's your husband? We haven't played together in a long time."

"Frankly, you just weren't much of a challenge to him. He's quite disappointed. Now, I'm leaving." Karen started to plot. *Hmm, so if Vaughn dies... then the Ethereal pretty much goes blind? I know Jargono would love this, but what can I do with it?*

As she faded away, Vaughn called out. "You could have planted that pear seed, you know?"

Grinchback burst out laughing again, even though everyone else glared at him, as no one knew what happened to the real Seed.

Standing *very* erect, looking very much like a true judge, Vaughn crossed his arms across his chest as he confronted the

Father, "Because you have *purposely* allowed your vile Black Oil and demon seed to propagate upon the Earth, the Seed to the Tree of Life shall also remain upon the Earth, though this one did indeed come down from Heaven! I don't care about your sense of justice. This is all about *my* sense of it so I'll deal with your Earth demons *myself* and destroy them! You'll follow all this to the letter or I'll permanently destroy all your orbs."

The Father just couldn't give in that easily. He had to attempt to save tail in some fashion. "What makes you think I'll agree?"

"Because I've decided I'm unwilling to live in a world less than what I've just set up, so if you don't like it, eat me! Either way is fine!"

The Alpha in the room shook their heads with a common thought. *He's crazy!*

But Vaughn continued. "Besides, what I've proposed isn't grievous to you at all. You really haven't lost any ground, just haven't gained any. It's not good Alpha sense to risk your orbs' destruction when you haven't even lost anything."

The Father stalled, beginning to gather his massive tail round and round himself so that its tip could tap in his thickly muscled arm. A good two thousand years of the Father's planning hinged upon this battle of wills. The Father had known the time would come when the fate of the Earth would turn critical and some saint or other would have to step on the line so close to the edge that he could be snatched, and with him, all the rest. The Father glared at Mafferan who once again shrugged his shoulders. *You didn't just step on the line, Mafferan, you* crossed *it!*

Vaughn began tapping his foot, and drew the Father's full attention back upon him. No one knew what would happen next, nor anticipated the downright spunk of this *kid*. Youth versus the ancient. Pride versus… one just didn't know the term for the other side of that relating to Vaughn. Brazen bluffing against the Father of Cunning? Or was it a bluff?

Extending himself over the boy then lowering his Great Eye, the Father let his malevolence threaten Vaughn who motioned to Mafferan to keep out again. The Father slowly increased the pull of his Great Eye, but the boy refused to fight though he was beginning to be swallowed by pure damnation. Sensing that Vaughn was freely sacrificing himself, the Father couldn't help but feel surprised. Never had even he experienced such a willing consumption. A softening morphed around the edges of the Father's Great, glistening Eye, and Vaughn knew it was time.

Still staring squarely at the Father, he pointed at HrorrarrAggrang. "One more thing. *He's* been behind a devious plan with Karen to upset my life considerably. The Highest Councilor hasn't done me any good either, but I'd like to stick with that old saying about 'The devil you know.' I think the Highest Councilor ought to consume him! In fact, I *insist!* This has *nothing* to do with the new truce. This is between me and *him!*" He pointed again at HrorrarrAggrang, who had barely acknowledged Vaughn through the whole proceeding, but was definitely focused on him now. Scorn would be too mild a description, but any hint that Vaughn's suggestion might be taken seriously simply didn't register with HrorrarrAggrang, the last of the original tribe beside the Father.

The Father's anger grew notably, and he chided Vaughn. "First you say I wouldn't lose anything, but now…" He stopped in mid-sentence. *This boy is too clever.*

Still facing the Father, Vaughn asked, "And what would you be losing? I thought you'd be glad to punish the real culprit behind upsetting the balance. I can bring up the records which I assure you are not forgery, records of all HrorrarrAggrang's dealings with Karen, Jargono, and other Alpha that are quite enlightening."

Vaughn paused, smiled, and then put on a look of deduction. "Oh, unless you had given him orders to do all those nasty things… hmm, then I guess you would lose a lot. It seems the one thing that never shows up in the orb is any of *your* communications with *any* Alpha, but I know I can bring them all into focus."

Vaughn also knew timing meant everything. He shot Mafferan and Grinchback a quick wink, waited to see a slight pause in HrorrarrAggrang's ripples, then resignedly ordered Mafferan. "Would you bring the orb back? I can see this deal is broken. Give my best to Stephanie."

The orb came back with the wave of Mafferan's hand and Vaughn plunged his hand deep into it. But then Vaughn felt the momentary *excruciating* pain of the Father's tail jerking him away even though he had rubbed a good bit of Light Oil under his shirt.

"Just a minute there, young man. You didn't give me time to respond."

HrorrarrAggrang couldn't believe the Father's words and

smelled betrayal in the ether. He began to change colors, a sort of angry purple, with raggedness in his ripples.

The Father found himself thinking deeper. *They already know HrorrarrAggrang is the last to be able to see into Heaven. I'd be giving up too much. Still, would all the orbs be destroyed a year from now if I consume this boy? There has to be some middle ground he's reaching for. Besides, I can't have this boy possibly expose all the secret dealings I've been conducting. The only one who knows even some is HrorrarrAggrang. But if the boy exposes them* all, *then everyone will be able to piece my ultimate plans together. I don't even think Mafferan knows!*

HrorrarrAggrang's amazement turned more into fright as the Father took longer to answer Vaughn. He noticed the Highest Councilor's Great Eye beginning to drool, and before he knew it, his question had blurted out. "Are you going to fall for this *ploy?*"

Highest Councilor ScrabaGag's and Grinchback's ripples stopped cold, hearing how HrorrarrAggrang questioned the Father. Seeing no response to his insolence only escalated HrorrarrAggrang's fear. He floated back a bit, his Great, glistening Eye growing wider. "I've been faithful to *you* from the beginning." The Father watched him in silence, disturbing HrorrarrAggrang further. "I should've known not to trust you!"

The Father tried to reach HrorrarrAggrang telepathically. "*Shut up, HrorrarrAggrang! What are you talking about? I have to come up with a counter offer.*" But something blocked the communication. Perhaps HrorrarrAggrang's fear.

ScrabaGag looked from a very proud looking underling to Vaughn. *I'm beginning to see what my offspring sees in this human. I never thought it possible for an Alpha even to consider admiring a human. It's too bad I can't consume him. He may even be tastier than his former wife.* He then studied HrorrarrAggrang's reaction, one he understood that Vaughn had strived quite hard to set up. *Wait… wait for just the right time.*

HrorrarrAggrang sensed how intently his adversary, ScrabaGag, focused upon him. Until this moment, he'd never felt vulnerable before.

Now! ScrabaGag's sympathetic tone set off the unfolding scene perfectly. "I'm afraid, my poor, poor HrorrarrAggrang, that your very long existence… will just have to continue within me. The Father has made up his mind."

No I haven't. I'm still thinking.

But before he could respond, Vaughn jumped in. "I guess I don't need to delve any deeper into the orb then. There are a few processes I haven't explored yet, but I believe I could uncover *all* of the Father's communications especially with HrorrarrAggrang. There's nothing done in the dark that doesn't come to light." Vaughn put on anger as he glared. "But I *suppose* you're off the hook, *Father.* Highest Councilor, do your duty!"

It was all HrorrarrAggrang needed to confirm his worst fears. "I'll not go down without a fight." He turned to the Father in a threatening tone. "There's a lot more to me than you know. I can be the Father then we'll see *who* will eat *who!*"

HrorrarrAggrang's tail lashed out with special barbs appearing along its lower third as it caught the Father around the neck. The barbs dug in while the Great Eye of the last of the original Alpha seemed to grow tenfold.

The Father had not tasted battle since no one knows because there's no record of it. He always has been, and no one had ever dared attack him. The Father seemed not to respond at all even as HrorrarrAggrang's Great Eye clearly began sucking in blackness from him.

Grinchback and his Master looked at each other. *It might be worse if HrorrarrAggrang wins.*

As the Father sensed the other's thoughts, and feeling pain in his massive neck, *and* losing a bit of his eternal essence, Mafferan asked him. "Do you need some help?"

HrorrarrAggrang doubled his determination to consume the Father, thinking Mafferan just might help. At every bit of gained essence, he gained more and more confidence, finally deciding to play with his food by taunting the Father. "I should have done this a long time ago!"

For the first time, finally realizing the supreme insult at being attacked, the Father's anger blew up. "Worthless *spawn!* Ungrateful *failure!*"

His tail plucked HrorrarrAggrang off of him like picking a flea off a dog. Though Alpha blood ran from the Father's neck, he dangled HrorrarrAggrang helplessly up in mid-ether.

Paralyzed in excruciating terror, slipping from the brink of victory, and now wretchedly poised over the Greatest Eye of Defeat, HrorrarrAggrang's long tail flailed uselessly as confusion clouded his consciousness. He could still taste what he had consumed of the Father, yet felt so powerless.

The Father's Great Eye enlarged as blackness radiated in waves from around it. No one here had ever witnessed the

Father consume anyone but now saw him merely drop Hror-rarrAggrang into the endless, bottomless pit of the Blackest Eye. There was no squeal, not even a painful moan, just dead silence as HrorrarrAggrang went head first into the Father, his great long tail slithering silently into oblivion, no longer the last of the original tribe.

As soon as the act was completed, the Father regretted his anger. ScrabaGag bowed his bulbous head while his tail thwacked Grinchback's back who immediately followed suit and also bowed. Even Mafferan was surprised by the Father's hasty consumption, giving him a hint of doubt concerning his ability to best the Father if he had to.

Vaughn applauded, saying with a smile, "*Well done*, Father! Well done. A fitting compromise! Finding the middle ground! It wasn't what I requested. The Highest Councilor doesn't get his meal after all. HrorrarrAggrang wasn't consumed by his hated rival, but by his beloved *Father!* Hmmm, such is Alpha life!" He then requested Mafferan with a wink. "Send the orb back upstairs, please. This *case* has been resolved!" He gave Grinch-back a slight nod communicating something then vanished.

No one had known exactly what would play out until Vaughn's resolution. The Father, who didn't seem to even grow appreciably from his massive consumption of Hrorrar-rAggrang, looked squarely at Mafferan who was scratching his head. "Well, what can I say? Sorry for your loss! The surprise of youth! They always seem to come up with something totally new and unexpected! I didn't know the boy was only out for himself!" After that comment, Mafferan disappeared.

Grinchback excused himself to do routine orb maintenance. Before vanishing, the Highest Councilor bowed again and said, "I'd better see about HrorrarrAggrang's replacement."

The Father was left all alone in his darkest room, thinking of all the times, the secret joyful times he'd enjoyed with the last of his tribe. He had consumed more than any Alpha, but try as he might, he couldn't shake the emptiness inside him. That feeling of hollow isolation would soon turn into a deep bitterness as he realized he'd been outsmarted by a human youth.

☙

Vaughn stood before the still naked Judge no longer restraining his ire. This wasn't anything encouraged by any Alpha but was his *own* anger, perhaps not even righteous. After all Vaughn had just accomplished, he somehow felt entitled to getting away with what he was about to do.

"Good Judge Matthew!"

Whether it was the surprise, or his nudity, or because the ominous tone in Vaughn's voice portended great evil, the Judge's heart leapt into his mouth. "Wha… What are you doing here?"

No question about it. The smile on Vaughn's face was wicked. "Making good on a promise to a friend." He placed his hand on Matthew and they both transported into the Dead Forest. The Judge fell to the gray ethereal ground so Vaughn pulled him back up by the hair he had left at the back of his bald head. "Where's your righteous black robe, *good* Judge? Is it true when we stand before God in Judgment that we stand naked before Him?"

Vaughn emanated vengeance to the supreme as images of Stephanie's humiliation played in his heart. The Judge's knees began to shake. Vaughn could *still* see the unbearable orb images of Stephanie, his truly God given wife being forced by this *bastard*. "I have a friend I want you to meet."

Grinchback came out from around a large dead tree with his Great Eye drooling profusely. True, the Judge wasn't the first human he'd hoped Vaughn would deliver to him, he only had guesses because Vaughn never told him who, but to consume anyone whole, soul and body alive, was most pleasurable.

Matthew backed up upon seeing the hideous form of the demon. Vaughn realized then he'd actually grown accustomed to Grinchback. He then chided the Judge about banishing the demon. "Come now, good Judge. Why fear? God has blessed you with power over the devils. Right? Remember how you sent Stephanie's father to oblivion?"

Grinchback delighted in Vaughn helping him play with his food. He knew then he had a true human friend. *Yes, friends forever!* He slowly floated up to Matthew, also desiring to help Vaughn in his sense of justice. "Yes, *good* Judge! Why don't you show me how you made my earthly demon brother cower at your power."

Matthew stood himself up straight, trying to stop trembling. He held out his hand, tried to muster his voice, but it came out with less power than he hoped. "I banish you, demon!"

Grinchback faked fear, and mocked. "Oh, good Judge, don't torment me with your great power!" Then in the next instant, he materialized only inches away from the Judge who immediately fell to the ground begging, sounding more delectable.

The demon lowered his Great Eye over him and tasted the Judge who howled from the shock. In desperation, the Judge groveled, and implored Vaughn who was leaning on a dead tree. "Please, have mercy! In the name of God, help me!"

"Help you?" Vaughn who had turned black, *deep* black, whispered, "I'm helping you by putting you out of everyone else's misery!"

Matthew vomited from the demon's contact, shrieked in untold agony as Grinchback started to slowly wrap his coil around the rather rotund man. "In Jesus name, stop!"

Grinchback taught the Judge. "You never had any power! That red head, *she* has real power, power from the one you *claim* to serve. Stephanie even burned my Great Eye once and left *this* scar on my neck, the imprint of her glowing hand as I shrieked in pain. I know her but *who* are *you*?"

The Judge peered at the handprint as Grinchback lifted his bulbous head so the fold of his hide opened. Matthew could hardly believe he meant his next words. "What have I done?"

Sensing God would not answer, he hoped she could somehow hear and yelled out. "Stephanie! Please forgive me! Save me!" But then he remembered she'd vanished with the children he helped torment.

"Look into my *Eye*." Grinchback commanded.

Mathew had to comply as the demon's will forced him to look up.

Vaughn interjected. "Slowly, my friend. Savor it!"

As his total essence was consumed by the demon, Matthew watched a multitude of his sins march by his awareness in a procession of confessions. Each moment brought excruciating pain as his ill-timed admissions fed his eternal condemnation. He didn't want to confess. He *had* to, as Grinchback, himself, brought everything of his life to his defeated mind and heart. As his last bit of essence was consumed, the Judge knew clearly that he had gone from a vision of seeming eternal power to infinite helplessness. Grinchback spoke his last word to him. "Don't worry good Judge, after all, no one can be perfect."

It is said that vengeance belongs unto the Lord, and that truly righteous people ought not to delight in it. Vaughn then justified his satisfaction. *Well, this hour, I guess I'm not righteous! I'm* neutral!

CHAPTER 17

Justice

Eve simply loved to tell stories from the beginning and there seemed no end to her capacity for talking lovingly, yet potentially embarrassingly about Adam. Her audience? She was first teacher to all the little children who'd entered heaven. What else would the first mother love to do? Not having a very long Earthly life, the children had so much to learn 'upstairs,' and Eve's first and most favorite job was to patiently teach them.

One boy with curly brown hair, of nine Earth-years sitting on the paradisal grass among many other children, all dressed in simple brown shirts, tunics, and pants raised his hand so Eve smiled, indicating he should ask.

"You said it was written that in the beginning, God created the Heaven and the Earth, but everyone talks about the Ethereal right now. And the Ethereal isn't Heaven or Earth … so what is it and how come it doesn't say in the beginning God created the Ethereal, too?"

"Does everyone understand his question?" our First Mother asked. This was your typical mixed-ages class. But all the little heads even bobbed in excited agreement. "Very well. As you know, I was there in the beginning, or at least that lengthy period of time which is called the Beginning, for it wasn't a moment but a whole time period." And she paused to make sure the boys and girls followed her.

"Well, Adam and I were told of the Ethereal and its wonderful purpose. After one-thousand years, if we'd lived that long on Earth, we'd be granted access to the Ethereal. We were shown its beautiful form. It was originally a magnificent court-yard made out of the same kind of shining stone as in heaven, but paths led to many, many open square mini-courtyards which had at their centers wonderful glowing crystal-clear blue orbs. They were to be the inheritance of the children of men and of course, the first to inherit them would have been my husband and me. Through these orbs, we would have been granted direct sight into both heaven above and the whole Earth, to offer us our next stage of eternal learning! The reason why the Ethereal was never mentioned in the description of the Beginning is because after my husband screwed things up ..." she paused with that playful grin they'd all come to know and love, "it was thought best not to mention it to mortals. But even Paradise isn't mentioned in the description of the Beginning, either, but still we know it's real and was mentioned later. And Paradise is actually part of the same *Middle Reality* with the Ethereal. The Middle Reality consists of Paradise, the Corridor, and the Ethereal.

Unfortunately, the first angel God created, whom you all know of, was in charge of maintaining the Ethereal, as well as using its orbs to minister for the Lord. Eventually, it would have been his and his angels' responsibility to teach the children of men all about the Ethereal's many mysteries."

All the children nodded and a little girl with long golden hair raised her hand. "Is that why the demons still live… ahhh… die… ahhh… is that why the fallen angels are still *there*? And how come they left God anyway? I would never."

Eve's smile beamed rainbows. "I'll tell you what. I want you all to think about her questions and use your imaginations to answer them! When we meet tomorrow, I'll listen to your creations then tell you the truth, if your imagination hasn't discovered it already!"

Everyone delighted in the game as all loved to use their imagination which Eve had taught them is a doorway into *many* worlds, and the greatest tool of investigation.

Mafferan popped beside Vaughn as the last of Judge Matthew disappeared. The saint's anger showed and his hard tone took Vaughn by surprise. "You probably think everyone should be grateful to you. But there's someone who wants to show you what this little *liberty* with your anger has gained you!" Mafferan pointed at Grinchback reveling in his first live meal. "Careful with that kind of friendship. The greatest honor that his nature desires is to consume you *too!*"

Grinchback nodded truthfully as Mafferan grabbed Vaughn's arm then both disappeared.

෴

Mandy and Carla, dressed in simple, long brown dresses, watched in stunned silence as three figures materialized in the living room of their apartment. But as soon as Stephanie arrived with the children, she excused herself. "I'll be right back girls." She rushed off to the bathroom, quickly closed the door tight, locked it, then vomited just as she made it to the toilet.

Carla slid off the red couch and fell on her knees next to the exhausted kids, proclaiming over and over. "Thank you, Jesus! Thank you, Jesus! Thank you for the dreams!"

Mandy looked at her with new understanding. "You knew."

"I knew what Lynnara had to go through. I even knew *this* little rugrat," she grabbed Rebekah's knee affectionately, "would attempt to save her best friend. What I didn't know was whether she'd succeed!"

Rebekah stared into Carla's deep, dark brown eyes, then leaned over and whispered to Lynnara who nodded. Mandy felt something terrible, but didn't comprehend why.

"Wait for Lady Stephanie to return, dear Mandy. She still needs us more than ever. She's kept *much* from us to spare us, but she can't bear such a burden alone any longer. She needs our help now just as we needed hers."

Stephanie kept retching, but it wouldn't release her from her shame, or the vivid memory of what she'd just done. Rinsing her mouth several times didn't seem to help either. She even thought about using soap in it as she pulled off all her clothes and threw them in the trash while avoiding her reflection in the mirror. Needing to mitigate the filthiness she felt, she ran the shower to wash it all immediately down the drain, but then, in total weakness, she despairingly sank to the tub floor knowing she'd have to return again. She was beyond weeping. The most barren desert landscape could not begin to analogize her feelings.

Images of her suffering people and the children began to temper her tears with resignation as the water ran over her. Wanting to die just wasn't an option. After finally gathering her sensibilities enough to join them, Stephanie came out wrapped in a large towel then sat down at the end of the couch away from the others who were sitting on the thickly carpeted floor. She tried thinking of what to say, but all her ideas evaporated when everyone's eyes turned to her.

Lynnara came to stand before her. "Mommy, why were you naked on top of that bad man? And he was naked, too."

Her mouth dropped open, and something within Stephanie wanted very badly to die right then. All the good she'd taught, all she had treasured had been violated, and what could be said to reaffirm any goodness now?

Though full of concern, Mandy heard her own decree against all evil in her head. *We are sisters*. Carla came over and sat down next to Stephanie then looked at her for but a moment then captured everyone else in the room with her loving gaze.

"I'm going to tell you all now, what I knew from my dreams. I couldn't tell before because the Spirit of God warned me that if I told, everything would fail." Carla then touched Stephanie's tears. "I know these tears, Stephie. You know I do."

Carla took the now bawling Stephanie in her arms, remembering how not so long ago that a very different Stephanie had done the same thing to a very different Carla. Lynnara, still staring at her third Mommy, the bestest Mommy she'd ever had, placed her little hand on Stephie's knee. Her loving touch made Stephanie squirm, feeling very unworthy of it.

"Your Mommy was told by that bad man and an evil woman that if your Mommy didn't have sex with him, you and Rebekah and all your people would die. So she went to sacrifice herself to save you all." Lynnara's eyes opened so wide, trying to process it all.

A shocked Mandy, knowing the utter depths of Lady Stephanie's integrity, how she had pulled Mandy out of such an awful life, sat down on the arm of the couch at Stephanie's other side. "I love you, Stephanie. We're more than sisters. I love you so much."

Coming to stand next to her best friend, Rebekah also placed her hand on Stephanie's other knee. She again whispered to Lynnara who reached her little hands around her own neck and took off a chain from under her white dress. Attached to the plain gold chain was the Seed to the Tree of Life that she had taken from her Mommy while under the bed covers. Lynnara held it out. "Mommy, it's time for you to take this back now."

Stephanie tried to shrink away. "No, *no*… I can't… It's yours… all yours!"

"Mommy, the Seed talked to me the whole time. It thanked me for hiding it, for telling you, you *had* to let me wear it. But even Rebekah said, I'm supposed to give it back now."

Rebekah wasn't supposed to know about the Seed to the Tree of Life, but it was now clear that Lynnara shared everything with her best friend. Or perhaps, the Seed wanted her to know. Rebekah studied Lady Stephanie. "She's worried she's going back to that bad man! That's why she doesn't want to take the Seed."

Stephanie peered through her puffed eyes at the child, stunned by her insight, then turned away with more shame as Carla hugged Stephanie tightly. Rebekah whispered to Lynnara anew and Lynnara nodded then Rebekah spoke to Stephanie. "I don't know for sure, but I just know Ranger Vaughn isn't letting you go back there anymore! He saved me, and saved you before. He'll do it again."

Stephanie shook her head. "You don't understand."

Just then a familiar voice sounded in the room, but it also had a tone that everyone instantly knew was profound. Something had happened to Vaughn. "Dearest Lady, I think Rebekah knows a lot more than you give her credit while I knew far less than I thought."

Rebekah immediately turned around and ran into him with a bear hug. "Ranger Vaughn, I *missed* you!"

"The Judge won't trouble you anymore!"

Beaming with joy, Rebekah turned again to Stephanie. "See? I told you!"

Stephanie didn't comprehend what she heard. Something prevented her from accepting it. All eyes fell upon Vaughn who put Rebekah down, then sat on a kitchen chair he set in front of everyone. "I can't tell you too much of what I've been doing. It's a secret between God and me that I'm sworn to keep, but I'll tell you what recently transpired."

Vaughn had known Stephanie years ago when she had been vile, and loved her from the beginning. His piercing gaze now reminded her of when they first met, and beckoned her again. He began his story. "I've had very deep dealings in the Ethereal! I can't tell you why but King Mafferan, Stephanie's ancestor, now a saintly spirit, needed me to… ahhh, make a case for him against a demon's accusations. Our *friend,* Karen, had also involved herself in a quest for power there. That's how she was able to get into your head, but Stephie, you knew that."

The faithwalker nodded. *I can't believe he knows all this!*

"What you didn't know was I discovered her by accident while conducting my duties for Mafferan. She won't be able to assault you that way anymore. I also…" Vaughn hesitated. "Stephanie, you and I go way back… so please bear with me. I also saw what she made you do."

Vaughn desperately wanted to hold Stephanie who shrunk away and wept again against Carla's breast. Vaughn shook his head mournfully. "I'm so sorry. I wanted to prevent it sooner, but I just couldn't make things happen fast enough." His pain was more than evident in his voice. Stephanie brought her head out from Carla to look into his eyes, but she just couldn't say a single word.

"Stephie, I fed that *bastard* Judge to one of the demons!"

All their mouths dropped open. Stephanie remembered when she'd struggled with the morality of whether Vaughn should set up the scheme that killed her former gang members, but there wasn't even a hint of conflict now. She wasn't at all sorry that such a horrendous thing happened to Matthew. He wasn't ruling her anymore. She sat up straighter, beginning to feel alive again, little by little.

Vaughn continued. "But it's what happened next that'll be most important to us." Everyone listened in sacred silence to his narrative.

"'There's someone who wants to show you what your little *liberty* with your anger has gained you.' Mafferan's hard tone jarred me into focus as we reappeared at a place which shined heavenly light. Standing upon a walkway of large, polished, multicolored stones that glowed up to my knees, I squinted to see where it led. The path seemed to ascend forever and reminded me of my vision two years ago of the endless tunnel with a floor that shined a gray light that hopelessly went on forever. Except this feeling of forever wasn't hopeless, it was dwarfing. My knees began to shake, and I realized the path I stood upon had a slow grade upwards that suspended itself within a crystal-blue, sunless sky but shining with golden light *everywhere*.

"I peered up the walkway at something very small at the farthest reaches of my sight and it was growing larger. And though it seemed millions of miles away, I still knew it approached, and came for me! I prostrated myself with no strength to stand, and in the next moment, bright fire with emerald greens, sapphire blues, and ruby reds so pure it hurt to see, shined around me. Mafferan bowed and stepped behind me as a soft voice, yet feeling like power itself, seemed to come from everywhere, though it came from the radiant ball of light over me. 'Where were you when I set the Heavens in place and the Earth below, the stars in the sky, and the seasons upon the Earth to *mark* the time of man?'

"I began to weep while I trembled as the voice continued. 'Thou who hast befriended a demon, and took it upon himself to wrest judgment out of *My* hand to deliver a soul that *I* made unto *your* judgment, stand up like a man and declare yourself!'

"I found myself standing at the command, though I didn't remember rising, but my trembling only increased. I didn't know how I kept standing, nor how I was able to look upon a throne, and upon One sitting there whom I felt I always knew and knew me, and yet I didn't know. A face I couldn't describe, like that of the most beautiful people, all there in one face, then the voice continued. 'Thinkest thou your judgment to be greater than mine? Or perhaps I had gone to sleep? Or was slow to act? Tell me now, where were you before I placed you in your mother's womb, or before your parents were born?'

"Suddenly, I found myself looking into the depths of that Light, beholding infinite thoughts, infinite goodness, all mingling together, yet each fine aspect of goodness had its own distinct will, yet all of it was one will together, and parts of it combined in infinite ways with various aspects of goodness. And some of these clumps of goodness became individuals and I knew all these clumps were the essences of souls, souls to be or gone on, or now, I couldn't tell. I wanted to cover my head with my hands, but had no strength to move my arms. I wanted to look away, yet wanted to look deeper, too, for the vision drew me in.

"The voice with a building anger in it, an unstoppable anger, asked me, 'Thinkest thou that your anger is *greater* than mine? Thinkest thou that your righteousness is more *timely* than mine? Behold, you have of your own free will done us a service because your love is strong, but think thou your love to be greater than mine?'

"I then beheld multitudes of souls standing before the throne, and their lives were open to me like books, lives all of suffering, and yet they rejoiced in God's mercy which had brought them into eternal peace.

'Behold, because you have treasured the love I made you out of and were willing to sacrifice yourself for mercy's sake for others, because you have done this thing, I also shall have mercy upon you.' Yet another crowd appeared before Vaughn, different from the first. These were suffering souls now present upon Earth. 'But because you have taken upon yourself to deliver a soul into eternal judgment, another shall take Matthew's place and your heart and the heart of your wife shall be crushed.'

"The throne began quickly to recede even as it had come, but from the distance I heard the voice calling from everywhere. 'After that, I shall hear you, and we shall begin again.'

Even Lynnara and Rebekah sat transfixed while Mandy's mouth still gaped, as if trying to catch her breath. Carla just kept nodding her head though no one wanted to move. But Vaughn wasn't done. He leaned forward, opened his vest pocket, and pulled out a scroll of what seemed like parchment that glowed. Stephanie's name in gold blazed upon it in a script she didn't and did know. "This was left at my feet upon the crystal path for you."

As soon as Lady Stephanie touched it, the scroll unrolled and floated in the air. Mandy made a slight gasp, wanted to shrink away, but also to see more. Stephanie knew she was supposed to read it but couldn't see through her tears. Part of her already knew in her feelings what it said, but part of her couldn't accept its message. Carla took Stephanie's hand, and then found herself reading the scroll aloud to all present.

"Dearest Stephanie,

There is none like you upon the Earth, who, though mired in the depths of sin, despair, and abuse, reached up into the heavens to declare the goodness of the Most High. You sought His mercy because you found goodness to be real in your soul, mind and heart. And that was before the events of this last year! Behold, I have heard you and I set an open door of prayer to be always before you—whatever you shall ask, I shall grant unto you. Therefore, take no more liberty with it as you did for your personal vengeance upon your father.

And behold, I have witnessed your sacrifice of this last year—a sacrifice from the utter depths of your heart for My Goodness sake and the sake of your brethren. Because you have done so, the sins which you committed, having done so without your heart in them for evil, are forgiven you for they are not what they appeared to be from the outside. I have also forgiven your personal vengeance, for in reality, you did no harm. You must take the Seed to the Tree of Life as the little child has offered to you. Lynnara has done well, but it is not her time to inherit it.

As Vaughn's forefather was sent to bless you, and as your forefather Mafferan, always My faithful servant, has blessed you, The Lord God, and the Giver of the Tree of Life blesses you, the Lord Jesus who came to Earth to do in human form what could not be done in Tree form gives you peace.

Eternally,

God of Truth"

The letter immediately began to disintegrate into tiny flecks of light, leaving all momentarily to wonder, asking if this event had ever even been, for the return to worldly perception left them all with a disjointed sense of the reality they had all just witnessed. For Stephanie, though, at the reading of the letter's last word, *peace,* peace seemed to move within her. And as the letter turned into light specks that drifted into Stephanie's chest, she knew its reality.

Vaughn then prayed over Rebekah, touching her head. "The Lord God of our fathers blesses you, because of your love and bravery, the Lord shall always be your Friend, Rebekah."

He also placed his hand upon Lynnara's head. "The Lord God of our fathers blesses you, because of your faith, and the ear you have to hear God, you shall always have His ear, Lynnara."

The little girl smiled, looked back at her Mommy and held out the Seed to the Tree of Life by its chain. Stephanie felt the Seed call to her to take it, and before she knew it, she had reached out her hands. Upon touching the chain, she felt the instant inundation of friendship and vowed to the Seed. "I renew my oath to protect you, and uphold you, with all that I am, all that I have." And she replaced the chain around her neck so the black seed dangled upon the towel she was wearing. Everyone in the room freely partook of her oath and reaffirmed it in unison. "Amen."

"I bid you all a peaceful good night." After his adieu, Vaughn vanished.

CHAPTER 18

Punishment

Ever since the little girl asked her questions, Eve positively radiated many colors not even found in the rainbow as she had been looking forward to their next lesson. "Well children, have you all done as I asked? The two questions were…" Eve waved her hand above her and the Tree of Life, under which they sat, turned into the vision of their last lesson ending with the little girl's inquiry. "Is that why the demons still live… ahhh… die… ahhh… is that why the fallen angels are still there? And how come they left God anyway?"

"Have you all used your imagination to try to answer them?" And when she saw vibrant nods, and raised hands, she picked on the same questioning girl first. "Since they're your questions, you go first, dear."

"The girl grabbed her long golden braids and began to twist them in her little hands. "Well, at first I thought because God gave the Ethereal to the fallen angels, and since God never says one thing and then does the other, I thought maybe He had to let them stay… to keep His word. But then I thought that since they were so bad, maybe they broke some kind of promise and then God could take it away from them and maybe make them a different place to live… ahhh, to stay."

Most of the children her age nodded in agreement, while the older ones began raising their hands, and an older boy got Eve's nod. The sharpness of his bright blue eyes almost seemed to cast a crystal blue light beam upon wherever he looked. "Except that God never really *gave* it to them, just like he never really *gave* the Earth to us. We were all given *responsibility* to care for the Earth, and them the Ethereal. I think this issue goes deeper. We were originally made *from* the Earth, and therefore we, in part, will always belong to *it!* Nothing can change that, so making a whole other different place for us that is *not* Earth, well, I don't think *that* would be right. God has never been one to approve crossing natures! In the same way, Lucifer and his angels and the Ethereal seem to be all connected from the beginning, so I think they all must have been made out of… the same *stuff?* In that case, they *belong* there!"

The eldest girl in the group, only days from graduating into adulthood, calmly raised her hand. Eve remembered her from fifty-four years ago when the girl first came up. "Marta, do add your understanding to this, and please see me later if you'd like to become one of my helpers in teaching."

Marta, with her long, luxuriously curly brown hair, had no idea such an honor would be offered to her. For a moment, it made her reconsider whether her reply was even worthy, but then she figured that she had thought her answer through very carefully and she can't be any different from what she thinks and feels. "I think the first issue is even deeper than *that.* The *fact* is there's no other place to send them! When the Lord God brought about *our* reality, the Heavens and the Earth, and the *Middle Reality,* that's simply all that could be possible, that being a full reality in which angels and humans and creatures all could be free. It *is* the entire reality brought forth by the Light, that Light being Freedom. Just like there can't be another Light, for Goodness will always be Goodness, there cannot be another reality. Even the new Heavens and new Earth will not be *different,* meaning outside of this reality now, but they are simply going to be made new. Purified, glorified, and *only* holy through and through. But I like Robert's reasoning."

Even though he was older than her, in that he entered *upstairs* being older, she had been here longer and naturally surpassed him most times. Marta continued, "In fact, the place where all of the ungodly will eventually end up, will be merely the same old place from where they came just like Robert felt they should because there's *no* other place for them. God's just going to *split* reality, allowing those who loved corruption to keep their corrupted portion, and those who allowed God to purify them will be given a purified part of Heaven and Earth." Then she looked around at everyone, raising her eyebrows. "It seems to me this really makes sense, and in fact, it goes along with what everyone else said though it's just deeper!" And Marta glowed just a bit pink, thinking her last statement needed a bit more humility to it, and not wanting to embarrass anyone else.

Seeing Marta blush, Eve delighted in helping her further. "I really don't think I could have said it better myself, Marta! And it's no shame to share your depth with others, just as it's no shame not to be as deep in understanding as another. Even this Tree of Life grows in seasons and stages, and at one time, we would've only found just two human beings upon it. There's no shame to be in different stages of life, dear children." All the children nodded at each other, and many came up to Marta, hugging and thanking her.

Robert expressed his admiration. "I really love what you explained. You helped me see further connections to what I'd already understood."

While Marta blushed even more, Eve adjourned their lesson. "My, my, but paradisal time still seems to fly …" She chuckled while many wondered at her age because no one else really acted like Eve. "At our next lesson, we'll consider the second question of how come certain angels fell. Use your imagination, children." And her voice echoed for a while as she slowly dematerialized. Many of her students lovingly rolled their eyes at her eccentric behavior.

Shouts roused Vaughn from the calmest sleep he'd had since he and Stephanie camped and dozed off in each other's arms well over a year ago. "Corporal Vaughn!" Groggily, he recognized Larson's voice coming from the other end of the barracks. Steps quickly grew louder, two loud knocks, then Larson barged in and pulled Vaughn out of his bed by one hand on his tee shirt. "Sorry! I don't know how Harris and Joshua made it but they're finally back. And Harris is in a really bad way!"

Larson then bolted out the door with Vaughn catching a glimpse at the wall clock displaying zero four-thirty hours while following at Larson's heels. After being awake for close to forty hours, Vaughn had managed to sleep for roughly four. Harris was laid out on one of the tables in the great hall, his shirt and trousers covered in blood. Joshua sat weakly in a wooden chair, his camouflage shredded, revealing scrapes and scratches everywhere that flesh showed through.

Vaughn brushed tears from his eyes, lifted Harris' head a bit then whispered. "I thought you said you could run fast!"

His eyes opened showing a heart desperately trying to hold on to life. Harris weakly shook his head. "Not from *this!* Not from what's coming."

Vaughn turned with a questioning look to Joshua who answered. "He told me some, but not all."

"Everyone out now!" Vaughn sternly commanded the growing crowd in the room. When they were hesitant to listen, he snapped. "That's an *order!*"

Joshua addressed the room, particularly those who looked at him. "I suggest you get used to following his orders without question, without hesitation! His promotion is in the works!"

The room cleared in seconds except for Larson and Joshua whom Vaughn instructed. "I don't have time to explain, and frankly, I don't want to. What you witness now must be kept to yourselves."

He still wore the Light Oil from his earlier ordeal, having immediately gone to bed after leaving Stephanie. After the two nodded their assent, Vaughn bowed his head, and stretched out his arms. "Lord God of our fathers Abraham, Isaac, and Jacob, take me where I bid." He vanished to reappear standing at Stephanie's bedside with his heart skipping a beat at the peaceful sight of Lynnara at her left and Rebekah at her right.

When Stephanie sensed Vaughn's presence, their eyes met in the dim moonlight coming through the window near her bed. He whispered, "Joshua's back, and Harris is about to die!"

She eased herself out of the children's arms, grabbed a robe from her closet, wound her long hair into a single ponytail, and turned to face Vaughn. Her soft scent, the very sight of her rising from bed, almost made him forget everything but he took only her hand. "This one's on me!" Vaughn said, then transported them both back to the barracks.

When they popped back in, Joshua and Larson looked even more dumbstruck than when he'd left. Immediately sensing Harris' imminent death, Stephanie pushed by Vaughn and asked, "Oh *dear* Harris, what have you gotten yourself into?"

"Save me… and I'll tell you." Then Harris passed out.

Stephanie bowed her head, but immediately gasped, shaking her head. "What *is* this?" Her hands, which she placed on his chest began to glow along with Harris, but a sickly blackness began to shimmer around parts of him. If the glow went to one area, the blackness went to another.

She looked up at Vaughn. "I need your help!"

He went to stand over the other side of Harris, and prayed silently. Angry sounds growing in intensity started to emanate from Harris's unconscious body. Both Stephanie and Vaughn asked each other, "What *is* that?"

"We need your help!" They summoned Joshua who walked to Harris's head and Larson who went to Harris' feet.

"This won't respond to my gifts. But it *will* respond to our prayers together!" Lady Stephanie lifted up her voice in profound prayer, eliciting both surprise and instant response from the whole military camp that had gathered outside. They all bent their knees in prayer as the military had never lost their respect for her, no matter what they had seen or heard others say.

In the deepest of emotions and power, Lady Stephanie's rich voice traveled throughout the room, through the walls, to the outside, and beyond. Lights turned on in waves throughout the town surrounding the military camp, and even many judges woke up as the spirit of her prayer roused souls from every quarter. Though the town outside the camp could not physically hear her words, all felt stirrings and not just a few recognized her spirit, and they all started somehow to pray with her.

"Dear Lord, what evil has come to trouble us? What suffering has been cast upon us? Oh Lord, not by You but the *vilest* of men. Because they can, they bring evil upon the Earth, *without* thought, *without* understanding. Turn them from our destruction, from their own *self*-destruction." She took a deep breath. "Oh Lord Jesus, they won't turn now and I know you don't force. They can't turn because they've sealed their fate. Help us, dear Lord, for we've no power against *this*. And this *be* but only the *first* battle, Holy Father, yet we were all asleep and didn't know. We had no idea evil hunted our souls this way to enslave us all. Now, Lord Jesus, when you walked here, you walked among the demons and their multitudes and their manifestations, of the demons and of evil men. Lord Jesus, now, against both evils together on a level unknown to us, what can we do about this joining of wills? But You, Lord God, Creator of Heaven and Earth, You know all things and of what they all consist. Look upon this man, being slaughtered by evil *against* his will through a device purely vile in Your sight, and have mercy. Have pity upon him and on us all, for if we don't win this first but small battle, how shall we win the next?"

Vaughn picked up where she left off. "Lord God, give answer to such evil. Defy its workings. Give us what we need to fight it, for we are here, Lord God, your servants upon the Earth *You* created for *goodness* sake. We have a *right* but evil does not! Rebuke this evil in your name Lord Jesus, and give us good answer against the storm to come!"

Larson continued. "I'm small, and don't know much. I've done a lot of bad things… too many, but Harris's heart I know to be pure. We would gladly die for Your sake, but *this* kind of death is not for us, dear Lord Jesus."

Joshua finished the prayer in tears, but his voice found strength to pierce through his exhaustion. "I carried this man on my back for fifty miles. Praying all the way for his dear life, for us all to know the dire knowledge he risked himself to gain. This knowledge we must have if we're to defend our homes, our wives, our children, our old and infirm, for our enemy has no mercy and no understanding of life. You've said that in the end of days Your saints would be worn out. Thy will be done but You have also said that in those days, your holy children would do exploits. Dear Lord Jesus, arm us, your children, against the battle to come and save this valiant man for he loves You with all that he is, all that he has."

At the conclusion of the prayer, the Amen was heard throughout the camp. And in the town, even souls who had not attained to the spirit of the prayer, strangely heard themselves say within, *Amen*, to a feeling they did not quite understand. Those who had attained the spirit wept in knowing the times had just changed drastically.

Harris laid unconscious and without much color. The four souls around him looked from one to the other, with a common thought on all their faces. *We've done all that we can do.*

Stephanie finally spoke up. "Has he been shot, as well?"

Joshua nodded, as he allowed himself to slump flat on his back on the floor. "Rifle, I think. It went in the back, out the front. But I think it missed the vitals or he'd be dead."

"But what *else* hit him?"

He weakly shook his head. "That I don't know. There was something black streaking … I don't know what."

Stephanie asked her husband. "Are you alright?"

His nod was *not* very convincing, but Stephanie turned back to Harris. "I could at least heal his gunshot wound, but this other thing in him is preventing that."

Vaughn spoke to Larson. "Get the medic back in here. Post double guards. And Larson, I need four of our deepest in Christ here *now!* I want them to also guard Joshua and Harris."

"Yes, King Vaughn." Larson knew no one there would object to the title, and knew which four to choose, those from whom Lady Stephanie had already baptized. But no sooner than he'd traveled halfway down the road, all ten souls met him, and wouldn't hear anything about selecting just four of them.

It was one thing to cast out a demon, and another thing to rebuke an evil man. But this poison in Harris came from the intentional and unforced combination of both abominations and posed a unique problem, for both had to be attacked simultaneously or else each simply transformed into the other that was not embattled. Plus, considering the dynamics of how each part of the hybrid poison worked, their processes being so different meant it was virtually impossible for only one soul to pray against them both. To untangle this mess from the soul it had wrapped around without destroying that soul, also posed extreme difficulties. That understanding began to settle upon both Queen Stephanie and King Vaughn as they knew all they could do now was to wait.

Vaughn went outside the hall, and dismissed everyone there. All nodded and went back to bed and he returned to Stephanie. *Dear God, he's grown up so much.* She hushed her thoughts from going further but caught a glimpse of Vaughn thinking the very same thing. She faintly smiled at him then vanished, so Vaughn went back to his bed in exhaustion.

☙

There was discussion all around about the feelings and events relating to Lady Stephanie's prayer. The reactions were variations on the themes of "I told you so", "I figured it was something like that" or, "I did feel something strange". The military was mobilized to watch more closely the border with their northern neighbor, the Country *still* with No Name.

There was no change in Harris who didn't die, but wasn't exactly living either. Joshua couldn't stand being cooped up under security so after just one night, returned to military duty, and his wife. The absence of Judge Matthew did not go unnoticed past the third day. On the fourth, general inquiry had been made, and by the end of the week, the news media was agog over the mysterious disappearance of the mighty Judge, the demon-banisher.

Speculation surfaced linking Lady Stephanie or the military to the mystery. "She was mad at him, that much is *obvious,* for exposing her to be a fraud." "The military tried to change this country by persuading people to grant them more power in government just because of a few corrupt judges. They did him in." "Maybe that's why Captain Joshua looks so terrible. Judge Matthew had a lot of power so maybe he *cursed* the Captain before a whole company of them finally killed him."

And the rumors continued to multiply and some accused the *heathen.* Vaughn began to realize his vengeance had unforeseen consequences. *Was it really necessary for me to feed the whole Judge to Grinchback? Maybe I could have just given him an arm or a leg!"*

But by the eighth day, the tension between the Judges, the military, and Vaughn's people quickly reached a critical level as each was accused of the Judge's murder. Vaughn had lost his sense of humor as squabbles throughout the country had become a serious threat. *If Jargono attacks, he couldn't hardly pick a better time.* But since he wasn't attacking yet, that meant Jargono expected things to get even worse.

Stephanie hadn't mentioned to anyone about Judge Mathew's threat of condemning her people if he disappeared. *What's the point? What's done is done. Maybe he was bluffing!* On her way to see Harris, Stephanie grumbled to herself. *I don't understand why Harris hasn't recovered yet. The longer this takes, the people's doubt increases. They've all been told I prayed for him. Lord, you said you gave me an open prayer door!* The same general despair that Judge Matthew had initiated when he was alive crept back more deeply into her. It's quite peculiar that once a rut is dug within a person, overly stressing that person digs the same rut much like a pot-hole in a road reappears in the same place.

The people were losing faith again, rendering useless any potential good Stephanie had done, reinforcing the lie that she was a phony, so what she'd told them wasn't true. Of the many outside people to which Stephanie offered prayers or healing, only one truly accepted. The common sense about her was, "Well, she works sometimes but mostly she doesn't. Not very godly!"

Eventually, Stephanie bitterly complained to herself. *It's almost as if every time something good happens, evil watches over it and covers it up. Is* that *the way it's supposed to be, Lord?* But to her surprise, the Holy Spirit seemed peacefully to reflect her question back at her. *Well…* idiot, *of course evil does, or tries to. What did I expect? That's what those damned orbs are for… still… goodness should prevail despite those orbs.*

"Watches over, watches over…" She kept repeating it. *I should run this by The Book of Wisdom, but then what would I ask? Why is this phrase bugging me?* She stopped cold in her tracks. *Damn! I've been such a* fool. *What happened to all that training Vaughn taught me from The Art of Fighting? Your enemy will always seek the higher ground for advantage. If you slacken and let him take it, you're more the enemy than your real foe.* Stephanie vanished from the street in mid stride, not caring if anyone saw her pop out.

Oh God, it's been so long since I simply walked around up here. Stephanie used the spiritual corridor mostly for instantaneous travel to different Earthly locations, but not for actually stopping within. She focused on Harris and found herself zipping to the corridor's parallel location just above him.

I've been such an idiot, *and* far *too slow at this game.* She walked slowly around an odd device, an orb the size of a basketball pulsed a blackness, and her red fire automatically flamed intensely all around her. Her first thought was simply to disintegrate it so that no more pulses left the corridor and invisibly entered into Harris. She raised her hand, but stopped. *I've been outthought every step of the way. I'm only thinking one move ahead.*

Stephanie knew what to do to destroy it. *The same gift which destroyed the gray scum left by demon Glen. Or would it?* Slowly, she paced around the device as she prayed. *Reveal wisdom to me, Lord Jesus.*

A blue shimmering within the small black orb became apparent. It didn't really glow, yet it had an intense brightness. *What is* that? *It's not demon though that orb is something like the ethereal.* She sighed not understanding the combination of powers.

The Seed to the Tree of Life began to glow hotly between her breasts and her hand automatically went up to rub it. Visions flashed of long ago. The people seemed so primitive, yet some flew, but not with machines! Giant beasts roamed the Earth, half earthling, half demon. A great flood annihilated them, but others, different from them, took their place. They too were destroyed… on and on, and there were giant men and creatures like her father, too.

A great King with powers appeared and Mafferan, too, but as a boy around eleven-years-old. His King, Lockula, laughed at him. "Go ahead, pick it up." It was an orb just like the one in front of Stephanie now. The boy shook his head.

"What are you afraid of? It won't hurt *you*. I've fixed it for Cranula. Give it to him as a gift. No, better yet, tell him you stole it from me and you want to sell it to him. Then tell that half demon that I've always told you that if he harms a hair on your head, I'll roast him and eat him for snacks. Now go!"

Mafferan picked up the black orb and raced away thinking, *Cranula's too smart and Lockula's a liar.* He walked along the path where he knew Cranula's flunkies hunted their victims. Mafferan, took off, running away, as hard as he could but he knew they were faster. They caught him and threw him to the ground. Mafferan cursed them in his thoughts. *These humans serving a half-human half demon Cranula. How can they be so pathetic? They're damned. At least Lockula is fully human… I think.* They grabbed the brown sack from Mafferan.

"This is ours now."

Mafferan laughed, assuring them. "You can have it!"

They looked at him warily. "Who you trying to kid, *kid?*"

"That's a trap for your Master. I don't know what it does but I'd like to be there when it goes off."

Gathering around the boy, they began to kick him then warned. "Yeah, right! Don't go anywhere. We'll be back after we've given this to Cranula."

The human demon, or demon human, took the sack and dumped out the black orb. "Hmmm, I like black. What is it?"

We took it from a boy trying his best to escape us. He told us it was a trap for you and wanted to be here when it goes off."

"Who does the boy belong to?"

"Your enemy, Lockula."

"Ha! That boy probably stole it and wanted to sell it."

Cranula turned his human hand into a demon's hand, and beams of black light shined from his fingertips to probe the orb from several directions. The orb pulsed outward once, shrunk, then exploded with a cutting sharp blue light. The flunkies' mouths dropped open as Cranula's head fell off with an odd look in his eyes. One of the flunkies separated into right and left halves while another split off horizontally.

Stephanie came back to herself. *Damn. I don't know what to do about this. What if it kills Harris as I destroy it? What if it kills me?* Stephanie shook her head then knelt down in the corridor. "Lord Jesus, please. I don't know what to do."

"Daughter." The familiar voice called to Stephanie who bounded up, and threw her arms around Mafferan and buried her face in his chest.

"Father, I've missed you *so much*."

The King hugged her tightly for several ethereal moments then eased her back. "What is it you'd like to know about that little toy?"

"Are you allowed to help me? What about the truce?"

Mafferan laughed. "That's on Earth, dear child, not here. I can tell you anything up here! Isn't that right, Highest Councilor?"

Just to the left of Mafferan, the corridor began to ripple like heat waves then ScrabaGag appeared, having been cloaked there somehow without Stephanie's awareness. She shook her head again. *How come I didn't know?*

Mafferan knew her thoughts. "You're just a child. Stop beating yourself up! You know very little though even it's a lot more than most! What say you, Highest Councilor? What do you think of that toy?"

ScrabaGag floated up close, but not with any threatening gestures or feelings. "Pity the Father ate HrorrarrAggrang, but I do appreciate you wanting to go with the devil you know!"

Mafferan bowed his head in good gesture, still waiting for the Highest Councilor's thoughts.

ScrabaGag narrowed his Eye at the little orb. "Seems your other offspring is up to a few cute tricks, but probably he *and* his wife combined."

"Jargono!" Stephanie spat out.

Mafferan followed up. "And you were just here to pick up the pieces?"

The Highest Councilor answered, "Well, we've been called worse names than scavengers.

"And it *never* occurred to you to warn my daughter of the danger?"

"Of course, after she was damaged I would have explained everything." And with that, ScrabaGag vanished with a smile.

Mafferan turned to his daughter. "If you get yourself killed, my wife will never let me hear the end of it! *But* if you get yourself *eaten, it'll be even worse!* She's quite fond of you, and actually, I am too." He kissed Stephanie on the forehead, then instructed. "Watch."

With his finger, Mafferan drew the shape of a square and a deeply red glowing cage appeared, much deeper red than Stephanie's fire. He lowered it around the orb and the pulsing of the orb grew suddenly more frequent. But the black pulses couldn't penetrate the red mesh, yet the orb didn't act as if it would explode.

"It'll keep increasing the pulse pressure until the cage is eventually stretched apart. Now use your gift against the orb. It'll pass unhindered through the red glow."

A bright beam of golden light shot from Stephanie's hand, disintegrating the black orb. As soon as it turned to ash, a tiny blue orb hidden inside shrunk violently then exploded. Before Stephanie could react, sharp blue light raced out, but the red mesh expanded almost right up to Stephanie's face and absorbed the blue light, turning it purple before disappearing.

Ancestor Mafferan turned to his descendant daughter. "Be careful, Stephanie. Jargono has far exceeded himself from when you last met. I don't think you can beat him. He's managed to, ahh, appropriate several orbs from the Ethereal and has made for himself several variations of it, among other things. They can't be used on Earth to spy but Jargono's using their energy and material. And you still have to clear out the human demons. There's less than two years now before they breed."

"Thank you, Father. Give my regards to Mother."

They both vanished from the corridor.

☙

When everyone heard Harris had revived, some said Lady Stephanie's prayers worked after all. Others said it had been too long so he probably got better on his own. Most neglected to remember that many of them had prayed with her.

It didn't matter what others thought about the prayers or her personally. Stephanie knew it was time to face the nation before a new Judge could hinder her. She was still a media favorite, and by the end of the evening news, the whole country knew that Lady Stephanie's long-awaited address would be the next day at high noon.

Stephanie wondered whether she would be told what Harris had discovered. Two days had gone by without a word and she started to be annoyed. Even Joshua didn't mention anything, and she hadn't seen Vaughn since their prayer. Recalling Harris' last words, *'Save me and I'll tell you'*, she made up her mind to probe her husband. When he finally walked in the door late, she smiled warmly. Not that she didn't feel warm to see him, but she added an extra kick to it.

Joshua smiled back, being always glad to see her face, whether happy, sad, or fishing for information. "What do you want to know, my love?"

"Let's get comfortable, then we can talk."

Joshua grunted, knowing he would have to tell her.

In bed, Stephanie snuggled close, propped her head up in her hand, then waited.

Joshua's eyes darted around, but he felt the heat of her deep stare, and sure enough, his will collapsed. "I can never hide anything if you want to know it. But you might not want to know this!"

The expression in his eyes unnerved Stephanie. As she snuggled even closer, she noticed his usual immediate expectancy wasn't there. *This* is *serious!* She placed her hand upon his chest. "I guess I have to grow up sometime!"

Joshua turned on his side to face her, and was surprised by the depth of acceptance with which she steeled herself. "I think I missed a lot since I was away."

Stephanie stared at him. *Oh dear God, he can't possibly know!*

Her reddened face and tears instantly made Joshua realize he'd made a terrible mistake. Being away for so long, he'd forgotten how quickly his wife could read him. He didn't want her to know he knew so he looked away, but said, "I know this. You're probably the most wonderful, most holy woman on the face of this whole God-given Earth, and I will always love you, no matter what."

Oh God, how could he possibly *know?* She dropped her head into the pillow, and cried thinking this wasn't at all what she intended.

Joshua kissed her head, and smoothed her hair. He whispered softly with humor. "What happened to growing up?"

She began to laugh through her sobs. "I don't *know.*"

"Stephanie, we all have limits because we're mortal. I think you're the most valiant human being alive." That was as close as he would approach to a confession of what he knew of her ordeal.

She lifted her head up and kissed him deeply. "God, I love you so much." But Joshua eased away so she prodded. "Go ahead, tell me!"

"We're doomed!"

"What?"

"Our whole country is doomed. Our fall will be soon, I think."

"But why?" She knew he wasn't joking.

"Harris got close, closer than anyone ever had. He saw Jargono training special men and women, giving or teaching each one a power! Some like you have, not nearly as strong I hope, and limited to perhaps a single power in each person. The blackness came from small orbs some of them carried. Harris said that when the first streak hit him, he instantly prayed so hard his gut wrenched but the blackness fizzled. But other streaks quickly replaced it as if he'd been marked and they overwhelmed him. He felt his insides being sucked out but focused on getting back to us, and pressed on by sheer will and devotion. He got through the fence where they shot at him and then hid. I waited for a long time for him to come to me but eventually I had to go get him. The enemy was waiting for me to go to Harris, but I first hunted down as many as I could. But one of them had that orb…"

Stephanie gasped. "Oh dear Jesus, did you get…"

"Yes, several times, but after I killed the bastard, I shot the orb and it shattered, and the blackness that had entered me fell out sort of like dead."

Joshua continued as Stephanie wondered at the mechanics of the orb. "But I tell you this, it wasn't a good feeling and I haven't felt right since. Somewhere, I think a part of me is missing!"

Missing! Oh dear God. "No!" Shaking her head strongly, fire now in her eyes and with her hand upon his chest again, Stephanie began to use a gift she didn't even know she had.

She probed into his inward spiritual parts with some special instantaneous knowledge. Finding the wound, she bowed her head, felt something in her fire that she'd never noted before, and it moved from her heart, through her hand into Joshua.

Immediately jerking up with a gasp, Joshua sighed deeply, thankful for the missing part's return, as well as for a good deal more understanding by virtue of that experience. *Oh God, I can feel again.*

He smiled but he needed to complete the story. "There's more! When I finally got to Harris, he'd been shot, was in and out of consciousness but I couldn't risk moving him then in the daylight. I gave him water, and bandaged his wound. That was all I could do except I kept praying. That's when he told me all I've told you. Once darkness fell, I knew we had to get away so I carried him. I think they summoned more spies from *here*, and I heard an infiltrator ask for special trackers. Those with the *power* to track. I decided I had to make a break before the trackers came so I ran blindly through the brush, and they did their best to chase the sound I made in the dark. They were quite intent that we didn't make it back alive, so here's what bothers me. Why? Why do they even care if we know? With that kind of power…"

"Because Jargono isn't your typical mad ruler, he's very, very careful and wise. He knows I'll seek a defense, a response, and Vaughn, too. We've fought him before."

Joshua nodded. "Vaughn told me."

"I didn't know."

"Yes. He even told me the bastard had killed you, but Vaughn's prayer to bring you back was answered."

This was part of her life she hadn't gotten around to telling her husband as she'd promised she would, and now was embarrassed. "I'm sorry Joshua, I should have told…"

He placed his finger to her lips, hushing her. "I love you, more than you know. Don't worry about it. So can you come up with a counter?"

"I don't know. All this hybrid mechanization stuff…" She waved her hand out and about. "This is all new to me. But if Jargono believes I can counteract him, then that must be within my abilities!"

Joshua laughed so Stephanie scrunched her nose at him. "Funny?"

"Yeah, in the way that Jargono's given us hope! Think about what you just said."

She realized he was right, and giggled too. He pulled on the chain around her neck and the Seed of the Tree of Life came out from under her nightshirt glowing. "The Seed seems to think so, too!"

His obvious connection to the Seed delighted Stephanie and she laid back with an admiration for Joshua she hadn't felt before.

CHAPTER 19
Justice For All

Eve always loved really slow fade-ins which invariably drew her students' patent eye-rolls. The same little girl could hardly wait for her to fully materialize before waving her hand right in front of her teacher, who said, "Oh, my! You seem excited. Very well, watcha got?"

"I did like you told us and used my 'magination. It was *very* hard at first, because it's hard to imagine leaving God. I mean, God isn't like a place you walk away from, God is… the goodness inside and outside us, so how do you leave that?"

"Mmmhmmm!" Eve nodded, and many of the other children repeated her intonation.

"Then I got a really good idea. I started remembering the times I was bad when I used to live on Earth… oooh, I *was* bad sometimes."

"Mmmhmmm!"

The child had her blond braids in her hands again and as she talked, she swung the braids around. "Well, I wanted things *my* way because… I just did. But I didn't understand there was more to think about than just *my* way. I was kinda selfish. So, I think that's why those angels left God. They were selfish, and

450

when the Father showed them they were wrong, they didn't wanna listen, thinking they could be bad and stay bad. I don't really know, because I still can't understand how you leave all that goodness and stay without that goodness because I always felt bad when I *was* bad."

A young boy, just a few years older, began jumping up and down to be noticed, his dark brown eyes looking quite urgent, and Eve gave him *the nod.*

"There's gotta be more to it than that! I'm not saying Cherri is wrong or anything, but…" He looked to see if others felt similarly but everyone just waited on him to continue. "Well, I think Lucifer thought he was better than God, because, before he got *kicked out…* A good many kids laughed at the way he said it. "There was this big argument in heaven. I actually went to our records and watched the whole thing, though I didn't understand some of it. But if you actually watched the records of *how* Lucifer acted even way in the beginning, he kept acting so important and… well, I suppose feeling so *important* tricked him, making him think he was even better than God."

Eve narrowed her eyes to challenge what the young man said, and when the other children saw it, they grew more excited. "Hmm, but aren't we *all* important? Is it wrong to feel that way?"

And many kids went. "Oh ! Hmmm… Yeah!"

It was interesting to see how certain children seemed to be de facto spokesman for the class, almost as if it was a natural order, and once again Robert got *the nod.*

"Of course we're all important so how could it be wrong to feel *that* way? I think he wanted to be *more* important than God, 'cause I also studied the records. I agree that's the way he acted from the very beginning but it really never made sense to me that he acted that way. I mean, *fine,* you're all super beautiful and all that, like no one else was super beautiful, but *who* made you that way and *why?"*

Eve then called the eldest girl up to the front. "Marta, dear, I have to go run an errand! Would you finish this lesson for me?" She disappeared rather quickly which was a bit odd for her! All eyes fell on Marta as she stood rather dazed until a lot of little loving hands began to push her gently to Eve's spot under the Tree!

Silence and expectation filled the paradisal air. *Well, this is a shock! Eve is so crafty! I so love how Robert thinks, but the most important part of this lesson is to learn the best way to think, not necessarily what to think.* "Do you all agree that he *really* felt *more* important than God? I mean, think about it. If you *know* you're important, that you have value, then can't you let that speak for itself and just *be?* And what really lets us understand how *very* important we are? I think this is a good place to end this lesson, with *these* questions , so… Until next time, *children!"* And Marta tried to speak the phrase as Eve does then to fade out Eve's way, but it didn't work. One arm faded, part of another leg, so she had to come back, and just floated away sighing.

All the kids rolled on the grass laughing, fading out a hand, or a foot, or at least trying to, but Robert followed Marta. "Don't feel bad. That was really quite well done, Marta! None of us has the courage to do what you just did."

She took his hand, and smiled. "Oh, I don't feel bad at all! I'm glad I amused them. If I was watching me, I'd be laughing and doing the same thing too!"

God, I really love her! And then it occurred to Robert. "You know, Marta, maybe that's where Lucifer screwed up! Because had that same thing happened to him, he wouldn't have acted like you just did."

Marta smiled, and asked, "Why not?"

At eleven thirty hours, the town center, including rooftops, and windows, had been packed to capacity, some even suspended themselves from light-poles. Stephanie had thought arriving thirty minutes early would be sufficient, but it wasn't. When one person in the back somehow heard her politely excuse herself, he somehow boomed over all the noise, "Lady Stephanie!" The whole crowd parted like the red sea, allowing her an open path. She couldn't figure out where they all had the room to move.

Finally, Stephanie felt like herself again sporting her three traditional braids, and her royal blue holy Appendaho dress in which she herself had been baptized. She seemed to float like an angel through the crowd, bringing cheer to everyone. Even her detractors caught themselves clapping and smiling. Smoothing her dress several times, feeling the deep blessing within the garment, she acknowledged that she always felt at her best when she wore it. That was the same dress the demon had begun to consume her in, shredding it without her knowledge, but she had used her powers after she'd escaped to mend it like new. *Why am I thinking about* that *now? I have to focus on the present.* But it flashed back to her the last time she'd been in this town square at high noon. Her father showed up and destroyed all the good she'd wrought for this country. *Maybe I can fix things… a little.*

Upon reaching the podium, the roar of all the people across the country sounded like an earthquake. Fifteen minutes went by before they were quiet enough to hear her request silence. Also, this time, she saw Vaughn in the very front with his special smile that she's treasured since their ice-cream-shop rendezvous. She smiled back, wondering why Joshua wasn't seated beside him.

"Dearly beloved people." The crowd erupted again, but seeing her hand up to hush them, they immediately complied. "I love you so much, so I'm here to tell you the truth. I've deeply studied you, and it's my conclusion that no matter how many miracles you see, they aren't able to give you faith. One can always find varied explanations for a miracle, and if you have more faith in a lie, or in your doubt, then the most plausible explanation to you can be the flatly unfounded, even illogical one. There's only one thing that gives faith. It's touching, feeling, understanding the true nature of Goodness for yourself."

Lady Stephanie paused a long while, somehow capturing the depths of everyone, even those watching on TV, and making them focus inward. "There are two great evils we must fight. The first is within you, which if you don't win that battle, that evil will make you lose to the second great evil that will attack you from the outside. My dear friend and protector, your Corporal Vaughn, has taught me that it's better to die fighting being what you are than lose the battle from within. This lesson comes from an ancient text, *The*

Art of Fighting, and it can mean many things. One of those meanings is if you're fearful, if that is *what* you think you are, fight it, because giving into fear is a losing battle. But truly, you *are* the goodness which God has made you to be from his Greater Goodness and it's better die while *being* that goodness, than to exist and lose it.

"The Most High has no evil within Him so He couldn't make you out of any evil whatsoever. The poison had to come in secondarily so better to die fighting against evil by being the goodness that you are than lose the battle from within. You fight the death inside and outside you for goodness sake. If we're faced with imminent destruction of this mortal body," she grabbed her arms in emphasis, "then so be it. But let us fight with every bit of energy we can muster against evil *even* as our bodies are being destroyed. We know that the body is made for the sake of the *person* inside and not the other way around. And we know that the life in goodness is a life greater than our mere flesh.

"Goodness cannot be destroyed even when our bodies are destroyed. Look deep enough into goodness and you will know this wonderful eternal life that preserves our persons even without our bodies. But even if you believe evil is you, the goodness in you will still tell you it's better to die fighting that evil than lose the goodness to corruption. Eventually, you'll discover you really are that goodness, and your person in that body will be free, even if the body is destroyed.

Some of our Christian theologians say there is no goodness in us at all! They grossly misunderstand certain Scriptures and unfortunately, through their misunderstanding, though they reach for God's Goodness, every time he brings it to them, they turn around and drive it away believing they can't be good! Does this make *any* sense *at all?* They confuse what the branch on the Tree is with the whole Tree of Life. The branch cannot of itself be good. Without the Tree it withers because the *sap* comes from the whole Tree, yet the *growth* this sap creates is... *what? Evil?* Of course not. In fact, the branch grows in a way to let *more* sap flow through it and also to help contribute to the Goodness of the whole Tree of Life. So while we cannot boast that we are Good with a capital G, we can take comfort that the Living God makes us good with a small g. All I can say is to let Jesus graft your branch back into the Tree of Life and let him prune it as he sees fit. And as I said, eventually, you'll discover you really are that goodness, and your person in that body will be free, even if the body is destroyed.

The hushed crowd heard little Rebekah chime in. "That's right! I see my Mommy now!" She pointed up in the air so the people looked up but didn't see. Even the camera's panned the air briefly.

"Thank you, Rebekah." Stephanie smiled at the child, then went on. "Now, unfortunately, many of you have doubts about me, but please don't doubt goodness. What I've just told you in non-religious terms, such *meaning* you all know is at the very heart of all our Holy Scriptures. As Jesus simply said in his parable- Either make the tree good, and its fruit will be good, or make it evil and its fruit will be corrupt. We are trees, dear people, for there is no better way to conceive of the intricate relationships of all the parts of our persons and of the Spirit of God Himself! Either make the tree, yourself, good, or make it evil. Better to die fighting for goodness sake, thus *being* good, so that our tree will not be corrupt, will not cause us to die eternally which is the true meaning of corruption."

"I'm going to tell you another truth. Judge Matthew had been…"

A single person clapped so loud that the entire crowd and the cameras tried to find out where the clapping was coming from. Once again Stephanie's father mounted the stage, and in everyone's presence, transformed his hand into a demon hand.

Dear Lord Jesus, not again! But this time the *faithwalker* knew what to do, or so she thought. The power in Stephanie's voice was unmistakable as she used a Scriptural verse, "What have I to do with *thee*?"

Throwing her hands open, her power ripped his garments away, showing a hairy body that began to grow and take on more demon form. The people began murmuring, with many fighting their fear. Demon Fred, covered in vile Black Oil, smiled and waved at the audience. Seeing his congeniality, some waved back!

A bright golden beam came out from Stephanie's outstretched hand and burned off some of the black fluid, but the creature's fur seemed to thicken and began to ooze more Oil as if it was his very blood. *Damn! Is this his maturity or something added?*

"See what I do to your *savior*. She's no daughter of mine. I'm of the *real* power and you *all* should know it!"

The crowd began hoping for their Judge, and Stephanie picked up on it. "I thought Judge Matthew banished you!"

Fred smiled again. "I escaped."

I need to keep him talking until I figure out what to do. I know the fire I used last time won't work. "Escaped, or maybe he never banished you at all."

"Maybe, but since you killed him, he can't be questioned, so maybe your killing him set me free."

Stephanie's anger flared up, looking at the foolish, thoughtless people who sided with Fred. "I can't *believe* you see a damned *demon* before you and still believe *his* words over *mine!*" Her rebuke caused quite a few to reconsider, and wonder at their stupidity.

Becoming aware of a voice from the Corridor speaking inside her father's mind, she cursed under her breath. "Damn Karen!"

"Do as I say or I'll slap you back into my husband's cage and never let you out again. Kill her!" Karen commanded Fred,

Radiating blackness, Vaughn leapt onstage and fired his revolver. Demon Fred laughed as the bullets were merely absorbed. "Well, I thought I'd try anyway."

Stephanie held her arm across Vaughn. "You can't fight him! He's a lot more powerful than Glen who almost killed you. Are you wearing any of your Light Oil?"

"I can't pop in and out, if that's where you're going."

Demon Fred suddenly stretched out his demon hand and a thick ragged blackness shot at them. Stephanie immediately shot her golden beam again, slowing the black stream's advance but it still drew closer, roaring and smoking as it approached.

Vaughn whispered at her. "You're thinking one-dimensionally. He's obviously well practiced in fighting. Have you?"

It had never occurred to Stephanie to *practice* her powers. She'd always thought their simple use would suffice. Mandy and Carla had their heads bowed in prayer, trying to send her their common thought. "Pray, Stephanie. You have an open door. *Use it!*" The crowd had become agitated and noisy, otherwise the sisters would have yelled their advice at her.

Stephanie wondered at the blue light she'd seen within the orb trap and her vision. Then she recalled Karen's words. *Cage! Karen mentioned a cage. There* must *be a power he bows to which the vile Oil doesn't counteract.*

From the corridor, Karen's thoughts appeared in Demon Fred's head again. *"Why are you toying with her?* Kill *that bitch!"*

Lady Stephanie concentrated. *Blue. What's blue? Gold is heavenly, but so is blue, but* what *is it?* She recalled Jargono's admonition when he'd tried to woo her. *'That* glow *is a waste of energy. It leaks all over the place. It needs to be controlled.'*

Then she realized the orbs are blue. *But what good does that do me. I need to be in contact with an orb to figure it out.* Desperately, she looked at Vaughn. "You were in the Ethereal. Were you in actual *contact* with any of those blue orbs?"

He laughed. "Ahh… I'm now an orb Master!"

Had the circumstances not been dire, Stephanie would have halted whatever she was doing from the shock of Vaughn's revelation. But Demon Fred was slowly advancing now, his thick blackness shooting from not more than twenty feet away.

I love this. It's important I take my time. When I was mortal, I was always rushing about. Foolish bitch ordering me around! 'And don't say anything to my husband.' One day soon, I'll kill her, too, and turn Jargono into my *pet. But first, should I eat my daughter in front of everyone or carry her to a more private place? Adding her power to mine will give me what I need to conquer Jargono and his bitch wife, and be God of the Earth as I should* be.

Stephanie increased the power of her light beam against the escalating pressure of the advancing black column, but sweat began to bead on her brow. Sensing her defeat, people began shaking their heads, concluding she was phony after all. Real children of God don't lose to demons. *Where is Judge Matthew? He was too kind to this demon before. This time he'd surely destroy him completely.* Those were the common thoughts.

With her free hand that she was saving for a different kind of attack, Stephanie grabbed Vaughn's head. "I need to enter your mind, to feel, to see."

It wasn't a request, but Vaughn was sworn to secrecy. "Stephanie… ahhh…"

His protest was too late. She searched for what she needed from Vaughn's orb experience. *Dear God, he's full of orb knowledge… well connected to them for* life! *Damn it! Focus!* She wasn't in his mind to study what he knew about or saw through the orbs. She had to find the actual feeling of contact with the blue orb, but there was too much orb information overshadowing it.

Vaughn was torn. *I shouldn't have let her in my head… but I have to trust her.*

With her confidence quickly waning, Stephanie began to beg. "Help me, *please* Vaughn! I promise I'm not after your secrets. I just need to find your basic *feeling* of the orb. *Please, bring me to it.*"

Only ten feet away. Demon Fred knew he could easily leap that distance. Vaughn knew it, too, from being battle hardened from fighting Demon Glen, but he kept calm. *The basic orb experience.* "Stephie, you can find that best when I first made contact with the orb. That's when I noticed its nature, how it felt. After that, I got used to it, and didn't really pay to…"

She zeroed in where he focused. "Got it! Now, what do I do with it?"

"Stay calm, Stephanie. Focus! If I have to, I'll buy you time."

Hearing *that,* she became frantic. "*No!* He'll kill you in one stroke. "

"Ha! I don't think the ethereal demons want that to happen. It's a secret, but let's just say that…"

"Vaughn, you *idiot!* My father doesn't care about *them.* He's just food for them, just like us! They eat their own, remember?"

He realized she was right. Part of his calm had come from his belief in the power of his threat against the ethereal orbs. *But to others, that threat just makes me their perfect target! Of course they'd want me dead! Damn it! Lord God, give me strength.* Vaughn rolled away from Stephanie, hoping to draw off Fred's attention, but he paid him no mind at all. Knowing that the Demon could kill her at any instant, Vaughn turned pitch black with righteous anger and burned with ferocious love then leapt at Fred.

Without even looking or slowing, Fred swept out a lightning arm to ward off the attack. But remembering how Demon Glen had fought, Vaughn leapt short, knew when to duck, and rolled under the demon's swing, then kicked Demon Fred in the knee, expecting to hobble him.

Fred howled in pain, not thinking any power on Earth could hurt him except Jargono's and Karen's. But Vaughn fought with a power that *did* harm him, but not enough. Before Demon Fred could stomp on his head, Vaughn rolled to the demon's other side, and tried to hit the other knee, hoping to at least slow Fred down. Expecting it, the Demon was able to kick Vaughn away, knocking him senseless.

Some in the crowd cheered! Mandy and Carla couldn't believe it. It became obvious that many were somewhat prejudiced against the foreigners. *Can they hate Vaughn more than a demon?* Knowing only precious seconds remained, Stephanie had to block almost everything else except that Vaughn had hurt Fred. *Righteous anger. Of course that's harmful to him. Black Oil can't neutralize* that. *But, damn it! Blue?*

The ethereal demons, all watching the battle, seriously worried about losing all their orbs should Vaughn die. Orb messages were sent, ordering their earthly offspring not to kill Vaughn, but Fred laughed them off. Karen had told him that if Vaughn dies, the ethereal all but loses contact with the Earth. *That's just fine by me.* But it was also part of Jargono's plan. He had promised the Highest Councilor that he would isolate the Ethereal from the Earth making the Alpha quite unreal!

There was nothing else to do except for the Highest Councilor to open a rare Earthly portal and destroy Demon

Fred. *I think even Mafferan would approve.* When the crowd saw the sky part, many went to their knees thinking Christ was returning. But as soon as the opening was set, bright blue bolts appeared out of nowhere, and shot into the ethereal, narrowly missing the Highest Councilor's precious Eye. Other Eyes drooled at the near miss, but the bolts exploded, sending lesser demons running for Black Oil that wouldn't work against the blue anyway.

Karen laughed at the result. *That ought to keep your filthy Eyes away for a while.*

Vaughn's efforts worked though, as Demon Fred kept turning around to check on his condition, further adding time that Stephanie needed.

A strange thought entered Vaughn's mind when it finally cleared. *If Matthew were here, he'd be trying to banish this demon right now. And every second makes a difference. Damn it!*

Finally, Stephanie regained some hope. *I've got it! I know the essence of blue.* She dared not drop her right arm until she knew her other hand would work. Raising her left hand, focusing on the nature of the blue energy she gained from Vaughn, she shot a thick blue beam that intersected Fred's column of thick blackness further up from where her gold beam fought it.

Clearly disturbed, Demon Fred reacted to the change in Stephanie's tactics by growling and speeding up his advance but Stephanie began backing up. When the crowd saw her retreat, they shook their heads. Some began betting on her losing.

Damn it! It's not focused sharply enough. Stephanie quickly narrowed the blue beam, multiplying its brightness exponentially.

This amused the Demon. *This is really fun. Let's play.* He responded by shifting his halted black column to a different angle.

When Stephanie tried readjusting her beams, the gold column crossed with the blue, turned it green, and BOOM! In a thundering green explosion, Fred's black column blew apart, knocking him over and throwing Lady Stephanie backwards, sliding her to the very edge of the stage. *Wow! I didn't know* that *would happen!*

The crowd had mixed emotions. Some cheered for the demon, others like Mandy and Carla for Lady Stephanie, but shouted, *"Get up!"* The rest of Vaughn's people were so far away they could only feel what was happening.

The cameramen all followed Fred's high arching leap at Stephanie, amazed at his power. With no choice except to fall off the stage twelve feet to the ground, Lady Stephanie realized her disadvantage. She didn't want to pop away in front of the whole nation. So knowing that righteous indignation would hurt Demon Fred, the *faithwalker* channeled all her anger through her hand into the blackest bolt she'd ever seen. It ripped into Fred at the height of his leap, sending him back halfway across the platform. But upon crashing onto the stage floor, the unfazed Demon jumped up instantaneously. "Is that any way to treat your *father?*"

In response, Fred's daughter, who finally got the hang of shooting bolts, let loose a hot blue bolt but the Demon simply dodged it. Her next shot, a golden beam, glanced Fred, making him smoke, but he made another, determined, long arching leap. Seeing his quick recovery, the failure of *everything* she'd done, and his new ferocious attack, Stephanie withered inside, knowing he would counter her next black bolt, knowing she'd definitely be overpowered by her father. She saw murder in her father's approaching red eyes, and it wasn't just the demon's rage but her father's rage solely focused upon her. Nevertheless, for some reason, and actually, a very *natural* reason, she sought some kind of mercy from him as he drew nearer. But she found none. *What could I have possibly done to keep him from loving me, even during his normal Earthly life?*

Soaring through the air, those glowing demon red eyes drew closer and Stephanie finally tried popping out although she knew fleeing was a concession to failure. But to her utter amazement, something prevented her from vanishing. *Oh dear God!*

She heard a jubilant Karen in her head, "*Got you, you bitch!*"

Stephanie remembered when she had fought Jargono, he'd boxed in or neutralized her powers. It's tragic when you can feel death coming unabated, and you're hopelessly going to lose everything, even your very soul. The Demon's eyes grew larger as his tremendous leap had almost brought him down upon her. Vaughn, just fully regaining his senses, witnessed in horror.

"Dear Lord Jesus, help me."

Carla and Mandy saw those words mouthed by Stephanie, though they couldn't hear them.

Something, someone, hit the Demon's side, knocking him off course and almost off the front of the stage as Stephanie screamed. "Joshua! *No…*"

"It's alright, I *expected* him! I knew that bastard Judge couldn't have banished him. It was surely a ruse." Joshua had slashed a gaping wound into Fred's left arm with one sword, and with the other had deeply pierced his torso.

Stephanie screamed again. "Joshua, *please!* You can't…"

But Fred rolled upright and immediately leapt at him. Though Joshua had mastered the saber, he had no idea of the Demon's lightning speed and ability to heal and neglect humanly mortal wounds. Both Vaughn and Stephanie yelled out. *"No!"*

Not even bothering to defend against Joshua's swords, Demon Fred bared his claws and ripped them across Joshua's chest, slicing through bone and lung. Stephanie's husband fell in a bloody heap as Vaughn's kick landed in Fred's face an instant too late. And the Demon ignored the pain, and as he fell backwards, he backhanded Vaughn, dazing him again, then Demon Fred leapt up, yet again, and strode across the stage to where he had knocked Vaughn over, determined to stomp Vaughn to death.

Stephanie had risen to her feet, not caring for her life anymore. "No! Oh, no! *No!"* While rushing toward her father, she gathered her full power and blazed a reddish golden fire but Fred knew she was going to die.

Karen sent her voice out to Stephanie from the corridor. *"That's right. Go ahead and get him. You can do it."*

As Stephanie rushed across the stage, she reached into her hidden pocket. "You scum! *Bastard!* You *destroyer!* I should have done this back in my village. In the name of our Lord Jesus, be condemned to the *lowest* of hells forever and *ever."*

Her arm whipped out at Demon Fred who expected some kind of light bolt and merely dodged away. But her hand didn't shoot a bolt, but followed his movement and threw the bottle of Light Oil that Vaughn had given her for a wedding present. Fred saw the puny object, and merely swatted it away, but he inadvertently burst the bottle so the Light Oil sprayed across him. Stephanie had stopped only a few feet away, and Fred thought. *What a pitiful…* But then he started to burn.

He tried to rub off the Light Oil but that only spread it. His hand began to burn, too, so he exuded much more Black Oil as his fur thickened. But he began to dance around from the pain, and grabbed the purple cloth covering the podium to remove the Light Oil which was now a golden glow far brighter than anything Stephanie had seen.

Fred screamed, roared, and smoked then quickly subdued his demon nature and turned back into a man. He stood naked before all, just as he naturally was, and the burning disappeared.

Joshua, who was still alive and had watched everything, summoned all his strength and shoved one of his sabers towards Vaughn so that it slid across the smooth stage. Coming to his senses, Vaughn rolled, grabbed the sword in his left hand, hid it behind him, took two more steps then leapt into the air.

In the back of his mind Fred heard the sword slide but a lot of his mind still identified with the demon so he placed very little interest in the sound. And he knew all he had to do was simply wash off the Light Oil while human then turn back into his true form. This all was, at most, a bit of a bother.

Even when he sensed Vaughn's attack, he didn't turn to see him leap, because he didn't fear it because even in human form, he still possessed great speed and strength. Just not as much as Demon Fred had, but he knew it would certainly be sufficient.

Vaughn faked a right kick to the head that he knew Fred would swat away. Vaughn also knew that Fred's counterattack would spin Vaughn around, and as he did, Vaughn brought out the hidden sword with a backhand swing that was made even faster because Fred had spun him around. Vaughn's sword stroke was so quick and clean that Fred's expression was still fixed upon his daughter even as his head fell from his body.

The demon nature in Fred quickly responded. All he had to do was simply pick up and put his head back on! But Vaughn had already anticipated this and rebounded and kicked Fred's head away. The Light Oil had also reactivated upon Fred's reanimation. The headless Demon's body and its transformed head began to smoke again. Fred had to maintain demon form long enough to make himself whole, but both parts burst into flames before he could do anything, flames driven by spiritual power, not mere physical reality.

Karen viciously screamed. "You *biiiitch!*"

Remembering Mafferan's deep red cage, Lady Stephanie immediately erected a similar shield between her and the corridor. Blue bolts streaked down at Stephanie, but they struck the shield which turned purple upon absorbing them. Now anger boiled through Lady Stephanie as she recalled actually healing Karen, keeping her from dying. "No, you're the bitch!" Lady Stephanie reached up her hand as if grabbing hard for something then pulled even harder.

Karen materialized out of the air in front of the cameras, and smacked down upon the stage only a few feet from Stephanie.

"Behold your enemy, dear people! This is the infamous *Queen* Karen, murderer of my mother and *many* more."

Karen stood up, smiled as she adjusted her fine blond tresses and black dress then bowed, and made to fade out, but Stephanie tried a trick. She threw a cage around Karen made of the same deep red glow, forcing her to rematerialize.

Now Stephanie smiled wickedly as she popped into the cage! "Let's do this the old-fashioned way!" She knocked the wind out from Karen with a punch in the stomach, pulled her down by the hair then climbed on top. Queen Stephanie scratched at Queen Karen's precious face then went for her throat with her hands glowing with the same deep red as the cage. Both had been in the same gang only two years ago but Karen had always avoided outright fighting.

Desperate to avoid any facial scars as she prided herself on her perfect beauty, Karen was aghast to glimpse her blood on Stephanie's arms. But her desperation increased when she found her powers neutralized and her ability to think scattered from being choked to death. *Queen* Karen squirmed and writhed and tried to pry Stephanie's hands free but it became evident from *Lady* Stephanie's fierceness that she meant to kill her. Karen tried to get her feet between them to kick her off but Stephanie scrunched lower to prevent it. That red glow from her hands seemed to penetrate deeper than the choking.

A man suddenly appeared on the stage and walked up to Vaughn who instantly shimmered in deep blackness. No one had ever seen such a sight with people falling out of the air, popping in out of nowhere, glowing… The cameras kept rolling as Jargono talked to Vaughn in a friendly tone. "No need to get all testy! I'm not here to fight… ahhh, just here to break up a *catfight!*" A huge basin appeared above the scrapping women as Jargono extended a hand toward them. He turned his hand over and so did the basin, dumping quite a bit of very cold water.

Both women disengaged quickly, and tried to catch their breath. After the red cage disappeared at a wave of Jargono's hand, Jargono threw his wife over his shoulder, and spanked her butt a couple hard cracks, causing her to yelp right in front of everyone. He put her down to face the people who had never seen such a red face, though whether from anger or embarrassment, they couldn't tell. His voice was uncommonly smooth as he turned to face his audience. "Dear people, as Lady Stephanie prefers to address you all, I am Jargono, and I will shortly be your new ruler of your new government. But don't worry, I'll still give you free health care!"

He bowed once to the crowd, bowed to Stephanie and winked, then turned to Vaughn. "Thank you for cutting off that bastard's head. I really never could stand him. He wasn't a very good pet either, and I've learned all I needed about his power. And now I've fulfilled my promise to the people to stop the Black Death!"

As Jargono and his wife vanished, Vaughn shook his head at the irony. The last of the vile Black Essence had created Demon Fred and it also was destroyed by the way he and Stephanie had killed him. *But all their offspring… I don't think Jargono knows about them.*

There was a moment of dead silence. The people simply had too much to process. Shivering, Lady Stephanie slowly brought her hands from above her head down the length of her body using her power to dry herself. Once relieved of that necessity, she whirled towards her husband. *Joshua… Oh God!* She and Vaughn reached him at the same time. She placed her glowing hands upon Joshua but he weakly pushed them away.

"Joshua!" Stephanie didn't understand and neither did Vaughn.

"You can't heal me."

"Yes I *can!*"

"No. I didn't tell you…" Joshua coughed blood. "There was a second black orb that infected me. Not by much, but I got enough that you won't be able to heal me. I didn't have time to search for it… had to get Harris back."

It must have hidden from me when I healed him before! But why was I able to heal him at all? Guilt slammed Stephanie again for not killing her father outright as the Lord had instructed, and these events of the day now condemned her selfish decision. "I'm so sorry… so very sorry. Oh God, what have I done?"

"Vaughn touched his Captain's head. "Let's pray. You don't know if…"

Joshua weakly whispered. "No."

"Look at me, my love. The Lord has given me privilege. If I pray for you, you *will* get better. My prayer wasn't at fault with Harris. They had a continual poison device hidden away and as soon as I destroyed it, our prayers worked. *Please!*" Stephanie implored her husband while beginning to weep.

"I don't want to! My time has come. This is my chance to set things right for you. I love you so much." He turned to Vaughn. "And I love you, too, my *best* friend. I want you to know, I never really knew her!"

Vaughn shook his head. "Joshua, I know Stephanie loves you. I don't understand. Of course you know…"

"I asked the Lord to preserve my life long enough to tell you, as God is my witness, I never knew your wife, we never consummated!"

Stephanie couldn't bear it. *He doesn't want to live because he doesn't think we're really married.* "Joshua, I love you. I'd have made love with you dearly. Let me pray for you and we'll…"

"I know, and I know you mean it." He smiled, then even gave a soft laugh that hurt. "What's not to love? Of course you love me, but Vaughn is your true husband by the Lord God." He turned his head back to Vaughn. "You're my best friend. I could never betray you, but I had to protect her, because I love both of you. I knew you couldn't keep her from Matthew. I just didn't know how to set things straight, but now I do."

Now Vaughn began to weep, falling apart inside, and he confessed. "If it wasn't for me, it would have been *Matthew* lying here, not *you,* Joshua. I know it, I just do, but I…"

Joshua sternly cut him off. "*Never* speak of it again. That's an order! I know, Vaughn! And I would have done what you did! Things have worked out as they're meant to be. My brother, a Colonel, will come and set things straight. He has… my last wishes." He coughed then convulsed a bit.

Stephanie pressed upon him. "Please, Joshua, let me pray. *Please.*" Part of her began to fill up to pray for him against his will, but the warning in the glowing letter Vaughn had brought back flashed before her. *Take no more liberty… Oh dear Jesus, would that be taking liberty, to pray for Joshua now? How can it be?*

But Joshua knew his wife, and asked. "Is it right to pray for another for something against their will? Please, dear Stephie, this is best for all. Both of you, give me your hands."

Lady Stephanie and Vaughn both placed their hands within Joshua's one good hand. "I'm a Captain and have the authority." He coughed again, feeling his life finally leaving. *Just a little longer, dear Jesus.* "The Lord Jesus Christ bless you both, husband and wife." Joshua's hand went limp as his head rolled back in peace.

Stephanie lowered her head to rest upon his shoulder and her tears mingled with the blood of her noble husband. She heard the word, *Sacrifice,* whispered softly by the Seed of the Tree of Life. "Sacrifice," she repeated, "Oh God, how I used to hate that word." Wracked with pains of guilt and love, she missed Joshua terribly, but also knew he spoke truly about Vaughn. *I would have made love to you, Joshua, if you had let me. I didn't want you to sacrifice.*

And she heard Joshua's voice answer back in her mind. *"Beloved faithwalker, I know your sense of justice and out of that sense, you most certainly would have made love to me. And you would have meant it, but you cannot fault yourself for loving the man God made for you. That night you read to me the letter from Mafferan then wept in my arms, I knew what I had to do, what God wanted me to do, and I did it. No one has enriched my life more than you. I thank you so much, but now,* quit my body. I'm no longer bound by it, and I'm at peace. You and Vaughn be at peace, too."

Joshua also spoke in Vaughn's mind. "You have much to face and the country will depend on you if there is any hope at all for us. No one knows better than you what needs to be done now. Listen to my brother when he comes and accept what he offers you. Do it in gratitude for my willing sacrifice. Now, take up your wife and comfort yourselves. It's been long overdue. My spirit will always watch over you."

CHAPTER 20

Conclusion
to the Beginning

This time Eve had sat on the lush grass under the Tree of Life long before her first pupil ambled by. As the students began to congregate, many inquired how long she'd been there and why, but she would only smile in silence. Whispers of such odd behavior continually filtered to the newcomers, with many responding, "That's Eve!"

As her silence continued, eventually every student followed suit and still Eve kept still. Eventually, everyone began to notice a special feeling settling into their midst. A still sense of being that all knew was always there but usually went unnoticed due to the crowding of many other perceptions.

"Dearest children, this last lesson of the season is the most important so I waited for you all to feel what you feel now. Only through that part of the Light may you see and understand the answers to the questions by which Marta ended our previous lesson. Why did Lucifer feel he was more important than God, or did he really? I, myself, am particularly knowledgeable of this matter because I, myself, partook of this egregious error. Because of *my* mistake, *my* sin, I caused all the suffering that befell the Earth."

It wasn't that the class didn't know this already, but to hear their first mother confess, to hear the pain, even after so much time had passed was heartbreaking.

Robert cleared his throat then spoke up without being asked. "Dear Mother, no one could have done any better than you. How can we be better than you and Adam? We came from you. We cannot rightfully begrudge you."

To that, all nodded in silence while Marta sighed. *Such a beautiful and wise answer!*

Eve bowed her head, and when she lifted it, all saw a single teardrop in each eye, brilliant like the clearest diamond. "This lesson shall set the foundation for next season's much deeper considerations of what Robert just expressed! But let's now finish with the questions at hand, as it is incumbent upon us to understand why Lucifer fell… how Adam and I fell. Contrary to popular *myth…*" A bit of twinkle escaped her eye with her half-attempt at humor. "Our sin started quite a bit sooner than when we actually ate the forbidden fruit. As it turns out, it wasn't the fruit at all that was forbidden … but something else that had to do with it."

Marta also spoke up without being asked. "Let's first regain our silence before considering further." And after the students did, Marta whispered. "Please continue, Mother."

"Dearest children, tell me from being in the midst of what you feel now, from this beautiful part of the Light, tell me what makes you important."

Many quickly answered while the rest nodded. "Being a part of *this*!" And they waved their hands about, but Robert qualified. "Not the surroundings we see, but feeling the full meaning of the Holy Spirit itself. It's like … it's like it's the most beautiful feeling in all Creation 'cause we feel *exactly* the same as its Being. At the same time, we feel how much greater the Spirit is than us, but we feel small only in one way, and it's not a bad small. In fact, the Spirit cherishes us so much we feel important! But we see that what's in us *is* important and actually, it *is* us!" He paused with an astounded look on his face. "Wow, I just said all that didn't I?"

And everyone nodded. "But you're exactly right. Well said!"

Eve stood up under the Tree of Life, reached up her hand then gently bent a branch level to her waist. She shook it in front of everyone as she smiled a tease. She also took hold of a twig and showed it separately. "Is this twig important?"

The class answered, "Yes."

"Is this leaf important?"

All said 'yes' again but Robert interjected once more. "I see where you're going. What's a branch if not all its tiniest parts which make it a branch? But from a different perspective, a single leaf doesn't seem all that important at all if you think that what's important is the whole tree. But… but…"

Marta saw how Robert began to struggle, and took over. "But of course the whole Tree is important, and of course, the Holy Spirit is more important than any of us since we're born *from* the Spirit. But in another way, from the viewpoint of Jesus, we are just as important! Because he said, 'He that is faithful in the least is faithful in the greatest.' And this naturally applies to God Himself, since in order to be Who He Is, God must be true in and toward even the tiniest aspects of Goodness, and that would be us! No tree can live if it despises its leaves! In the silence we just had, we could feel, and understand both perspectives to be in agreement, so we are both important and humbled at the same time. The Tree as a whole gives us both our identity and our humility!"

Eve sighed in recollection. "Indeed… if only I had been so wise when I was your age!"

Lutan, another young man near Robert's age but from the Earth's Far East, added. "Lucifer was one of the three main branches to the heavenly Tree, but unlike anyone else, he was in charge of the Ethereal, of ministering to the Earth in a way that no other angels had. That focused him so much on his importance that he lost sight of the purpose and meaning of life, which is only known and *felt* by knowing the *whole* Tree… just like what we felt in the silence."

Robert nodded and quickly picked up where Lutan left off. "I see, I see that as soon as he began to feel that his branch had an importance *other* than being part of the *whole* Tree, Lucifer would have lost the understanding we have in the silence! Then he actually would have felt very unimportant at the same time he was feeling overly important."

Lutan picked up again from there. "That sense of unimportance would have made him try to be even *more* important, to try and make up for his increasing loss."

Marta turned to Eve. "Dear Mother, is this what somehow happened to you and Adam?"

"That, dear Marta, is the lesson you shall help me teach next season! It's also the lesson unfolding right now upon Earth. For at the very heart of the battles that our dear Stephanie and

Vaughn are fighting is the dire struggle for the people to properly define the word *power*. Does power mean importance?"

Rivalry aside, every judge across the nation knew that losing Captain Joshua wounded the country deeper than they actually could afford. Though his rank didn't show it, he was indispensable in his role in security. He also couldn't be replaced easily, as even the Judges found Joshua's sharp sense of integrity inspiring. They were cursing him with one breath, doing their best to emulate him with their next.

From all across the United for Christ, Judges and the highest military personnel went to the funeral. When top secret people from a very elite intelligence agency showed up, the hunches were confirmed of the dear Captain's involvement in the innermost workings of their country's defense.

Judge after Judge stepped to the podium, first declaring they would never yield to their enemy to the North then with sincere gratitude praised the Captain's life and work. Some even drew chuckles at their candor when they alluded to their rivalry with the good Captain. A new feeling, a new spirit began to grow between the Judges and the Military as both listened to each other's' heartfelt words and realized they were on the same side. The love and respect for this man in his death drew them together whereas his mortal life had seemed to fan flames dividing them. Both sides even made allusions to certain unspeakable, deplorable activities of some Judges, sincerely agreeing that such things could not be tolerated, especially in a time when purity and strength were so desperately needed.

Colonel Asa had been given the express privilege to conclude the funeral. Far more low-key than his younger brother Captain Joshua, the Colonel possessed a rare presence that simultaneously commanded respect and fear. It wasn't fear of evil though, but rather the certainty that whenever Asa spoke, no matter how difficult, it would be the unquestionable truth. Their mother was the daughter of a high Judge and their father a General, so the first born, Asa, had been given the rare privilege to do Judge apprenticeship while concurrently studying at the military school. At the ceremony for his confirmation as Judge, where he would have received his righteous black robe, Asa confessed he could better serve his country in the military, starting at the bottom and working his way up. He had been bold enough then to contrast the military meritocracy to how Judges inherited their robes and even suggested that new judges ought to earn their Judgeship from scratch as well. The straightforward honesty with which he delivered his first national address won him the ever-growing admiration of his people. And only ever so often, he would make a public appearance concerning some national crisis or deep concern. People across the country knew Captain Joshua was his brother, but many felt there would also be more to his forthcoming speech.

Close cut black hair, and a sharp black military uniform added emphasis to his blue-eyed stare that riveted all into focus as he waited for complete silence, which took only seconds to achieve. Vaughn's family and Harris sat dressed in black at the front row along with all the high Judges and Military.

Lady Stephanie could now be heard weeping because of the silence of the crowd. She still found it difficult to reconcile all the strange twists that conspired in her husband's death, as certain actions even predated their initial meeting. There were many cases of 'if only' that played in her mind. For sure, both she and Vaughn had made some critical errors, if not outright wrong decisions.

Colonel Asa spoke softly. "I want you all to listen closely right now." All across the nation, people in front of their televisions heard Lady Stephanie's plaintive sobs more clearly as he paused. A camera even zoomed in on her but she was still unaware of her public display of grief. "That weeping says more than I could ever say." Asa paused again and even the Judges began to wipe their eyes.

Finally realizing, she asked, "Forgive me, I'm so sorry…"

"Nay, dear Lady, it is everyone else in this country, including me, who should be begging *your* forgiveness!"

Now the fear of truth began to creep into the audience and Asa waited awhile in silence to let it build. The conscience is quite a mysterious entity, truly having a mind of its own, though unfortunately it seems to communicate in a foreign language at times, yet the heart can discern its emotional component.

Colonel Asa pulled out from under the podium a rather thick manila envelope stamped top secret, held it before the cameras to focus upon then set it down upon the podium. For some reason, the people began holding their breath, and that inner foreign language suddenly seemed on the verge of being translated.

"What I'm going to tell you is the truth. In this envelope is intelligence that I fought to declassify so I can share it with everyone. It is absolutely necessary for us to understand the events at hand, who our friends are, and who our enemies are." He paused again, and goosebumps began to surface upon all his listeners. There seemed to be so much implied here, but what?

"That man there," The cameras zoomed in as Asa pointed at Harris, "along with several others and my brother, Captain Joshua, undertook a dangerous mission, knowing full well that the likelihood of survival was nil. As it happened, only Harris and my brother made it back, but a secret weapon wounded Joshua long before he died valiantly.

"That wound that my brother kept hidden prevented any possible recovery, because he prioritized delivering intelligence and saving Harris who had been more seriously wounded. My brother carried him on his back for fifty miles, and refused any special attention for himself, desiring all healing power to go to Harris for the good of our country. The intelligence Harris has provided perhaps gives us a chance to survive as it at least lets us know what we're up against."

No one had realized the seriousness of the times until now, and if any other had spoken, it was doubtful whether anyone would have believed.

"Captain Joshua has had a very important and well deserved relationship with our new people from the North, not just because Lady Stephanie became his dear wife, but also *Sergeant* Vaughn saved his life, and even more than that. Captain Joshua was not a man to suffer anything evil by lying down, nor to give respect lightly, but due to the impeccable character of *Sergeant* Vaughn – you *are* a Sergeant now, Sir

– even before he had any rank at all, Joshua had long since signaled to me his importance.

"Before our newcomers came to us, Vaughn had earned through valiant deeds and tenacious character two titles. He was appointed Ranger for life among a group of men that I would dearly want fighting at my side when all hell breaks loose. They are here among us in secret as it should be. But Vaughn had earned himself another title."

Vaughn's eyes widened even as he looked at Stephanie. Neither of them, nor anyone else, knew where all this was going.

"He tried to refuse such a title many times, but his people flatly told him it was their right to appoint whom they wanted to serve. When King Jargono – the dashing young man who very recently appeared to inform us he would be our ruler – when he confronted Vaughn's people just before they were to cross into our country, Vaughn alone stood against Jargono. And Jargono, thinking he had won, demanded Vaughn's people to bow down to him."

Stephanie leaned into Vaughn's ear. "Did you tell him?"

"I don't think anyone did. I think they've been watching and know more than we realized, which means…"

"Now let me tell you about the strangers whom many of you have ridiculed, because I *hope* when the time comes, we shall have as much bravery! When Jargono demanded them to bow, they instead began to hail Vaughn as their King. They shouted it over and over. So enraged was Jargono that he began killing them, but they still chanted hail to King Vaughn, telling Jargono they would die before they would bow to the likes of *him*."

The crowd murmured, most nodding their heads in deep respect and approval. Vaughn became aware of the cameras, began shifting around in his seat, but had no place to hide.

"Vaughn took advantage of the distraction and almost killed the bastard, but instead wounded his *lovely* Queen so Jargono had to rush off to save her. Dear people of the United for Christ, the foreigners who have come under our shelter do not belong to the country up North. They do not belong to us either, and rightfully so as they are Jews!"

Vaughn and Stephanie's mouths dropped open, feeling quite exposed, still not knowing where this was all going. The United for Christ knew no Jewish people, and in fact knew no differentiations at all since everyone had long since intermarried and everyone was Christian. Even more complex than that, since all their populations were stiflingly reduced by both The Great Religious War and the Second Civil War, disunity simply could not be tolerated and so through the fifteen-year-long Civil War, anyone who felt they couldn't unify had fled to the North. The only Jews the United for Christ knew were those they read about in their Holy Scriptures.

"If you read your Holy Bible, and you all know me, that I do, you will find that when King David was driven out by his enemies, he came to live with a people not his own and fought for them honorably and they prospered. Now these Jews, who knew *nothing* about God or Christ because the North robbed them of their heritage, now they have come to not only serve God, but many are beginning to understand who the Lord Jesus Christ really is." He paused to let this all sink in. Many knew the signs of the times. Those who didn't were quickly informed by those who did.

"I don't know about you. You all have your own minds to make up. But my mind *is* made up. I could not think of any people I would rather have fighting by my side than these Jews who have come under our wing."

He waited again to see which way the crowd would go. Many of the Judges were shocked, but many nodded their heads in approval. Judge Peter, Supreme Judge, promptly stood up, and began to clap slowly, and sharply. The other Judges also stood up and did the same. Then the crowd began to respond, and minutes later all were standing, clapping in respect and assent, all except Vaughn who stayed seated, head in his hands.

Asa finally held up his hand for silence then continued. "I am very glad to have a King, a highly deserving *King*, in our presence."

The crowd went ballistic, cheering, chanting, "King Vaughn! King Vaughn…!"

The cameras again zoomed in on Vaughn who had forgotten all about them. Vaughn sat with his head in his hands, shaking it from side to side, and when the people at their television sets saw his reaction, they commented. "What a humble lad. He truly *is* a King."

Asa raised his hand again, and silence returned. "My brother, Captain Joshua, loved these people with all his heart, soul, mind and strength. His last wishes are as follows…"

Everyone now focused so intently that the air seemed to crackle with each one's concentration. "Joshua requested that

King Vaughn take Joshua's place as Captain. I can think of no other."

All the military officials stood and saluted Vaughn, who didn't know anything about it because he still hung his head, shaking it. The cameras zoomed in on him just as Lady Stephanie elbowed him sharply in his side. Catching that little scene caused not a few chuckles across the nation, while Vaughn's expression at all the military saluting him added to the humor.

"Come up, Sergeant Vaughn. You don't have to accept this extra promotion if you feel it wrong or that you're not up to it. But I desire your response to the nation!"

The camera's caught Lady Stephanie pushing him forward and more chuckles were elicited.

When Vaughn reached the stage, Colonel Asa firmly grabbed his hand, taking his arm as well, and he spoke privately. "I know you were my brother's best friend and I never got a chance to thank you for saving his life. I've known about you from the beginning. Your secret service is invaluable and I wish you to operate it independently, however you see fit. We will be in contact with you and you with us to do the best we can under the circumstances. Deal with the infiltrators among you as you see fit. Now, what say you?" Colonel Asa grabbed Vaughn by the shoulders and firmly placed him at the microphone.

Vaughn stood before the people a bit dumbfounded. He shook his head. Silence remained. The cameras focused. He sighed. "First, I want to say that I dearly miss my Captain, my best friend." He had to pause. He bowed his head a moment.

"I wish…" He paused again and sighed. "I wish I could have gotten there just a bit sooner… maybe he wouldn't have died." He shook his head again.

Everyone could feel his emotions and knew he was real. But also, everyone had witnessed all these events for themselves and they knew Vaughn had exceeded what any other man could and would have done.

"I've been put in a rather peculiar position. Captain Joshua's last words to me while I held him were to accept what his brother, Colonel Asa, would request of me." Speaking became far more difficult for Vaughn than ever before. It didn't seem right to step into Joshua's place, but it didn't seem right not to, either.

"But I have to consider for myself this responsibility. I cannot accept such a thing out of honoring my dearest friend, nor out of gratitude to Colonel Asa." Vaughn turned and saluted him crisply then Asa saluted back. Vaughn turned to the people with more force, and a stronger voice. "I cannot accept such a promotion for my own personal or political gain. Because such a position is very well the *life* of this country, and that life is also my life and the life of my people. I cannot take such a thing lightly. *My* Captain Joshua, for whom I would gladly lay my life down, would only want me to accept this if I knew I can do the job well. I haven't his experience. I don't know, everyone else seems to know me better than I know myself, I guess. They see something in me, I guess."

He paused in reflection. Everyone could see this was a young man truly baring his soul and all were riveted, craving more.

"I'm no King, really, though I understand at the time, what Colonel Asa described really did happen. I wish I hadn't have missed Jargono… but I did." He shook his head. "All that you've seen…" He waved his hand about the stage. "The demon, Jargono, and all that, I've been battling even before I came into your country. I have personally fought Jargono two other times." There were exclamations of wonder and astonished expressions as Vaughn added, "As you can see, I didn't win."

Someone from the crowd shouted, "You didn't lose, either!" And many agreed with that remark.

"This is true, I suppose. Lady Stephanie and I have both fought that bastard. I think we know him better than anyone."

Someone else shouted from the crowd, "Take the job!" Then others began to chant. "Take the job! Take the job!" All across the country, people joined in. "Take the job…!"

Vaughn couldn't restrain himself and the camera caught his tears. He remembered seemingly so long ago when he defiantly vowed to come to this country to seek support to fight the terrible injustices done up north. *I had no idea my prayers, my vow, would be answered… only that I had to make them, and live them, anyway.*

Vaughn held up his hand for them to quiet then pointed at his tears. "I'm not accustomed to this in front of so many people, but I love Joshua dearly, and he loved this country, its people dearly. I want to do what's best for all. That's also why my tears. I *don't* want to disappoint or let you down. These tears be my witness, my oath between thee and me that I pledge unto you all, that nothing short of *death* will prevent me from giving my all to do right in protecting you. It is with a heavy heart, but a *determined* heart that I accept the promotion to Captain. Thank you."

Vaughn turned again to Asa, saluted then made to leave but the Colonel caught his arm, and pulled him back to the podium. In the meantime, the people ecstatically cheered, but Colonel Asa asked for and got silence. "Captain Joshua had other last wishes. I must convey… the *truth*."

He paused again while all got a feeling in the pit of their stomachs, again. "It is said that a nation divided against itself cannot stand. We no longer have the luxury of the petty squabbles between Judges and Military. You all know my family background, that my feet are in both worlds, as my mother is the daughter of a Judge, and my father is a General. I love both sides so it is with a heavy heart that I must tell you about Matthew. I cannot call him a Judge!"

The people's eyes widened. Many had of lately grown to love the good Judge.

"But before I tell you about Matthew, I must tell you of Lady Stephanie!"

He beckoned with his hand for her to come up. She shook her head, but he nodded his then fixed her with a drilling stare, still beckoning her. Stephanie had no intention of complying so she wondered what she was doing when she ascended the stage. He placed her in front of him at the podium beside Vaughn.

Asa, towering over the couple, stepped to her side and turned to Stephanie. "First, I want to thank you for being so dear to my brother. He told me quite a lot about you." He lifted his head back up to the people. "Lady Stephanie is a *faithwalker!*"

Stephanie's eyes widened. She couldn't believe he just told her secret to the whole country.

"I think by now many of us, having heard her, having seen and heard of the miracles she's done, I think we all know she's something special. My brother wanted me to know the truth about her so that we could protect her, because she has already given her all to protect us."

Stephanie's eyes continued to widen. *How much does he know? Dear God, will he tell* all?

"When Lady Stephanie came into this country, two men immediately noticed her. My brother who fell in love with her, and Matthew who lusted for her. And learning of her abilities, Matthew lusted even more. Under threat of destroying everyone that Lady Stephanie loved, Matthew commanded her to his bed, knowing full well she was wife to my brother."

Colonel Asa was a man known not to show anger, so when he showed it, the people cringed inside especially those who had rooted for the good Judge Matthew.

"I have surveillance that proves it all!"

The crowd went ballistic again, but this time in anger. Asa held up his hand but they didn't calm immediately. "There is more! Matthew told her he would have Joshua killed if she told him anything."

The crowd turned fierce against the Judges on stage.

Asa continued without trying to quiet them, but they hushed to hear what he would say next. "To save everyone, Lady Stephanie chose to sacrifice herself in giving herself to Matthew."

Hanging her head, shaking with tears, neither she nor Vaughn understood why this all should be told. Feeling all those eyes upon her person, Stephanie began to collapse, her shame too much to bear. And when the people saw it, that confirmed Asa had spoken truthfully. Colonel Asa, like a dear father, quickly stepped back behind her, held her up and turned Lady Stephanie away from the crowd. Taking her into his arms, he continued to speak. "My brother's wife is brave and valiant beyond measure. I did not tell her terrible secret to embarrass her, but to make you *hardheaded*, *stubborn* and *foolish* people understand and to love her. We *need* her on our side. As I've said, she is a rare human being, a *faithwalker*, and though not as experienced or seemingly as powerful as Jargono, she far excels him in love and good character."

The crowd, with many tears in their eyes and many with much shame for their mistreatment of her, cheered for her now. "Lady Stephanie, Lady Stephanie …"

After a bit, he continued. "But there is *yet* more. As you know, I am next of kin to Captain Joshua and have the right, the responsibility to take Lady Stephanie as my wife, though she would be my second."

The crowd hushed even more, thinking that might be a good thing. "But my brother confided in me that he loved Lady Stephanie and his best friend, *Captain* Vaughn. He became aware that these two souls had already been secretly married before they came to this country, but feared to tell anyone because of their young age and our laws."

He wrapped an arm around Vaughn now then pulled him

toward Stephanie. The two looked at each other wondering what would happen next as did the crowd

"My brother married Lady Stephanie to protect her from Matthew, and had hoped to somehow reunite her with her true husband, his best friend." The crowd hushed in utter amazement. "Make no mistake about it. My brother truly, deeply loved this young woman, but being the honorable man I am *proud* to say I knew, he would not touch her though she be willing out of her sense of justice and love for him as well."

With so much of her intimate, private life now known, Stephanie's mind seemed to blur. Like a father, Asa still held her in one of his arms so she didn't know whether to bury her head further into his chest weeping, or to use her abilities to burn him to a crisp, or to just vanish forever. It didn't seem right for him to bare her secrets.

"I tell you all this, so that you may fully understand the true nature and character of these two souls that stand before you now. And I remind you that our law is Biblical Law. We execute adulterers when it's proven. But Matthew did far worse. He stood before you all and thoroughly tested Lady Stephanie, and after she proved to us a depth of faith that even I, myself, found inspiring, he proclaimed her a Christian. All the while he plotted to turn her into… I cannot say the word. When Vaughn became privy of Matthew's blackmail, Vaughn did what Captain Joshua or I would have done. He killed that bastard!"

The crowd erupted in the loudest cheering, yet. Vaughn hung his head along with Stephanie, but Asa let them cheer for a good while.

"As I've said, the truth, the *brutal* truth… but there is also another reason why I have revealed such deeply private and personal information. These two souls are vital for our national security and I did not want our enemies to be able to distort or use the truth in any way to detract from or hinder their best efforts to aid us. Make no mistake about our perilous situation now. Our enemies will seek to undermine us in any way possible. But now you know the heroic efforts, the noble hearts of these two souls. Now *you* have entered into their pains, into their struggles by understanding and sharing their burdens."

Stephanie and Vaughn looked at each other, both thinking the same. *Asa's right! I see that now. There's a lot more to the saying that the truth will set you free.*

After allowing his words to settle deeply within all souls, Asa continued. "Now, I decree the following: As is my God given right as next of kin to Joshua, and as his sacrifice entailed and his last wishes described, I pass my right to take Lady Stephanie as my wife, and I pass it to Captain Vaughn. Also, since they were already previously married by God, this is a just decision, a right decision, and since my brother's honorable chastity upheld their union, there is nothing more for me to say except to make it official here in our country. Lady Stephanie, Captain Vaughn, will you please, in honor of my dearly beloved brother and his sacrifice for you and in honor of both of your mutual courage and love, will you please turn and face each other!"

Both Vaughn and Stephanie wept openly. They never could have dreamed of any such thing happening so, and happening so *very* openly. They *still* couldn't believe it, even though it was happening right then and there.

Asa began to perform the ritual. "Do you, Lady… *Queen* Stephanie…" Upon hearing the official title, and the respect Asa inflected into it, the crowd exploded into a roar, shouting louder and louder with that same respect. "*Queen* Stephanie, *Queen…*" And Asa paused, and for the first time smiled broadly as he looked at Vaughn and Stephanie's stares and then to the crowd below.

Soon the crowd's voices waned, as no one wanted to delay any further. No one wanted to miss a word, a tone, the softest whisper. "Take *King* Vaughn, this man, for your true husband by Christ Jesus, our Lord and Savior, and to be all that God means for you to be for him?"

She simply nodded, but Asa prompted her. "Say the words, dear." Stephanie put her face in her hand, shook her head, then lifted it and said, "Oh, yes. Of course I do with *all* my heart, *all* my soul, *all* my mind and strength."

"Captain Vaughn, *King* Vaughn. You know Lady Stephanie is a true Christian. Will you let her baptize you also, so that you may complete your conversion to our dear Lord and Savior Jesus Christ?"

Both Vaughn and Stephanie were shocked with the same thought. *He knows about* that, *too?*

And in answer to their thoughts, the Colonel smiled. "Oh yes, I know, and so did Joshua." Colonel Asa glared at the Judges a moment then turned back to Lady Stephanie. "You do *not* have to worry any longer to hide that the Lord has sent you to baptize and bring souls truly to the Lord Jesus. Where

Matthew thought to make you an *honorary* Judge, I say we have no right at all to say *anything* to you! Just, let the Father in Heaven's will be done through you and *cursed* be the man who would come against you!"

Asa turned back to the Judges on stage. "Supreme Judge Peter, I know you as an honorable man. If I have erred here, please let us all know *now* and correct it." Colonel Asa wanted everything to be perfect, as well as out in the open.

Judge Peter stepped forward. "The only thing I wish to correct is the corruption I have learned about, and I pray that the Lord's anger against us might be stayed by us now doing the right thing. Please proceed as you are."

Colonel Asa turned back to Vaughn. "I know you as a man of integrity and I take you at your word, Sir, as to your walk with Christ Jesus. Will you let Lady Stephanie baptize you to truly receive Jesus Christ?"

"My dear Colonel, I will, and soon."

"I take you at your word, Sir, to set things up in due time as the Holy Spirit allows. Thus I am permitted now to ask you. Do you take Lady Stephanie to be your God given wife and Queen forever and ever, to love, honor, and protect always, never to part till your bodies go back to the dust?"

Vaughn first crisply saluted Colonel Asa. "Thank you, *Sir.*" Then he turned to Stephanie. "Yes. I *do*. I take Lady Stephanie to be my Queen, my wife forever."

"You may now kiss the bride. I pronounce you duly joined in holy matrimony."

Suddenly, the couple felt as if in a dream as they took each other's arms while the cameras focused narrowly upon them.

As their arms slowly wrapped around each other, their lips touched tentatively, gently, slowly drawing each closer into a kiss that all could tell had totally absorbed them.

☙

"Touching!" Jargono exclaimed.

"Call it whatever you want, but this wasn't *my* idea of suffering." Karen spat out as they both watched from the corridor.

"You're too caught up, too fixated on your vengeance. If you have patience, let our destinies unfold naturally, the kind of suffering that will slowly engulf them will please even you, I think, my dear, lovely wife."

Karen simply frowned. *I owe that bitch... and I owe that bastard for almost killing me.* She eyed Jargono. She saw how he concentrated on Stephanie and she knew he knew she knew. *One day I'll pay you back for your little fun and games, my dear husband.*

Jargono turned, and smiled at her. "Now that's *exactly* the kind of patience I'm talking about!"

Queen Karen did her best to hide the fright in her eyes at realizing Jargono had heard her thoughts, and changed the subject. "The people seem quite unified now. Look at them. Judges and Military all on the same page. I thought you wanted disarray."

Jargono casually shook his head. "Don't fret over their happy feelings. Happy feelings never last long. But fear and sadness, now those have shelf-life. Those are the feelings that stick around to control people, and they're all going to have plenty of that shortly. They'll soon be at each other's

496

throats and wanting to crucify even their new Captain and his Queen."

Karen eyed her husband. Try as she might, he never told her his plans, and many times she wasn't even sure if certain events were his doing or not.

Jargono turned and smiled at her again without speaking a word.

She suddenly thought of something that finally got that twinkle back in her eye. "Well, at some point I need to pop into the former Judge's chambers and see if *my* surveillance survived! I want my porn video of the good *Queen* Stephanie! She actually did a fairly good job of acting like she enjoyed it!"

Jargono smiled more deeply than pleased his Queen. "Now that the Colonel has told the *truth,* it probably won't affect the people at all. In fact, you might even bring them closer together if you show that."

"Dear, I don't give a damn about showing it in *their* country, although if people were to actually see for themselves how much fun she had, they might even second guess their Colonel as well as her. Anyway, I want to make it prime time in *our* country! Then let her try and show her face here again! After we take control in the South, I'm going to make it required viewing."

☙

Highest Councilor ScrabaGag wrapped his tail around his trusted offspring. "Well, are you happy for your *friend,* Grinchback?"

"Master, please don't mock me. You know if it was possible, I'd eat him in an ethereal second. Don't get confused between my meaning of the word friendship and the human's!" Grinchback spoke with just the hint of an eye smile, knowing his Master knew those were also Mafferan's words to Vaughn.

When his Master caught it, he burst out laughing. "So, how did the good Judge taste?"

"*Did* Master? I taste him continually, forever, and I have to say I'm quite pleased with the level of his suffering. I hadn't thought such a one would supply me with so much energy."

"Very good, Grinchback! All in all I think things worked out well for us! They've lost a year and a half to no gain. Another eighteen months and our Earthly offspring will be ready to mate and turn the Earth into a glorious feeding ground. Whatever *glow* is around then, won't be for long. Though, to be safe, we now must turn our attentions to the recent outbreak to make sure it won't spread further.

"Master, they know the greater threat isn't Jargono. They'll surely seek to destroy them."

The Highest Councilor shook his head. "Jargono should serve our purpose handily by keeping them busy, so it doesn't matter if they know if they're too busy trying to stay alive."

"Are you sure Jargono doesn't know about them? He's become quite powerful, stealing our orbs and invading our files."

"He's only acquired what I let him have so that he can cause the people more trouble than they can handle. The files I left on those orbs were only those I meant for him to have. Besides, Queen Karen has plans for our Earth Demons!"

"Master, she knows?" Grinchback Eyed his sire realizing his Master had hidden the plot. *What else has Master hidden?*

"She knows, and will protect them if she has to. She's part of *us* now!"

"But… but Master, how could she…" He saw the twinkle in ScrabaGag's eye. "*Master!*"

"Learn something well, Grinchback. Human women are peculiar creatures. Some you can trust, others you can't."

∽

Standing by the lake edge, her long black hair gently blowing in the wind, Marissa exclaimed, "It's about time!"

Since for so long things had gone from bad to worse, she had thought she'd never be baptized by Lady Stephanie. She didn't want anyone else to do it. *Right hands,* the thought kept coming to her. *It's got to be done by right hands.* She hadn't known what was wrong with her Queen, only that each time she'd visited her, she appeared worse and worse until she didn't feel she could pester her any more. That's partly why she challenged Judge Matthew at their last meeting. *Someone had to stand up for what's right.* But now, since the Colonel's national speech, she knew. *Dear Jesus, how could she have endured all that? Make me so I won't fail, no matter what.*

When Marissa had met Mandy over at Lady Stephanie's apartment, she eyed her narrowly. "What about *you*? You look like *you* need to be baptized! I'm already seventeen, and I've waited *far* too long. Have you thought about it? What it would mean?" Marissa was never one to mince words, and to her, this wasn't a religious proselytizing, but simply straight from her heart.

Mandy, at first, had a deer-caught-in-the-headlights look

about her. *I can't believe she's so* rude *as to ask me that! Even Stephanie never even mentioned anything… I mean, she told me about herself and all… but she never asked me. I wonder why. I mean, the way Stephanie described it really made sense. It was so beautiful, but… how come I never thought to be* truly *baptized? Even after I saw all those miracles and her glowing letter Vaughn brought back.*

Mandy's memory hearkened back to when, as an obligation, her parents had carried her at seven-years-old to be dunked in the water with a lot of other seven-year-olds. She did it to please her Mom and Dad. She hadn't thought so clearly about them in a very long time, and this memory rekindled her longing for them. *I'm older now, am twice that age so pretty much grown. I can think for myself, but Stephanie shows what it* really *means to serve God. If Jesus was going to pick anyone to represent him on Earth, it would be* her! *In fact, I think He really did!* And with that thought, Mandy realized the flood of real feelings she now had. *No, I think I've always felt this way… somewhere.*

Through the powerful love Mandy had for Stephanie, her *sister*, she understood that all Stephanie did for everyone was a direct result of her real love for God, which Stephanie often referred to as Love or Life or Light with a capital L. *I've always wondered why she mostly called God by those names. Now I think I know why because when all the Judges call God I get no feeling from them. But when Stephanie says, Love, or Goodness it makes so much sense and I can see she lives Love, she lives Goodness. But… they're all calling the same God… aren't they? Why the difference then?*

Mandy slowly began to nod her head to the realness of the answer to her question. Feeling the love her sisters had for her and she had for them, that love made so much sense. But then it was as if that sense suddenly revealed more of itself as Love. *Just like Stephanie calls God Love! And I see that it's also Life.* The clearness of that picture now caused Mandy to see how her sisters got their unwavering strength. *That's so real!*

Mandy addressed Marissa who had sat down on the couch beside Carla. "You're right! But I think I need to give it a lot more thought first 'cause I don't want it to be *fake* at all."

Marissa acted in mock defense. "Well, I never meant to suggest anything less."

Carla was glad for the opportunity Marissa had created to seek Lady Stephanie's service, also. "I feel, though the Lord has already blessed me, I just feel I need to be baptized again, with my *full* understanding this time."

Marissa smiled with victory, turning to Stephanie at the other end of the couch. "You're not getting out of this now. No putting it off any longer."

Sitting in the comfort chair across the living room, Vaughn's broad smile beamed. "Can't put it off any longer. We all know what must be done."

Stephanie bowed her head. "As you wish, Lord Jesus. This is by your Spirit's hand, *not* mine."

Within the week since their auspicious nuptials, Lady Stephanie had been inundated with requests for baptism. On the third day after the televised wedding, she again went on television to explain that she was only one person and needed to first organize some faithful help, see to a few personal matters and then she would serve all to the best of her abilities.

Fortunately, Supreme Judge Peter had informed his fellow clergy to be happy for such occasions, and to answer any request from her with *sincere* help. Lady Stephanie requested the registry of all the Judges across the whole land and with the help of certain local officials, sent letters informing them that she would shortly organize a set of meetings all across the country to work things out between her and them. So far, all seemed to be proceeding smoothly between all factions.

One week later, Carla, Mandy, Marissa and Vaughn, and six others stood together in prayer at the edge of a pristine lake surrounded by pine trees and rocks. However, they no longer worried over secrecy but still enjoyed the privacy of the location.

Mourning doves sent their haunting calls though the air while Lady Stephanie, in her holy dress, clasped her hands together in prayer. "Dear Lord Jesus, I cannot fathom how I got through what I went through to be standing here now to do Your service. Even what You blessed me with had seemed to have left me, but You made a way out of no way for me. Now, we're gathered here with one accord to partake in the reason for Your sacrifice so that Your blood should not have been shed in vain for them."

Lady Stephanie reached for Carla's hand. "My dear sister in suffering, would you please be first?"

Out into the water they went, then stood face to face with their shared knowledge of sin and sacrifice. When they both knew it was time to begin life anew, then Lady Stephanie uttered words only for Carla and God as she placed her into the lake.

Under the blessed water, Carla set free her heart and let go of all her pain. "It's more important to focus on Your Goodness, dear Lord Jesus. In You, all things are made new."

With that firm understanding and knowledge, she completely released herself to all the newness that the Holy Spirit contained… believing it, trusting it, *knowing* it.

When the Spirit rushed into her, she spread her arms out as if trying to gather in more and more. Dark black streaks oozed into the water from Carla's body that Stephanie could feel as they floated by. *Oh God, it's her pains, the evil of those pains that were forced into her against her will.*

The fiery ball lingered within and around Carla until no more blackness came from her, then its bright glow slowly faded. When Lady Stephanie saw its departure, she brought Carla up who then walked peacefully to shore with hands still outstretched, basking in what the Holy Spirit wrought over her and within her, thanking God in whispers and private conversation.

Still waist-deep in the lake, Stephanie playfully called out. "Marissa, you've pestered me to death! In my time of terrible darkness, your tenacious uncompromising will inspired me! No, you will never compromise, as it should be. Come, dear Marissa. The Lord is anxious for thee!"

Marissa smiled as tears rolled down her cheeks, and confessed. "You know, I used to be quite arrogant, even controlling. I couldn't keep from bossing people around. I suppose I meant well, I thought I was right all the time, but what good is it without being guided by true knowledge? I'm sick of my selfishness, of trying to control. It's why I felt so empty. I just want to *be*, and I know the Lord Jesus can set my heart straight. I know it."

'So be it' was all Lady Stephanie said. She called upon the Lord to do his will as Marissa went underwater.

"Take all of me, dear Lord Jesus. Leave nothing in me that's not good in Your sight, and do with the good as You see fit. I control no longer." Marissa prayed in her mind, expecting a fiery return from God, but found none.

"I know the Lord has heard me. I know He'll answer in truth." Then she realized she was *still* trying to control by the way she prayed so she stopped waiting, stopped expecting, and noticed a certain peacefulness floating nearby to which her heart immediately agreed.

As their agreement grew deeper, so did the peace grow while everything seemed to stop. This standing still of time was the antithesis of controlling or trying to. *It's just simply being! I'm simply being!* It wasn't what she'd expected at all, but she already lived forever in *that* moment. When Lady Stephanie brought her up, Marissa didn't want to come up, and stood very still as Stephanie and everyone else stared at her. It was quite uncommon for Marissa to be so *quiet*, but she finally walked off silently, except for her half whispers. "So much peace... so real."

Stephanie then turned to Mandy. "When I first saw you in the underground, I saw myself, dear Mandy! Thank you for standing so steadfastly by me. The Lord shall teach you about yourself and so much more."

Mandy hugged her. "I love you, Stephie!"

"I know, but you must forget all about me if…"

"I know, if I want my love to be truly real. I understand. Put me under so I can finish hashing this out!"

"Mandy, it's alright if you want more time. We can…"

"Oh, no! *Definitely* not! Ever since Marissa opened her…" Mandy glanced at the still so quiet girl, "Ahhh, her formerly big mouth, I've been reaching for this. If we're truly sisters, and we *are*, then the Lord is even more there for me! He'll help me get through this. Put me underwater, please!"

"As you desire, Mandy, so be it."

"I've really made a shameful mess of my life, Lord. I can't stand to look at myself. I didn't mean to, but things happened. I don't know what to do. I can't change what I've done, but I'm so, so sorry. Let me begin this life again. Forgive me, dear Jesus, and let me be as if I were just born. Let me begin again." Mandy kept repeating her prayer over and over. The others began to wonder, to watch Mandy for any sign of struggle but saw none. Lady Stephanie, her eyes closed in peace and prayer, showed no concern either, but they all began to look at each other.

Mandy focused on the meaning of beginning again, looked way past what she had done, and become, and in this process she saw her whole life in large pictures. She then instantly let the memories and the pains go because she knew she was here to put a true end to all this for goodness sake. As if re-entering her mother's womb, she focused only on the essence of herself that is the goodness the Lord God made her out of at her beginning. And when she arrived at this naked place, Mandy prayed. "Now dear Jesus, I'm not worthy to think past this point, take my goodness back and do with me whatever You will. I'm not worthy to even think any further." And as she left her little goodness open for the Lord to take, she heard a great voice, having a distinctly feminine feel. *And you have always been my sister!*

Mandy was no longer underwater, as her person dwelled somewhere in a place of pure meaning. Feeling the presence of this Great Sister, Mandy answered within herself. *Who are You? I feel like I know You.*

I am often called the Spirit of Wisdom. I am that part of the Lord Jesus sent to bring you His gift. Because you have been a true sister, I shall always be yours!

With her heart weeping with all of her being, Mandy reached out to love, cherish, and hold inside her that Spirit of Wisdom. She was at the same time loving and being loved, and the Love had fire in it. The Fire mixed with Wisdom, and were One, different aspects of the same Good Spirit teaching, giving feeling, enlightening. Inside herself, Mandy gave her full appreciation and worship, then yelled of release and exhilaration, of letting go, and taking in.

The next thing Mandy knew, she was standing before Lady Stephanie, dripping water off her nose, and quite unaware her eyes glowed. Stephanie, whose eyes were glowing, too, wrapped her arms around Mandy. "My dear, *dear* sister, how I love you."

Stephanie wept, thanking God, remembering how Mandy fought her at first, and all the toils that led to this point in time. Finally Stephanie released Mandy. "Now, go and embrace your other sisters."

Mandy nodded, walked off, then hugged and startled the still very sedate Marissa. "Thank you so much for speaking up to me when I needed it." She went to Carla with no words at all, but they held each other in silence.

Carla suddenly faced Mandy. "We have much to battle together, all of us. This is only the beginning!"

Stephanie then began to glow all over and Vaughn's eyes turned fiery. This intensity of spirit drew everyone's attention. Mandy nodded her head, remembering his beautiful gut-wrenching poem she had furtively read before.

"Sir Vaughn." It was his honorable title she'd used when he started calling her Lady Stephanie before they'd entered the United for Christ.

Vaughn bowed his head in respect to her then petitioned his Queen. "Would you do me the honor of baptizing me in the name of the Lord God of my Forefathers, of Abraham, Isaac and Jacob? For truly, only the Light from the Beginning is able to save, and is truly Master of all. No man is worthy to be our Master, except that Light that took on the form of a human being so that He could make us a new heart, a *new* spirit within our humanity, the only place it could have been made to overcome all darkness. For the Lord God is not a God to be outdone even amidst all evil. And He is able to make us perfect *right here*, in *this* lifetime so that evil cannot boast against God, saying, 'You might create, but I shall destroy upon this Earth.'"

When everyone else heard, and felt the ripples of power moving through the air when Vaughn spoke his words, they all knelt on one knee to praise God. They also had the common thought, *He's someone* very *special! What is God going to do with him? And he's so young! What's he going to be like* after *he receives the Holy Ghost?*

Vaughn extended his arms out from his sides, looking heavenward. "Behold me, Lord God who took the Earthly name of Jesus, for truly there's no other salvation than that new heart and new spirit that You purchased by Your own blood and suffering. For how else could You prepare against all evil in the flesh except You *lived* it, *felt* it *Yourself*. For the Holy Ghost is made *not* for the angels in heaven, but for man on Earth to overcome all evil here, and thereby being made able to enter into Your glory. Oh yes, dear Lord Jesus, I *understand* the Oneness of God and I come before Thee for that Oneness."

Vaughn paused as a deep blackness came over him, through which a fire shined like the most brilliant star, then he raised his hands higher as his voice carried more power. "Be warned, oh world! On this day after thousands of years, the Tree of Life and her people of true meaning are rejoined to the people who keep her true words. And what power can withstand *that?*"

He turned to Lady Stephanie, who now also glowed black and gold. "It's time. Put me under. From this day forward, I am neutral no more!"

"So be it. In the name of the God of the Tree of Life whom the Appendaho have protected for true meaning's sake, and in the name of the Lord God of your Forefathers, of Abraham, Isaac, and Jacob, in that singular name which now unites us into one, in the name of Jesus, I baptize you unto the Lord God."

And under Vaughn went. "I know my many sins, Lord Jesus. I know my anger, and how I thought to raise it above Yours. Forgive me. I'm but the tiniest speck of your Goodness from which You made me. But I'm so thankful for that speck."

And Vaughn felt himself so very small amongst a Greater Goodness that grew in greatness exponentially until he felt himself disappear, and willingly disappear into that infinity, willingly surrendering to the Lord God Who *is* that Goodness.

Infinity entered his mind and heart. It was as if he were in ten thousand places all at once, feeling special goodness in and loving each and every place, but every place lived deep within God, and letting go further, Vaughn embraced fully the Lord God by yielding fully to experiencing all that the Lord Jesus brought him. And he wasn't just experiencing it, Vaughn *became* that experience!

A voice everywhere, was inside of him, though all heard it thunder on this clear day while Vaughn was underwater. *You, who have searched for meaning and truth when there was none around you. From the inside out have you searched with all your heart, all your strength, all your mind, all your soul. From the inside out You shall be mine. You, who discovered the spirit of courage amidst abject fear, I shall be your everlasting shield. You who have burned with pain for Justice's Sake, despising the cruel, the evil, and the unjust, and suffering innumerable pain to protect the innocent, the downtrodden, and the remorseful… I shall place in your hand the Staff of my Indignation, as well as the Staff of Life. Receive the Holy Ghost.*

The water had lit up and boiled during the thundering and then slowly calmed. Amazed, Stephanie let go of Vaughn who was still submerged! Arms outstretched, he floated to the surface. Mafferan and a seemingly old man with a long white beard appeared at Vaughn's side, and raised him out of the water.

Stephanie recognized the bearded man from when he appeared to her with Mafferan just after they escaped from the North. While Stephanie despaired for her slaughtered people, the Appendaho, while Vaughn had just discovered his heritage, this bearded father of Vaughn's people had placed his hands upon her head and blessed her. Now Stephanie watched as they held Vaughn upright.

"Lord God, Lord God of my Forefathers, of Abraham, Isaac and Jacob …" Vaughn kept repeating.

The bearded man smiled then spoke. "Well, King Vaughn, you can stop calling the Lord God of me. He's *yours* also! My son and grandson send their regards as well!"

Vaughn only stared, not understanding, so, Stephanie smiled, then lovingly took the old man by his arm and introduced him to Vaughn. "Did I tell you I met Abraham, your father, before?"

Now remembering she had, Vaughn became fully aware as Abraham stretched out his right hand and prayed over his heart. "The Tree of Life lives in here forever. As I walked in the days of Sodom, so shall you walk, and fight, and win until it's your time to go the way of the Lord." He turned to Lady Stephanie, blissfully smiling. "And in yours, too, dear Lady! You two shall never be apart any more, even in death! You are *forever* married. You are one." Mafferan, smiling, nodded to them all and they disappeared.

Shocked by what they all witnessed and wondering at the meaning, everyone stood motionless, listening to the still calm and the mourning doves cooing.

❧

Freedom. Never before had the Jews, including their King Vaughn and Queen Stephanie, known such a wonderful feeling, for not only were they granted permanent citizenship, but were now held in high esteem. No longer segregated, no longer stigmatized, the people mingled more than ever, and fast friendships began forming. And the newly baptized holy people began to befriend many. Having been given such excellent kindness and gifts, they worked skillfully, cleverly, to bring the Judges and common people to better understandings.

Freedom. It wasn't just the newcomers to the United for Christ who felt it so dramatically, but all across the nation, new feelings stirred to life. Lively and healthy discourse quickly grew between the Judges, the Military, and the common people. The underground movement that Stephanie had started also suddenly surfaced. Her sermon at the underground bar was revitalized with even more strength after she was publicly vindicated. Suddenly, many more marriages were being celebrated, and new businesses requested legitimate licenses to go with a slight modification to their former clandestine services.

Three precious products, which for so long had only been smuggled due to severe restrictions on trade, now surfaced above ground at a reasonable price. Coffee, tea, and chocolate. The impact of such commerce was not to be underestimated as suddenly the world became a much larger place to the common man.

The gaping, tragic, world wound from the Great Religious World War of one-hundred-seventeen years ago, suddenly showed signs of healing. Once international trade re-opened for the United for Christ, people from all over the world began to visit her. The media found a healthy pre-occupation with international news stories and their public ratings surpassed anything ever imagined as the common man's hunger for world knowledge increased with each new international vignette. Only one unnamed country remained ominously silent after the United for Christ officially rejected its generous healthcare offer.

Breathing out his words as if releasing a lifetime of stress, Vaughn noted. "Freedom… it's a lot more than crossing a border."

As Vaughn back-kicked the door to their apartment closed, Stephanie took hold of his strong arms. He looked so handsome in his black Captain's uniform. She gazed seriously into his dark brown eyes. "Freedom, my dear, dear husband. You know, I feel so much older than sixteen. I don't understand. Why does our old country hold teenagers down so much? We're capable of so much more than we're allowed. But even here, their school system doesn't allow the youth to accomplish nearly anything close to their potential."

Vaughn appraised his wife. She had *created* another beautiful dress, this one was pink with blue Appendaho embroidery around the hems and neck. "At least here they allow us to marry as adults." Vaughn was referring to the law that let citizens marry even as young as fourteen.

"True, but mostly only the women marry young. The young men don't usually have the means to care for a family at that age. You're probably the absolute youngest person ever to accomplish a number of things. Look at Joshua at twenty-three. He was six years older than you, Vaughn. Most young men at seventeen are either still in school or at the very bottom of the workplace where their potential is simply wasted."

Vaughn smiled with suspicion. "True, but why do I get the feeling you're going somewhere with all this, my dear lovely wife?"

Stephanie smiled mischievously. "Ahhh… I think I want to reform their educational system, too! Vaughn, the changes we've inspired might very well bog down under the strain of a broken educational system! There are too many unskilled, ignorant people suffering too harsh conditions. And frankly, I think a lot of their current education is one big money scam! Most appear to graduate but then get most of their training *on the job!* How does *that* make sense? I mean, the waste of time in phony education."

Vaughn nodded, but with a sharp glint in his eye, and Stephanie knew he was about to make another of his points. "I don't know. Did any of that hinder us? Look at all we overcame in spite of everything."

Stephanie shook her head. "But can we expect others to do, to suffer as we have? I don't know. Do many others have that capacity? Is it right to expect…"

He touched her lips, hushing her. "We'll help everyone to the best of our ability. That's all we can do, my dear. Let's see, you're now the head of the formerly underground reform movement. You've called for all Judges across the nation to form groups whom you're visiting personally within one month's time. You have more requests to baptize people than is humanly possible even in a whole year… requests to visit the sick, and to speak nationally. You've got offers to lead your own TV show, and now you want to reform the school system too! You're still the Queen of our people and a Mommy, and now a sister… ahhh, and oh, my wife, my dear Queen."

And he drew her into the deepest, fullest kiss she'd ever had, preciously holding her cheeks as all the goodness he'd just cited about her increased his love. During this kiss, the knowledge that they now had a full, unrestrained life together drew them closer in ways they never knew before. Yet, Stephanie's heart also mulled over Vaughn's narration of all her responsibilities, of all that people needed from her, and they all seemed to echo in her heart. But as she continued in their passionate kiss, the more she noticed what almost seemed to be a growing selfish rebellion against the noise. *But is it really selfish to want my own life, too? I mean, to just relish and enjoy? Just like this kiss! Mmmmmm… so* delicious!

Suddenly flooded with all the hopes and desires for just her own life and for what she loved dearest, Stephanie grabbed Vaughn by the shirt with such force it almost made him feel small. "I can't wait any longer! I love you *so much.* And we've been denied *so much.* Too many times others have almost had me before you! Well, not anymore!"

And as she kissed him so tenderly, truly, the Seed to the Tree of Life began radiating a warm glow that seemed to feed her passions even more strongly.

Wrapping his arms around her, Vaughn squeezed her tightly, feeling the Seed's glow enter him, too. But finally, he managed to disengage as they both caught their breath. "Wait just a moment."

Vaughn turned around, slipped the bottle of Light Oil, still a third full, from his inner vest pocket and placed some upon his hands. After replacing the bottle, he turned to his wife, placing his hands upon her cheeks. Feeling the Oil, she smiled in utter contentment as her passions only deepened further as she rejoiced with the peace, and feeling purely feminine.

"What?" She suddenly perceived her husband deep in thought.

He reached around her neck and pulled out the chain to reveal the glowing Seed. "It's time for us to plant this!"

She shook her head. "But where? Is it really safe to…?"

"When I was in the Ethereal, I did extensive research on my forefathers' lands. I'll show you!"

Holding her by the cheeks again, with Vaughn smiling with knowledge, they vanished. Stephanie recognized traveling through the spiritual corridor speedily. After a few moments, they reappeared on top of an ancient mountain, but it was barren and dry. Spread across the land down below, nestled lush valleys with small farms and herdsman and small towns sending smoke. Way beyond that, desolation, as if the lands beyond had been permanently scorched with fire.

Having done quite a bit of orb historical research, Vaughn pointed, "Out beyond is where the former United States and the other nations retaliated with their nuclear missiles to destroy the countries of the terrorists that had sent the plague upon what they called the heathen."

Lady Stephanie had tears in her eyes. "Dear Lord, it still lays in waste."

"As so it should! Those bastards were all guilty, *knowing* what their fanatics planned but doing *nothing* to prevent it. The Lord God has punished them, as He had promised He would." Vaughn pointed to the people dwelling peacefully in the valleys. "*These* bastards are the *descendants* of those who came into the land of Israel and slaughtered all the Jews when they knew Israel had no more effective allies. They slaughtered the men, women and children and still to this very day laugh and mock about it, teaching their children about their *great* victory against the *sub-humans!* But since this, *here,* is the Holy Land, the United States didn't want to blow it to hell with everything else, and all agreed."

Stephanie groaned. "You want to live amongst *them?* Plant the Tree of Life *here?* On this barren mountain?"

Vaughn smiled. "Think about it. The story Mafferan told you in his letter. It was on a similar mountain where he found the Tree. But we don't have to have this mountain be barren, do we, *Faithwalker?*"

The look in his eyes and calling her Faithwalker communicated his deeper thoughts, his deeper vision.

"My God! I see what you're thinking. But if I do that, the people down there," she pointed in disgust, "will surely come up *here.*"

"Not if there's a protective barrier!"

Lady Stephanie shook her head. However, the Holy Spirit over showered her with a word. "Truth!"

"My *God!*" she exclaimed again, walking a little away from Vaughn.

This is simply amazing! Staring at the utter desolation of the mountain, the *faithwalker* had the uncanny sense of history repeating itself. Remembering the stories from Mafferan's legend that Arlupo had told her… *Vaughn is right. I bet Mafferan found the Tree on a mountain just like* this! *But this time it's going to be different. I vow it!* With determination, Lady Stephanie bowed her head and began to glow as she reached back into the memories, the visions that Abraham had placed into her distant mind of the Holy Land when he walked upon it. "My God!"

She walked away still further and opened her mouth in prayer. "Lord God of Vaughn's Father's, of Abraham, Isaac and Jacob, I'd ask *You* to do this but I see the power is being put into *my* hands! So be it. Since it pleases You for me to do so, it pleases me to ask You to guide me."

"SO BE IT." The Lord's voice resounded in a booming thunder which rolled down into the valleys, causing the people below to look up to the mountain and to a clear sky.

Lady Stephanie stretched forth her hands. "Restore your land, Holy Father, as in the days of old!" And with her eyes closed, her head bowed, she raised her arms and began to turn in a slow circle.

A thick dark cloud materialized, enshrouding the whole mountain, and time disappeared. They could have been standing in that thick darkness forever or for a moment. It didn't matter, as Lady Stephanie gave herself over to the vision, to the Lord's guidance, and to the tremendous power she had never felt before. She knew the feelings of destruction, the feelings of life, of all the miracles she had worked up to this time, but even if she could have imagined all of those feelings all at once, that picture wouldn't have even come close to what now manifested within her of Life, of Creation. At some point, the cloud dissipated as dear Stephanie felt very small.

"Dear God!" Vaughn and Stephanie exclaimed together. The smell of a lavish fertile land rose in their nostrils. A deep sweet spring gushed from the top of the mountain which had leveled and broadened considerably with enough space for a large town, or even a small city. Everywhere, birds of all kinds, rabbits, squirrels, and plants, the likes of which neither of them had seen, flourished as if having always been there.

The people down below in all the various valleys began to run towards the mountain and Vaughn turned quite dark, then raised his right hand with his voice thundering with power not his own. "Behold the Mountain of the Lord God."

And that thunder rolled down the mountainside and when it hit the people it knocked them flat. Lady Stephanie extended her arms out from her sides with her palms outward and she spun around again, slowly. "Place your holy protection around this Mount, dear Lord Jesus, that Your Tree of Life may flourish free of the ungodly."

The air around the whole Mount began to shimmer and suddenly everything for ten feet outside the shimmering burst into flames and turned to ash. Of course, there had to be a few people who just had to tempt fate, expecting the worst to be a burned hand, but as soon as they touched the shimmering, they immediately burst into intense flames and became a pile of charred powder.

Vaughn smiled when he witnessed it, and nodded his head, as he turned to his wife who was shaking her head at the needless loss of life. "You feel bad for them."

"Of course! Vaughn, do you understand what the Lord just did through me? He used me to *create!* I mean, not like I've done with a few dresses or a bottle or even healing. I mean really create!"

In response, Vaughn reached around his wife's neck, to which she instinctively bowed her head as he undid the chain holding the Seed. He looked deeply into her rich brown eyes. "My dearest Stephanie, such a wonder of Creation that I just witnessed comes with consequences. I understand your compassion for them, but I also understand the Lord's Judgment in protecting this."

And he dangled the Seed to the Tree of Life in front of their faces, and it glowed with increasing warmth. In one hand he took his wife's hand, in the other he sacredly held the chain in front of him as they walked to the center of the top of the mountain. There in the center, at the head of the origin of the spring that ran down the mountain, was a small hill of freshly cultivated land.

After briefly looking each other in the eye, King Vaughn and Queen Stephanie knelt together. Together they dug into the soft, rich earth, after which Vaughn held the chain up to her. Lady Stephanie placed her fingers upon the Seed, speaking softly to it with a tear and a sob. "It's time, my friend!" She had once died to protect the Seed, and even though this one came down from Heaven, Stephanie knew that *all* the Seeds were exactlythe same, possessing the *same* Spirit with the *same* experience.

And in response as it dislodged itself, it spoke softly, "Thank you Lady Stephanie for carrying me."

And as the *faithwalker* placed the Seed into the hole they'd dug, Stephanie prophesied, "This be your new place to root, *forever!*"

Vaughn held up the empty chain to her, wondering what she wanted to do with it, and surprisingly, Stephanie placed it back around her neck, but this time not feeling so badly about it being empty. Vaughn covered over the seed, speaking, "We plant thee together in the name of the Lord God Jesus Christ. This is the *Lord's* Tree."

"Amen." Lady Stephanie seconded.

The day was warm, and the breeze was delightful as the birds chirped sweetly. The grass was thick and soft under their feet and they disrobed carefully, folding each garment and placing them in two piles beside each other. With no restraint left, they took each other in their arms and kissed passionately. Memory came of how they'd felt this before, but now that the right time had finally arrived, their fire burned joyfully.

Vaughn suddenly scooped her off her feet and Stephanie continued to giggle in joy as he slowly knelt down to the grass and laid her there. As soon as Stephanie felt the gentleness and the slight tickle of the living carpet, she laughed in delight and pulled Vaughn over beside her so he could feel the grass, too. Smiling amorously into her eyes, he proclaimed, "My dear wife forever," and he rolled over, scoping her into his powerful arms.

They experienced the freedom to explore further, this time knowing that their prayers, their hopes could finally be fulfilled. As Sir Vaughn and Lady Stephanie achieved their first real unity and she flinched, she whispered in his ear, "I told you so," hearkening back to when Vaughn had thought Demon Glen had violated her. And when Vaughn had still doubted her, she grabbed his hand and told him to check for himself. Whereupon he jerked his hand back and turned deep red in embarrassment, saying that he believed her. But now he knew without any doubts at all.

Vaughn paused to look deeply into her eyes and saw how much she cherished her reborn virginity and the meaning of having been made new and now sharing herself only with him and no other forever. A new feeling poured down upon them together and both their eyes look inward to examine it. They both said within themselves, *Sacredness! That's sacredness we feel. The sacredness of being one life, one heart, one home together.* Vaughn whispered in her ear as he squeezed her tightly, "I am home in your heart." And he remembered way back, after she had dragged him home after her gang almost beat him to death. She had placed her hand upon his chest and that's when he first noticed that he could feel her heart through her hand. He loved it then, and he loved her even more now. Every time he squeezed her now and she squeezed back, it was as if he was engulfed within her wonderful heart.

And for Stephanie, she remembered after Vaughn had carried her down the ladder, saving her from her gang, they ran and hid behind a bush. Vaughn had scooped her up in his arms to comfort her. She felt his wonderful goodness and strength then, as she felt it now, and she pressed even tighter into him, seeking ever greater union with the goodness that is Vaughn, treasuring her husband. She felt so at peace, so whole within his goodness and strength that wrapped around her so perfectly.

Both gasped with the unfolding of their sacred promise, their growing sense of pleasure matched with an equally intense meaning of life, of eternal love. No longer just a dream, just a hope, but reality. The reality of truly being fully one. And then they laid beside each other both reflecting on their new sense of each other that had just deepened so wonderfully. With the sun lazily warming them, Vaughn began to doze when suddenly…

"Oh *God!*" Stephanie shrieked.

Vaughn lazily opened his eyes. "What?"

"I'm pregnant!"

Vaughn laughed so hard he felt just a bit guilty, but Stephanie looked at him sternly so he had to explain. *I really thought she understood this.* "Dear, we *just* made love. You *can't* be pregnant that fast!"

"You don't want me to be pregnant?"

Vaughn did a double take, not expecting such a conversation at all and certainly not *that* question. "I just meant that…"

She looked steadfastly into his eyes. "Vaughn, I know the biology, and I'm *telling* you…" She dropped her voice to a whisper. "I'm pregnant. Oh God, I'm sixteen-years-old and I'm pregnant."

Vaughn turned on his side and took her cheek in his hand. "Then my dear wife, *we're* pregnant! That's what can happen when we make love. Ahh, although I didn't think it'd be that fast, but frankly, well, I can't wait to see our baby! How could I not want a child with *you?*

"Oh Vaughn," she started to cry. "Do you realize the bad timing of this? Look at all we still have to face. My *God,* we have to slaughter all those damned demon offspring in about… Oh God, our baby will only be like, nine months old. I'll probably still be *nursing!* Do you realize how vulnerable having an infant will make us?"

Vaughn showed mock fright. "*Yeah*, and think of all the *hormones!* I mean, I've heard these terrible stories of how crazy women get while *pregnant!*"

She smacked him on his chest. "That's *not* funny!"

"Well, though it seems impossible to me that you'd be pregnant so fast, I've learned to have faith in you so I believe you! And I'm telling you, I will do all in my power to be the greatest husband and father."

Hearing his words ignited her passion again, and she pushed him onto his back and then she moved over. Laughing, Stephanie teased. "Well, I told Lynnara that either one could be on top!" She purred as Vaughn began to caress her.

"We might as well go for twins!" he said with a big smile.

"Vaughn!" She smacked him on the chest again, but didn't stop making love.

"Be it unto the Tree of Life, my dear wife."

"So be it, my dear husband," Lady Stephanie whispered.

www.TheFaithwalkerSeries.com